"I have always d[...]
bravery, courag[...]
Kincaid. This bo[...]
—ANNA [...]
bests[...] [...] of Prairie

"A superbly crafted novel, *ME AND THE BOYS* is
witty and gritty and downright great fun!"
—*Rawhide & Lace*

"The wild, raucous adventures of Gini Kincaid weave
their way through the tapestry of Arizona history,
coloring it brighter than a Navajo blanket . . . the
story has something for everybody."
—Marshall Trimble, author of
Arizona: A Calvalcade of History

"Many stories have been told about me, all of them
wrong. The dime novels call me a Heroine of the West;
the newspapers make me out a whore and worse. I'm
not a heroine and I'm sure no whore, though it is true
that I've undertaken perilous quests in the company of
celebrated men. I have strutted the stage in notorious
haunts and sought the company of outlaws. I have held
in my hands a fortune in stolen gold, loved a gambler,
and fought for my life against villains. It's because of all
the folderol and outright lies that I take pen in hand to
set the facts straight. I have got three weeks before they
hang me, so if I write fast, maybe I can get the most
important parts down . . ."

Me and the Boys

"An adventure that will make you laugh and cry,
cheer and jeer, and yearn to be the cheeky Gini.
Buy two copies—you'll need a spare when the
first copy is worn out."
—*GEnie RomEx Reviews*

ME AND THE BOYS

or

The Glorious Adventures of Gini Kincaid:
My Perilous Times in the Territory

A Novel by
Ellen Recknor

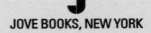

JOVE BOOKS, NEW YORK

ME AND THE BOYS

A Jove Book / published by arrangement with
the author

PRINTING HISTORY
Jove edition / November 1995

ISBN: 0-515-11698-X

A JOVE BOOK®
Jove Books are published by The Berkley Publishing Group,
200 Madison Avenue, New York, New York 10016.
JOVE and the "J" design are trademarks
belonging to Jove Publications, Inc.

PRINTED IN THE UNITED STATES OF AMERICA

10 9 8 7 6 5 4 3 2 1

Contents

Author's Note

I love the American West. I cut my teeth on TV Westerns like *The Lone Ranger* and *Cheyenne* and *Maverick* and *Bonanza* and *Wanted: Dead or Alive*. At the movies, I cheered for "the Duke," and was always proud that he'd come from my home state, Iowa. When I was eleven or thereabouts and deep into my Jesse James period, my Uncle Clark and Aunt Tot drove me all the way down into Missouri to see the house where Jesse was murdered by that "dirty little coward," Bob Ford. A few years later, my parents, my sister, and I took a family vacation through the Southwest, with stops to visit relatives in Arizona and New Mexico, and lots of (demanded by me) side trips to every nickel-and-dime roadside Wild West attraction. I'm sure I drove my long-suffering parents crazy.

Years later, my love of the West drew me again to Arizona. Considering all the fashionable shops and exclusive resorts that line it now, it might be difficult to believe that as recently as the 1950s, cattle were regularly herded up Scottsdale Road, the main drag in the town where I live. But all one need do to rediscover the wildness of this place is drive a few miles out of town on one of the old, lonely highways that skim a blistering line through the desert or snake through the shadowed mountain passes. The sky is big and the terrain infinitely varied, its beauty simultaneously subtle and grand. After almost twenty years here, I still ogle the land as I travel through it, fascinated that Geronimo or Tom Horn or Wyatt Earp may once have passed by the same saguaro, ridden down the same arroyo, crossed the same sparkling mountain creek. Here, the Old West seems not so far away.

It is impossible for a writer (well, this writer, anyway) to live in such a place and not write about it.

While the historical backdrop for *Me and the Boys* remains reasonably true to fact, I have taken some liberties — although probably not so many as the old dime-novel crowd so admired by Gini Kincaid. Towns like Oro Tiempo and Hanged Dog and Mendacity originated solely in my head, as did all but one song title; and I allowed Geronimo to jump the reservation a bit sooner than he did (on that particular occasion) in real life.

Where possible, I've tried to stick to the facts. The murder of Tombstone's Marshal White and its aftermath, for example, is much as was reported at the time. Miss Nellie Cashman did indeed operate the Russ House at the corner of Fifth and Tough Nut, and was such an interesting character that she undoubtedly deserves more books of her own than have been written about her. As for the Earps and Doc Holliday, it's so difficult to separate the fact from the many fictions (at least insofar as their personal demeanors go) that I have simply written them as I always thought they *should* be.

Most of the main locations in the book are, of course, actual places, and I've attempted to paint them as they were then. Phoenix was a dusty little farm town, and Tombstone (which, roughly a year after the OK Corral excitement, would be more or less civilized by the Reverend Endicott Peabody — and, of all things, baseball) was, in 1880, a politically corrupt boomtown and a risky place to be. Killings in the saloons and brothels were so commonplace they

attracted little attention, and the place was so barbarous—
and so ore-rich—that it earned the nickname Helldorado.

Prescott, too—particularly Montezuma Street—was just
as wild and woolly in those days as I have described it, and
continued to be for some time thereafter. Legend has it that
when Montezuma Street caught fire just after the turn of the
century, somebody hauled a player piano out of a burning
bar and installed it on the Plaza. Obligingly, the piano
played "There'll Be a Hot Time in the Old Town Tonight"
while the boys drank "rescued" beer, played roulette and
faro in the open air, and watched over two dozen saloons
and all the brothels burn to the ground.

Arizona is blessed with a plethora of historians, among
them Charles Lauer, Odie Faulk, and Frosty Potter, who
have written wonderful and highly readable books on the
subject. My thanks to them, and anyone I may have
forgotten. My gratitude, especially, to author and Arizona
historian Marshall Trimble, whose fascinating and entertaining books make history spring to life. I highly recommend his works to any reader interested in tales of Old
Arizona. Another book which helped me greatly in understanding the mind-set and prejudices of the time was the old
standby *Life Among the Apaches*, by John C. Cremony.

My thanks to friends and family, who had faith. Thanks
also to the denizens of FidoNet's WRITING echo and the
ladies of GEnie's RomEx for their electronic moral support.
My gratitude to my agent, Oscar Collier, who believed in
Me and the Boys and in me; and to my editor, Gary
Goldstein, not only because he loved this book, but because
he once said to me the four most beautiful words any writer
can hope to hear: "Write anything you want."

                                        Ellen Recknor
                                        Scottsdale, 1995

Prologue

Many stories have been told about me, all of them wrong. The dime novels call me a Heroine of the West; the newspapers make me out a whore and worse. I'm not a heroine and I'm sure no whore, though I admit it runs in my family.

It is true that I've undertaken perilous quests in the company of celebrated men. I have strutted the stage in notorious haunts and sought the company of outlaws. I have held in my hands a fortune in stolen gold, loved a gambler, and fought for my life against villains. I do not believe I ever acted in malice except in the case of Weevil Jukes, and he deserved worse than I gave him.

Also, I only ever lit but two of those fires on purpose.

It's because of all the folderol and outright lies that I take pen in hand to set the facts straight. I have got three weeks before they hang me, so if I write fast, maybe I can get the most important parts down.

Executing a lady—especially a sixteen-year-old lady—is a rare thing even in the Territory, so they figure to do it proper. They have sent all the way to Kansas City for a certified hangman, and they plan on a big crowd for the festivities. I've had my picture taken I don't know how many times, and I hear they're printing them up into commemorative postal cards. They're going to have fireworks and souvenirs, and concession stands with pies and barbecue and cotton candy.

I hope they all choke to death.

I know I plan to.

1

At Home in Hanged Dog

I first drew breath in the Year of Our Lord eighteen hundred and sixty-five, in the hellhole town of Hanged Dog, Arizona. My mother was a whore who went by the name of Paris LeFleur, though I have got genuine doubts it was the handle she was christened with. Only the Good Lord knows the true identity of my daddy, and as far as I am concerned the Lord can keep it to Himself.

Hanged Dog lies on the hot and dusty edge of a chunk of Arizona Territory the Spanish named *El Despoblado*, meaning "uninhabited land." Close by to the east are the piney White Mountains, onetime stronghold of the murderous Coyotero Apache tribe. Folks say those mountains are filled with the ghosts of pilgrims who didn't remember to bring spare lead and powder or to post enough lookouts in the nighttime. To the west is desert, haunted by those who didn't think to haul extra water or to kick over a rock before they reached a hand to it, and found a scorpion nest instead of gold.

In the Territory, you've got to do a lot of thinking if you want to stay alive.

Only two important things ever happened in Hanged Dog, and both of them happened a long time ago. The first was the silver strike that got the town started. The boom was before I was born, and the big mines were pretty much played out by the time I was five. Oh, they kept on digging, but it wasn't like the old days.

The second thing was that a famous outlaw named Tuck Brennan used to make the Thirsty Buzzard Saloon his home away from home. Tuck Brennan shot up many a town in his day and robbed a few banks and stages, too; but he knew enough not to foul his own blanket, and he never broke the law in Hanged Dog. People still remembered him real fond, even though he got arrested by U.S. Marshal Bob Kember and twenty-three deputies back in 1866 and got sent away to jail—and later the territorial prison—in Yuma.

The Thirsty Buzzard was where my ma used to sing on the stage and do other things upstairs. I don't remember much about her, as she got herself accidentally shot in the head, which is what can happen when a person spends too much time with drunken *pistoleros* who like to street-brawl. That happened when I was three or thereabouts. Right after, I went to live with Gam.

Gam wasn't my real kin, but she was as good to me as blood and did her best to raise me up a Christian lady. If some folks think I didn't turn out to be one, they best not try to lay blame at Gam's feet, for a finer woman never lived.

Gam was short for Grandma, but when I think back on it, I guess she couldn't have been as much as thirty when she took me over, and was still a fine-looking woman. She didn't have any suitors lining up, though. Even as low a town as Hanged Dog, Arizona, has got its standards, and neither Gam nor I measured up: me because of Paris LeFleur being my true mother, and Gam on account of her having once married up with an Indian, which is something nice people don't do in Hanged Dog, or any other part of the Territory.

Gam's first husband was Mr. Homer Washburn. He and Gam were headed for California and the Land of Promise, but they ran into the Mescalero Apache first. They killed Mr. Washburn right off, but they took Gam for a slave. That is what the Apache used to do with a lot of ladies, be they white, colored, or Mex. I have heard the Texas Comanche tribes are even more partial to captives than are Apache, but I have never met any Comanche and cannot say for sure.

Anyway, it was terrible bad for Gam; but after about a year things got better because the Mescaleros sold her to the Chiricahuas, and she took a Chiricahua husband. I could never pronounce his Apache name, but he was better known as Cuchillo Rojo, which means Red Knife, and he was an infamous cutthroat down around the border country and parts south. He and Gam were wed four years before he got killed by another Apache in a fight over some ponies what were thieved off the Pimas in the first place. I guess she really got to love Cuchillo Rojo, but by then she was pretty sick of living on the desert with a bunch of people who treated females like dray horses and who'd cut off a squaw's nose for sparking with a brave who wasn't her husband. Not that Gam had her nose cut off—she stayed true blue to Cuchillo Rojo—but she'd seen it happen.

After he got killed, Gam just walked off and nobody tried to stop her. She headed toward Fort Buchanan, but after the second or third day the sun fuddled her brain so bad she got lost. She would have died out there in the nowheres if a good-hearted bandit named Mescal Mort hadn't happened along. Trouble was, when Mort delivered her to civilization, a couple soldiers recognized him and turned him over to civil authorities for the reward. On account of imminent Indian troubles (those being some of the early and worst days in the Apache Wars), the army sent Gam on her way before she was proper back in her head, and the bandit was tried in a barroom and hanged quick. Gam never even got to tell him thanks. She guessed he knew, though, because he left her his beat-up Bible with his name inside. Gam still had the Holy Bible of Mr. Morton "Mescal Mort" Scobie, and she kept it right up on the mantel.

Anyway, there weren't more than ten people in Hanged Dog who'd stop to pass the time of day with Gam, and only two we could count on as true friends, those being Pearl Scrimm, who my mother worked for before she got shot, and Doctor Benjamin Winslow. Doc Ben used to spend a lot of time at our house, and I was twelve before I puzzled out the reason. Up till then, I just figured Gam had some mysterious disease that only came over her on Friday nights.

Even though Gam had been both Mrs. Washburn and Mrs. Cuchillo Rojo, she still used the name she'd been born with; and when I got to be about ten, I took it on, too. Geneva LeFleur seemed just a little highfalutin for Hanged Dog, Arizona—and a tad fancy to suit my tastes, too, when it came down to it—which is how I came to be called Geneva Kincaid, Gini for short.

We had a little three-room adobe on the edge of town, with a cactus garden in front and a vegetable patch in back. We kept a cow, two sheep, and a few chickens. We had a good paint gelding named Jigsaw, and a pet desert tortoise that Gam was real fond of. We called him Malachi. Between the garden and the chickens and Gam's little semiannual from her gold shares we did just fine, though we never lived fancy.

Even back then I hated wearing dresses, so the britches aren't any "recent affectation," like some of those newspaper scribblers say. When I lived with Gam, I had to wear skirts most all the time—we already had enough animosity coming from the townsfolk—but she made me up some buckskins that were so thin and butter-soft they were like wearing nothing. Some nights I'd slip into those bucks and crawl up on Jigsaw bareback, and we'd range out over the desert by moonlight. Gam never worried about me when I rode. She said if she didn't know better she'd have sworn I was part Apache.

It also helped that the horse was Jigsaw. Gam bought him off a trader when he was seven and I was just turned eight, and she got a good deal because he was terrible thin and half-lame and head-shy from being abused by some fool. Gam used Apache ways on him—mud and herb poultices, soothing chants, and some trinkets she braided into his mane for magic—and in six months he was dollar-sound and seal-sleek and would let you flap a blanket around his head. So much for head-shy!

I do not want you to think he was a dullard, for he had fire and courage, too. He just wasn't one to spook and skitter at every jackrabbit, the way some ponies do. He was tall, just past fifteen hands, and good-trained. He had dark, kind eyes—wide-set—and a stout heart and no bad flaws of conformation, though he ran a little goosey through the rump. He wasn't schooled to cut or rope, but he reined real slick and could spin on a bottle stopper. He also possessed the smoothest jog-trot I have ever had the pleasure to sit.

Some people do not like a spotted horse, but that is their loss. Jigsaw wasn't a regular pinto, but the kind of paint that has more dark splotches and less white, with the edges of the dark being jaggedy instead of smooth. I have also heard this type of coloring called skewbald or *overo*. Jigsaw's splotches were deep chestnut, about the color of polished cherrywood, and he had a Crown P brand on his left hip.

He was so sweet-tempered that even when I was little he would have been steady for me to ride to the one-room schoolhouse in Hanged Dog had I been welcome, which I wasn't. The schoolmistress, Widow McBride, was a die-hard, starched-up Presbyterian. She didn't approve of the produce of fallen women, and said I would taint the other children.

It was just as well. Gam kept me home and taught me my three R's, and lessons in the garden in spring or in front of the parlor fire in winter sure beat a hard chair in a drafty schoolhouse, even if Gam was all business when it came to ciphering and geography. She showed me the way to card wool, and how to loom rugs and blankets like the Indians do, and how to run a thread out of the pattern and off the edge so the spirit can escape. I stitched a sampler, too, with all the alphabet and numbers and a homely verse. It was mostly in red. That's my favorite color. Gam also made me read the Bible on Sundays to make sure I got Jesus, and one time she took me all the way down to Tucson just so I could see some of the world.

Book-learning was an easy thing for me, though I can't take credit for being any more than average smart. What I did have was a knack—a God-sent gift, Gam called it—for being able to remember anything I saw on paper, right down to the last comma, period, and flyspeck. Pearl Scrimm used to come over every Wednesday morning to play poker for matches with Gam and me, but by the time I was seven, Pearl wouldn't let me sit in at blackjack anymore on account of me remembering exactly what cards had been used up, even when she triple-decked them.

One thing Gam didn't teach me was how to fight. I learned that for myself. I found myself in a lot of scrapes when I was a kid, about half of them because of Paris LeFleur and the other half on account of Gam. I got real weary of all the remarks about being a cheap floozy's bar-brat and being raised by a white squaw, which was just one of the things they called Gam. They also called her an Apache's whore, or, most often, Injun Mary. When I was eleven, I beat the Holy Hannah out of Chester McCleave for using that "Injun Mary" business just one time too many. Chester was two years older and a half-foot taller than me, but I was a good bit madder. It was the last time he or any of the other kids maligned my Gam, at least to my face.

Some nights she'd brush my hair till her arm must have ached, but she never minded. "Gini," she'd say, "a girl with all this sorrel hair would be mighty popular with the Apache." Gam knew from whence she spoke, having been greatly admired for her own hair, which was a sort of wheat-blonde.

"Oh, Gam!" I'd say, since we both knew she probably would have murdered me before she let me run off to live on the desert with a bunch of nose-choppers.

She'd just laugh and say, "Well, you're growin' up a looker, child. With all that red hair, I'll just bet your daddy was an Irishman. Maybe we should oughta change your name to O'Malley or Dingle or Magee."

Now, that Irish business narrowed down my father's identity to roughly half the West, since it seemed to me that near all the 50 percent of the Christian population which wasn't Mex or Negro was either Irish or Scots or English or those three mixed up. I'd say, "Gam, I think Kincaid is already Irish."

"Is it?" She'd give a shrug. "Well, it don't sound Irish to me. And besides, my papa—who is prob'ly fast-steppin' on Mr. Scratch's fiery coals by now—was a dirt farmer and a Virginian, and his daddy was a Virginian before him. No, I think Kincaid's a Virginia name."

I'd usually let it drop about then, since there was no arguing with Gam. But if we had that conversation once, I'll bet we had it five hundred times.

She always used to talk to me about what she called the Adventure of Life, and as hard as hers had been, what with being kidnapped by Apache and then being scorned by her own kind, she used to get a funny sort of smile when she said it. The Adventure of Life. Looking around Hanged Dog, I couldn't see much adventure in store for me, but when I'd ask her about it, she'd say, "It's not somethin' you plan, child. You take it as it comes, and build it up from there."

I guess you never understand some things until they run right over you.

I didn't realize it at the time, but for me, the Adventure of Life commenced in 1880, about four and a half weeks after my fifteenth birthday.

It was the middle of July and as hot a day as we have in Arizona, which is pretty dang hot. What made it worse was that the summer wets were just starting up. Dry heat, like we usually have, is one thing; but along about in July and August the air gets so squish-thick with promised rain, you feel like you're boiling in your clothes and breathing in steam. Most of the time the rain doesn't come and you get those mean black dust storms and dry thunder, but when it does let loose with water, it lets loose with a vengeance.

We'd had one of those gully-washers the night before, and the air hung so heavy it was near as hard to wade as the mud. For my part, I would have been happy to sit in the front room in my underwear all day, sipping on a limeade and fanning myself with a seed catalog; but along about eleven in the morning, Gam came in from the garden looking peaked. She was kind of hunkered over and she half-fell down on our old sofa. For a minute I thought she'd been scorpion-bit.

"I think you best run and fetch Doc Ben," she said, and her voice sounded all swallowed up. "I've got somethin' terrible wrong with my belly."

Well, I grabbed the first thing I could find to throw on

over my drawers, which was a pair of Doc Ben's pants Gam had been mending the night before, and I hightailed it up the street. I guess I got more than a few stares, but I can't say I cared much. Doc Ben's office was over the mercantile, and I took those rickety steps two at a time. I started in banging on the door as hard as I could.

I don't know how long I hammered and hollered for him to wake up before I heard a voice from down the sidewalk. It was Amos Malone, one of those dang snooty Malone brothers who owned Hanged Dog's mercantile plus three others in the Territory, with plans for expansion. They lorded that over everybody, said they only kept the store in Hanged Dog out of sentiment and Civic Duty. "Hey!" he called, like I should be real honored by the conversation. "What you doin' up there?"

"I'm takin' tea with Rutherford B. Hayes," I yelled back. "What's it look like I'm doin'?"

"Well, you're sure dressed for it," said Amos, and started in laughing like an old donkey. I started in pounding on the door again.

"He ain't there, y'know," he said.

My knocking hand was pretty scuffed up by then, and I stuck it under my armpit. "Well, do you know where he is, or do you just wander up and down the streets makin' sport of ladies?"

He snorted at the "ladies" part, but he said, "He's out to the Lawson place. Rose is expectin' her tenth."

"Well, thank you very much for sayin' so in the first place," I said, and I ran down those stairs so fast I knocked him splash in the street.

I was out of breath by the time I got back to the house, but Gam was in a lot worse shape than me. She lay on the sofa, hunkered up and crying, and I don't mind saying she had me scared close to death.

"Don't worry, Gam," I said, as brave as I could. "I know where Doc Ben is. I'm goin' to get him real quick. I left word at the Thirsty Buzzard, and Pearl is comin' straight down to sit with you till I get back."

She just nodded and cried a little. I ran outside, threw a saddle on Jigsaw, and started for the Lawson spread at a gallop.

Going hard on a good day, it used up an hour to get to Ike Lawson's, but what with all the mud and slop and the air being near as thick as okra water, it took almost two. By the time we skidded into the barnyard, poor Jigsaw was clay mud to the shoulder and looked more solid dun than Indian paint. He was also pretty well spent and blowing hard. I tossed his reins to one of the Lawson kids—with orders to keep him walking—and marched on up to the house. I didn't bother to knock. I just tramped in the front door and hollered for Doc Ben.

Ike Lawson came out of the back room. "Who's that trackin' half the Territory into my parlor?" he said, trying to sound grumpy even though a big smile was practically splitting his face.

"It's Geneva Kincaid," I said, "and I need Doc Ben Winslow in a hurry." Just then I heard a baby cry in the back room, and I knew Doc Ben would walk out any minute with it in his arms.

But Ike said, "'Fraid you missed him. He'd just delivered Rosie of a fine baby girl when Roy Turner's boy galloped in here and took him up to their claim. Said Roy busted up his leg pretty bad. That was near two hours ago. What you need Doc Ben for, anyhow?"

Because of all the sliding and slipping we'd done to get there, I was as yellowed up with mud as my horse, and Ike kind of stared me up and down before his eyes settled on the little bow at the front of my camisole. He said, "Ain't you got a proper shirt?"

It was a pretty stupid remark, and I ignored it. "It's my Gam," I said, "Mary Kincaid. She's terrible sick. My horse isn't used to all this rough-ridin', Mr. Lawson. I'd be obliged if you'd give me the loan of a mount and let me leave my paint here for a spell. That claim's halfway up in the mountains, and it's another good hour, even ridin' quick."

He lent me a bay mare he said could go, and he barely had the girth cinched before I leapt on her and headed up into the trees. The mare was fast, all right, but she was just as used up as Jigsaw when I galloped into Roy Turner's camp. Right off, I saw Doc Ben: squatted under a pine sapling ramada, pouring whiskey down Roy's throat, and just finishing up setting his leg.

"Why, Gini!" Doc Ben said, and took himself a healthy swig on the bottle. He tucked a blanket around Roy Turner's splint and rolled his own sleeves back down. "What in thunder you doing clear up here in your underwear? Are them my Sunday pants you've got yellow mud all over?"

I told him about Gam as quick as I could, and a darkness settled over his face. "Where's she feelin' pain?" he asked, and made me point. "Did it come on all sudden-like?"

I nodded.

"Pain like a knife?"

"Yes, and she's white as milk."

He stood up quick, grabbed his bag, and told Roy Turner's boy to bring up his horse. "I expect it's her appendix, Gini."

"Is that bad?" I asked, knowing it was, but wanting him to tell me she'd be fine in the morning.

He just said, "Mary, my Mary," climbed on his old gray gelding, kicked it into a fast canter, and took off down through the woods.

Roy Turner was too drunk to talk reason, what with all the whiskey Doc Ben had been pouring in him, and his no-account son wouldn't let me borrow a horse. I had to jog Ike Lawson's mare back down to his place and pick up Jigsaw, who was well-rested enough that he gave me a decent lope on into the desert flatlands and back to town, but I still didn't get there till just past dusk.

Our little house looked awful still when I rode up, and I was almost scared to open the door. When I did, I found Pearl Scrimm sitting in the front room, crying all the rouge off her face. Doc Ben stood by the cold fireplace with his arms on the mantel and his head in his hands.

I took a long look at them, and then at the closed bedroom door, and all I said was, "No."

Besides the undertaker, the three of us were the whole crowd at the funeral. Doc Ben was pretty well drunk from mourning inside a liquor bottle, and wandered off right after. Pearl walked me back to the house.

"Why doncha come on up to the Thirsty Buzzard, Gini?" she said, and stepped around a leftover mud puddle. "You could even have your ma's old room. We'll fix it up all fresh 'n' purty."

I shook my head. "No thank you, Pearl. I don't think I'm cut out for that trade. Besides," I said, looking down at my chest, of which there wasn't much, "I don't think I've got the proper equipment."

She was still weeping a little from the burying, but she managed to laugh some at that. "That don't much matter. I seen the way you turn heads when you walk down the street."

I hadn't noticed any heads turning, but I figured if they had been, it was more on account of my being Paris

LeFleur's daughter and Gam's ward than anything else. I had learned to ignore rude stares a long time ago.

I said, "No thanks, Pearl."

"Well, just come up and sing in the bar for a while," she insisted. "You got your Mama's pipes as well as her looks. Why, when you sing 'A Blue-Eyed, Black-Hearted Man,' you make me cry every time."

We had got to the house, and I put my hand on the latch. "I don't believe so, Pearl."

She was a little put out by this time, since she figured to be doing me a favor and also since she'd walked all the way from the cemetery in her good shoes, which pinched her bunion. Pearl always was one for flash over comfort. "Then what you gonna do for money, child?" she said, a little testy. "How you gonna live?"

I shrugged. "Gam and me always made it fine before."

"That's only 'cause she had them little checks from her gold stock, and you won't be gettin' that 'cause she didn't leave no will. It'll go back to her brother in Virginy. Doc Ben and me looked into it."

"Well, I'll have this place."

She shook her head and shifted her weight to her good foot. "That goes to her brother, too. Fact is, girl, you ain't got nothin' but your clothes and personal things, and you only got two options I can think of. One's to work for me, the other's to get hitched. And I don't see nobody champin' at the bit to do that last one. Course, Frank Malone's been droolin' after you since you turned twelve. He ain't the marryin' sort, but I s'pose he'd pay your bills till he got tired of you."

Now, Frank Malone had money but he was a certified lecher and just about the last person you'd want to be stuck in a room with, let alone married—or anything else—to.

"No, Pearl," I said, "I believe I'll just stay on in the house for a bit. I've lived here practically my whole life, and I'm in no hurry to move. If this brother of Gam's wants me out, he can just come and toss me out on the street himself."

As it turned out, that was pretty close to what he did. Two months later, and just as we were starting to get some halfway decent weather, one Mr. Evert Fairbanks—complete with gold-rimmed glasses, slicker suit, and black bowler hat—showed up on my front stoop.

"I represent Mr. Reuben T. Kincaid and the estate of his sister, Mrs. Mary Kincaid Washburn," he said after he took off his hat and sat down in Gam's good rocker. Pinched and pasty, he had this look on his face like he had to use the outhouse real bad but was too proper to give in to the urge. Lips pursed, he said, "I believe you worked for her in some capacity?"

"Worked for her, my foot!" said I. "She raised me up like family."

"I see." His mouth puckered a little more, and he sorted through some papers in his case. "You realize, of course, that you have no claim on her estate. There was never any formal adoption, per se."

He acted so self-important and pompous that he made those stuck-up Malone brothers seem like just folks. I said, "Where're you from, Mr. Fairbanks?"

He looked kind of surprised, but he said, "Virginia."

"Well, they may do things 'per se' in Virginia, Mr. Fairbanks, but this is Arizona. You can ask anybody in town, and even though they might not have thought high of her or me, they'll tell you Mary Kincaid was like my ma. She even let me take her name. We do what's right in Arizona Territory, even though we don't always put it on paper in front of some fancy-pants lawyer who runs around spoutin' foreign languages."

I guess I shouldn't have used such stern words, because he pulled his little shoulders back and said, "And in Virginia, missy, children are seen and not heard. In any case, you will have to vacate the premises." He paused and looked around our little parlor. "I admit I am somewhat disappointed in the structure, but I suppose it is worth something."

"You're goin' to sell Gam's house?"

"I am empowered to sell Mrs. Washburn's real estate, as well as all her personal belongings, on behalf of her brother. I understand there is some livestock as well? A horse and so on?"

If there was one thing Gam was death on, it was a lie; but this time I think she might have forgiven me. "There's livestock, all right, Mr. Fairbanks, but the horse is mine. Gam gave me Jigsaw for my fifteenth birthday."

He shuffled through some more of those papers of his. "I see," he said, and pushed his glasses up his skinny little nose. "Have you any documentation?"

"Mr. Fairbanks, the last time somebody gave you a birthday present, did you ask for a bill of transfer?"

He puffed out a little snort that made his glasses slither back down his beak. "I suppose I'll just have to take your word. Now, I'd like to make an inventory of the remainder of the estate. . . ."

Well, we spent the rest of the afternoon going through Gam's things, and Mr. Fairbanks wrote everything down in a little book and made notes about how much he thought each item might be worth. Finally, along about nightfall, he closed his notebook, pushed up his specs for the umpteenth time, and said, "I'll schedule the auction for Friday week,

Miss Kincaid. That's ten days. You'll have to vacate by the preceding Thursday."

"And just where do you suggest I vacate *to*, Mr. Fairbanks?"

He put on his hat and stepped out the front door. "That is entirely up to you."

I mused on it for a whole week. At first I thought maybe nobody would buy Gam's adobe, since it was a poor thing and clear on the edge of town. But the three Malone brothers had their eye on it for a warehouse, and it was told to me that nasty old Nadine Pinchot from the dress shop had already cleared out a space in her parlor for Gam's breakfront. Frank Malone even had the gall to knock on my door and ask to come in and measure the rooms—and maybe a few other things, if I got his drift. I shut that door in his face pretty dang fast, I can tell you.

By the Wednesday before the sale, I decided I had best go see Pearl about singing in the saloon. I didn't have anything against the singing by itself, but I knew Pearl's avaricious heart well enough to figure she wouldn't be satisfied with just that for too long. I wasn't too proud to go to Doc Ben Winslow for help, but since Gam died he'd been practically living at the Thirsty Buzzard, and his practice had gone to pot. Folks didn't even try to send for him anymore. They took their aches and pains over to the medical man in Flat Rock, a good half-day's ride east.

I put on a dress, fixed my hair nice—piled high to make me look older, with ringlets round my face—and took myself up to the Thirsty Buzzard. Pearl was busy abovestairs when I got there, but the bar was pretty much deserted. I ordered a sarsaparilla and waited for her at a corner table, figuring to pass the time by counting the slug holes in the walls. I didn't get counted higher than two dozen, though. Doc Ben Winslow had seen me come in, and within three minutes he staggered over and dragged out a chair.

He didn't speak more than two words to me before he started to cry. He kept saying how much he loved Gam, and how sorry he was. "I would'a give anything if I could'a saved her. I would'a give anything if she'd been my wife," he wept. "I asked her, oh, I asked her a thousand times, but she wouldn't have it. She'd just say, 'What do we need with some piece'a paper, Ben?' and tell me I was bein' silly. What'll I do without my Mary? What'll I do, Gini?"

I am ashamed to say it now, but as good as Doc Ben had always been to me, right then I was disgusted with him. That's the arrogance of youth for you. I thought he ought to be acting a little more grown-up about the whole thing, and I was feeling superior. After all, we'd both lost Gam, but I had faced up to my responsibilities and he was trying to kill himself with bourbon whiskey. I figured he couldn't have done a much better job if he'd just climbed into a barrel of John Barleycorn and pulled the lid shut over him. If I'd known then what I know now about life, I would have been a good bit kinder to him, at least in my thoughts.

I was just sitting there, watching him mutter with his head on the table, when I realized somebody had come up next to me. I noticed his clothes first. His pants had some road on them and his boots were scuffed, but above that was a plain red vest and black suit coat, and even a black string tie. None of it looked too pressed, but he still appeared a sight tidier than the Thirsty Buzzard's usual riffraff. He was smiling like he knew some secret joke on the rest of us.

"You're looking pretty haughty for a body so young," he said.

"And you're pretty forward for an old coot with a beer

belly," I replied, though he probably wasn't sixty and his belly didn't pooch over his belt buckle more than a couple of inches.

He grinned at me and sat down. "Mind?"

"Does it matter? Seems to me you're already sat."

He'd brought his beer with him, and he slid it on the table. He had these real white, even teeth, and that smile of his never broke. "What's a fair young thing like you doing in such a low establishment?"

"You just make that up?"

He gave out with a laugh, kind of barking and refined all at the same time. He was clean-shaved and sun-browned. Light blue eyes burned cool out of his face, welcome as ice in summer. "You're a sharp one," he said, "but you didn't answer my question."

I took a draw on my sarsaparilla. "Didn't plan to."

Just then Doc Ben lifted up his head, and his rheumy eyes drifted into focus. He looked over at the stranger, gave a thoughtful lick at his lips, and slurred, "I know you."

"Of course you do, friend," the stranger said with just about the most soothing tone I'd ever heard. "We'll talk about it later. Now, go on back to sleep." Doc Ben nodded and put his head back down on his arm. The stranger waited till Doc Ben started breathing deep and regular, which didn't take more than a few seconds, and then he turned back to me. "You put me in mind of someone, Brown Eyes," he said. "I don't suppose we've met before?"

I laughed and tried to look sophisticated. The old man had plenty of brass, and I decided I might just like him. "That's a new one," I said. "I never seen you in my life, mister."

"I suppose you're right." His voice had a streak of real charm in it: kind of fancified, but not so much as to sour you on it. It was the kind of voice you'd like to hear read a good story out loud. "I forget how the years have left me behind. Person I'm thinking of was from a long time ago. But my goodness, you sure do favor her."

Well, he had me curious, which is probably just what he wanted. "Where'd you know this lady?" I asked.

"Right here in Hanged Dog," he said. "A fine lady by the name of Perry LeFleur." He held his hand over his heart and he looked genuinely sad. "They tell me she's passed on to God's greater reward. I am deep in regret."

That got my ears perked up. "You mean the Paris LeFleur who was a whore in this saloon?"

For just a second, his brow knotted up and looked a little mean. "Perry LeFleur may have been a soiled dove, but I won't have her called a whore in my presence, young miss."

"I reckon I can call her anything I want, old man, seeing as how she was my ma."

Just like that, his face went mushy as a hound dog pup's. "Well, I guess I should have realized," he said. "Perry's girl."

"The same."

He just smiled at me. "I'll be damned. You're not employed here, are you?"

I figured since he was an admirer of my ma's, he was thinking about taking me upstairs to do a little comparing. Real quick, I said, "I'm goin' to be a singer here, but that's all, mister. Don't go gettin' any ideas."

He laughed again. "I'm too old to get ideas, girl. You got a name?"

"I might ask you the same question."

"Yes, you might, but I asked first."

"That's fair," I said. "I go by the name of Geneva Kincaid. Gini for short."

He finished up his beer. "That your daddy's name? Kincaid?"

"Don't know my daddy's name, wouldn't use it if I did. Now it's your turn."

"Well, I tell you, Miss Gini, I—" He twisted in his chair. "What is it, boy? Can't you see this young lady and I are hip-deep in the social amenities?"

A young cowpoke had tapped him on the shoulder. He was blond and kind of scruffy, but probably not bad-looking underneath the dirt. He leaned down and whispered, "C'mon, Tuck, let's get outta here 'fore you reminisce me into jail. I think that deputy got an eyeful when we rode in, and him and the sheriff's conferenced across the way."

My friend waved his hand. "Settle down, Pete. Nobody's going to bother us in Hanged Dog, least of all Ezra Wanamaker."

It sunk into me all at once. "You're Tuck Brennan, aren't you?" I said. "Nobody told me you were fat!"

"Holy cripes!" Pete hissed. "Keep your consarned voice down!" He needed a haircut real bad, and now that he'd been standing there a couple of minutes, I realized he didn't smell too good, either.

"I'll keep my voice any dang way I want it," I said before I turned back to the old man. "Why, you're a hero in this locality, Tuck Brennan! I have heard stories and read books, and I know the names of all your gang from back in the old times. There's the murdered Jinx Danahoe and Elroy 'No Thumb' Chavez, who got back-shot over to Yavapai City. Young Tyrone O'Neill, too. They say Tyrone could charm a diamondback out of striking, then win the rattles right off him at cards."

"My goodness," said Tuck, in such a manner that I couldn't tell if he was impressed at my knowledge or just humoring me.

I couldn't seem to shut up, though. I had never met a famous person before, and I guess I was besotted by the presence of greatness. "I read in *Boss Brennan's Final Freedom: Blind Justice Takes Its Toll* that Tyrone did a couple years' hard time up in Colorado," I went on, "but neither newspaper nor dime novel has mentioned him since. Folks say Tyrone's dead, now, too. They say you're the last one left."

"And how do you figure it, Miss Gini?"

I cocked my head to the side and tried to appear wise. "I figure that to be highly likely, myself."

"You're not so smart, Miss Girlie," said Pete.

"Smarter than you, if that's all you can think to say. Plus, if you two are countin' on the kindness of Sheriff Wanamaker you are out of luck, since he got shot by a drunk Dutchman four years ago. Now we have Sheriff Cyrus P. Russell, and he doesn't take kindly to outlaws. Although if you served your time, I don't know why you should be worried."

"Miss Gini," Tuck Brennan said as he scraped his chair back and stood up, "there are times when an intemperate man is liable to happy-go-lucky himself into a five-foot cell with no window."

It didn't strike me till just then how tall he was. Still grinning, he made a little bow. He lifted up his hat when he did it, and I saw that his hair was red, near as red and wavy as mine, except for the gray streaks.

"It was good to meet you, Miss Gini," he said. "Good to meet the daughter of Perry LeFleur." He turned around to Pete and said, "Just calm down, boy. I never saw a body so nervous over next to nothing. Now, you amble on out there and mount up like you've got all the time in the Lord's Creation."

I went to the window and watched while they got on their horses and jogged away. The sheriff and Deputy Riggs didn't pay them much mind, so I guess they hadn't recognized Tuck or Pete after all. But it was while I stood there watching Tuck Brennan ease down the road that I got my idea.

I went back to where Doc Ben was passed out and kissed him on the forehead. I told the bartender I'd changed my mind about seeing Miss Pearl, and then I went home and put on my buckskins.

It was getting toward sunset, and the light faded fast as I packed my carpetbag. Some clothes and my sewing kit went in along with things that had sentiment for me, like the Good Book Gam got from Mescal Mort Scobie, our few photographs, and Gam's garnet jewelry that had been her grandmother Kincaid's. I filled up an old flour sack with boiled eggs and coffee and the rest of the ham and such, and pulled down Gam's old squirrel rifle from behind the kitchen door. Then I saddled Jigsaw and tied the baggage on behind.

It seemed like it took forever to locate the dang tortoise, especially since it had got dark by that time, but I finally found him snugged up underneath the pump stand. I carried him out to where I had Jigsaw tethered, and tucked him inside the carpetbag.

"See you don't make a mess on my clean underwear, Malachi," I said before I closed it up. Not that he'd listen to me, but I felt better for having warned him.

I turned out the sheep and the cow, shooed the chickens out of the coop. Then I went back in the house, took a long last look at all those things Mr. Evert Fairbanks planned on auctioning off come the day after next, and started splashing kerosene.

Adobe is dang near impossible to burn, but we had a thatched roof and a good bit of stuffed furniture, and by the time I got two miles out of town, it fairly lit up the sky. I have never before or since seen such a glorious conflagration, and I'll warrant Mr. Evert Seen-But-Not-Heard Fairbanks hasn't either.

2

On Tuck's Trail

I suppose it would have been wiser to wait for a daylight start, but seeing as how I wanted to make sure Mr. Evert Fairbanks didn't get his hands on Gam's things—and since somebody'd be sure to catch me in the daytime—I trailed Tuck Brennan and his smelly friend by moonlight.

It wasn't hard, for they had turned off at the old Lode City road and stuck to it at an easy pace. Plus, Pete's horse was plenty sloppy in front, so she was easy to track. I figured Pete for a man more set on dazzle than substance, for though that mare of his was a real looker standing still, she'd be sure to wear herself out quick in a dead run.

The road wove on out into low foothills, and the tracks kept to it for a good five miles before they veered off into the scrub. By then it was late and the moon had started to cloud over. I reined Jigsaw off the road and up toward a nice cluster of rock that had some ironwood and mesquite around, all silvered by moonlight.

After I got Jigsaw seen to, I rescued Malachi from the carpetbag. He had messed on my clean drawers, and I gave him a good scolding. I don't think it had much effect, because when I sat him down and told him he was free and I was glad to be shed of such a silly-looking, turd-making critter, he just sat there yawning, with his neck craned up.

I aimed him out toward freedom, but he wouldn't budge.

Tortoises can be real stubborn, even after they've had things explained to them. Finally I gave up on him and gathered kindling for a little coffee fire. I must have been more beat out than I thought because, as unaccustomed as I was to sleeping without walls and roof, I dozed off before I even got it lit.

I don't know exactly what woke me, but I came to pretty sudden. The first thing I saw was Malachi. He'd only taken about two steps from where I'd put him, and he was blinking at me from a long pool of shade that wasn't cast by any tree.

"I figured when I spied somethin' movin' around up here that it had to be that paint horse of yours, Gini Kincaid."

If there was one person I didn't want to see right then, it was Frank Malone; but there he was, standing right over me and casting his nasty shadow on my tortoise. Through the upside-down V of his legs, I could see the little bald-faced sorrel he always rode. Frank had ground-tied it about fifty feet out, which is why I hadn't heard him ride up.

"Go away," I said.

He smiled down at me. He had this way of smiling, all kind of superior and smarmy, that made you want to slap him, then go take a bath. He said, "'Fraid I can't do that, Gini. Folks in town aren't happy with you. Mr. Evert Fairbanks is madder'n a wet cat, and my brother Amos isn't exactly thrilled, neither. Looks like we're gonna have to build a new warehouse from scratch after all."

He didn't even have the decency to look me in the face. He stared straight down at my leather leggings, and a kind of tic twitched at the corner of his left eye. The whole business made me a little nervous, but mostly it made me mad.

"Chris Mitchell's fit to be tied, too," he said. "It sparked over and burned his brand-new shitter right down to the seat. Sheriff's got Deputy Riggs and half the town out lookin' for you right now, and as a Civic Leader, it's my duty to take you back. Those're sure mighty tight britches."

I would have sat up, but with him standing over me—feet on either side of my knees—I didn't like thinking about what I'd be sitting up into.

"I'm real sorry about the Mitchells' privy," I said, "and that's the truth. It's also the truth that if you don't clear out of here and let me be on my way, I'll have to shoot you." I had my hand curled around the stock of Gam's squirrel gun, which I'd laid down next to, in case of snakes.

He gave out with a laugh, and said, "Gini Kincaid, you couldn't lift that thing, let alone fire it. Where'd you get those britches, anyhow? Old Injun Mary make 'em for you?"

Well, that rifle was near as long as I am tall, and at the moment it still lay alongside me with the business end against my ankles and the stock butt under my armpit. What with Frank standing over me, about the only thing I could shoot was his horse.

"I'm warning you, Frank Malone, you best not speak foul of Mary Kincaid. You don't want to mess with me today."

He wasn't taking me at all serious, because he said, "How do those britches fasten up, anyhow?" He started bending down like he might have the bark to actually try and find out, and that did it. I reached over, grabbed the squirrel gun's forestock in my left hand, and, hard as I could, levered that long steel barrel up betwixt his legs.

Old Frank let out a whoop. His eyes kind of screwed up and he had both lips bit hard between his teeth, and he folded up on the ground.

I jumped up quick and grabbed Malachi and my gear. By the time I threw on Jigsaw's tack and got scrambled into the saddle, Frank Malone, Civic Leader, had wobbled up to his knees. He made a grab for my stirrup when I went past, but a good crack to the top of his head with the rifle butt settled his hash.

"That'll teach you to speak unkind of Mary Kincaid," I said as I rode out, though I don't know if he could exactly hear me. "And don't try to follow. You come after, you'll get more of the same!"

I started right out on Tuck Brennan's trail. I looked back over my shoulder every few minutes, but I didn't see hide nor hair of Frank Malone. After a couple hours I got to wondering if maybe I'd killed him, but then I decided his skull was likely too thick to dent, let alone bust. And if I'd whacked him good enough to put him out of commission for a while, I'd probably done the town of Hanged Dog—or at least the part of it south of Main Street—a service, since Frank was known for prowling around over there at night and walking with señoritas who didn't always want to be walked with, if you get my meaning.

Anyway, along about ten in the morning I came to where Tuck and Pete had camped for the night. They'd met three other riders there, and the five of them had set out northwest. I was glad Gam had taught me so much of the Apache way. Right off, I knew the new horses were all males, and that they'd just come from around Tucson: the first because all three had made water between their hoofprints instead of behind, like a mare; the second because their manure was full of grama grass, which everybody knows you find mainly down on the tableland outside Tucson. Well, Dragoon Springs, too, but that was too far away for them to still be dropping it. Of course, none of this helped me find Tuck faster or figure out who the new riders were, but thinking about it and congratulating myself for being so clever helped pass the time.

There was a lot of time to pass and not a lot of scenery, because pretty soon the trail led back out into scrub desert. Scrub is flat as anything and goes for miles. It's got nothing to recommend it. It's just rocks and brush and prickly pear, snakes and scorpions, and jumping cholla. I steered around the cholla, for it is a calculating kind of cactus: it knows when something warm-blooded, like a horse or human, is near it, and pops out little clusters of nasty spines that are death on your clothes as well as your hide.

I kept an ear cocked the whole time for rattlers, too. Now, pilgrims who have only heard the sound a dead snake's dry rattles make don't live long if that's the warning they expect. When those rattles are still on the original owner, they go so dang fast they sound more like the hiss of steam when you drop cold water on a red-hot stove lid, only more drawn out. That's what I listened for. I was plenty scared of snakes already, since I'd nearly got bit by a big old sidewinder when I was about six and playing out by the garden. Gam whacked off its head with a hoe, but boy howdy! I had nightmares on that one for years.

Come late afternoon, the trail took a curve toward higher ground, and by nightfall we were almost up in the trees. That's how it is in the Territory sometimes. There are places where you can go from bare desert to dense pine forest in two hours if you know where you're aiming. Of course, this wasn't exactly forest I was riding up into, but there were low trees and grass.

I didn't push Jigsaw past dark. I settled him in, shared a boiled egg with Malachi, and had myself some ham and coffee. I was just about as tired as a body could be, what with only getting three hours' rest the night before and riding all day, and I nodded off directly.

Well, the Lord must have had it in for me to not get

enough sleep, because right along in the middle of the night, I felt something whack my boot.

I hollered "Snake!" and grabbed for my squirrel gun. But before I could get it off the ground, somebody stepped right down on my wrist.

"Look at all that hair!" said the one who had kicked my boot. "I believe we caught us a gal!"

"A gal with a rifle," said the one with his foot on my arm, "and it's nigh on big as she is."

"Get your messy boot away!" I said. There wasn't quite a full moon, but I could see halfway decent. "I know who you are. You're Pete that rides with Tuck Brennan."

"How you know me?"

"By your stench, which has not improved since we last met. Now, leave me go!"

While the boot-kicker laughed, Pete stooped down and popped a match with his thumbnail. He held it over my face and squinted. "I'll be jiggered. You're that jabber-mouth saloon gal, ain't you?"

I gave a jerk and tried to get my arm free, but he just stepped down harder. "I might'a been in the Thirsty Buzzard," I said, "but I'm no 'saloon gal' and you best not call me one. I'm Gini Kincaid, and I tracked you up here."

"I do believe she's after the reward on me," Pete said, kind of proud.

The other one laughed again. "If she's smart enough to trail you this far, Pete, seems to me she's not so dumb as to go to all that bother for just thirty-five dollars."

"Forty!" Pete said, and shook out the match. "Zack said the last poster he seen said forty!"

"All right, then. Forty. Now move your damn foot before you break her arm."

"Aw, cripes." Pete got off my wrist, but not before he

grabbed away my squirrel gun. He hauled me up by the elbow. "What you think we oughta do with her, Mace?"

I was tired to begin with, but these two had me downright fatigued. I said, "The least you can do, if you're goin' to come sneakin' in here and rob me of my rest, is to stand downwind."

Pete gave my arm a hard pinch. "You got an awful smart mouth for such a skinny gal! How come you're dressed up like an Injun?"

"How come you don't take a bath?" I said, and shot my free elbow back into his ribs. I didn't aim it too good and it glanced off, but he cussed under his breath. He also pulled back his fist like he planned to slug me.

The one called Mace caught his arm. He was grinning. "You don't want to go hitting her, Pete. She looks kinda frail to me."

Pete still had me in a lock, but I said "I'll show you frail!" and took a kick at Mace. My boot sort of skidded across his shin, but at least it hit. "Now, you two penny-ante players better take me to Tuck Brennan, for I've got important business with him."

Mace was still grinning, from what I could see in the moonlight, but he'd taken a step back out of range. "Business?" he said. "What kind of business could you have with Tuck?"

"It's between him and me, and has got nothing to do with forty-dollar desperados."

Pete gave me a good tweak for that one, but Mace said, "Why, miss, I'm no forty-dollar desperado. That honor belongs solely to my brother. Personally, I'm not worth a wood nickel on the open market. Let her go, Pete."

"But Mace!"

"Let her go. You've got her gun already, don't you? You don't even come off worth forty bucks, actin' scared of a little redheaded girl. That hair is red, isn't it? Hard to tell by moon."

Pete let me go and I gave a good shake. "Yes it is, and I thank you for callin' off your brother, as the stink from him was about to turn it a whole new color."

Pete still had ahold of my squirrel gun, and he swung it up in the air, ready to bring it down on my skull. "Lemme whack her, Mace! Lemme whack her just once!"

But Mace just laughed. He had a nice laugh. He wasn't bad-looking, either, for a clean-shaved man. Now that I knew he was Pete's brother, I could see the resemblance; but Mace had dark hair, trimmed short, and he did not smell. "How you know Tuck Brennan?" he asked.

"It's enough for you to know we're acquainted," I said. "He was a good friend to my mother as well."

"That ain't no lie," Pete admitted. "I heared Tuck say so himself."

That seemed to satisfy Mace. "Get your gear," he said. "I'll take you to see Tuck, though Lord knows what he's gonna think once he gets a look at you."

I grabbed my blankets. "He's goin' to think you're a Christian gentleman," I said, and scooped up my tortoise.

We started higher into those brushy trees, weaving through the splinters of moonlight that filtered through. Either the growth was getting thicker or Mace was taking the hardest path on purpose, because it seemed like I spent half my time bent low in the saddle and the other half getting smacked in the face with paloverde needles or worse.

We hadn't got more than ten minutes from my camp when Mace reached over and grabbed Jigsaw's reins. When I tried to yank them back, he swatted my hand and hushed me. "Listen!" he whispered.

Pete reined in, too. "Reckon it's a bear? Cougar, maybe? Remember the time you and me and Daddy cornered that catamount on Big Bone Hill, and her with a litter of—"

Mace shook his head. "Quiet. If it was a cat, that mare of yours'd be tangle-footin' her way to the next county by now. Shut up and let me listen."

This time I heard it. Pete did, too.

Mace tossed my reins to his brother. "You two just keep on going." He backed his horse away, and Pete led me on ahead.

"What's he doin'?" I asked. "And give over my reins!"

Pete raised his arm, ready to backhand me. "Shut up or I'll brain you, gal! Mace ain't here to hold me down, and I've got me a powerful temper."

"With forty whole dollars on your head, you must be some kind of cutthroat, all right."

He twisted round on his saddle real fast and changed his open hand into a fist, which he waved in my face. "I mean it! If you don't start showin' a little respect for your betters, I'll—" His head cocked up. "You hear that?"

"I didn't hear a thing besides the sound of your blamed arrogance, and furthermore—"

There was a cry behind us, then the rustling crash of bushes being bent and broke. Well, that mare of Pete's might have been slew-footed, but she reined awful dang good. She wheeled round so fast she nearly knocked me and Jigsaw into a big old ironwood tree.

We took off the way we'd come at a smart trot, and came upon the source of the ruckus in just a couple minutes. Mace was waiting for us, slapping his hat against his thigh to get the dust off. He pointed to something dark back in the bushes. "Either one of you know this fella?" he said as Pete and I slid off our horses.

Pete got there first. He bent down and twisted his head to

squint. "Ain't never seen him afore, Mace. Maybe he's a bounty hunter after my reward."

"Don't get your hopes up, Stinky Pete," I said, for I was beside him by then. "That is Frank Malone of Hanged Dog, Arizona, and of the Malone Brothers Mercantile stores. He is after me, though I'm surprised he's still on the trail after the harsh measures I treated him to this morning."

Pete gave out with a real sarcastic laugh. All superior, he said, "Why would anybody be trailing a scrawny thing like you?"

"I don't know what 'scrawny' has got to do with anything. But he's after me for arson and destruction of private property," I said proudly. It didn't come to me till just then that arson was just what I'd done. All of a sudden the proud in me got pushed aside, and I felt kind of ashamed.

Mace looked at me real odd. He said, "Well, whatever he's here for, I think we'd best decide what to do with him. I didn't thump his head all that hard, so he's gonna be comin' round soon. Horse took off yonder, Pete. Go catch it."

While Pete went after Frank's gelding, Mace dragged Frank out of the bushes and tied him up. "Those aren't very good knots," I said.

"I don't recall asking your opinion," Mace replied as he snugged up the last one, "but they're tied that way on purpose. I only need him trussed till tomorrow, not till Judgment. Course, I suppose we could do it your way and just set fire to him."

That riled the shame right out of me. I felt like giving him a kick, but instead I said, "I'll have you know I didn't burn one critter, human or otherwise. What I lit was my own dang house. It's not my fault it spread a little."

He took hold of my wrist. "Don't go stompin' your foot

at me, girl. You start a fire, the damage it does is on your soul and no other. A firebug's a sorry thing to be."

I tried to pull my arm free, but he wouldn't turn it loose. "If you're trying a-purpose to get on my bad side," I shouted, "you're sure doin' a good job of it! You just don't know—"

"All I know is a child as spoilt and sassy as you needs a serious visit to the woodshed." He let go of my arm like he was tossing away a piece of rubbish, and I felt bad all over again. He turned his back on me and leaned Frank up against a tree trunk. Frank groaned like he might be on the edge of waking up, and Mace said, "He gonna have any friends comin' after him?"

I sniffed a little bit, but tried to keep it quiet, not wanting him to know my feelings were hurt. "Far as I know he's got no friends. But he said there were others lookin' for me, if that's what you're aimin' at."

Pete came up on us then, leading Frank Malone's gelding. "This is one horse that just don't want to be caught," he panted, and mopped his forehead with a grubby sleeve. "He ain't bad, though. Got a awful purty mane, don't he? My Loula, she likes her a bald-faced horse. Maybe we should take him along."

"Just tether him over there," Mace said, disgusted. "If you're gonna add horse-thievin' to that poster of yours, you best learn to discriminate in what you're stealing. That thing's calf-kneed and ewe-necked, and is generally worse off than that worthless mare you're ridin' now. Giving him to Loula would be the next thing to an insult even if she liked horses in the first place, which she don't. I swear, Petie, about all I ever remember our daddy talking about was horses. How you managed to go your whole life without hearin' one blessed word is a bafflement."

Frank Malone opened his eyes. He looked down at his

ropes, then straight up at me. "I might'a known it was you, Gini Kincaid. You're a wicked child in need of reprimand! You set me free this instant or it'll go that much harder for you!"

It wasn't till I glanced over at Mace that Frank realized we weren't alone, and all of a sudden he looked scared. "Who are they, Gini?" he whispered, all choked-like. "What are they gonna do?"

It struck me that old Frank had spent a pretty rough day, what with getting hit once between the legs and twice over the head. "Frank Malone," I said as kind as I could, considering how worthless he was, "it is none of your nevermind who these men are. It's enough you know we won't hurt you unless you try and follow. I warned you before and you didn't care to listen. You best mind me this time."

"You oughta be able to work your way loose by morning, mister," Mace added. He had pulled his hat down low over his eyes so the moon couldn't show his face. "If you're smart, you'll hop on your horse and get yourself back home. Seems to me 'bout all you really want to do is give this brat a good hidin', anyway. That's not worth gettin' yourself hurt over, 'specially since I'm about to save you the trouble and swat her myself."

"I'd just like to see you try!" I said, and put up my fists. I figured I might not be able to whip him as good as I'd whipped Chester McCleave when I was eleven, but I'd be danged if I'd let anybody get away with that many insults, even if he did have a fine smile and knew his horseflesh.

But before I could level a punch, Mace snatched me up and slung me over his shoulder. I started beating on his back and kicking and hollering for him to let me down, but he grabbed me round the knees and snarled, "Judas Priest, but you're wearin' me thin! Shut up, or I swear I'll bend you

over here and now, and after I've paddled you raw, I'll leave
you roped to your friend Frank."

Nasty old Frank liked that idea, all right. Even trussed
like a pork roast, he had the gall to smile. Personally, I
didn't fancy the notion one bit, and I made myself go limp
over Mace's shoulder. He carried me to Jigsaw and dumped
me in the saddle like a sack of turnips. Then he wagged his
finger and growled, "Now stay there, dammit, and stay
still!"

Real quiet, I said, "I'm goin' to remember you did that."

"Shut up!" he barked, and smacked me on the leg: not so
bad it really hurt, but enough to make me bite my lip and
mind him.

"Har, har," was what came out of Pete. "Guess he told
you good, Miss Smarty Mouth!"

"You shut up, too!" Mace said.

About twenty minutes later, we came into Tuck Brennan's camp. He'd set up near a little stream that probably
got a lot bigger during the flood season, since the whole of
the valley floor was boulders and river rock. Orange dawn
was just creeping up over the hills by that time, and Tuck
and his boys were rising with it.

One older fella, who I took to be the sentry, was squatted
next to the fire, a rifle across his thighs. He had a rag
wrapped round his hand, and he held an iron skillet packed
with just-done biscuits. Tuck Brennan was sitting up in his
bedroll and stretching his arms. The sentry stood up slow,
like his joints needed oiling, and called, "Danahoes is back!
Carryin' an extra!"

Tuck got right to his feet, grabbed his red vest in one hand
and his rifle in the other. He gave a kick to the third fella,
who was still snoring, before he walked out to meet us.

"Who's that you got there, boys?" he said, real friendly,

though he had that Winchester pointed toward us. I was glad to hear the sound of his voice. It made me feel like I was someplace important, even if it was only some godforsaken riverbed in the middle of nowhere.

"It's all right, Tuck," Mace said. "We ran across this girl. Says she's got business with you."

Tuck grinned and let his rifle swing down real casual. "You believe everything everybody tells you, Mason?"

He came on over and gave Jigsaw an appreciative look and a pat on the neck before he smiled up at me. "Well, if it isn't Miss Gini, the daughter of Perry LeFleur. If I'd known we were entertaining lady visitors today, I would've pressed my shirt and had a shave." He slid that red vest on over his shirt and suspenders, then reached up and took my arm. "Let's hop on down from there, Miss Gini, and have ourselves a palaver."

"Best not make it a long one," Mace said as I jumped off Jigsaw. "She had a feller on her tail. We discouraged him some, but he looked bullheaded to me."

Tuck nodded. "You boys get yourself some chuck, then start breaking camp. I'll be with you shortly."

We walked a ways upstream before he sat me down on a smooth boulder by the water's edge. The old sentry, a gap-toothed, mostly bald coot named Zack, brought us gritty coffee and some of the biggest, hardest, and worst biscuits I have ever set a tooth to. While we took a stab at breakfast, I told Tuck about Gam dying, and what I'd done since.

"Nobody wants me back there," I said by the way of closing. "Nobody except Pearl Scrimm, who's mainly interested in starting me a-whoring so as to make her some ready cash, and Frank Malone, who I already told you about. I thought it all over, and I decided I'd like to ride with you for a spell."

Tuck hadn't said a word up till then. He'd just sat there sipping his coffee and trying to make headway through one of those doorstop biscuits. I don't mind saying he had me a little worried, as I had hoped for more enthusiasm.

Finally, he tossed away the last of his biscuit, gulped down the rest of his coffee, and said, "You just thought you'd ride in here and join up, did you, Miss Gini?"

"That's the size of it."

He pulled out his pipe and held a match to it. "I suppose there's no sending you back to Hanged Dog."

I tilted my chin up. "No, sir. There sure isn't, being as how I'm now a wanted woman."

He rubbed his chin stubble and took a puff on his pipe. "Well, I'd venture you're wanted in a somewhat limited sense, Miss Gini. And after hearing the sort of treatment you and the Danahoe brothers handed him, I have true doubts that your friend Mr. Frank Malone will give you any more grief. But I'll tell you what I'll do. These gentlemen and I are headed north on business, but we can detour over to Bogen Flats without losing too much time. You can ride that far with us, but that's it. I don't carry children, especially girl children who start fires, even if they are the daughter of Perry LeFleur."

Well, I stood straight up at that one. "I've had fifteen summers, old man! I'm no child, and I'm weary of the label. I can ride as good as anybody here, probably better. I can track like an Apache and use a gun if need be. I know how to stitch busted tack and mend a stove-up man or beast, and how to find the herbs that'll fix you when you're fevered. And I can sure as Holy Hannah make a better biscuit than these rocks you men have got the nerve to call breakfast!"

Tuck Brennan busted out laughing. "Well, you have most assuredly got some bark on you, Miss Gini, I'll say that! I can understand the herbs and the tack-mending, but just how do you figure you can track like an Apache? That doesn't seem a likely skill for any young lady, let alone an orphaned one from Hanged Dog."

I guess I stuck my nose up in the air some, but I sat back down on my rock. "The lady who raised me taught me how. She taught me a lot of things. Plants and herbs and such, and how to tell weather by the animals. How the Chiricahua Apache track, and how they make rock signals by the side of the trails, that being a skill even Apache squaws do second nature, but that the whole dang U.S. Army can't figure out!"

"Glory," he said, more to himself than me. "Gini Kincaid. I don't know why it didn't rise to the top of my brain before. This Gam who brought you up wouldn't have been the one who was wife to Cuchillo Rojo, would she? The one folks used to call Injun Mary?"

I jumped back to my feet. "I'll not hear you nor anybody else call her that, old man!"

He motioned me down. "You keeping hopping up, Miss Gini, you'll wear yourself out before we even get started. I didn't intend any insult to Mary Kincaid. I am sorry to hear she is dead. It seems I'm losing a great many old friends of late." He stared out over the valley floor toward the trees and chewed on his pipe stem for a couple minutes. I thought it passing strange that Gam had never mentioned knowing the famous Tuck Brennan, and I hoped he'd shed some light on that for me; but what he said when he looked at me again was, "You say you make decent biscuits?"

"Feather-light," I said, for I took pride in my cooking. "Flapjacks, too, and tortillas if you want 'em. I can bake a skillet cake and make the best jackrabbit pie you ever slid lips around. Corn fritters, enchiladas, fried squirrel with wild onions and gravy . . ."

"Enough, enough!" He grinned wide and said, "I suppose

Bogen Flats might be a tad far out of our way, after all. I'll tell you what, Miss Gini. You can ride with us as far as Prescott if you'll take over the cooking. Zachary's the best one of us with a skillet, and these poor biscuits are his pièce de résistance."

I found out later that Tuck was always throwing some French or Mex or Latin at you, though not snotty like Mr. Evert Fairbanks. But I didn't know that then, and I figured I'd just heard him funny. "They're pretty resistant, all right," I said, and dropped the last of mine in the stream. Even though the water ran strong, it sank straight down. "I'll wager that sorry thing'll still be sittin' there come spring."

"I wouldn't be the one to take that bet, Miss Gini." He signaled Stinky Pete to bring up our horses, then got to his feet and offered his hand like a true gent. I stood up, but he didn't give me back my hand. He held it in his, studying it. He said, "You've got Perry's hands. Beautiful hands, she had. Long, slim fingers . . ."

For a second, he looked like his thoughts had floated to the long ago times, and then he caught himself. He patted my wrist and smiled real warm.

Even though the gesture was purely wholesome, I was kind of embarrassed. As I slid my hand away, I said, "You said Mace and Pete are Danahoes. Would they be kin to Jinx Danahoe that rode with you?" It seemed a good change of subject.

"His boys," he said, his eyes twinkling like he was chuckling at me on the inside. "I suppose you know all about Jinx? I mean, seeing as how you seem to have devoted yourself to an intensive study of my life and times."

The way he said it made my face go a little hot, but I said, "I sure do. I know that Jinx Danahoe was a celebrated scout for the army, and a well-known horsebreaker, too. But he married up with a gal named Opal Wilbeck, which ticked off her daddy, the Oro Tiempo Mine King—"

"One Mr. Harlan Wilbeck," Tuck muttered around his pipe stem.

"I know all about him, too. He's got offices in practically every town that digs bright metal. He had a place in Hanged Dog till five or six years ago, but I guess our boys were not bringin' out enough to make it worth his while. I used to spit every time I passed the Wilbeck branch office."

Tuck arched a brow. I guess he did not consider expectoration very ladylike.

"It was on account of what he did to Jinx Danahoe," I explained. I glanced over Tuck's shoulder toward Pete, who had just tripped himself flat over a rock and was cussing a blue streak. "If that's what old man Wilbeck ended up with for grandsons, I guess I understand why he was worried."

Tuck chuckled. "I wouldn't be too hard on them, Miss Gini. They're good boys under that swagger."

"My Gam used to say smart-minded and good-natured go seldom hand in hand."

"Mary Kincaid was a wise woman. I'll grant you Pete'll never be a scholar, but once he gets a few years on him and marries that little gal of his, he'll settle down into a fine citizen. And Mace? He's like his daddy. He's wild-coltish now, but he runs deep."

"They're both rude. Mean, too. That Mace threatened to spank me, just like a kid!"

Tuck grinned and twisted at his pipe. "Did he now?"

The way he said it made me feel petty, and I said, "Well, I guess maybe he's got a right. I suppose I might be cranky and mean, too, if my own grandpa had cut my mama out of his will and got the law after my daddy on a trumped-up charge."

"'Magnanimous' should be your middle name, Gini

Kincaid. And I see my faith in your knowledge of important historical facts has not been ill-invested."

"Maybe you're makin' fun of me, Tuck Brennan, but I know what I know. And I *also* know that it was around then that Jinx took to ridin' with you. I know how Jinx Danahoe died, too."

"Here comes Pete with the horses," Tuck said, like he hoped I was done.

I wasn't, though. "Jinx got killed a few years after you went to Yuma. They say some of Wilbeck's boys took him out back of a Tucson saloon and beat on him till he died."

"You heard right. But if I were you, I wouldn't bring it up in front of Mace or Pete."

"Talkin' 'bout me?" Pete handed over our reins and shot me a nasty look.

Tuck gave me a boost up on Jigsaw. "I was just telling Miss Gini what a sweet lady friend you've got in Miss Loula Mahoney, boy, and Miss Gini was telling me how she is the champion Apache-rock-signal tracker of all time." And then, like he had all the time in the world, he buttoned up his vest, put on his coat, and swung up on his horse.

He rode a handsome black-bay gelding he called Zeus, and I thought he sat that horse majestic, though how he looked right then might have been colored some by the way the morning light slanted across him. He sat ramrod straight in the saddle, not slouched over like most cowpokes, and when he pulled his hat down over his forehead, he looked so dang inspiring I wished I were a painter.

By then the others were all mounted and waiting. Tuck held up his hand and said, "Gentlemen!" They all snapped to, so I guess I wasn't the only one who saw him that way: like a great general or maybe even a king.

"It's a fine morning!" he said, all grand and joyous. "Smell that air! Savor the pine in the breeze, the unmined silver in the earth! Fill yourself up with the Lord's clean perfume!" He stretched out his arms and swelled his chest out so far I thought his lungs might go *pop*. "That's the smell of freedom, boys, freedom on a fine, brisk, Arizona morning."

They all puffed out their chests right along with him, except for Pete, who stopped in the middle to whine, "How come we gotta do this every blamed morning, Tuck?"

"Because—like I tell you every blamed morning when you ask me that same blamed question—it's good for you, boy. Now breathe!" He just sat there smiling till Pete sucked in enough air to suit him, and then he said, "This is Miss Gini Kincaid, and she will be honoring us with her company as far as the Territorial Capital. Miss Gini, I believe you met everybody already, with the exception of young Bobby Lee Caulfield. Bobby, say hello."

Bobby was a wiry little dishwater blond with a scraggly mustache and hairy goat-hide chaps. He appeared near as scruffy as Pete, and I doubt he was even a year older than me. He half-tipped his too-big hat and mumbled, "Ma'am."

"Cripes, Tuck," Pete piped up. "How come we gotta go haulin' her along? She ain't got no respect for her betters."

Tuck looked at him real even, without breaking that white smile of his, and said, "You know where the road is, Pete."

Pete smacked his hat against his leg, but he shut up.

"As Miss Gini is a youngster and a lady," Tuck continued, "I expect you boys to act gentlemanly and keep your cursing down to a tolerable level. Zack, she'll take over the culinary department."

Zack said, "If that's the cookin', it's fine by me," and let loose with a stream of tobacco juice.

That coffee and bad biscuit rose straight up in my throat. "I'm afraid I will have to ride in front of Mr. Zack," I said once I got my breakfast swallowed back down. "His disgustin' habit is one that turns my stomach, and I will not spend my days watching him spit foul brown juices."

"It's just Zack," he said, and spat again. "No 'Mister' to it. I al'ays ride drag anyways." His teeth, where he had them, were stained a real unpleasant shade.

"See?" shouted Pete. "She's a troublemaker, Tuck! You know what she's got in that carpetbag'a hers? A turtle! A goddamn turtle!"

"You better be careful, Pete," Mace smirked. "She's liable to set fire to you."

I stood in my stirrups and shook my fist. "I've about had it with you and that fire business, Mr. Mace Danahoe! And as for you, Stinky Pete, up till now I thought any fool would know a turtle from a tortoise, but I guess you are the one fool who doesn't!"

Tuck reined Zeus into Jigsaw, mostly to get my attention. "Let's get a move on."

We started up the riverbed, me riding off Tuck's shoulder, the others stringing out behind. "Pete took my Gam's squirrel gun," I said. "I'd like to have it back."

Tuck hollered up into the air, "Pete!"

Pete skittered his mare up next to Jigsaw and yelled "What?" across his neck, like I wasn't there.

"Give Miss Gini her firearm."

"Cripes, Tuck! She's like to murder us in our sleep!"

"Give it over, Pete."

He made a face, but he started tugging at the latigo that tied it along his rifle boot. While I waited for him, I turned back to Tuck. "Why you goin' up to Prescott?" I asked. "You goin' to rob the bank there? The stage office?"

Pete shoved Gam's gun at me. "I told you, Tuck! Nosy, nosy troublemaker!"

3

Whiskey Row

Frank Malone must have taken the hint, as we had no more aggravation from him. Of course, we did a little fancy sidetracking that entailed riding a couple miles up a stream and doing a loop-back over hard ground, but I just had a feeling old Frank had tucked his Civic Leader's tail and gone on home.

We rode north, in a general sort of way, and the countryside just got handsomer and handsomer, along with rougher to travel. We wove our way around thickets of live oak or manzanita and skunkbush turned scarlet. Those gave way to juniper and piñon pine and gnarled, twisted cypress; then gray-barked oaks and sour cherry trees and the first real forest pines, all dark green and craggy and smelling like Yuletide. There was plenty of water to be got and wildlife in abundance, but the land was often thickly treed and always rocky, and we spent a lot of time scrambling our horses up and down rugged ground. When the land gets like that, it takes you two or three times as long to get anywhere as it would on the flat, sometimes longer.

Tuck and the others didn't seem to mind. In fact, they acted like they had all the time in creation, for we started late in the mornings and stopped early in the afternoons. In between, poor Malachi had to stay in my satchel, as I was too busy hanging on to the saddle to lap-carry him. Come

47

nights, though, he got plenty to eat and I suppose, for a tortoise, he got enough exercise.

Tuck was good to me, and even if he wouldn't answer a straight question, he sure talked a lot. Most of it was around the subject, but I didn't care. He could have made outhouse-digging seem pure fascinating.

It seemed to me he knew something about practically everything. He talked about far-off places with magic names like Baghdad and Constantinople and Cairo, and people who lived a long time ago. He knew the names of the stars, too. A couple times, when he saw me lying awake in my bedroll, he pointed them out.

"Gaze upon Cassiopeia," he'd say. "Ponder on the wondrous wings of Pegasus, the gird of Orion's Belt. Drink in the sparkling wonder of it, Miss Gini!" Then he'd tell me stories about the olden days in Greece, when they had lots of gods instead of just one, and put their dead heroes up in the sky in star pictures.

I did more than my share of gabbing, too, mostly to fill up the empty air when Tuck wasn't speaking. I did not have such educational things to say as he did, though during one lull I did recite a poem I knew, about a tiger. When I finished, Tuck thumbed back his hat and said, "Why, I do believe that was word-for-word, young lady. You memorize that at your little school in Hanged Dog?"

Since Gam had always said a body shouldn't boast on what he didn't have a hand in getting, I didn't mention my special talent. I just said, "My Gam gave me my schooling, and it was one she liked." That was no lie, though her very favorite had been one about an old sailor with a dead albatross tied round his neck. That one was real long, though, and I thought it might be showing off to say it.

Of course, when it came to my accomplishments at the homely arts and Apache lore I was on safer ground for bragging, and I guess I did some. I think I can be excused for it, as I felt like I needed to make it more interesting; not that the others seemed to care.

Mace barely had a word to aim in my direction, though I caught him taking a stare at me from time to time, and once he carried water for me without being asked. Young Bobby Lee Caulfield spent most of his time acting like he was a hatchling goose and Pete was his mama. If the human brain was a machine, I'd've had to say that somebody had forgot to grease up all that boy's gears.

I found out that Pete's forty-dollar reward was on account of he had swiped two pedigreed breeding sows from a man down by Union Wells who had a pig farm. He did it on a dare and made a bad job of it, for the sows got away from him and went back home, and the pig farmer didn't understand about jokes. Tuck and Mace teased him about it something fierce.

Zack was pretty quiet, but when he did let fly a sentence, the others—even Tuck—paid attention. Maybe the reason he didn't jaw much was that he always had something in his mouth, either tobacco or hard candies; sometimes both at once, though I don't know how he stood it. He had even passed on his habits to his roan horse, Jelly. Jelly was so spoiled to sweets that if Zack didn't give him lump sugar or candy before he mounted up, that old horse would just stand with his ears pinned and kick with his off-hind hoof till Zack got back off and did right by him.

I did a lot of listening and spouted my share of words, but mostly I cooked. Tuck seemed appreciative, and always let me know when he found a dish especially toothsome. The other boys didn't comment, but I noticed the vittles always ran out fast, and there was usually quibbling over the last ladles of rabbit gravy and partridge skillet-pie. After the first day or so I doubled all the receipts, but that was as far as I was prepared to go, as I had joined up with Tuck to see the world, not cook for it.

It was the fourth morning on the trail and we were climbing up into the Bradshaws when a loud disagreement broke out back in the line. Tuck whoaed his gelding and hollered, "What in the blessed name of Hera is going on back there?"

The others caught us up and kind of circled in under the trees, and it was plain right off that it was Stinky Pete making the fuss.

"We're gonna miss it entire!" he simpered. "Tuck, we oughta ride down into the Basin." Bobby looked to be on Pete's side, since he nodded along with him. That was about the most life I'd seen out of Bobby in days, and it kind of worried me.

It was Mace they were arguing with, and he was so disgusted that those eyes were practically shooting sparks. "The Basin doesn't take us closer to Prescott, you fool," he said. "Besides, like I been tryin' to tell you, it's probably full of rustlers that'd just as soon shoot you as say good morning, plus which you wouldn't know what to do once you got down there. Horsethief Basin's full of horses, not hogs!"

"Silence!" Tuck thundered, and they all shut up. "There's to be no detour through the Basin. They'd pick you off before you got over the rim. Hell, there's probably some wise young man with a spyglass sitting up on the piney ridge right now, watching you idiots bicker. I'm half-embarrassed to be seen with you."

"Aw, cripes!" Pete said, like a kid after more candy. "Tuck, we could slide in there and take them horses! Why, they's five of us, six if you want to count that gal, not that she'd be much good."

"I'd be plenty good!" I shouted. I wasn't sure what they were yammering about, but I knew when I was being insulted. "I can ride, I can shoot, and I can—"

Tuck waved his hand at me. "We all know what you can do, Miss Gini, as you have told us innumerable times. But there will be no detours, side trips, or picnic adventures."

"C'mon, Tuck!" Pete said. "Why, we could run 'em south, back down to Mendacity. They'd make a fine start on a herd for me an' Loula, for after we get the—" He flashed me a look, and said, "I mean, once Loula an' me start our ranch."

Tuck just stared at him.

"Well . . . Well, maybe not," Pete allowed. "But we could drive 'em on up to Prescott and sell 'em, couldn't we?"

"I swear, boy," said Tuck, all exasperated, "sometimes I'm convinced you have used up all the Danahoe family foolishness. First off, you don't know what the situation is down there. . . ."

"Well, I know they's got to be horses. Ever'body knows they's always horses in Horsethief Basin!"

Tuck closed his eyes for a half-minute, like he was willing himself out of cracking Pete upside the head with the stewpot, or maybe something bigger. He shook his head real slow before he said, "The reason for that is because it's so easy to guard. Doesn't that tell you anything at all?"

"But—"

"Plus which, how you know those horses weren't stolen from Prescott in the first place? You'd look pretty ignorant trying to sell some gent back his own buggy horse."

Mace was grinning, now that he had Tuck on his side. "Aw, he's used to lookin' ignorant."

Pete twisted toward him. "You wanna step down off that horse?"

Zack, who hadn't done anything the whole time but wag his head, worked his chaw to one side and drawled, "Mebbe you should oughta go ahead and let 'em murder each other, Tucker. Make things a lot more peaceable-like."

Tuck grinned wide. "Friend Zachary, that is a perspicacious insight. I'm close to agreeing with you, save for the singular fact that I promised myself to take on these boys in their daddy's stead. You wouldn't want me breaking a solemn oath, would you?"

"Reckon not," Zack said after some consideration. He spat out a stream of coppery juice, at the sight of which my throat just about pushed up against my teeth.

Pete was still whining, and Tuck said, "Hush, boy! If you want to forsake our errand to play nickel-and-dime outlaw, it's your affair. But if you do, nothing from it—moral justice included—is coming to you, even if you do get out of the Basin in one piece. Those are my rules, and they are one hundred percent steadfast."

Well, that stoppered Pete's jug, but it took the cork out of mine. It was the first time Tuck had made any remark concerning his purpose, and it was just enough to prime me for more.

As soon as we started forward again and the riders were fair strung out, I goosed Jigsaw up next to Tuck. "What job is it? What errand? Is there a good deal to be made?"

He thumbed his hat back and crossed his wrists over his saddle horn. "Lord, Miss Gini, I don't believe I have ever known any human person so brim-full of questions."

"And I have never known anybody so disinclined to parcel out satisfaction! Tuck Brennan, I think you have got plans. I think you should confide in me."

He laughed, loud and with his head back, white teeth flashing. "Poor Miss Gini," he said at last. "The whole of life is just one deep, dark mystery after another, isn't it?

Where are we going? Why are we going? What will we do once we get there?" He tugged his pipe out of his vest pocket, lit up, and puffed for a minute. "I'll tell you this much, Miss Pandora Kincaid. We're not going to Prescott to rob or steal or break the law in any way. Fact is, Zachary and I have paid what is called our debt to society, and, aside from yourself, young Pete is the only one of us to scrape up against the legalities as of late. We are a plain and simple group of law-abiding citizens, going to Prescott to meet an associate, strictly on business."

"I find that hard to believe," I said. "If you're on the up-and-up, why don't we ever go near a civilized place? We have gone the long way round every town in our path, and I haven't seen a real road since I left Hanged Dog. That's not the way an honest citizen travels."

He was still smiling, but he shook his head and let out a sigh. "Old habits die hard, Miss Gini, and my habit is not to advertise. And we're taking our time about it because our associate won't be arriving until this Saturday. The capital city is an expensive place to bide, even for an extra day or two."

Well, I was disappointed, I can tell you. All those stories I'd heard about Tuck Brennan and how he was the Robin Hood of the Territory, all those tales of romance and adventure in the wild country: they all just sort of went splat. I guess it showed on my face, because Tuck got to chuckling again.

"Don't worry, Miss Gini," he said. "I reckon there's still a Santa Claus."

Now, I have got a powerful admiration for Tuck Brennan, but right then I was mad enough to spit. "That's not a bit funny," I said. "And it's not very gentlemanly of you to make sport of me. I guess you're just not the man you have been cracked up to be."

He chewed on his pipe stem, kind of thoughtful, and said, "Few men are, Miss Gini, few men are."

We neared Prescott the next afternoon, and that's when I found out that, like me, Bobby Lee Caulfield was getting dumped off there. Young Bob had got himself in a spot with some rowdies down on the Gila, and Tuck, being acquainted with Bobby's mama, had taken it upon himself to make sure Bobby got back home in one chunk instead of several.

Anyway, about two miles outside of town, we stopped at a frame house with a big truck patch and a falling-down hog yard with three sows in it. Tuck called out "Queenie! Queenie Caulfield!" and a skinny blond woman came out and started right in to weep. Bobby got down off his horse and went to her and they both cried a bit, though Bobby tried to keep us from seeing. While the Danahoe boys tended the horses and Tuck and Zack jawed with Queenie Caulfield, I went to Queenie's room and took myself a good sponge bath and washed my hair.

After I was cleaned up and Tuck was about talked out, we were invited to stay for a celebration supper of pork chops and applesauce and yams and beans with bacon and good brown bread, the whole of which tasted all the better to me because I didn't have to cook it. She had rhubarb pie for dessert, and Zack ate near half of it by himself.

We left Pete at the Caulfield place, too, though with him it was only temporary. Since he had a price on his head, albeit a little one, Tuck didn't think it was too smart for him to go riding big-as-you-please into the capital city. Pete wasn't exactly joyous about the situation, as he had planned to drink his way up and down Montezuma Street, which is celebrated far and wide as a place where a man can drink and whore nonstop if he's of a mind.

I feared they planned to leave me at the Caulfields', too,

but nobody said anything, so after supper I mounted up along with the rest. Bobby and his ma waved us good-bye and Pete slumped on the edge of the porch, looking sulky. Mace hollered back at them, "That little brother'a mine's a crafty thief, Miz Caulfield! I'd guard those sow-hogs with a shotgun and some rock salt if I was you!"

It was good and dark by the time we rode into town—chilly, too, on account of the altitude as much as the time of year—but it sure wasn't quiet. Now, I am sure that a city the size of Prescott, A.T., has got a refined side, but that was not the part I saw that night. Montezuma Street bustled with miners and cowboys and troopers and whores, both painted up and plain. The air was wispy with breathed-out, laughed-out vapor and woodsmoke and steam rolling off fresh manure. Bawdy music spilled from the bars, of which there were a multitude. Somebody was having a little gunplay down the road, too. What with so much yelling and shooting and laughing and out-of-tune piano-banging coming from everywhere, I didn't know where to look first.

Tuck called a halt out front of the Select Hotel. All that noise and carousing didn't faze him in the slightest degree. He just swung down off his horse and motioned for me to do the same.

Mace and Zack stayed in their saddles. "See you at the Blue Jennet," Mace shouted over the din, then he and Zack jogged away.

I jumped down off Jigsaw and looped his reins round the rail. "What's the Blue Jennet? Would that be a saloon?"

Tuck held out his hands. "Give over your things, Miss Gini."

He got a room for me and a second for himself, Mace, and Zack to share, and then he walked me upstairs. I was in number 14, which was cramped and dark and falling apart

from what I could see. It wasn't at all what I'd expected
from a room Tuck had paid ten dollars gold for, that being
almost enough to buy a green-broke colt if it's not fancy.

"Tuck Brennan," I said, "you have been gypped!"

He set my carpetbag and squirrel gun on the bed. "This is
a full-tilt mining town, Miss Gini. Prices are in accordance.
You would not want to stay at one of the less expensive
establishments. Better let your tortoise out." Somebody shot
off a couple rounds right out in front of the hotel. Tuck just
struck a match and said, "I'd stay back from the window if
I were you."

I opened my satchel and rescued Malachi. He was
moving slow on account of its being so cool. "Is he goin' to
be safe while we're gone?" I asked.

"No need to trouble yourself, since you'll be here to mind
him." He lit my lamp and set it on the bashed-in chifforobe.
It was missing a leg and blocked up on one corner with
mouse-chewed Monkey-Ward catalogs. "I would have left
you with Pete and Bobby, except I knew you and Pete'd
probably murder each other, and that would spoil Queenie
Caulfield's day. I admire Queenie too much to put her
through that turmoil."

"I thought we were supposed to meet Mace at that Blue
Jennet place," I said, a little angry. "We have come a long
way, and I do not plan to spend my evening staring at this
bad wallpaper, which, if you have not noticed, is mostly
peeled off the walls. I want to see some town."

Tuck shook his head. "You've got no business in Sodom
and Gomorrah on a Saturday night, Miss Gini. Even dressed
in those bucks, somebody's liable to mistake you for one of
the local *filles de joie*."

Well, I didn't know what the Holy Hannah he was talking
about, but I didn't have time to get an explanation as he was
already out in the hall.

"Hold on a minute, Tuck Brennan! You're not leavin' me in this sorry place! And what about my horse?"

It was too late. He slammed that door and locked it from the outside, and when I banged on it and rattled the knob, he said, "Don't get yourself in an uproar, Gini Kincaid. I'll see your Jigsaw's taken care of. You just quit ruminating on the wallpaper and get yourself some sleep. Have yourself some fine, rich dreams, but keep your bag up off the floor so the mice don't fray it."

I can tell you I was pretty dang mad. Here I'd come all this way through cactus and piñon pine and Frank Malone and baking up Lord-knows-how-many biscuits over a dang campfire: all that just to see something of the world. And now that it was right outside the door, I couldn't get to it. I went to the window and watched Tuck lead Zeus and Jigsaw off toward the livery. I was still watching when he came out and headed down the street.

Finally I sat down on that mean, hard little bed and started rummaging around for something to feed Malachi. I had a boiled egg left, and though it was old enough that I'd have thought twice before I ate it myself, he didn't seem to mind.

"Malachi," I said, "if you were me, would you stand for this?"

He was busy slow-chewing his rubbery old egg yolk, but he looked like maybe he was thinking it over.

"Well, Tuck Brennan is not my boss," I said, "and he's not going to make me spend my night starin' at a wallful of sorry pink rosebuds. You can stay here if you want, you old stub-foot, but I'm goin' to see some'a Prescott!"

The window came up easy once I got the latch unjammed, but the porch roof wasn't near as solid as it looked. I made the fool's mistake of stepping between the braces, and I let out a yelp when my foot broke through. The rest of me followed right after, but the Lord was with me, because my fall was broke by two cowboys.

Once we got untangled, we all stood up and picked the pieces of roof off us. One of them cussed me out, since his whiskey bottle had got busted when I landed. The other one grabbed my arm and said maybe I ought to make it up to them and why didn't the three of us go on upstairs?

"You leave me go!" I said, and stomped down hard on his foot.

He let go, all right, and started hopping around on one leg, but his friend grabbed me round the waist and lifted me clean up off the ground. He was laughing. His breath stunk like fried onions and cheap whiskey. "She's a wild 'un, ain't she, Dinny? Maybe we oughta get a couple more fellas to help hold her down!"

He had me hoisted so that I couldn't do much more than pound on his shoulders. "Let me down, you rancid-mouthed son of a she-wolf!" I hollered. "I am here with dangerous men, and they will make you sorry you ever messed with me!"

With all those people milling on the street, you'd think at least one of them would have come to my aid, but most of them didn't pay any mind, and the ones who did just sniggered and moved on. Right then, I wasn't too crazy about Prescott in particular or the state of humankind in general.

"Dangerous men?" snorted the one who had me up in the air. "And just where would these dangerous men be, honey-girl?"

"Ye'd best be puttin' her down, boy-o." The voice was real commanding but kind of soft-spoke, and for a second I couldn't figure where it had come from. Neither could the cowpokes, because they both craned their heads to look through the crowd.

"Not too keen on listenin', are ye?"

That time I found him: a tall, strong-built man in a black suit. He leaned against the hotel doorway, all kind of slouched and casual with his hat pulled down low on his forehead. One tail of his suit coat was tucked back behind the gun on his hip. It was a fancy rig, and he tapped the holster with the tip of his thumbnail. He said, "Put down my baby sister. I'll not be tellin' ye again."

Well, the cowboy stopped laughing, and he let go of me so fast that I dang near fell over. "Didn't mean nothin' by it," he said. "If she's your sister, I 'pologize, but you should oughta know better than to let her loose on the street in a place like this."

The one named Dinny backed away, too. He said, "That's right, mister. We was just funnin' her a mite. Didn't mean no offense."

The man in the doorway eased his coat back over his pistol. "None taken," he said, still real casual, but he kept his eye on those two boys till they disappeared into the crowd. Then he stepped on over to me and picked a wood chip out of my hair. He did it the way you see fellas pretend to pluck a two-bit piece out of some kid's ear, like they're getting a real kick out of it. He said, "I've seen some high-drama entrances in me time, darlin', but that was a prize. Would ye be wantin' a boost back up on the roof, or are ye satisfied with ground level at present?"

Well, I just looked at him, stuck for something to say. He was pretty old, thirty-five or maybe forty; but smiling or serious he was deadly handsome in the face, with near-black hair and a thick mustache and dimples. His suit was clean and pressed, and a fancy brocade vest peeked through the coat. The brogue was on his tongue, so his words came out near as much song as talk.

"Ye didn't damage yourself in that fall, now did ye?" he

went on, like he was really concerned. "Would ye be needin' a physician?"

That kind of shook me out of it. I pulled my shoulders back and stood up real straight. "I'm fit enough," I said, "and I'm obliged for your help with those roughnecks. Aside from one of the men I traveled here with, I think you may be the only true gentleman in this whole excuse for a civilized town."

When he smiled at me, his dimples sank furrows in his cheeks and his eyes winged out into crinkles at the corners. He said, "It's no gent what lets a bit of a colleen like you go gambolin' about the rooftops. I dinna know that I ought to let him have ye back. If ye dinna mind me sayin' it, that's quite the garb you're wearin'. Would this be the latest fashion where ye come from?"

Later on I wondered if maybe he was being a little sarcastic, but right then I was so busy looking at him that it didn't occur to me. I said, "I don't know about fashion, but it is a good outfit for riding, and I have been doin' a fair amount of that lately."

"I see. Would ye be wantin' an escort back to your lodgin'?"

If any other stranger had said that to me, I would have taken it for the worst and given him what-for, but with him it came out gallant. I said, "No, thank you. I'm lookin' for my friends, sir, and I'll be able to find 'em on my own."

He tipped his hat. "Well then, seein' as ye've come to no harm, I'll be bidding ye a good evenin'. Take me advice and keep off the roofs in future!" He took a step back, and wove himself into the crowd.

It took about three more people bumping into me and one nearly knocking me flat before I remembered the reason I'd climbed out the window and fallen through the roof in the first place. I set off to scout out the Blue Jennet.

Although Hanged Dog was still a wild town, it had nothing on Prescott. Just about every door I passed opened into some low establishment, and what excuse there was for a sidewalk was crammed with men rushing into or falling out of them. I got elbowed and squished and a couple times I got pinched. I passed the Palace de Oro and the Silver Belle and the Horny Owl and some place the sign had fallen off of before the crowd got the better of me and shoved me right through the swinging doors of the Quartz Strike Saloon and practically to the back wall.

I was brushing myself off when a female voice, crackly and hard, said, "If you think you're gonna work this place, honey, you're sad mistook." I looked up through the smoky yellow air, and there she was: a great big, black-haired, rouge-cheeked floozy, sitting atop an upright piano, swinging her doughy legs and wearing nothing but her underwear. I always thought Pearl Scrimm dressed cheap, but this whore made Pearl look like a Methodist.

"I'm not workin' anyplace," I said, "and if that was you I heard a minute ago tryin' to sing 'My Love Is Up the Pecos for a Spell,' you had best find yourself a new line of business. Why don't you go put on the rest of your clothes and quit botherin' decent people?"

She hiked up her chins and laughed. "Least my hair's combed and I ain't decked out like no boy Injun. Now git afore I have Harvey toss your skinny bones on the street." She pointed to a fella stoking the woodstove. His shoulders were wide as a draft mare's behind, and he didn't look one bit friendly.

"I'm Fat Nell," said the whore, like she expected me to be impressed, "and this here's my stompin' ground. Don't need no flat-chested no-name girl-children hornin' in."

"I'm Geneva Kincaid, Gini for short, so I guess I've got a name some better than yours," I said. "And I have got no interest in stompin' your ground or anybody else's."

I would have stayed and told old Fat Nell what-for, but I still had the Blue Jennet and Tuck Brennan to find; plus which, between her and that Harvey, I reckoned to be outnumbered about six to one. I settled for sending her an evil look before I shouldered my way toward the front door.

When I spotted the Blue Jennet, I was down the road a piece and the crowd had thinned out. I had also twisted my hair up under my hat, thinking I would likely not get pinched quite so much if I looked like a boy. I climbed up on the bench out front, stood on my knees, and pressed my nose right between the front legs of the turquoise mule painted on the glass.

Compared to the places up the street, the Blue Jennet's business wasn't brisk. There weren't more than a score of patrons, all too busy jawing and playing cards to be rowdy. Tuck sat way back at a corner table with Zack. They were about ten feet away from the stove, and appeared a good deal cozier than I felt. Mace Danahoe was bellied up to the bar, his arm around a whore who looked just a little less used up than Fat Nell. It dawned on me that maybe coming out after Tuck hadn't been such a good idea after all.

I was deciding whether to go in or just walk back to the Select Hotel when I realized there were two fellas' faces reflected above mine in the glass. The closest was a rough man, thickset and maybe forty or so, with a bad-broke nose running a crooked ridge down his face. He and his friend were so busy staring in the window and getting bumped by the foot traffic that they hadn't taken note of me.

"By Gaw, Ronnie," the crook-nosed one said under his breath, "that's him, all right. That's the one and only for-real Tuck Brennan in there."

"Let's us go on in and get him, Vince," whispered the other one, who appeared some younger. He had close-set eyes and a fat, wet lower lip that stuck out like an old mule's. He sounded half-drunk and dumb-eager.

"Gaw, you're a mooncalf, Ronnie! Just shut up and go 'crost the road and keep an eye to this place. That old bastard comes out, you follow him, and don't you let him set an eye to you. I gonna ride over to Mr. LaFouche's hotel, let him know it's comin' together."

It took about all the temperance I had not to turn around and ask those two cowboys just what the Sam Hill kind of business they thought they had with Mr. Tuck Brennan, but I managed it. I stayed still and kept that way till broke-nosed Vince was clear gone and his mule-lipped friend had dodged across Montezuma Street and leaned up against a post.

I was chilled through and my knees ached from that hard bench, so I sank down on my heels and wrapped myself up in my arms to do a little mulling. Tuck had told me he wasn't wanted for anything, so those boys couldn't be bounty hunters unless they were real stupid ones. Course, judging by the looks of Ronnie, that was sure possible. I was mid-ponder when all of a sudden somebody caught up my arm.

I took a wild swing, and I would have hit him good and hard in the stomach if he hadn't caught my fist.

It was the Irishman again. He laughed. "Easy, lass!"

It seemed there was no getting rid of this fella. I stood up. "Sorry, mister, but you should announce yourself before you go grabbin' people who might not want to be grabbed."

He said, "Apologies. Still on the scout for your friends?"

I half-wished he'd stop smiling at me, since I didn't much care for the way it made my innards all queasy. When Pete or Mace Danahoe got on my nerves, I could give them a good swat and not feel bad about it, but this fella didn't look like the sort that you'd want to go around hitting. I said, "No sir, they're found. They are just inside this saloon."

He took my hand and put it on his arm. "Come along, me brown-eyed darlin'. Your teeth are a-chatter. Let's take ourselves inside before ye ice up and freeze to death. Ye shouldn't be about without a cloak or jacket. And ye shouldn't be hidin' those bounteous red tresses away." He lifted off my hat and my hair all fell down into a mess again, but he said, "Lovely," and walked me through the doors.

4

The Gold Map

Mace looked up from the whore he was mostly wrapped around, took one look at me and one at my friend, and hissed, "Judas Priest!"

Tuck got up on his feet and gave me a queer look.

"Now, don't be mad, Tuck," I said. "I just couldn't stay up in that pigsty of a hotel by myself, and furthermore——"

My new friend hiked his eyebrows. "Dinna be tellin' me this old miscreant is the same gent ye were out after!"

Tuck was to us by then. He stuck out his hand and I gave a little jump, thinking he was ticked enough to smack me. Instead, his eyes got all misty and he pounded my friend on the shoulder. "Ty, boy!" he cried. "Is that you? By all the saints of Rome and Ethiopia, these past fifteen years have surely been your loving mistress!"

The Irishman laughed, and he and Tuck hugged each other like brothers. They were both ignoring me, but I got swept along to the table. Mace was in such a rush to get in on the whole thing that he dropped his whore flat on the brass foot rail, and when she threw her shot glass at him, he didn't even notice it bouncing off his rump.

Well, everybody was knee-deep in back-pounding and handshaking and saying things like, "By Christ!" and "I'll be double-dogged!" Near five minutes passed before anybody remembered I was drawing breath.

"Ty," Tuck said, pointing to Mace, who had leaned so far over the table I thought he might crawl across, "this eager young gent is Mason Danahoe, Jinx's oldest."

The two of them shook hands, and Mace was so impressed he even took off his hat. "Proud," he said. "I'm right proud to know you."

"I guess you've already met this enterprising child," Tuck said. He nodded toward me. He didn't look all that mad anymore, but I sure noticed that "child" remark.

"Not so as t'be formal," replied my friend, and he was gentleman enough to leave it at that and not mention the business with the busted roof.

Tuck said, "Then I'll be the one to do the honors. Miss Gini Kincaid, late of Hanged Dog, Arizona, and the best campfire cook in the Territory bar none, be so kind as to say how-do to Mr. Patrick Tyrone O'Neill, originally of County Kerry, late of Lord-knows-where, and the fancified vestige of an ace highwayman."

"That's Geneva Kincaid," I said. "The Gini is for short. If you're the same Tyrone O'Neill they write about in the books on Tuck and the one they say is dead, it seems to me you're fleshed out pretty good for a corpse."

He laughed, and there went those eyes and dimples again. He had nice straight teeth, too. Between him and Tuck, it looked like a dang dentists' convention in there. He said, "I'm findin' m'self in dire need of a whiskey, Miss Geneva Kincaid. Would ye be joinin' me in a wee drop?"

He said it kind of like a dare, and though I had never tasted whiskey in my life, I allowed that I would.

Tuck put a stop to it. "Best get her a soda pop, Tyrone. You go giving her a taste for bourbon and branch, she'll be hitting every fast house on Whiskey Row before the night's over."

Well, they all thought that was pretty funny, but as it

turned out, the Blue Jennet didn't stock anything so tame as sarsaparilla. Ty ordered an egg and sherry after he convinced Tuck it would take the chill off me.

What with all the excitement, I had forgot to tell Tuck about those two ugly jaspers outside and how one was watching from across the street. I was just about to open my mouth when Ty said, "It's glorious to be seein' your face again, Tucker darlin'." He had finished his whiskey by then and was nursing a beer chaser. "But outside of the reunion, I'm sorry to say we've both had a wasted trip."

Tuck leaned forward. "You didn't turn up Sam Gonzales?"

"Oh, I found the poor beast. About two days before his wake, Lord rest his soul."

Tuck appeared shocked. "They hanged him?"

"'Twasn't the rope what took him," Ty said sadly, and had another draw on his beer. "I tracked him all over Montana and Wyoming. Trailed him like a basset, I did, and finally turned him up in the town of Cheyenne. He'd changed his name to Moreno and wed himself an uncommon fine temperance-minded lady by the name of Tottie Ann. Bakes a toothsome apple pie, Zachary. I thought'a ye with every tender bite."

"Well, what happened?" Mace demanded. He was a little skunked, and Tuck shot him a look to remind him to respect his betters.

Ty didn't seem to mind, though. "Sam was a man with a terrible sickness," he went on. "A tumor in his bowel. Poor sod was guzzlin' the laudanum like water, for all the little good it did him. He said the Wilbeck job had been too long ago, and even when 'twas fresh in his mind, he couldn't've got back to the proper locality. He was too scared and t'were too many Apache."

I was halfway through my egg and sherry, and feeling

pretty warm. "What Apache?" I asked. "What place? Did I tell you I can read rock signals? Remind me to tell you about Vince and that Ronnie with the old mule lip."

Tuck patted my hand, but other than that he paid me no mind. He looked over at Ty. "What about the map?"

Ty shook his head. "Sam said he didn't hold it, and I'm convinced he spoke the truth. He was a destitute man, Tucker darlin'. If he'd owned Mort Scobie's map, he'd have been makin' proper use of it."

Well, my ears perked up at the mention of Mescal Mort Scobie, he being the hero who had brought my Gam out of the wasteland and then got himself hanged.

"Judas Priest!" Mace said, so loud every head in the place turned toward him. "All that dreamin' and hopin', and now not a pin! Not a goddamn pin!"

"Settle down!" Tuck snapped.

"I should'a known," Mace muttered, mostly to himself. "I should'a known it was too easy. A fortune just for the pickin' up and no way to tell where. I should'a known a man's got to work for his money, not like you and Daddy and—"

Zack, who so far hadn't done much but spit, barked, "Close your hole, boy."

"I won't close nothin' and I won't settle down! It's ours—mine and Pete's through our ma! I got a right to—"

Tuck grabbed him by the elbow and jerked him flat into his chair. "You clamp your mouth, boy, and you keep it that way, you understand? When we parked Pete at Queenie's, I thought I had divested myself of the Danahoe family fool." He looked madder than I'd seen him.

Mace gave the table a rap with his fist, but he did what he was told.

Ty O'Neill twirled his empty beer mug, making wet loops on the tabletop like he was above it all. "The factualities are as follows," he began. "When Mort Scobie was picked up back in sixty-five, he knew 'twas the end, but he wasn't about to give Harlan Wilbeck the satisfaction of recoverin' that gold. So he dispossessed himself of the map."

Zack scootched the chaw around inside his lip. "Well now, Tyrone, I reckon we all knowed that. We also knowed that Sam was the last of Mort's pals to see him breathin'. Which is why he's supposed to have the consarned thing!"

Ty shook his head and ran a line through all those wet circles with his little finger. "Ah, but Mort was laborin' under the misconception that he was the last of the crew left livin'. He got quite a surprise when Sam turned up. He told Sam the tale—at least what of it he could with a guard hoverin' about and only five poor minutes allotted for the visitation—but he couldn't hand over the map."

Zack missed the corner spittoon, then wiped his mouth on the back of his sleeve. "On account'a the guard? Some half-ass tin badge get our gold map, Tyrone?"

"Nothin' so easy. When the law caught up with Mort, he was after bringin' in a heat-stroked white woman, an escaped Chiricahua captive he found on the wander. Before they hauled him away, he pressed his Holy Bible upon her as a partin' gift. 'Twas where he kept the map, y'see. I'm supposin' 'twas his joke on Harlan Wilbeck, givin' the key to all that Apache gold to some hatter-mad white squaw. By the time Sam bade Mort good-bye and hied himself to Fort Buchanan, the woman was gone. He never did find her, though he spent the next three years scourin' the better part of New Mexico and half of Arizona."

Well, I looked at Tuck, and Tuck looked at me, and right then we both knew exactly who that white squaw was and who had that very Bible. He made a quick grab for my arm, but I jumped up before he could catch my sleeve. A big grin stretching my face, I hollered, "Boy howdy, Tuck Brennan, you're not leavin' me off no where, no how, no way!"

"Stop her!" he yelled as I sprinted for the door. "Head her off before she gains the hotel!"

I ducked between miners and whores; raced past cowboys, drummers, and assorted revelers; scrambled under wagons and rigs when I couldn't get round. I knocked a few folks sprawling, but I didn't have time to beg pardon. I just hotfooted it toward the Select Hotel as rapid as I could, by any path I could make.

Halfway there, I made a rolling dive under a hitched horse. That old cayuse must have swung its butt back toward the water trough right after, because a couple seconds later I heard a big splash, then Mace hollering at the top of his lungs that killing was too good for me.

I skidded up to the Select, panting like a rabbit with a coyote closing in. I leapt up on the hitching rail, grabbed the rain gutter, and hauled myself up to the porch roof. This time I was careful to stay on the supports, and cut a wide berth around the hole I'd made earlier. As I edged along, I looked down through it and saw Mace pass under me. He was dripping horse-trough water and was followed in a big hurry by Tuck and the others.

I hopped in my window and did some quick digging for Gam's Bible. I was back out on the roof, Good Book in hand, when I heard Tuck's boys crowd into the room. As I swung down to the hitching rail and jumped the rest of the way to the street, Tuck bellowed, "Idiot! She's not under the goddamn bed! Out the window! Out the window!"

I skinnied into a throng of drunk troopers, popped out the other side. I heard Mace yell something not very nice at me just as Tyrone called out, "Watch your step, boy-o!"

Mace must not have listened, because just then I heard a big crash. I didn't look back.

Twenty yards later, I ducked into the Quartz Strike. It was still packed and Fat Nell was still perched on the piano, except now she was singing a bad job of "Violets Are the Flowers I Love, 'Cause You Laid Them on Mama's Grave." Most everybody was too busy to notice me, so I hunkered down and sidled along the front window. I wormed my way into the front corner opposite the doors (that being the only place with more than two square feet of floor available), slid down on my haunches with my back to the wall, and started going through that Good Book.

There wasn't a thing at the front, but inside the back cover I found a folded-up piece of real lightweight paper, almost tissue. My fingers were shaking so bad I feared I'd tear the dang thing.

It was the map, all right, drawn in lead and kind of smeary. A main map was in the center, with an arrow pointing out of it to another sketch, enlarged for detail, in the corner. There were lots of instructions writ out in longhand, too. Some of the places were spelled wrong, but I didn't hold that against Mescal Mort: when a man has saved your Gam's bacon, he's entitled to a flaw or two, to my way of thinking. Anyway, I gave it a good stare and got it set in my head, and then I got up to my feet. A youngish cowhand stood with his back to me, and I tapped his shoulder.

"Why, how-do, little miss!" he shouted over the din. "Where'd you come from?"

"Hanged Dog, if it's any of your nevermind. You got a spare match?"

He allowed that he did, and dug one out. "Don't tell me a bug-sized thing like you's got the tabaccy habit!"

I snatched away the sulphurtip, which he had held up kind

of high to tease me, and scratched it lit. "You might want to stand away, mister," I said, and touched it to the corner of Mescal Mort's map.

It whooshed up into flame, and that cowhand gave a hop at just about the exact second Mace and Tuck pushed through the swinging doors of the Quartz Strike to stare me dead in the face.

"Judas-over-the-cliff!" Mace hollered. He was covered with little bits of wood and tar paper, stuck to him all the worse for his being soaked through. His hat was gone and his torn, soggy shirt flapped. A red scrape as wide as my hand ran down the side of his neck, and he was mad as a bag full of badgers. He climbed right over a table to get to me, and the fellas who had been trying to play stud at it jumped up cussing. He made a grab for the map, but by then it was all burned up and fluttering down like black snowflakes, so he grabbed me instead. I think he would have sent me home to Jesus directly, except that right then one of the boys from the poker game took hold of his shoulder, spun him around, and slugged him square in the jaw.

Well, I am here to tell you it was one monumental fracas. Just like that, the air filled with bottles; chairs, too. Fat Nell stopped trying to sing. She long-jumped from the piano to the top of the bar, so natural that she must have done it a few times before. When she lit, she pointed at me and hollered, "The whelp Kincaid!" A blond-headed fella got his face shoved into the piano case. Some fancy squirt in a charcoal suit scrambled along the floor between everybody's legs, picking up cash money that fell off the upturned poker tables. Big Harvey, the bartender, got sight of him and climbed right over two fistfights to pick him up by the heels and shake the cash from his pockets. A couple rock-breakers hopped the bar and tossed full bottles until three other fellas went after them and knocked Fat Nell into the middle of the brawl in the process. Somebody shoved a table through the front window, and then they started pitching each other through the hole.

I lost sight of Mace and Tuck, and I couldn't do much besides duck and try to stay clear, though I did crack one fella upside the ear with a beer mug. About halfway along in the proceedings, I managed to hop out the hole where the window used to be.

A goodly crowd had gathered on the street to cheer the fight. Several of the most unsavory types were right out front, picking up the boys that sailed out the Quartz Strike's window and tossing the conscious ones back in. The fellas that were out cold got dragged off toward the alley, and it was a safe bet they'd wake with their pockets sucked dry.

The spectators were counting as the bodies came out. They were up to nineteen then, though they did not count me.

All that broken colored glass on the street was almost beautiful, the way it picked up the lantern light, but it grated underfoot. I made my way to the edge of the mob and found a seat on a hitching rail, figuring that when Mace or Tuck came flying through the window, I'd see to it that no cutpurse dragged them off. I had Gam's Bible clenched tight under my armpit, but just as the crowd yelled "Twenty!" I felt somebody tug it away. I whipped around so fast I dang near fell off the rail.

Zack stood right behind me, the Bible in his gnarly hand. "Why you wanna go out of your way to give a tired old man so much grief?"

"Gimme that back!"

He stuck it inside his belt, that being a place I had no intention of reaching for. "Ain't givin' you nothin' back. You made me swaller my chaw."

That struck me as pretty amusing, but what with the

discouraging look on Zack's face, it didn't seem the time to chuckle over it. He nodded toward the Quartz Strike's busted-out window, which was just spitting out two more chewed-up cowpokes. The spectators called out, "Twenty-one! Twenty-two!"

Zack said, "Tuck and Mace in there?"

"Give me back my Bible and I might just tell you."

He raised up his arm to backhand me, but right then Mace came kiting through the window. He landed flat in the street to the cry of, "Twenty-three!" Several fellas ran over, hauled him to his feet, and started to shove him back inside. Zack got there first and half-dragged him past me to a water trough.

Mace was soaked already, but Zack shoved his head down under that old horse-spit water. Mace came up sputtering and cussing. "What'd you do that for, you bald-headed fool!"

Zack still had him by the shirt collar. "I'm revivin' you, boy!"

Mace shook himself free, and his gaze came to rest on my face. "I'm gonna kill her!" he hollered, his eyes fair bugging out of his head. He almost made it to me before Zack took hold of his arm.

"It's all right, Mason," he said. "I got it." He patted Gam's Bible, still tucked in his belt.

Mace's eyes got even bigger. He screamed like a wildman and lunged for me again.

I jumped off the hitching rail and tried to back my way into the throng. "You harm me, Mace Danahoe, you're never goin' to find what you're lookin' for!"

A hand took hold of my shoulder and hung on tight. I swung around with my fist cocked and punched Tuck Brennan right below his belt buckle.

I heard him give out a little "Oof!" before he stood up tall again, jerked me half off my feet, and hauled me through the crowd.

I told him I was sorry, but he didn't say a word. I told him I wouldn't have done it if I'd known it was him, but he just kept dragging me, and he didn't stop till he got me clear of the mob and a half-block up the way.

"Tuck, I swear I—"

"Silence!" he roared, and slammed me up against the building so hard it near knocked the wind out of me.

I had never imagined Tuck Brennan capable of such mistreatment of a lady, and I was about to tell him so when Mace and Zack caught us up. I guess Zack must have heard about the map by then, because he ripped that Bible out of his belt and threw it down on the ground like garbage.

"That's my Gam's," I said. "You pick that up reverent-like and hand it over!"

"Figures she'd burn it," Mace sneered. Steam rose off his wet clothes into the cold air, making him all the more fierce.

Tuck looked me square on, and the way the fire burned in those icy eyes was a terror to behold. Real quiet and right in my face, he said, "Do you have the smallest notion of what you just did?"

"I got a large notion," I said, though I admit my voice shook a tad. "I'd do it again, too."

He looked at me like I belonged in an asylum. "You figure this little prank will endear you to me? You are a spoilt child, Gini Kincaid, and daughter of Perry LeFleur or no, you are in dire need of corporal punishment. Mace, it seems only fitting that you do the honors. Besides, I am too angry to do it myself."

Mace's face lit up like a nasty sort of Christmas, and he took a grip on my wrist. "Leave me go!" I hollered. "I'm tryin' to tell you—"

Mace dragged me two steps up the walk, plopped himself

down on a barrel, and swung me across his wet lap. When I kicked and yelled, Zack grabbed hold of my legs. Mace brought his hand down directly, just as hard as he could.

"That's for the water trough!"

"Let me loose, you sodden son of a—"

Down came that hand with another fierce crack. "That's for the roof!"

"Leave me go, I tell you!"

Crack! "For near gettin' me killed in the Quartz Strike!"

"Help! Murder!"

"And this is for the Bible! And the map! And the match you set to it!"

After a minute I was crying just like a kid, and dimly, I heard Tuck say, "Enough."

Zack let go of my legs and Mace stood straight up, which dumped me hard on the sidewalk. It wasn't till then I heard the laughing and realized we'd drawn away a share of the spectators from the saloon fight.

Tuck reached down to me. "Get up," he said. He looked a little sorry, but not much.

I brushed away his hand and got up by myself. My backside and legs were like fire, and if there hadn't been all those people around, I would have sunk my rump into one of those icy water troughs. I rubbed at my face with the back of my hand and sniffed before I said, "I got a good mind not to tell you, now."

"Tell me what, Miss Fire-Setter?" Mace barked.

"I wasn't talking to you, Mace Danahoe. Why don't you get a job with the teamsters and go beat some mules for a while?"

"You stopped me too soon, Tuck," Mace said. "I didn't get near all the sass whopped outta her."

The spectators were moving away kind of grumbly. I guess they weren't happy unless they saw a person get clobbered clear to death instead of only halfway. Tyrone O'Neill was just cutting his way through the crowd. "What have I missed?" he said, and stepped up on the boardwalk. "Why, Miss Geneva darlin'! Are those tears?"

"Your friends have practically beat me to a mince pie, sir, and they very near whipped that gold map right out of my head."

"Your head wasn't the part I hit," Mace said with a mean laugh.

I balled my hands into fists and looked right up at him. "You just hit me where you thought my brains were, seeing as how your backside is where you keep yours." When he took an angry step toward me, I said, "Fine! Hit me again! Hit a defenseless lady who was only tryin' to make you a rich man! I won't forget this night, Mr. Mason Woman-Hitter Danahoe. I'll get you back for it someday, if God doesn't beat me to it!"

That just made him madder. "You burned up my money, you brat!"

"All I burnt was a piece of paper. I swear, Mace, you should not drink, as when you do you come off stupider than that brother of yours, though it hardly seems possible. That map's safer than it ever was, but I have got a strong inclination not to share it with you."

Tuck crossed his arms and sighed. "Miss Gini, just what in the name of Hera are you talking about?"

I set a finger to my temple. "It's here," I said, "all right in here. I remember things, and that is no brag. I can remember every wanted poster up at Sheriff Russell's office, every word from every book I ever read, every sign, handbill, newspaper, or magazine I ever saw. And I can sure as Holy Hannah remember somethin' as simple as a misspelt map!"

Zack looked away, real disgusted, and Mace thrust his arms up in the air like he was asking for God to just strike him dead and get it over with. "I never heard such a load of pig manure in my life!" he said.

Tuck gave his chin a rub. "Maybe," he muttered. "Maybe not."

A few of the riffraff who'd watched my whipping were still hanging around, hoping for more excitement, and Ty put his arm round my shoulders. "What would ye say to unravelin' this in private, Tucker?"

After Ty picked up my Bible for me, we walked to the Select Hotel, me doing my best not to limp. As we passed under the porch roof, Tuck looked up and said, "That's quite a good bit of damage you did there, Mace, though I'll be damned if I know how you made two holes that far apart."

We went to my room. Tuck dragged a straight-back chair out from the corner, turned it around and straddled it. Zack leaned up against the wobbly old chifforobe, Mace perched on the windowsill, and Tyrone sat on my bed with his back against the headboard and his legs stretched out. Even if they'd left me a place, my backside smarted too much to sit.

Tuck thumbed up his hat brim, folded his arms over the chair-back, and propped his chin on his wrist. "So you know things once you've had a look at them. Is that it, Miss Gini?"

"That's it," I said. "That map is not gone. The fact is that from here on out, I am the map. You want Mescal Mort's gold, you got to take me along, though I don't know if I want to be in the company of the likes of Mace Danahoe, now that he's shown his true depraved nature."

"Aw, geez, Tuck!" Mace went to jerk off his hat, and when he remembered he'd lost it, he settled for slapping himself on the leg. "She don't know a blasted thing. She just don't want to get left off, and she burned up that map out of pure meanness. She'll be setting fire to the hotel next!"

Tuck ignored him. He looked right at me, kind of half-smiling. "I've heard of folks that can do what you're saying. I even knew a boy, a long time back, who was possessed of that particular talent."

"I can quote to you if you want me to prove it," I said. "There's the Bible, which I've read most all of. Or any World Almanac for the last five years. More of those Blake poems, like the tiger one. Or a page from *The Mustang Hunters,* or *Bob Woolf, the Border Ruffian*. Or maybe one'a the ones about you. *Rivals of the Mogollon Rim*? *Boss Brennan and the Navajo Whoop-Up*? Or how about—"

"It's a t-trick," Mace said, too loud. He hugged himself tight, and his teeth had commenced to chatter. I hoped he was coming down with the double pneumonias.

Tuck raised one hand and waved it. Still looking at me, he said, "Zachary, do me the favor of strolling across the hall to number fifteen. Pull a book out of my pack." He tossed Zack the key. "Any one'll do."

Zack got right back and handed Tuck a beat-up volume. Tuck opened it without looking, then held it toward me. "Gaze on that for a minute, Miss Gini."

I did. "Tuck," I said, "these folks talk awful funny. And this room is sure gettin' gamy. Somebody in here has the odor of a wet cowdog."

"Never mind," he said with a smile. "Just give it a look. Both pages."

I handed it over. "Already did."

He stuck his finger in the place to mark it, then opened the book again, right to the beginning. "Save that place, now, and look here."

I did, and gave it back again.

"All right, Miss Gini," said Tuck, "from the first place you looked, give me, let's see . . . Start at the fifth line from the bottom of the right-hand page."

I clasped my hands behind my back like Gam had taught me was proper, and started. *"Life's but a walking shadow, a poor player that struts and frets his hour upon the stage, and then is heard no more; it is a tale told by an idiot, full of—"*

"Full of sh-sheep shit!" Mace cut in with a mean laugh that broke down into a cough. "A tale told by an idiot? That's the most truth we've heard out of her tonight!"

I gave him a dirty look. *"Full of sound and fury,"* I finished up, *"signifying nothing.* Which is about what you signify, Mace Danahoe, you lowlife woman-beater. Just exactly squat-nothing! Don't you even possess the common sense to change your clothes? You don't smell so bad dry, but soaked down you are near as rank as that brother of yours."

Well, Tuck was smiling wide and I could hear Ty chuckling, but Zack was about to twist his hat in a knot. "Stop that bickerin' or, so help me Christ, I'll pistol-whip the both'a you! Tuck, I'll be danged if I ain't half-forgot what we're doin' up here in the first place!"

Ty stretched his arms out along the headboard. "Why, Zachary darlin'," he said, real grand, "we're readin' the Scottish play."

Tuck broke out in that big, singular laugh. "Just to be sure, Miss Gini, tell me the words from the front of the book."

"Starting where?"

He glanced down to where he'd marked the place, and said, "On the left, at the top of the page. Right after where it says *First Witch.*"

I clasped my hands behind me again. *"When shall we three meet again in thunder, lightning, or in rain? Second Witch: When the—"*

Tuck shook his head. "You don't have to say that part."

"What part?"

"Where it says *Second Witch*."

"Seems to me you're awful nitpicky about this, Tuck Brennan." He didn't answer, so I just went ahead. *"When the hurlyburly's done, when the battle's lost and won."*

"That's enough," he said. "If I were to give you a piece of paper and a pen, could you draw me that map, Miss Gini?"

"I could, but I will not. I won't be left off on Montezuma Street or at Queenie Caulfield's or by the side of the road. I am the only way to that gold, which I figure is part mine, too, since it was to my Gam that Mr. Mescal Mort Scobie left his one and only Holy Bible and map. If you men want your share, you'll have to take me along, no two ways about it. And in case you're interested, Tuck Brennan, I'm not the biggest burr under you blanket, for in this town there are two no-account drifters, Vince and Ronnie by name, who were watching you down to the Blue Jennet Saloon. One of them is probably outside this hotel right now, and the other rode off to tell somebody named Mr. LaFouche."

Ty swung his legs off the bed. His boots hit the floor as sharp as a gunshot. "Burl LaFouche is in Prescott?"

Tuck had me tell them all about Vince and Ronnie, what they looked like and everything they said, and then he stood up. "Mace," he said, "I suppose your pack's still on your horse?" When Mace nodded, Tuck gave a resigned sigh. "All right," he said, "get across the hall and change into dry clothes. You'll find some in my roll. Zack, take yourself out the back way, then saunter on over to the livery and pick up our horses. Ty's, too."

Ty told Zack what his horse looked like and where she was stalled, and then Tuck said, "Miss Gini, gather up your bag and your tortoise. I want you to take Tyrone downstairs and see if you can't point this Ronnie out to him."

• • •

It didn't take more than a few seconds to get Malachi squared away and grab my squirrel gun. Ty carried the satchel downstairs for me. He said, "Miss Geneva, when ye catch the sight of this character, I'd be appreciative if ye wouldn't go pointin' or callin' out. A little tug t'me sleeve will do lovely."

I was about to tell him that if he thought I was that much an ignoramus he was in grave error, but just then the crowd outside the front door parted for a second, and I saw that mule-lipped Ronnie. He wasn't much of a spy, for he was leaned up about three feet from a lantern and lit up plain.

I pulled Ty's sleeve, just like he'd said. "He's at the mouth of the alley across the way. What are you goin' to do?"

He ignored the question entirely. "After that donnybrook down the street, Geneva darlin', he's sure to know you're with us. Take yourself out to the porch and stand by a lamp so he can see ye."

"And where are you goin' to be?"

"Dinna worry, darlin'. I'll be about." He gave me a little shove toward the door. When I looked back around, he was gone.

It took a minute to fight my way through the milling bodies on the sidewalk, but when I got to the street Ronnie was still planted in the same place. I put myself where he couldn't help but see me, and I stood there a couple minutes, hugging myself against the cold and trying not to look over at him. That was pretty easy, because there was a good fistfight about a half-block up, mid-street, to keep me entertained. But every once in a while I caught Ronnie from the corner of my eye. Just as I sneaked my fourth or fifth peek, I saw an arm snake out of the alley, lash round Ronnie's throat, and jerk him off his feet and out of sight.

A few seconds later, Ty stepped into the light. He was

alone, and brushing dust off his coat. He looked up the road and gave a nod, and it wasn't till I followed his line of vision that I realized Tuck was out there as well, about a quarter-block away, and carrying his Winchester in a very serious manner.

Just as they reached me, Zack brought up the horses. Mace, wet hair matted to his head, was on the street by then, too. The borrowed clothes in no way fit him. The pants were cinched in at the waist and rolled up at the bottom, the shirt cuffs almost covered his fingers, and he looked about to drown in the jacket.

"Just shut up," he hissed as he grabbed his reins from Zack and mounted. "I'll brain the first man—or child—that so much as snickers."

Zack twisted in his saddle and looked away. Ty was busy checking his mare's girth and his hat was pushed down so low you couldn't see his face; but the way his shoulders were shaking, I knew he had a chuckle caught inside him.

Tuck was on the hotel porch, eyeballing the throng. He picked out a good-natured cowpoke and after a bit of haggling, bought the hat right off him. Then he carried it over to Mace and handed it up. "I just paid that boy way too much for his lid," he said. "Thirty dollars, to be exact. If you have to misplace this one, try and do it in a town with an all-night haberdasher."

I was waiting by Jigsaw, wondering if Tuck had gone clear crazy (and if my britches would ever stop feeling like they were full of branding irons), when somebody grabbed me by the shoulder in a none-too-gentle manner.

A rangy fella had ahold of me. He was sporting a shiny silver badge, and he was not smiling. He said, "Your name Kincaid?"

Before I could answer, Tuck was at my side and prying the lawman's fingers off me. "You're mistaken, friend

Deputy," he said, so slick I almost believed him myself. "This is my niece, Miss Katherine DePadua."

I started to open my mouth, but he stepped on my foot. Zack and Mace sat quiet, and Ty pretended he was real busy fiddling with his tack.

"I think she's Kincaid," said the lawman. He had one hand on the butt of his gun, and looked like he was trying to place Tuck but couldn't quite do it. "Fat Nell over to the Quartz Strike says a gal named Kincaid started that riot earlier. This one fits the description."

"This child?" Tuck said, and raised his bushy brows in disbelief. "Why, my little Katherine has done nothing in this wild and heathen village but sit in her room and read the Lord's Word. Katherine, show this gentleman your Bible." I opened my satchel and started to poke around, and Tuck continued, "That fracas down the road is why we are leaving, as a matter of fact. I had no idea the capital city was such a hellish town, and I do not want my sweet niece exposed to such riffraffery and unchristian influences."

I had my Bible out by then, and handed it toward the deputy. He took it without looking. "Sure fits the description," he said. "Redheaded gal in bucks."

"Why," said Tuck, "in a metropolis the size of Prescott, there's bound to be dozens of them. Hundreds! My little Katie doesn't fritter time in low establishments, I can guarantee that. Her daddy and my dear brother, the Right Reverend DePadua, keeps as tight a rein on his daughter as he does his flock. Katherine, quote something godly for the deputy."

I clasped my hands behind my back and started spouting off the top of my head. *"Cast in thy lot among us; let us all have one purse.* Proverbs, one-fourteen. *But the eyes of the wicked shall fail, and they shall not escape, and their hope shall be as the giving up of the ghost.* Job eleven-twenty. *He leadeth counselors away spoiled, and maketh the judges fools. He—"*

"All right, all right!" The deputy shoved Gam's Bible back into my hands and looked up at Tuck. "Get her outta here."

"My intent, sir," Tuck said solemnly. "My perpetual intent."

The deputy stalked off, and Tuck put his arm round my shoulders. He gave me a squeeze. "I believe you'll do, Miss Gini-Katherine. Now, up on that paint horse. But first . . ." He paused and reached inside his coat. "That leather looks pretty uninviting." He brought out one of those skimpy little hotel pillows and put it up on my saddle.

As he boosted me up, I said, "Did you steal that, old man?"

"Haven't you heard, Miss Gini Kincaid? That's the business I'm in. Besides, seeing as how I have paid the management a small fortune for rooms I barely used, I believe they owe me the goodwill."

"I'm surprised you bothered to pay that hand a nickel for his hat, let alone a month's cowpunchin' money. Why didn't you just grab it off his head?"

He gave a thoughtful rub to his chin. "Miss Gini, for somebody who has chosen to ride with the likes of me—and who has just flimflammed a sworn officer of the law—you have got a serious high-and-mighty problem. And if you don't know the moral difference between a hotel pillow and a man's own hat, I could never explain it to you."

5

Trouble at Horsethief Basin

It was a handsome night despite the chill. You could see the stars and moon real clear where they peeked through the trees, and once we got outside of town, the quiet was as crisp as the air. The cushion on my saddle gave me some comfort, though I found myself shifting every few minutes and cussing Mace Danahoe under my breath just as often. We were almost to Queenie's before I remembered to ask about Mr. LaFouche.

"He's partner to Harlan Wilbeck," Tuck said curtly. I think he was still a little mad about that pillow business.

"P-partner come l-lately," Mace added through chattering teeth. He had started to look downright miserable. I can't say I was too upset about it.

"He wed Wilbeck's younger daughter," Tuck went on. "That'd be Mace and Pete's Aunt Ruby."

"I d-don't count none of them as k-kin," Mace grumbled.

Tuck gave a low chuckle. "And here I thought we were going to all this trouble just to pick up something in the way of inheritance for you boys. Regardless of how your Aunt Ruby's changed since she married Burl LaFouche, she was a straight-headed woman in her youth and did your daddy a favor or two. But if you're rejecting your Wilbeck blood, this whole thing boils down to a pure mercenary operation.

That being the case, you two young hotheads might just be a detriment."

"All right, all r-right," Mace stuttered. "Just don't go rubbin' it in."

"How come this Mr. LaFouche is so far north?" I asked, wishing Tuck would get back to the subject. "It'd seem natural for old man Wilbeck to be shovin' his pockets full of Prescott diggings, but I always heard he never leaves his big house down in Oro Tiempo. I don't know why his partner'd be any different."

Tuck shrugged. "It's a curiosity, Miss Gini. I've no inkling why he'd have his boys scouting after me in particular, for there's no way in Hades he could guess our purpose." His pipe had gone out, and he paused to strike a match and puff twice. "Now, once upon a time I would have expected Pinkertons and scoundrels. Almost felt ignored when there weren't at least a few on my heels. But these days the population's majority believe I've long since shed this mortal coil. Ones that know different are of the opinion that I'm too out of practice to pose threat to any payroll or bank vault. They are undoubtedly correct."

Zack jogged up from his usual place at the rear and reined his old strawberry roan even with Ty's horse. Somewhere along the way he had cut himself a fresh plug, and I heard the splat of juice on leaves before he said, "You take good care of that feller in town, Tyrone?"

When Ty replied that he had indeed, I said, "You didn't hurt him bad, did you? You just hit him on the head or tied him up or something, didn't you?"

He smiled at me, his eyes and those white, even teeth glinting in the moonlight. "Why, Geneva darlin', I'm destroyed that ye'd ask."

I was so busy trying to decide what he meant that when Tuck reined in his gelding, I nearly ran Jigsaw smack into him. "We're here," he said. "Let's roust out Pete and get on our way."

But Pete wasn't there to roust. Queenie Caulfield was sitting up by the hearth when we walked in. The whole house smelled like pinewood fire and her good coffee, and she poured us each a big steaming cup. She didn't look happy, and she told Tuck that the boys had ridden south about an hour after we'd gone into town.

"They didn't expect you back till tomorrow night," she said as she dug out a wool jacket for Mace and an old duster for me. "Pete was sore at the lot of you for leaving him, I guess. Kept sayin' he'd show you he could rustle more than hogs. I tried talkin' them out of it, but that Pete wouldn't listen, and . . . Well, Tucker, you know Bobby Lee. They went south, toward the Basin."

Tuck looked like he wished he could figure how to kick himself in the hindquarters. "This is my fault, Queenie, and I'm regretful your Bobby got caught up in it. I shouldn't have teased Pete so hard, and I shouldn't have let you other boys prod him."

I scrambled into the coat she'd handed me. It was a decent fit, if a little short in the sleeves. Gam used to say I was all arms and legs.

Queenie had poured us each a second cup, and Mace gulped the last of his. "Could I have another c-cup, please, Miz Caulfield? It's fine coffee."

"I put in eggshell," Queenie said, and got the pot for him. She didn't have me fooled. I knew she was adding a short scrape of nutmeg, too.

"Drink it fast, boy," Tuck said. "I don't know how, but we've got to catch those two before they get where they're going. Sometimes, when I think how prone to foolishness youngsters can be, it seems a solid miracle that any human makes it past the age of thirty."

Queenie Caulfield went paler than she already was, and Tuck put his arm around her narrow shoulders. "Now, Queenie, I reckon we'll catch them before they do anything rash. You just get yourself some sleep, and we'll send your youngster on back to you. I warn you, he may come home with his backside tanned." I guess I flinched some at that, because Tuck grinned. "We seem to be having a rash of misbehaving children lately. Must be something in the stars."

Tuck had a comforting way about him, and as Queenie stood in the lantern light waving us good-bye, she appeared a little more peaceful.

But Tuck didn't seem relaxed at all. As soon as we got out of Queenie's hearing, he said, "If those two lunatics don't get themselves shot solid with rustlers' leadball, it'll be the biggest intervention of the Almighty since Daniel stepped from the fiery furnace with frost in his whiskers."

Mace had stopped shivering so much, but he looked pretty agitated. "They've got at least four hours on us, Tuck. How're we gonna catch 'em? Bobby can't help being slow in the head, but damn that Pete!"

"We can catch 'em if we hurry." Zack was staring up through the trees at the night sky. "They's a back way that I'll just betcha neither one of them lamebrains knows of. If the moon don't cloud over and we can keep to a good trot without somebody's horse pullin' up sore or bustin' a leg, we can be there by dawn. Hell, Tucker, we might even beat 'em."

Tuck pulled the hat off his head and made a sweeping motion that ushered Zack right up to the front. "By all means, friend Zachary, lead on!"

Tuck declared the Fates were with us, because the moon stayed free of clouds and the going, he said, was easy. I guess he did not mind skittering up and down dark and slippery breakaway grades and getting slapped in the face with pine needles every two minutes, but I did. Still, despite all that ducking and jostling, I was dozing in the saddle by three in the morning. Even the cold in my hands and the pain in my sitting-down parts wasn't enough to keep me full awake. Sometimes I'd rouse to find myself half-off poor Jigsaw, with him fighting to keep from going down to his knees on a gravel slide, and I'd have no idea how far we were or how we got there. All I knew for certain was that I was sure mad at Pete. I'd been all set to head south for a real adventure and a fortune in gold, and on account of him I was having to ride all night on a side trip in the freezing cold.

It seemed like that night would go on forever. We stopped a couple times, as much to relieve our bladders and restart the blood flow in our legs as to give the horses a breather. Zack passed out chunks of jerky, and we gnawed it while we rode. Nobody said much. Mace sounded pretty thick in his lungs. He was coughing more all the time, and I could hear his wheezes over the horses' labored breath.

To keep myself from dozing too often, I thought about Mescal Mort's map, made the picture of it bright in my head. The place-names on it sounded magic and distant, like Jaguar Hole and Squaw Circle Rock, and the locality that would be our destination if I didn't get us lost on the way: *Cañon de los Espejos*. I knew enough Mex to translate it: Mirror Canyon.

When the sky started turning pink with first light, Zack stepped up the pace, and just as the sun hit the halfway mark at the horizon, he whoaed us. He pointed out at an angle through the trees. "Other trail runs down yonder. Boys'll be comin' in that way, if they ain't already. Reckon we'd best cut across and fan out, start lookin' for track and hope we don't find none."

Mace looked so sick by then that we didn't know if he could get back on his horse once he got off, but the rest of us did like Zack said. I spotted sign first. "Here!" I called to Ty, who was closest. "Twigs are snapped off." I lifted up the branch. "Fresh breaks."

Tuck's voice came through the green. "It's our boys, all right. That slew-footed mare'a Pete's left her track."

We were barely remounted when the shooting started. We galloped toward the sound, zigzagging through the trees. The men had pulled their rifles, and I remember Tuck yelling at me, "Keep back! Keep back!"

That was when Mace got shot. He was riding about five yards off my flank, and he flew off his gelding like he'd been tied to a tree and the rope had just caught. I hauled Jigsaw into a skid, vaulted off the wrong side, ran to Mace. I had been thinking some pretty sour thoughts about him but I sure didn't want him dead.

The others jumped off their horses, too. We were still in the woods, but at the edge of an old beaver meadow. Ty's black mare came loping past without him, reins flying as she shot out into the clearing and jumped the creek. All around was the thin whine of bullets and the cracklings and thuds of lead splintering live wood. I couldn't see any of the men.

I crouched over Mace. He was bleeding some but still breathing. His thirty-dollar hat and Sharps rifle were gone, lost in the brush. I yanked the beat-up Peacemaker from his holster, pointed it blind at the trees across the meadow, and braced myself. I got off four rounds before I heard Tuck call, "Stop shooting, goddamn it!" then louder, "Hold your fire up there! Parley! Parley!"

There were a couple more shots, then silence, and then I heard a new voice: gravelly, but loud. It came from the woods across the way. "Why should we parley with you? Ain't no man lower than one thief who'll steal from another!

Get your band'a secondhand crooks outta here, mister, or get 'em shot!"

"Get them out is all we came to do, friend," Tuck answered. "I've got a couple of hotheaded young game-cocks that ran off on me, got the notion they want to be in the equine requisitions game. If you'll give me back my youngsters, we'll get on with our business and leave you to yours."

Mace moaned and coughed a little, and I moved his head into my lap. There was a pause, and then the rustler called out, "Mister, your way of speechifyin' sounds some'at familiar to me. Would you have a name?"

"I would. This is Tucker Brennan speaking, and I ask you once again to hand over those brash youngsters if you have got them. Elsewise, leave us in peace to locate them on our own."

"Is that *the* Tuck Brennan? The one what was in on that Canyon de Chelly deal back in eighteen and sixty-one?"

"The same," Tuck called back.

"You remember a shy yeller-headed boy what took a Navajo lance a-skitter along the ribs?"

While Tuck thought on that, I checked Mace over. He was only hit in the upper arm, but during the night's ride he'd come on with a terrible fever, and that kept him on the ground more than the flesh wound. He was still out cold, and I let him stay that way. I figured he needed the rest.

"Yellow-headed boy, you say?" Tuck called after a minute. Then I heard him laughing big. I could just see him in my mind. I bet he had his head thrown back, all his teeth showing. "Mount Olympus! You wouldn't be old Bashful Ben Lamar come back to haunt me, would you?"

The other fella laughed, too. "That I would, you Harvard polecat! You can have your boys back, but I can't guarantee what shape they's in. Last I knew, they was shootin' at us from mebbe twenty yards to your right."

I heard Zack shout, "Bobby? Bobby Lee! Pete boy! You hear me?"

Nobody answered.

Tuck hollered for them, too. Still no answer.

Bashful Ben yelled down, "Tucker?"

"I'm still here."

"I sure hope you ain't gonna hold no grudge if them boys is banged up a mite. They come sneakin' in here aimin' to drive off our ponies, 'cept they weren't sneakin' none too good. We didn't know 'em from spit."

"I'm aware of that, Ben. I would have done the same in your boots. I bear you no malice."

With that, Bashful Ben and his boys started down through the trees. I could hear them cracking branches underfoot and scraping against pine boughs before they stepped into the clearing, their rifles a-swing. Off to my right, Tuck stood up, then Zack. Ty came up beside me from somewhere to the left and knelt down. "How is it with him?" he asked, and touched Mace's shoulder.

I had Mace clear of his wool coat by then. "Just hit the meat," I said.

Out in the meadow, Tuck stepped over the little stream, and he shook hands with a big, checker-shirted man that appeared more hard-luck farmer than desperate horse thief. His boys were a pretty ragtag lot, too.

I pulled a bandanna from Mace's pocket and wiped the sweat from his forehead. "He's awful sick, Ty, burnin' up. I need to get some herb tea in him. Sage, catnip, or pennyroyal, with some whiskey and honey in it. He should be under a stack of blankets to help sweat out the fever."

Tuck and Zack, along with Bashful Ben and his four boys, fanned out into the woods to look for Pete and Bobby.

Ty stayed with me, and whistled up his mare. She was as well trained as she was handsome, and she trotted right over.

"This'll help for now," he said, and pulled a flask from his saddlebag. Mace had come round enough to swallow, but after he took a couple sips, he set in to a coughing fit. When he finally stopped, I held the flask and made him take a little more while Ty checked his arm.

"Ye've got the luck, young Danahoe," he said in that singsong voice. "Slug whistled straight out the other side, sweet and clean. A good tight bandage and a bit a'bedrest for those sniffles, and ye'll be fit as Murphy's mouser."

I knew it'd take more than a "bit," but I kept my mouth shut. I felt a little low, seeing as how it was sort of my fault old Mace had got dunked in the horse trough and near froze to death, but by the same token I wondered if maybe this wasn't the Lord's way of punishing him for having whipped me so bad. Either way, I supposed we were even, as his fever would likely last as long as my bruises.

"Bring your mare, Ty." Zack stood over us, squinting down at Mace's bloody arm. We'd been so busy getting Mace comfortable that we hadn't even heard him walk up.

Ty got to his feet. "What is it, Zachary?"

"'Tain't good," Zack said, and turned to shoot a stream of brown juice on a sapling. "Just bring the mare. Boy all right?"

"Fine," Mace croaked, and started in to cough.

"He'll mend," Ty said, and gathered up his mare's reins. Then he and Zack walked off, Ty's mare between them. I hollered after them to find out what the trouble was, but they didn't answer.

I called for Jigsaw, thinking it wouldn't hurt to put a cool cloth on Mace's head and clean up his arm. Jigsaw didn't obey so quick as Ty's mare, but after a couple clucks and whistles he ambled out into the clearing and started grazing his way toward us.

While I waited, I made Mace drink some more whiskey, and when Jigsaw finally got near, I opened up my satchel, lifted out Malachi, and found a pair of drawers he hadn't messed on. By then, Mace had passed out again. I washed his arm, got the bleeding slowed to almost nothing, and ripped the drawers up into strips. I was just tying off the bandage when I heard the men coming back.

Zack and Ty were in front, leading Ty's mare. Bobby Caulfield's body was slung across the saddle, his hatless head thumping against the stirrup, lank hair swinging. Blood covered his side, soaked his shirtsleeve, dripped off his fingers to spatter the yellow grass and make long shiny runners on the horse's leg.

Next came Tuck and three of Bashful Ben's boys. They were walking careful, for they were carrying Pete between them on a blanket sling. All I could see of Pete was his hand flopping over the edge of the blanket, but Tuck's face was the color of ash. Another of Ben's boys followed at a distance, leading Pete's mare. She was limping bad.

They laid Pete down by the creek. Tuck sent one of the boys for water and rags before he knelt down. I could see him talking soft as he opened Pete's shirt. Pete stirred a little, lifted his hand.

Tuck looked terrible sad. I guess he was thinking about Queenie Caulfield, and maybe that promise he'd made to look out for the Danahoe boys. Zack's face was all sort of twisted up. Neither of them would look me in the eye. Bashful Ben mopped at his eyes with a big stained handkerchief.

"Lordamighty," he sniffled, "if I'd'a knowed it was one'a Jinx's boys and the Caulfield kid, I just would'a let 'em *take* the gol-dern horses. Why, Reid and Queenie Caulfield stood up at my weddin' fifteen year back, and Jinx, well, I guess ever'body knowed Jinx. Lordy, Lordy! Shoot me, Tuck! Jes' put me outta my misery!"

He stopped to blow his nose, which was a good thing, because I could tell Tuck was half-tempted to take him up on that shooting part. Ty must have sensed it, too, because he put his hand on Bashful Ben's shoulder and said, "There, Ben, that's enough. Ye'd no way of knowin'. We're holdin' no blame to ye or the lads. And the Danahoe boy may make it yet."

"You'll tell Queenie how terrible sorry . . ."

"Aye, Ben." Ty smiled at him kindly. That was when I noticed that Ty was the only one of us who didn't look even slightly torn up by the situation. I supposed that since he'd never met Pete or Bob, that was probably natural; still, a killing is a killing and you'd expect a person to react to it somehow. I told myself Tyrone O'Neill had probably seen so many dead bodies in his day that he was immune to them.

Bashful Ben's boys rounded up the rest of our mounts, then set to work lashing together a travois for Pete. I helped Tuck get him cleaned up. He had taken a slug in the chest and lost a lot of blood, but we got the wound packed and the bleeding slowed up. Pete's mare had bowed a tendon. Ben said he'd keep her, and traded Tuck his own nice buckskin saddle horse to pull Pete's litter.

For the time being, they laid Bobby Lee by the stream and covered him with a blanket. Ty and Zack stripped and watered the horses, tied them on a picket line, and grained them good. One of Bashful Ben's boys made a fire and got some coffee going, then rode over the ridge to Ben's camp and brought us out a big hunk of venison from the haunch they'd roasted the day before. I was almost too wrung-out with fatigue and sorrow to chew, but my stomach appreciated what of that meat I could get down.

I must have napped for a good while, because the next thing I knew, the sun had climbed well past the noon mark and Tuck was squatted down next to me. He looked a good five years older than he had the night before.

"Wake up, child," he said, real soft. "The horses are rested, and so are you. It's time we got on our way."

"How's Pete?" I said with a yawn.

"He's rested some, Miss Gini, but to tell you true, I cannot promise he'll make it back up the hill."

"Maybe we should stay here a spell."

Tuck shook his head. "He needs a real doctor."

I started looking for Malachi. What with it still being pretty cool, he had gone exactly nowhere, and I stowed him away in my satchel.

Mace was already mounted. His rifle was back in its boot, but I guess they hadn't found his expensive new hat as he was bareheaded again. Half-conscious, he was tied in the saddle and talking, in mumbled spurts, out of his head. "I'll get that for you, Ma," he said, then, "I believe he's to the stock pen." I didn't know whether it was from the fever or if they'd got him that much drunker.

Pete was roped into the travois. He looked awful white and awful small, and he was either unconscious or in too much hurt to open his eyes or talk. Bobby's body had been bound up in blankets and strapped across his horse. A little snatch of furry goat-hide chap poked out the edge of his shroud.

I felt tears coming on, and made myself get busy tying my satchel behind Jigsaw's saddle. Tuck had managed to find my little hotel pillow, and he put it on the seat. As he gave me a leg up, he said, "I'm sending you off with Zack."

"What?! What do you mean, old man? Did you forget what was decided last night?"

He put his hand on my leg, real firm and fatherly, and

said, "I know, Miss Gini. But this . . . misfortune has put just a little bit of a hitch in the proceedings. I've been talking it over with Zack and Ty, and we're in agreement that the minute I show up around Prescott, LaFouche'll have a man or two on me again. Situation might get unpleasant. The best thing is for us to go our own ways and meet up again later. It'll give me time to shake the watchdogs."

"But Ty and Mace and Pete are goin' with you!"

He shook his head. "Mace and Pete can't help but go where they're taken. And after we see to those poor boys, Ty'll be setting off on his own, too."

"Well, where am I goin'?"

"I'm having Zack escort you south, toward Goose Flats and Tombstone. That's a prime jumping-off place for our little treasure hunt, isn't it, Miss Gini?"

I think I colored up a little. "Tombstone's not even on that map, Tuck Brennan."

"Course not. It's too new a tent city. But it's a fine location for a start-out."

Well, he was just exactly right, and I couldn't do much more than glare at him for being so clever.

He managed a smile. "I know a bit more about most things than you credit me, child. Zack'll keep you clear of mischief until the rest of us can catch up."

"And just when would that be?"

He shrugged. "When we can. Two months. Six months. A year, maybe longer."

"But Tuck!"

His brow furrowed, and I knew not to push him. "Enough, Miss Gini. Now you go on with Zachary and don't complain. I have a child to bury." His eye fell on Pete, and he added, real soft, "Maybe two."

• • •

I bade my fare-the-wells to Bobby, Pete, and Mace from Jigsaw's back. And as Zack and I started south, I got to wondering what kind of marker or monument poor Bobby would rest beneath. Most like, it'd be a wood cross, period.

Me, I always favor a stone marker. A good, thick slab or big fat angel carved of marble or limestone is that much harder for the elements to erode or the drunks to shoot up or the pranksters to lasso and dump in the arroyo on All Hallows' Eve. Doc Ben Winslow had got Gam a king-sized pink marble headstone—practically the biggest in Hanged Dog's whole little cemetery—that said:

> *A spirit brave, yet kind and mild,*
> *Constant friend when others waned,*
> *Sweet mother to a dear lost child:*
> *Our loss is the Christ King's gain.*

Doc Ben wrote that poem himself. And the letters were not carved small, which will give you an idea of how hefty Gam's marker was.

But what sort of epitaph could you write for a boy like Bobby? If the deceased had been a man like Tuck, why, a person would have been hard pressed to narrow it down to a paragraph.

For Bobby, the stonemason would probably be stuck with *Beloved son*, period. I didn't know what they'd do if Stinky Pete didn't pull through. A person couldn't go engraving *Here lies Pete: We always smelt him before we saw him,* or *Pete Danahoe: A fair hog thief but a bad horse rustler.* The more I thought about it, the more I figured Tuck had better stick with wood crosses, small ones to boot. Just enough room for a name and the dates of entry and exit.

I had quite a bit of time to think this over, because Zack was not what you'd call an entertaining traveling companion. We were both awful sad about Bobby and Pete, I guess, and since it was all I could think to speak of and Zack wouldn't talk about it at all, the nightly conversation stayed limited to *is the biscuits done yet* or *rain don't seem likely*. Days, I settled into riding along behind him, shifting on my little pillow, thinking about the gold (and going over and over Mescal Mort's map in my head), and watching Jelly's tail end. By the end of the second day, I figured I knew every red and white hair on that old roan's rump.

On the third day, I finally asked Zack a question that had been preying on my mind. We'd been riding in silence for the past couple hours, so when I asked "Zack, does *shave-tale* mean anything to you?" he looked kind of surprised. Also irritated.

"Shavetail? That's a brand-new second lieutenant in the U.S. Army." He stopped to take a spit. "What you want to go askin' me that for?"

"Is it anything else?"

"Green mule," he said, like I was an idiot. "Army used to mark the wild ones by shavin' the tops of their tailbones till they got broke good. Mebbe they still do. Anythin' else you can't live without knowin'?"

"Never mind."

He didn't pursue the topic, which was just as well. I had already known both those things, so he hadn't helped me out any, and I did not want to explain that my reason for asking was the gold map of Mr. Mescal Mort Scobie.

The landmarks on most of the map had been marked plain, though misspelt in many cases; but our final destination, the place where Mort had made the X to mark the gold, was smeared. It was in the second map, the one of Cañon de los Espejos that he'd drawn bigger for detail. The map showed a winding path ending in a place I couldn't quite read the name of. The best I could make of the smudged writing was *Spinit Hettle*.

Now, that didn't sound like American or Mex either one, and made no sense to me. The closest I could figure was that maybe something there looked like a spinet piano. But inside that Spinit Hettle place was the X, and right next to the X, marked over two or three times so the writing was heavy, it said *shave-tale*. Mort must have thought it was pretty important.

Zack didn't seem in much hurry. We traveled down out of the mountains about as slow as we'd ridden up into them. Malachi was appreciative, since he could ride in my lap most of the time. He thereby got plenty of fresh air, even though he still moved sluggish. Actually, I was some worried about him, as I don't imagine horseback travel can be too natural for tortoises. He should have been set free to wander around on solid ground and do whatever tortoises do, but even after we rode down into scrub I kept putting it off.

I was still carting him four days after we left Prescott. By that time, my backside bruises had healed up and we had moseyed to within spitting distance of Phoenix, which is on the Salt River, called by some the Rio Salado.

Phoenix, once we finally rode into it, was kind of a letdown. It claimed over one thousand souls in residence and was sure a lot more peaceable than Prescott, but it was a plain and dusty town. Zack got us hotel rooms and paid extra for me to have a bath, then he went off to buy supplies.

The bathtub had a room to itself at the end of the hall, and after a couple kids brought up the water, I locked the door good and soaked for a whole hour. The water was pretty cold by the time I got out, but I used it to wash out my bucks. That was sure a jolt. I had not realized how hog-dirty they were. They turned the water close to black and killed off any hope I'd had of scrubbing the satchel things Malachi had messed.

After I wrung my bucks good and rolled them up in towels, I put on the only other outfit I had brought, that being a calico dress. It felt strange to wear after living in buckskin for so long, and when I got back to the room, even Malachi looked a little shocked at the sight of me.

Zack was pretty surprised, too. When he came back from marketing, he walked into my room, peeked over the brown-paper packages he was half-staggered with, turned bright red, and mumbled, "Pardon me all t'hell, ma'am, I have got the wrong room."

He started to back out, and I said, "You aren't in the wrong place, you old geezer. Haven't you ever seen a lady in a dress before?"

He took a good long squint at me. "You plannin' to horseback-ride in that getup?"

I had a stare at him, too. For some reason I could only guess at and be thankful for, he'd taken it upon himself to get cleaned up. He'd had a bath and a shave, and what few hairs he had were trimmed and oiled flat to his head. Except for those crookedy brown gap-teeth, he came across real nice, like maybe your grandpa or great-uncle would look of a Sunday.

As slick as two townies, we went out for a good restaurant dinner, during which Zack got relaxed enough to tell me some stories he knew about an ex-reb officer who'd practically started Phoenix single-handed (anyhow, that was how Zack told it) and who had died in the penitentiary at Yuma while Tuck and Zack were there. Arizona is funny like that. Sometimes it seems to me like we throw every-body in jail sooner or later, just in case. Anyhow, it wasn't till then that I found out Zack and Tuck had only met five years previous, while they were both serving time. I don't know why, but all along I'd assumed they went way back. In truth, Zack knew Ty first.

"First met Tyrone in a Santa Fe cantina," Zack told me. "That were back in, oh, mebbe seventy, seventy-one. I was gettin' a slug dug outta my hip in one room and Tyrone was dealin' stud in the next. He come in to see what the screamin' was about, said it was wreckin' his concentration. Course, I was on the dodge in them days. Spent the next week hid out in a shed back of the bar, healin' up and swattin' black widders. Afternoons, Tyrone used to come out and play a few hands with me, keep me company. That Tyrone is a powerful storyteller once he gets started, and he spun me some fine yarns 'bout his old days with Tuck and Jinx and the rest of the lot, back before everybody else got kilt off or split up and Tuck got sent away to Yuma. Did you know it took U.S. Marshal Bob Kember and twenty-three deputies to take him in?"

Since that piece of information was known by practically every Territory resident over the age of five, I found the question just a little insulting and I told Zack so.

He swallowed the last of his second roll, slathered some butter on the third, and said, "I'll bet you don't know what happened to U.S. Marshal Kember, though, do you, Miss Smarty?"

When I confessed I didn't, Zack grinned kind of wicked and leaned across the table. "He met up with a little accident," he said with a wink. "Least, that's how it got recorded. But the fact of it's that about one year later Tyrone come up on Mister Big Important Marshal Kember one night as Kember was exitin' the public outhouse back of the Ox Bow Saloon down in Crystal Springs. 'Marshal Kember?' says Ty, and when Kember—staggerin' drunk and fulla hisself—says 'Yes, by Christ, and who wants to know,' Tyrone says, 'Robert Kember, you have arrested my best friend by unfair advantage and sent him to that shithole in Yuma. I am about to do the same to you, only without the help of twenty-three armed brigands.' Brigands! Now, ain't that a word for you? Course, Ty said it more Irish than that, though likely not near as brogue-ified as he talks now. That Irish'a his gets thicker with the years. Y'know, I think he must practice it a-purpose. Hell, he come to this country when he was somethin' like eight years old. You'd think he'd be talkin' American by this—"

I grabbed his sleeve. "Holy Hannah, Zack! You've got so out of practice with conversation this past week, you forgot how to come to the dang point! What happened to the marshal?"

"Why, Tyrone knocked him cold and shoved him down the shitter, headfirst. T'weren't dug very deep, and he was good an' dead by the time somebody seen his boots stickin' up through the seat. Folks figured he was so drunk he just fell in."

Well, I had a hard time believing a gent like Tyrone O'Neill would do any such thing, but it didn't seem the time to say so. I was just glad Zack had decided to talk to me.

I must have proved a good audience, because then he got to talking about the really old times, and about how he had fought, for a year or so, in the War Between the States. He said he rode off to war from down at Florence, Arizona, where he used to have a scraggly ranch with no water, a dry-goods store he didn't like, a wife he couldn't stand, and a one-legged best friend named Ethan Forrest. Ethan couldn't go to war on account of his leg, but one night, over a bottle of tequila, he talked so pretty about the Glory of Battle that the very next day, Zack took himself east toward enlistment and away from his wife and store.

I guess he soon found the war wasn't quite the romance

his pal had led him to believe, because he deserted right after the second Battle of Bull Run. He told me this real factual, without any sense of shame or cowardice. Maybe he figured that since the South had got beat anyhow, it didn't matter at what exact point a body had given up.

Anyhow, what with the army having all the decent horses and him having to do a good share of the journey on foot, it took Zack clear till halfway into 1863 to make it home. When he got there, he found out his wife—certain he'd get killed sooner or later—had prematurely announced his death, put on black for a month, then married up with the same Ethan Forrest who talked him into defending the Glory of the South in the first place.

"It weren't like I was heartbroke about losin' Eudora," he told me over his beef stew. "It were the principle of the thing. Here I'd been a year hunkered up in wet holes with lead flyin' overhead, dead and grievous wounded all round, and the whole time, Ethan had been warmin' up them big, bony feet'a Eudora's. Fact is, if I'd'a knew he craved the old bat, I would'a just give her over, and been glad to be shed of her. But no, he had to resort to whatchacall, one'a them Tucker words. *Subterfuges*. So I pulled out my service pistol and shot him in the face. No subterfuge in that. Pass the salt."

That's what put Zack on the run, though he found out later he was never charged with the killing. Since he'd bypassed town and gone straight to the ranch, everybody still figured him for a dead hero. Eudora was the only witness, and she was so overcome with latent remorse that she told the sheriff it was Mex bandits that did the deed.

"It was a couple years afore I heared 'bout Eudora fibbin' for me," he said around his last mouthful of creamed corn, which was not a pretty sight. "By then I had fell into bad company and got used to it. Not long after, somebody I

knowed from the old days was in a New Mexico stage I
happened to be holdin' up at the time, and he says, 'By Jing,
it's the ghost of Zack Ruggles!' I was knowed by that
name for a while in New Mexico. Ghost Ruggles, that is."
He pushed aside his dirty plate and started in on his dessert
like he was afraid somebody'd steal it.

Well, I had sure heard of Ghost Ruggles. I'd even read a
book about him, though the worn-out codger sitting across
the checkered tablecloth (and signaling the serving girl for
more peach cobbler, please) sure didn't bear a resemblance
to the steely hero on that old book cover.

"I read about you," I said. "In *Ghost Ruggles, Phantom of
the White Sands Wasteland*! Did you really hold off all those
Kiowa single-handed?"

He looked at me like I'd gone crazy. "What Kiowa?"

"The ones that attacked you along the Rio Vermejo!
There were twenty bloodthirsty braves against you, and you
licked 'em all!"

He pointed at my dessert, of which I'd only eaten half.
"Shame to waste that pecan pie," he said. I pushed it toward
him.

"Seems I got a terrible sweet tooth in my old age," he
mumbled, his mouth full. "Must be a tapeworm. That book
didn't tell you no truth, missy. I never been up the Rio
Vermejo. Only dealin's I've had with the Kiowa have been
peaceable. Near cordial, accordin' to Kiowa standards." The
last gooey pecan went into his mouth. "That whole book
full'a such nonsense?"

I was shocked. "You mean you never read it?"

He shook his head. "I heared of it once or twice. Never
set eye to it, though." His second cobbler showed up right
then, and he set to work on it.

To tell the truth, I was all of a sudden kind of impressed
with him, now that I knew he was the famous Ghost

Ruggles. Counting Tuck and Tyrone, Zack was the third famous person I had met in the last half-month. I wondered if that was some sort of record.

I felt bad he had never got to read his own biography, and I asked if he would care to, if he got a chance. When he nodded, I said, "I tell you what, Zack. I have got that whole book here in my head. Word for word, comma for comma, paragraph for paragraph. I'd be pleasured to say it out for you as we ride along south."

When he allowed it would suit him, I said, "And in trade, you can do me the blessed favor of tossin' out your chaw."

He had scraped up the last of his cobbler, and he held up his hand to signal the girl. She came right over, and he ordered himself a slice of chocolate cake, seeing as how he hadn't tried that yet. He must have had a whole string of stomachs, like a cow.

"Much as I'd like to have me a listen," he said, "can't do 'er. My chaw has stuck by me through Eudora and the war, not to mention a life of thievery, wild times, and prison. Been my only constant and true companion. Ain't gonna desert 'er now."

Well, I was pretty disappointed. I didn't know how much longer I could stand the day-in, day-out spitting and the sight of that wadded-up thing under his lip. After a minute I said, "Well, would you consent to turn your back with each and every spit?"

Well, he finally agreed to that, though within three days he had forgot the promise entirely. I guess I wasn't so mad at him. I had plenty else to occupy my thoughts. We were south of the Gila by then, and into Maricopa and Pima country. The stiff had gone out of my clean bucks, I was still mulling over *Spinit Hettle* and *shave-tale*, and I had about come to the conclusion that Mescal Mort had been just as sloppy a writer as he was a bad speller: if I bent the letters in my mind a little, the *n* in Spinit could be an *r*, and the *H* in Hettle might maybe be a *K*. I can't say that *Spirit Kettle* made much more sense than *Spinit Hettle*, but at least it was in American. And I liked it better.

We made our way south, Zack spitting tobacco and chewing peppermints, and me trying to stretch my recitation of *Ghost Ruggles* long enough to keep him entertained till Tucson.

I should have told it faster.

6

A Fateful Journey South

The Ghost's smoking pistols glinted like glory in the New Mexico sun. "Stand down, Bart, or meet your doom!" he cried, eyes ablaze with righteous fury.

Blue-Fingered Bart threw back his loathsome head and roared the Devil's own laughter. "No, Ghost Ruggles, I'll not be the one to die today! You may have freed fair Belle Weston from my grasp and saved her family from ruin, but this afternoon you will not shield yourself from disaster!" With that, he drew his six-shooters and fired.

The air was rent by flying lead as—

I grabbed the skillet just in time to save the last bite of quail stew.

"Hey!" Zack grumped. "What you quittin' for? Do I get kilt or what?"

"Course you don't get killed," I said after I swallowed. It was good stew. "You're still sittin' there, aren't you? And from now on I am not goin' to storytell durin' meals, as during the time I'm recitin' you eat all the vittles."

He furrowed his forehead in a frown. "I mean, did I get kilt in the consarned book! They's been so many lies in there already, I wouldn't be surprised if they murdered me off, too. Hell's bells, I never met nobody called Blue-

Fingered Bart. How you reckon a feller *gets* a blue finger, anyhow?"

I set down the skillet and stared out into the cold black night past our little fire. "You hear that?"

Zack twisted toward where I was looking. "Coyote."

"You sure?"

He gave his head a disgusted shake, then picked up a flat, fist-sized stone. He listened careful for a half-minute, then hurled it. I heard a yelp and the sound of something four-footed skittering away through the brush. "Happy? Now go on and give me s'more book 'fore we turn in."

I finished out the chapter, but I still kept an ear cocked. Zack always complained I was too nervous, but I figured I had reason.

Our next real town would be Tucson, and between Phoenix and Tucson there is not much of anything except what the maps call "open plain" and everybody else calls desert. Most all of it is Indian country. The Pima and Maricopa tribes live there, and they are good people indeed: farmers, mostly, who are fair-and-square traders. But any time you got this far south you had to keep an eye peeled for Apache, and that's what had me nervous.

A few years prior, the Apache Nations—or what members of them could be rounded up—had been moved to San Carlos. San Carlos is also called Hell's Forty Acres, and for reasons you can guess by that name, Geronimo or somebody like him jumps the reservation about every five minutes. Usually they head for Mexico to hide out and raid, but you never could tell when you might run across some Apache with a grudge. More likely they would run across you.

That last one was a situation I in no way wanted to experience, and I thought Zack was being way too lackadaisical about watching for Indian sign. Gam had told me so much of the way Apache can sneak up on a person that I had been seeing imaginary Mescalero and Chiricahua and Coyotero behind every cactus and clump of sage or mesquite. I still thought I knew it all, thought I was going to keep us safe.

We could not have asked for better traveling weather, for though the nights were cold enough that I made good use of both my blankets, the daytimes were balmy. We were only a day out of Tucson and just five skinny chapters away from the end of the Ghost Ruggles book, which I had been stretching thin so as to make it last. We were riding at a slow jog, not far from the dry bed of the Santa Cruz, and I had just recited the pages where Ghost Ruggles escapes certain disaster at the hands of twenty Kiowa by using his last powder to start a rock slide.

To tell the truth, even I was a little surprised at how easy that story flowed out of me. I had never tried to recall a whole book in order before (and to be honest I had a little trouble with the first part of chapter 12), but once I got the picture of each page clear in my mind, it was just like having the book in front of me all over again.

Zack enjoyed the recitation about as much as I have ever seen a body relish anything. He especially liked grousing about the parts he said were so wrong they couldn't have happened to anybody, let alone him. I kept a keen ear to his grouch sessions, for along with the complaining, he mixed in all kinds of exciting true stories by way of illustration.

He was happily remarking as to the impossibility of two shells' worth of gunpowder owning enough blasting power to avalanche forty tons of rock (and telling me how he and a tough customer named One-Ball Jackie Pead once tried for a day and a half to blow a Herrick & Sons safe and dynamited three-quarters of the town of Proviso, New Mexico, in the process), when I heard a kind of soft whoosh and a little thump. Zack stopped talking. He tipped sideways off Jelly, right into me.

I reached for him, but lost my grip. He slid down between the horses. Then I saw the arrow in his side.

Malachi was in my lap, and I snatched him up in order to jump down quick. Before I freed boot from stirrup, there was another little whoosh, then a whip-crack sound. Malachi was gone. It felt like somebody had just jerked him away.

I hit the dirt with Gam's squirrel gun in hand, and crouched over Zack. He was on his side and bleeding some, but he wasn't hurt bad enough to wipe the cantankerous off his face. He reached down and, with a disgusted grimace, snapped the arrow's shaft off. "Where's my Henry?" he muttered before he realized it was still in his rifle boot. His hand went to his holster. "After all them invisible Injuns you been spookin' at, how come you didn't—"

He stopped then, because another arrow took him low in the back and sank in deep. Our horses had wandered on ahead, like nothing had happened and we were just being nice to let them graze. The cover was spotty and even then no higher than two feet, but I guess it was enough for those Apache. I could not see them anywhere.

I went to bring up my squirrel gun, thinking that lead flying blind was better than no lead at all, but Zack put his hand on my arm and tried to pull it toward his handgun. That last arrow had done him bad and he was terrible weak. He said, "No, child. Pistol. Don't let 'em—"

Hands clamped my shoulders, jerked me away. Zack rolled facedown in the dust. The invisible Indians were solid enough now. There were a half-dozen braves. Two of them already had our horses. Three more were scattered out in the scrub, none farther away than thirty feet. The sixth had me.

I shouted out Zack's name, and the brave behind me let

go of one shoulder long enough to smack the side of my skull. It was no gentle cuff, and for just a second everything went blurry and dim.

I gave my head a shake, shouted "Leave me go, you heathen coward!" and shot my boot heel back into his shin just as hard as I could.

He jumped, and a couple of the others laughed. He shouted at them in Apache, and they shut up quick enough. Then he hit me again. This time my ears buzzed and I started to fall. He let me drop.

I landed, face in the dirt, right next to Zack. He was still drawing breath, and he signaled me with his eyes to take his pistol. That brave must have seen him, too, because he grabbed the gun before I could. He waved the barrel under my nose and said, in Mex, that I was much trouble for such a small and worthless girl.

That was the first time I saw his face. He was youngish, maybe not more than a few years older than me, though it is hard to tell with people who live on the desert all their lives. His skin was deep bronze and already weathered, and he had the high cheekbones and broad, clean forehead of many of his race. Above a wide, thin-lipped mouth and a long, straight nose, his eyes were narrowed and dangerous, but they were not Apache eyes. They were light gray. I guess I stared.

He stared back till I had to look away. About then, one of the others shouted at him. He walked off, leaving a flat-faced, bowlegged brave to stand guard over Zack and me.

I eased Zack onto his side and pillowed his old bald head on my leg. He had lost his chaw, and I wiped a few shreds of tobacco from his chin stubble. He tried to say something, but it only made him cough. I put my fingers over his lips.

The bowlegged brave looked bored, but he managed to

give a sharp kick to my ribs or backside every couple minutes. He was probably mad he'd been left to watch us, as the others were having a fine time going through our bedrolls and baggage. They remarked over our horses, feeling their legs and peering in their mouths.

I watched them throw my treasures on the ground. Gam's Bible, her favorite earrings and garnet necklace, my dress and good shoes, the pictures of me and Gam: all were tossed in a heap. They found the jerky and passed it around, as well as the extra johnnycake I'd made at breakfast and what was left of the smoked turkey we'd got in Phoenix.

Zack looked awful bad. My Mex was not very good, but, as best I could, I asked our guard if I could have some water for my friend. I guess it was too much trouble for him to say no, because he kicked me in the leg.

I said, real soft, "Zack Ruggles, don't you go and croak on me."

He didn't open his eyes. A little blood oozed from the corner of his mouth, and then he said, "Sorry . . . Sorry I et up all the fried ham this mornin'."

"I didn't want it anyway, you old coot." I ran my fingers over his brow, wiped away the sweat and dirt as best I could.

The light-eyed brave was back. He and an older Apache, hair streaked to gunmetal gray, were standing almost over us. They were having quite a discussion in their own lingo. I didn't look up long. I was too busy watching Zack.

You know, it's funny that after all those years with Gam, I had none of the Apache language. But Zack Ruggles did, and because of that I did not die.

There they were, having this big palaver about three feet away, when all of a sudden Zack's eyes popped open. He took hold of my wrist so hard I thought there'd been a miracle and he was well again. He looked me in the face and whispered, "For your life, say she's your ma."

"What? What are you talkin' about?"

I guess the bowlegged one had tired of abusing me, because this time he reached down and grabbed the arrow in Zack's back. Grinning, he gave the shaft a mean twist and thrust it in so cruel and deep that the arrowhead burst through Zack's belly.

Zack screamed. It was a sound like I never heard before, and pray I never do again.

Bowlegs laughed. I cried Zack's name and threw my arms around him, but a hand closed on my elbow and hauled me up. The gray-eyed one pushed something at me. Half in Mex, half in American, he said, "This woman. She is known to you?"

Well, I thought he'd gone crazy, or I had.

"Here!" he said, and made me look down.

It was a picture. My eyes were so flooded it was hard to see, but I finally realized it was one of Gam, taken the year before I came to live with her, when she was new to Hanged Dog and not long off the desert.

"She's known to me," I said, and made myself not cry. Gam had said they took it for weakness, and I would not give them the satisfaction.

The older one grunted. He seemed to be the leader. "Say her name," he said.

Right then it dawned on me what poor Zack had been getting at. Cuchillo Rojo had been pretty well-known, so maybe Gam had been, too. If the older Apache had recognized her picture, he might be of a mind to leave me unharmed. Plus, by the looks of it, the light-eyed one was the son of a captive himself. Maybe his mama had even been a friend of Gam's.

I stood up tall, though I was sore from being kicked so much by that villain, Bowlegs. "Her name was Mary Kincaid," I said, right out. "She was once wife to the great

Cuchillo Rojo, and later mother to me." I put it mostly all in American with a little of my bad Mex tossed in, but they seemed to understand. It started a whole new conversation between the two of them, not one dang word of which I understood. I was bending to Zack again when the older one caught my arm. He gave me a shake, as if he did not already have my attention.

"How are you called?" he demanded.

"I am called Geneva Kincaid. Why have you killed this good man? He did not harm you. He had nothing worth stealing."

He motioned to Bowlegs, who knelt down and put his hand on Zack's chest, said something in Apache, then spat.

The older brave nodded. "He lives still," he said, "but not for long." He took the picture back and waved it in my face. "How do we know this is your mother? How do we know you have not stolen it?"

I pointed toward the pile of my things the others had thrown aside. "There is another picture. The two of us together."

The light-eyed brave made a signal to the others, and after they picked through the debris for a minute, one of them dog-trotted over with the rest of my pictures. There was one of Gam in her Sunday dress, another of me at seven, and my favorite, taken the previous summer: Gam sitting in the photographer's fancy armchair, me standing alongside, my hand on her dear shoulder.

"You have broke the glass!" I said, and grabbed for the frame.

Light-eyes snatched it back. He took hold of my face and held the picture up next to it. He and his friend studied both me and the photograph for quite some time. Finally, he let go of my jaw and said, "Yes, this is your image. She is your blood. She is my blood, too."

Well, you could have knocked me over. I couldn't think of a blessed thing to say.

He said it for me. "I did not know of you, Neva Kin-Kay. the Mexicans have named me Asesino Pequeño, the Little Assassin. But you and I share blood. You will know my true name." He said it in Apache, and I guess I looked blank because he added, "In your tongue, it means Sees Silver. I am son of Cuchillo Rojo and Glows Like Sun, who whites name Mary Kin-Kay. Our mother lives still?"

I could hardly make my mouth move. It seemed to me that neglecting to mention a whole, entire son was more than just an oversight on Gam's part, and I was just a little ticked at her for it.

"No," I said finally. "She died some weeks ago. I am going to Tombstone with . . ." It occurred to me I'd better make Zack into kin, too, if I wanted to get him good treatment for what time he had left. "With my uncle," I finished up.

Sees Silver looked down at Zack, who groaned a little. "This man was brother to Glows Like Sun?"

I crossed my fingers behind my back, though under the circumstances I figured the Lord would most likely forgive all these whoppers. "Yes," I said. "He is my Uncle Zachary. That makes him your Uncle Zachary, too."

Right about then the bowlegged brave started looking real nervous, and it didn't take a genius to figure he'd been the one who'd shot up Zack in the first place. When Sees Silver took a step toward him, Bowlegs hollered near loud enough to bust my eardrums, and took off at a run.

Sees Silver was faster and caught him in ten yards. The two went down in the brush, rolling and kicking. A hand came up, a knife flashed bright.

Sees Silver stood up. He walked back alone and stopped in front of me. He ran his thumb along the side of his red-smeared blade, then pressed it to my forehead. He said, "The brother of Glows Like Sun is avenged."

You may think low of me for it, but I was glad.

Manuelito, the older brave, turned out to be brother to Cuchillo Rojo, making him Sees Silver's uncle on the other side, and he seemed to be pretty much in charge of the others. Zack could not be moved, but while he was still passed out, Manuelito snapped the butt off the arrow Bowlegs had kicked through, and slid it free.

Though Manuelito's boys had no horses and little food, they did have a small amount of *tiswin*, that being a kind of alcohol the Apache brew. After Zack came round again, I made him sip at it. It eased his pain some, though he groused about it and whispered to me that it tasted like pony piss. I thought it best not to ask how he knew to compare. He had a few peppermints and horehounds in his pocket, and I dropped the mints in his *tiswin*. That seemed to make it easier for him to take.

I rigged a blanket on some sticks for shade, and then I sat down beside him. "Zack," I said, "I promised to say out all your book. If you'd like, I'll start in again now."

He nodded, stiff-like. "I'd admire it," he whispered. "Somethin' else . . . Maybe you could get word to Eudora. Tell 'er I kicked for true this time." He tried to laugh, but it just made him choke.

I said I would, and I began his story right where I'd left off.

Now, those Indians were still hanging round. It seems the Apache have what is called a matriarchal society. They owe allegiance to the woman's clan, be it mother's or wife's, and therefore Sees Silver was honor-bound to be my protector. Zack's, too. And I guess he figured that if I was crazy

enough to sit out there in the middle of nowhere and tell
. stories, he'd just have to stay and watch over me.

Zack stayed pretty much conscious, and I talked steady,
only pausing to give him a swallow of *tiswin* now and then.
Pretty soon I noticed the Apache were creeping in closer and
closer, but not in a menacing way. They were listening. I
don't mind saying I was awful glad we had already finished
the part where Ghost Ruggles kills off all those Kiowa, as I
wasn't sure how these boys would take to it.

It was coming on dark and getting chilly by the time I got
to a good temporary stopping place. My throat was raw, and
I had a terrible craving for coffee. Also, I had missed lunch.
After some persuading, I got Manuelito to make a little fire
and I set the pot on to brew. While I waited on it, Sees Silver
asked me why I told this story to Zack.

"Our uncle was once a great warrior in the lands east of
here," I said. "This is the story of his time there."

"He is the one the story calls Ghost?"

I said yes, and Sees Silver nodded. He was real solemn,
but you could tell he was proud to have added such a heroic
relative as Ghost Ruggles to his family tree. Now that he
was trying to be friendly, I thought I could see a bit of Gam
in his face. I took some comfort in that.

I was pretty hungry by then. I must have looked it,
because he said, "There will be food soon, Neva Kin-Kay.
Roberto has found a fat tortoise."

I stood up so quick I near knocked the coffee into the fire.
"What tortoise? I have just lost one!"

Sees Silver pointed, and there was long-faced Roberto,
about to sink a blade right into Malachi.

I jumped over the fire and snatched Malachi out from
under his knife. That was not smart, for Roberto nearly
stabbed me instead and appeared disappointed when he

missed. Malachi was still alive, peering out from under his lid and blinking. I clutched him to me.

"He's my pet, Sees Silver. Gam—that is, Glows Like Sun—she was real fond of him."

Roberto was fair irritated at having lost his supper, but after a few words from Sees Silver, he went off to look for something else to kill. I carried Malachi over by Zack and set him down. He accepted a piece of cactus that I skinned for him and he seemed well enough; but the arrow that'd knocked him out of my hands had scarred his top shell with a jagged groove. It hadn't sliced deep enough to crack his back, but I guessed he'd always carry the mark.

I drank my coffee black and bitter (the Indians having found and gobbled the sugar early on), gave Zack another sip of peppermined Apache moonshine, and started in on the last chapter of *Ghost Ruggles, Phantom of the White Sands Wasteland*. All during it Zack held my hand. He was slipping away, and I just talked faster and faster. Every time I'd have to stop for the two or three seconds it took to wash a little coffee down my throat, he'd give my fingers a feeble squeeze to hurry me along.

When the book was through, Zack kind of smiled up at me. His lips moved a bit, and I leaned over and put my ear close. He whispered, "'Twere a fine book, child. Don't let them sonsabitches eat my horse." Then he died, just like that.

I do not know what they did with the body of the bowlegged murderer Sees Silver killed, and I did not ask as I didn't much care. But we buried Zack at first light.

The gravelly kind of desert we were in is hard to dig deep, especially when all you've got for a shovel is some sticks and a couple frying pans. The other braves sat around acting useless, but Sees Silver helped me scoop out a shallow trough and put Zack in it. I had wrapped him in a blanket first. I did not want to think of dirt going on his face.

After we filled it in, we gathered up all the big rocks we could find and built a cairn on top of the grave to keep coyotes and such from profaning it. Afterwards, I spoke the Twenty-third Psalm. I had it in my head, of course, but I used the Bible to read from. Somehow that seemed more proper. Sees Silver and Manuelito made the others stand up and act reverent—at least, as reverent as an Apache can act at a white man's ceremony.

After, I made breakfast. While I sizzled up some flap-jacks, Sees Silver told me about how he had lost his daddy and mama in the same day. I knew about Cuchillo Rojo getting killed in a fight over some horses, of course. The way Gam had told it, she had just set fire to Cuchillo Rojo's possessions (that being the custom), said good-bye, and walked off. According to Sees Silver, the tribe figured she was just strolling out into the desert for some solitary mourning; thinking it might be some crazy thing white people did, they didn't interfere. But when she didn't come back after a decent time, Manuelito and some others went to look for her. They trailed her to where her tracks met up with Mescal Mort's, then they trailed him and Gam both. Of course, they thought Mescal Mort had kidnapped her and they were closing in to the "rescue," but the troopers picked up Gam and Mort first.

All in all, I guessed Mort Scobie had got the best of it by getting hanged. I would not want to have Apaches as mad at me as they had been at him for stealing off their Glows Like Sun. Here it was, better than fifteen years after the fact, and Manuelito and Sees Silver were still talking about ripping out his liver and making him eat it.

I just let them keep thinking Gam had been spirited off against her will. It would have served no purpose for Sees

Silver to learn his mama had deserted him; and to be honest, knowing Gam the way I did, I didn't understand how she could have just walked away and left her four-year-old baby behind. I sure wished she was there to explain it.

The reason Manuelito's band had attacked me and Zack was for our horses, guns, and food. I gave them the breakfast leftovers, saving back only what I'd need for my lunch. I also let them take the rest of the beans and lard and dry goods, but I would not give up the horses. Though Sees Silver greatly admired Jigsaw, he would not take him, as he was mine; but I had a hard time convincing them to leave Jelly. It helped that they did not know to offer sweets first, for when Roberto tried to ride him off, Jelly would only stand and strike out with his off-hind leg, no matter what that brave did. Finally, I said I had to take the horse to Zack's widow, she being a poor old woman who would starve without a horse to sell. I suppose they figured Eudora must be in dire straits indeed if she could make use of what little cash such an ill-trained, obstreperous pony as Jelly would bring, because after that they let him be.

In addition to the foodstuffs, I gave Sees Silver a picture of Gam: the old one Manuelito had recognized her from. By rights, the squirrel gun should have gone to him, too, but since his pals had requisitioned Zack's pistols and Henry rifle, I figured there'd be enough mayhem already. Instead, I gave him Gam's jewelry, thinking that someday he might give the set to his wife. That option did not seem to occur to him, for he dropped the earbobs into a little leather pouch on his belt, then had me fasten the necklace round his own throat. I daresay he was the only Chiricahua Apache in the Territory to wear a garnet and gold-filigree necklace. The others thought he looked real fine.

"You had best take good care of that," I said. "Our mother brought those jewels all the way from Virginia, and they have been in the Kincaid family for three generations; four, counting you."

I almost set Malachi free near Zack's grave. It would be a good place for him, and I liked to think he'd keep Zack company in that lonely place. But in the end I couldn't do it. I had of late lost every person I called friend or loved one by reasons of death or leave-taking, and that tortoise and Jigsaw were all I had left. It was a selfish thing, but I put him back in my satchel.

After Sees Silver and I said our good-byes, I started south on Jigsaw. I led Jelly, who finally moved for me after I slipped him a horehound drop. He was pretty balky. I don't think he understood what had happened to Zack.

Manuelito's band veered off to the southwest at a ground-eating trot. Now, there are no people tougher than Apache. I have heard it said that they pride themselves on being marathon runners, and can make as good time on foot as a white can make a-horse, better sometimes. Gam once told me that a motivated brave can cover seventy miles in a day, even over harsh territory. Judging by the way those boys moved, I believe it.

I guess Sees Silver was still keeping a brotherly eye on me, because I saw them once more that day, when I was south of Picacho Peak and not far from Tucson. He and the others were sitting up on the crest of a rise, five specks in the distance, one with a glint of gold and red at his neck. They just squatted there for a spell, watching. I waved to them, but they didn't wave back. I glanced away for a second, and when I looked up again, they were gone.

Tucson was bigger and busier and there were some fancy new wood buildings mixed in with the old adobe, but for the most part it was just as flat-roofed and dusty gray a place as I remembered. I found the Cactus Wren Hotel, that being the place me and Gam had stayed at before, and took myself a room. The Cactus Wren was mostly as I recalled, except they had added on some rooms at the back and covered over the packed dirt floors with red clay tiles. It was nicer underfoot, if a little noisier. They also had running water in the new bathroom, with a spigot smack over the tub. They charged extra for the use, of course, but I had no immediate money problems as I had slipped Zack's purse from his pocket the night before, when no one was watching and Zack was past caring.

The first thing I did was reserve a bath, and the second was have a good cry right there in the tub. The third was to write a letter to Zack's widow. It wasn't a long one. Judging by what Zack had told me about Eudora, she was not worth too much ink. I just told her that he had died brave, that I'd seen him buried proper and Christian, and that she was free to marry again if she hadn't already. I had Zack's pocket watch, having snatched it at the same time I got his purse, and I wrapped that up, too. I put the whole business in a little box I got from the desk clerk and took it to the Butterfield Overland Mail Company; and it was in the Butterfield lobby that I first met Miss Elma Justice.

There she sat: this little bit of a blonde-headed thing in a mint-green dress and matching parasol, perched on a bench at the Tucson P.O. and crying her eyes out. After I paid for my postage, I sat down next to her.

"If you think you have got bad troubles," I said, "I will tell you mine and then you'll feel better."

She sniffled and rubbed at her nose with a little green hankie. She was sure one for matching her clothes up. Even her shoes were green. She was also a lot more spiffed up than me, as after my bath I had put on my dirty bucks again, not having had time to clean them. She eyed me up and down like I just might have a disease or maybe nits.

"You don't need to stare," I said. "I have been on the trail, and that's not a place where a lady can dress for show. My name is Geneva Kincaid, Gini for short, and I thought I might be able to help you. But if you're too fine to talk to me, you can just help yourself."

I started to leave, but she put her hand on my arm. "Forgive me, Miss Kincaid," she said. "I fear I have been so intent on my own woes that I have misplaced my manners. I am Miss Elma Justice, and I have journeyed all the way from St. Louis to teach school in the town of Amulek, Arizona. And now that I am only forty miles from it, they write to tell me my services are no longer required. I've no money to get home, and I do not know what to do."

"You got my sympathy," I said, and sat back down. "Though I'm a little confused. I thought Amulek was a Mormon town."

She daubed at her eyes. "I don't see what that has to do with anything."

"If you don't mind my sayin' so, Miss Justice, for a schoolteacher you are not very educated. We've got lots of Mormon settlements here in the Territory, and a good number of those towns don't take to outsiders 'less they are also of the Latter-Day Saints persuasion. I have heard tell that some practice what they call the Gospel Plan, and the whole dang town takes meals from the same table and they all dress just alike. I don't know why they would hire a schoolteacher all the way from St. Louis."

"Well, all the same," she said, "they did. I have the letter right here if you don't believe me." She looked a bit put out, and started ferreting through her handbag. It was green, too.

The postmistress had been soaking all this in, and she leaned out the service window. "Amulek ain't like that," she said. "They's just regular Mormons, so regular most of 'em ain't only got but one or two wives. It's a mixed town—

now, anyhow. Methodists moved in." She lifted up her eyebrows like me and Miss Justice and probably everybody in the U-S-of-A should know what happens when the Methodists take root.

"Well, I'm sorry," I said to Miss Justice. "I didn't mean to doubt your word. It seems to me your future is not as black as you paint it, though. Why, there's bound to be a school or two in Tucson. Maybe you could find employment here, if you don't mind garbage in the streets and alkali dust."

She shook her head and started leaking more tears, and the postmistress butted in again. "I already told her, it's middle of term and there ain't no openings. My brother-in-law, Mr. R. C. Wittenhouse, is on the school board, so I ought to know. And the garbage ain't so bad as it used to be. They're pickin' up the dead animals faster these days."

Well, I hadn't planned on carrying Miss Elma Justice, but it looked like I was stuck with her. Sorrow had clamped her fingers to my arm, and I figured if she didn't cease her weeping pretty quick, we'd soon be hip-deep in saltwater.

"Miss Justice?" I said, but she just kept crying. The second time didn't get her attention, either, so on the third try, I added in a nudge with my boot.

When she stopped weeping to scowl at me and check her shoe for a scuff, I asked where she was staying.

"Just around the corner and up the street at the Cactus Wren Hotel," she sniffed, "although this will be my last day there. I lack the funds to stay longer." She set in to weep again, then checked herself long enough to slide her feet to the side. "And don't you kick me again, Miss Kincaid!"

I guessed she must have led some kind of genteel life if she thought that little bump was being kicked, but I said, "I'd appreciate it if you'd call me Gini." I got up and brought her with me. She wasn't much taller standing up than sitting down. "Now, you and me are goin' to the Cactus

Wren, seeing as that's where I'm booked, too. We are goin' to have us some supper—my treat—during which I will tell you my problems. If that doesn't make you feel better, nothin' will. And in the morning, you and me are startin' south to Tombstone."

She shook her arm free and kind of rose up on her toes, which might have made her all of five foot, even. "Tombstone! Why Tombstone? Wouldn't you rather just kick me again?"

I ignored that last part, as I figured she was just upset about losing her job. "Tombstone's a brand-new town, Miss Justice, so new and fast-growin' that I bet they haven't had time to think about hirin' a schoolmarm. I'm goin' down there myself to meet friends, and I'd be glad for the company. Besides which, you got anything better to do?"

Well, she allowed that she didn't, and in the end she elected to go. I bought supplies (including some lemon drops for Jelly) on the way back to the Cactus Wren, and then me and Miss Justice had a good hotel dinner, during which I told her some about Tuck and Zack and the others, but no important details, and about Gam dying and leaving me all alone. We had that in common. She said she had lost her brother to fever three months past, that being the reason she had contracted to teach school in Amulek.

I cried into my dessert a little. It was peach cobbler, and it reminded me of Zack.

Miss Justice was a real pretty little thing, once I took the time to look at her close. She had big brown calf eyes and these tiny hands that sort of fluttered when she talked, like white moths. I reckoned that even if she couldn't get a teaching job in Tombstone, she could likely have her pick of the eligible bachelors.

I got a better night's sleep than I expected, and in the morning I packed up Malachi and met Miss Justice in the lobby. She had a big trunk, which she told the desk clerk to keep till she could send for it, and two small bags. Those were fit for horseback travel, but I was not so sure about her, as she had on a peach-colored dress and pump shoes and toted a matched peach parasol with white rickrack on the edges.

"You sure you can ride a horse in that rig?" I asked.

"I suppose I will have to," she replied, "since I certainly have no trousers, and would not wear them in public even if I did."

We had a little argument about it, but she was just as obstinate as could be, and in the end I gave it up. I brought the horses down from the livery, and we drew quite a crowd while Miss Elma Justice—petticoats, bustle, and all—tried to get on Jelly. Several fellas, a couple of them real gentlemen, came along and offered to boost her, but she'd have none of it. When one of them tried to pick her up anyway, she said "Remove your hands from my person this instant!" and smacked him with her parasol. That pretty much wiped out any doubts I had about a frail thing like her teaching a roomful of rowdy kids. She was probably a prize knuckle-whacker.

Anyway, it took about fifteen minutes and her hat got turned sideways in the process, but she finally made it into the saddle. Her skirts had ridden up to mid-calf, and she kept tugging them down and falling half-off on account of trying to balance that danged parasol at the same time. I will say for Jelly that despite what those Apaches had thought of him, he was a good-trained horse. He did not shy once at that silly umbrella, even though she waved it all over creation and accidentally banged him in the head with it at least three times.

We were on our way out of town, going slow with Miss Justice death-gripped to the saddle horn with one hand and clenching her rickracked parasol and Jelly's reins in the other, when I heard somebody call out, "Kincaid! Gini Kincaid! That you, come all the way from Hanged Dog?"

I looked up, and there was bushy-faced, potbellied Joe Malone, elder brother to Frank and Amos. I don't mind saying a cold shiver swept me. I remember wondering what would happen to Miss Justice's parasol if I had to kick the horses into a canter all of a sudden. I took a deep breath and said, "Yes, it's me. How do you come to be in Tucson?"

He crossed over to us. He was smiling, so I guessed Frank and Amos must not yet have written to tell him about me burning down what was to be their warehouse. Joe was gone from Hanged Dog a good deal on business.

"Why, we've got a store here, Gini. Thought everybody knew that!" He had a big cigar in his mouth, and he yelled around it. When he was a kid, Joe Malone had got kicked in the head by a speckled ox and lost part of his hearing. He always shouted like everybody else was half-deaf, too. "But I been down to Tombstone," he went on, "settin' up a new mercantile. Place is booming! Lots of trade! Miners by the hundreds, all in dire need of the Malone brothers' inventory. On my way back home to Hanged Dog tomorrow! Riding along with the troopers, y'know. Apaches on the loose again, can't be too careful. Nice to see a body from home!"

I cocked my head at him. "I guess you must be homesick, all right, Joe. That is about the most you have said to me in maybe five years."

It was the truth, and he colored up some.

"If you'll excuse me, Joe, me and my friend have got to be on our way."

He looked kind of mad by then. Those Malones were used to being kowtowed to, and they didn't like it when a person stood up for themselves. He said "Good day, then" and turned his back, just like that. Those Malones were a rude bunch, as well as stuck-up.

"That wasn't very polite of you, Miss Kincaid," Elma Justice said as we rode down the street. She had got brave enough to leave go of the saddle horn, which gave her one hand each for her reins and parasol. "That man was quite cordial. In addition, you did not introduce me."

"The Malones are only cordial on the outside, Miss Justice. They are too big for their britches, tryin' to be like the Goldwater boys, who have got stores all over the Territory too, but who are genuinely public-spirited persons, and who brought the telegraph into Phoenix out of their own pocket and without being asked. The Malone brothers would not have pitched in more than a nickel for something like that, and would have grouched about it all the way. No, the Malones are trash, and you don't want to know them. And, like I have already told you three times yesterday and once this mornin', my name's Gini."

"I am fully aware of your Christian name, Miss Kincaid," she said, parasol high, eyes straight ahead. "But as we have known each other less than twenty-four hours, I think it prudent to keep things, for the time being, on a formal basis. In a land as new and unpolished as the Arizona Territory, I believe it is up to the women to maintain the civilized aspects of society and set the standard for others."

Well, that shut me up. I could hardly credit that this was the same teensy woman that only yesterday had been crying all over my bucks in the Butterfield Overland Mail.

"Boy howdy," I said under my breath. "Wait till Tuck Brennan gets a load of you."

7

Tombstone

Miss Elma Justice might have been a fussy dresser and a stickler on formalities, but she had pluck. Not many a back-east lady would have traveled such wild country on horseback, especially when she might have made the same trip by Wells Fargo in under a day. But then, she had no cash for the fare, and for my part, I had Jigsaw and Jelly to think of.

Our first day was slow, but we thereafter averaged about twenty-five miles a day. That is not too bad, I think, for two ladies going it alone, especially when one of them is a newcomer to all-day saddle-sitting. I let Miss Justice use my hotel pillow, and we kept mostly to a walk, stopping every hour or so to let her stretch her "limbs."

The weather grew more wintry all the time, but I suppose I did not mind the cold so much. It had at least got rid of the flies and sent the snakes under cover. Malachi had commenced a state of torpor, too, and stayed tucked hard inside his shell, like a tortoise-shaped rock. He would not eat and barely opened his beady old eyes. I still lap-carried him during the afternoons, though, just to get him out of my satchel and into the fresh air.

Miss Justice did her fair part with the cooking and camp-breaking. She also got some better about mounting up, though even at her best you couldn't call her graceful.

Old Jelly didn't seem to care, so long as he got his sweet beforehand. She was even nice to Malachi, and sometimes asked to let him ride on her lap. She turned out to be a real talker, too, once she got started.

She had an opinion on flat everything. She went on about the Germans in Zanzibar, the British in the Sudan, the French in Tunis, and the Congress of Berlin. "Allow me to illuminate," she'd say, and there'd be no stopping her. She talked all over the world: past, present, and future. Of course, Tuck had done his share of that, too, but at least when he did it, a person was interested. I sure missed him.

Anyway, after a while I got so that I just let her voice turn into part of the rhythm of travel, like the whistle and billow of wind, the creak of leather, or the crunch of gravel under the horses' hooves. It made a good music by which to spy out lurking Apache. I saw not a one, though that does not mean there weren't any out there. It was also a good backdrop for thinking, and I had a lot of that to do: about the gold and Tuck and the Danahoes, and about how a person might go about towing a nice stone marker out to Zack's grave site. I admit I thought about Tyrone O'Neill, too, especially about the way he looked when he smiled.

I also did a fair bit of pondering on why Gam had never mentioned her son. It was the second morning before it struck me what Doc Ben had meant by having *Sweet mother to a dear lost child* carved on her gravestone. All along I had thought that "lost child" was me, and I was real let down to realize it wasn't. It also hurt me to think she had told Doc Ben, but not me.

We kept off the roads in order to avoid the ruffians and riffraff that lurk along them. Two ladies traveling unescorted in the Territory cannot be too careful, and I doubted Miss Justice would be of help if the situation went to gunplay or fisticuffs; though if it came to talking some assassin to death, I would have laid money on her.

I have been told recently that any normal person would have just stayed on in Tucson and started a new life there. After all, I had a bit of Zack's money, and no assurance that Tuck or the others would ever meet me in Tombstone like they had said. I also had no assurance, even if they did arrive, that they would give me a share of the gold once we found it. But not one of those things crossed my mind, and that is a fact.

I have also been told that if I had stayed in Tucson I would not be in all this trouble I am in now, and maybe that's true. But to my mind if the Lord has you scheduled for Adventures, He is going to give them to you one way or the other.

Early on the fourth day out, I was scouting for the Tombstone road (thinking we must be near our goal) when we heard a commotion which could not have been produced by any self-respecting Apache or highwayman. We rode toward it, over the crest of a little rise. Right out in the middle of what looked like nowhere was a lone man: a lunatic, by his general appearance.

He drove a rattletrap, short-bed Conestoga wagon. The canvas cover had been removed, so the supports for the top hooped up in the air like so many ribs. They were not bare, though, being strung with rafts of brass cowbells, clusters of jinglers, and strings of those little silvery fairy bells like you hang on a Christmas tree. There were twenty times more clappers on that wagon than I have ever seen in one place before or since, and it made some kind of racket, I can tell you.

Otherwise, his rig was not loaded heavy. The only things

I could see in the bed were a stack of beat-up gunnysacks, tied together with twine, and an old wood plank.

One horse and a pony pulled the wagon. The horse was a sunburnt sorrel, about fourteen and a half hands tall. He didn't look too old, but his back was so terrible swayed you could have laid two sacks of feed in there and still not brought it up to level. The pony hitched beside him was a fat, shaggy, black and white pinto mare, hardly ten hands high. She had a thick, roached mane that stood straight up. Her legs were so stumpy that she had to take two strides for every one of the swayback's, and she had her ears pinned flat. Both she and the swayback had bells tied all over their harness, which was as much cotton rope and baling twine as leather.

I was so busy trying to figure out those dang horses that I didn't take a real close look at the driver till we got within conversing distance.

"Howdy-do, folks," he said as he reined up his team and threw on the brake. He was a scrawny little runt, maybe fifty or fifty-five. He had a floppy, old-fashioned wool hat, patched clothes, and eyes so light cornflower blue that it was a wonder that the sunlight didn't strike him blind. He was smiling, and he looked to have most of his teeth.

"How-do, yourself," I said. "I am Geneva Kincaid, Gini for short, and this is Miss Elma Justice. We are looking for Tombstone."

"It's as reasonable a location to be lookin' for as any, I reckon," he said. "Where did you ladies start from?"

"Tucson," I replied.

"Then I would say you have come pretty close to it. Now, if you had said San Pedro, I would've had to comment that you are sorely off-course. But Tucson, that is another matter. No, you have come pretty close. Congratulations, and good day." He gathered his lines, picked up his ratty buggy whip, and flicked the air just above the swayback's ears. "Git up, Comanche, you rapscallious villain! You too, Gracie!"

Little Gracie didn't like the idea and tried to sit down in her harness, but Comanche took a step forward and dragged her along with him. The whole contraption started in to jangle and clank.

Miss Justice had charge of Malachi, and she almost dropped him when she clapped her hands over her ears. I hollered "Hold up there!" and reined Jigsaw to block him.

He whoaed up his sorry team. Gracie took advantage of the halt to sit down all the way.

"Now you've done it," he said, his smile gone to grimace. "She's only good for one 'git up' in a row." He jumped to the ground, went to the rear of the wagon, and came back toting that long wood plank. "Now I'm gonna have to convince her back on her feet."

Well, I goosed Jigsaw, and he jumped right between that man and little Gracie. "Don't you go hitting that poor tiny thing," I cried.

"And don't you go trying to run a man over!" He looked a little shook, what with Jigsaw bounding so quick to block his path, and now both me and Jigsaw glaring at him. "I do not beat my horses," he added, "even though they are spiteful and quarrelsome creatures and probably deserve it."

"Then what do you aim to do with that board?"

He put his hand on Jigsaw's nose. "What did you say you were called by?"

"Geneva Kincaid. Gini for short. Though I don't see what that has to do with pony-beating."

"Well, Geneva-Kincaid-Gini-for-Short, if you will move this fire-breathin', wild-colored hoppy-toad out of my path, I will demonstrate my purpose."

I gave him the benefit and reined Jigsaw to the side. He strolled up to Gracie, the plank balanced under his arm, and pulled a big wad of cotton out of her ear. "Grace," he said, "you are the most obstreperous excuse for a pony that mortal man ever set eye to. I don't know why I was cursed with your ownership. I ask you, will you take your feet again?" When she only snorted and gave him the evil eye, he poked the cotton back in. Then he dropped the plank, jammed his hands in his pockets, and walked off ahead, whistling "Plant Me Near the Apple Tree When I Go, Dora Dear." He had a robust whistle, and was right on pitch.

Miss Justice put a hand down to steady Malachi, then reined Jelly over next to me and whispered, "I believe he is quite mad."

He had got about twenty yards away from us, and just then he stopped whistling to throw his arms in the air and whoop, "Halloo!" Just as quick, he dropped down on his haunches and began digging in the dirt.

"Miss Justice," I said, "I suspect you have got him pegged."

We watched while he freed up a good-sized rock and staggered back with it. Miss Justice leaned toward me again to whisper, "I am certain he is probably insane and possibly dangerous. Any directions he gives are likely to take us straight to the dead lake of Mexico City."

"Ain't crazy," he piped up. He had put down his rock a few feet away from the little mare and positioned it just so. "Ain't deaf, neither. Got ears like an owl."

That didn't make much sense to me, but I didn't dispute it. "All we want to know is how to get to Tombstone."

He picked up the plank again. "So you said." With that, he put one foot on Gracie's hip. He shoved her off-kilter just enough to slide one end of the board under her rump, so its middle sat on the rock and the other end stuck up in the air to make a little seesaw. Swaybacked Comanche just stood by, looking bored and drowsy, like this must be a real common occurrence.

"Might want to stand away, ladies," he said to us before he pulled the cotton out of Gracie's ear again. "This is your last chance, your midgety she-devil. Will you take your feet?"

Gracie pinned her ears that much harder and jutted out her top lip to bare her yellow choppers.

"So much for you, then," he said, and poked the ear cotton back in. He stepped a few feet away. Then, all of a sudden, he leapt into the air.

He landed, both boots, on the upraised end of the board. Well, he went down and Gracie went up, all of it quick as a cardsharp's blink. Truth was, I think Gracie had it timed pretty good, as it seemed to me she started up just a tad before he landed, and his end of the plank hit the ground fast and hard. But he looked fair satisfied and so did the pony.

"Well then," he remarked as he picked up his lever and tossed it back in the wagon, "I'll be off." He climbed to his seat and eased off the hand brake.

"What about Tombstone?" I said.

He scratched at his chin. "Couldn't say how to get there. I am bad at directions. Suppose you could follow me, though; I'm goin' for supplies. Long as you don't make me stop these quarrelsome critters again for no purpose, and you keep that nervous Indian horse of yours away from my Comanche. He's a bold one, and will fight another horse at the drop of a hat."

I looked at the drowsy swayback again. "No offense meant," I said, "but I don't believe that horse could fight a three-legged sheep and win."

"It's a ruse," replied the man. "Inside, he's all hellfire. Now, if there is nothin' else I need to stay stopped for, I'll be urging my team on their way."

He did, and the bells commenced to clank and tinkle. We started along beside him. Over the clamor, Miss Justice said, "Excuse me, sir, but if you do not know the location of Tombstone well enough to give us directions, how do you propose to find it yourself?"

"Oh, I know how to get there good enough. Just can't say it out. No good with streets, either." He scowled at his team. "Hi there, Comanche, you rogue! We'll have none of that!" I couldn't see that Comanche was doing much more than plod. Gracie trotted along beside him, ears flat, head down.

Miss Justice didn't look much happier. "How much farther is it to the town?" she asked. You could tell she thought it wasn't very genteel, having to raise her voice like that.

" 'Bout as far as from here to there," he hollered right back.

She twisted her parasol. "That's hardly a decent answer, sir, when you have been asked a civilized question. And by the way, you are in possession of our names but you have not favored us with yours. I fear your manners are sadly lacking."

He looked over at me and poked his thumb toward Miss Justice. "From back east, is she?"

I nodded.

He turned to Miss Justice. "If it's any of your business, missy," he shouted, "my name is Horatio Montgomery Beldon, but folks call me Jingles. And it is my considered opinion that any person who goes ridin' through Indian country carryin' a pink umbrella and wearin' a pink gauzy hat with little white jiggers on it, and totes a tortoise in her lap to boot . . . Well, a person like that has got no call to go round sayin' other folks are unsettled in the brain."

"The tortoise is Miss Kincaid's, not mine," she said, kind

of huffy. "And it's peach. Fresh Georgia Peach is the exact name of the color. It certainly is not pink."

"Peach, pink, orange, it's all the same. T'ain't none of 'em a good, honest Kansas City red. Where you ladies and your tortoise plan to bide in Tombstone?"

"In a clean hotel or boardinghouse, if there is such a thing to be found," I shouted. I thought I'd best jump in before Miss Justice gave him a lecture on the history of cloth-dying. "We figure to stay a while and cannot afford high rates."

"Then you'd better see Nellie Cashman," he replied over the racket. "She has a nice place at the corner of Fifth and Tough Nut Streets. It's clean and she'll treat you right. They call her the Angel of Tombstone on account of she's so good to the miners, and a finer woman never drew breath nor baked a biscuit." He took off his hat for that last part. He had short sandy hair with a lot of gray through it, and a funny bald spot—scarred over and as big as a baby's fist—right on the top of his head.

"We will take your advice, Mr. Beldon," I said.

"Call me Jingles," he hollered.

"And you call me Gini."

He nodded, then cocked an eye to Miss Elma Justice. She was still mad about him calling her outfit the wrong color, and she was staring straight ahead with her mouth all set into a line.

"I think you best call her Miss Justice," I added. "She does not believe in familiarities."

He put his hat back on. "Then she is not going to like Tombstone."

I did not like it much, either, when we first saw it. The outskirts of town were jammed with lean-tos and shacks and tents made of canvas or hides, and swarmed with tough-looking cowboys, scruffy dogs, miners, Mex, and Chinese. What few decent buildings existed were so straight and shiny that they looked to have landed there by accident. One of the biggest and newest had a bold sign that read *Malone Bros. Mercantile*. I ducked down in the saddle until we got well past it, just in case.

However, the farther we went down Allen, which is the main street, the more civilized things got. The carpenters and painters had been working overtime to turn it into a real town, and they even had wood sidewalks with overhangs. Some of the buildings were so grand that it was hard to believe that just a couple years ago there hadn't been a Tombstone, A.T., at all, just a few shacks and wickiups on a scrubby meadow called Goose Flats.

On one side of Allen there were cafés and specialty stores, a telegrapher, and several mining company offices, one of which was marked *Wilbeck & LaFouche, Tombstone Division*. I guess Mace and Pete's granddaddy had his fingers in the Tombstone silver pie, too.

But the other side of the street was another story entire, being a solid row of saloons, casinos, and brothels. Even though it was the middle of the week and not even dark, loud piano music and bawdy laughing came from the saloons we passed. Each time we rode by a bar or sporting house (which was pretty much nonstop), Miss Justice averted her eyes. It seemed to me that this did not bode well, as it looked like practically three-fourths of the whole town was low establishments. I figured if Tombstone kept on building up like this, Miss Justice would soon run out of places she could look and we would have to get her a blindfold and just lead her around.

Anyhow, Jingles Beldon and his noisy team and wagon led us right into the thick of it. About everybody we passed looked up on account of the racket, but several folks waved and smiled at him, and some whore in her underwear leaned out of a second-story window and threw him a kiss. When we turned the corner at Fifth and Allen, a round-faced, mustachioed man hailed us from the sidewalk.

"Afternoon, Beldon!" he shouted. "How's the blasting?" He acted friendly, but he did not look to me like a man with much humor in him.

Jingles tipped his floppy hat and hollered, "Tolerable, Virgil, tolerable. My mare only set on me once comin' in, but I am still beset by bats."

The man, who wore a black hat and frock coat, did not seem much interested in bats or ponies. "Still working on your shack?" he called.

Jingles nodded. "I am grievous short on bottles. It's what I come to town for. That and lard. Short on lard, too."

"After you get stopped at Nellie's," the man yelled back, "you best park that hellacious rig at the livery and leave it there till you go. Otherwise I'll have to cite you for disturbing the peace."

Jingles nodded and waved him good-bye.

"How does he know where you're headed?" I asked. "What business is it of his where you put your wagon?"

"I always stay at Miss Nellie's," Jingles replied over the din. "And that fella that looks like a church deacon is Deputy U.S. Marshal Virgil Earp."

I knew the name Earp, and asked, "Would he have a brother up in Dodge City by the name of Wyatt?"

"Never been to Dodge City," Jingles replied, "although I once was in Wichita and been twice in my life to St. Louis, so don't go thinking I'm not a man of the world. Virgil does not care one whit that a man has giant bats in his shaft, he's that single-minded. It seems to me his time would be better spent if he'd quit bothering folks about their bells and concentrate on tracking rustlers and murderous highbinders.

I've seen the Staked Plains of Texas, too. Now there is some rough territory."

I was about to ask about the bats when we came to another cross street and Jingles reined up his team in front of the Russ House Hotel. It is no lie when I say that even after we had dismounted, tied our horses, and walked in the front door, I could still hear those dang bells of his clanking inside my head. I guessed that maybe Deputy Virgil Earp had a point, after all.

A little bit of a lady, just a smidge taller than Miss Justice, came out to meet us. She was young and pretty, with dark hair and big dark eyes, and she had a cameo brooch at the collar of her dress.

"Why, Mr. Beldon!" she said. "I was just saying the other day that we hadn't seen you for a long spell. We have a goodly number of bottles saved for you out by the back stoop."

He yanked off his hat and hugged it to his chest. "Yes ma'am, Miss Nellie," he said, all sheepish.

"Are you having good luck?"

"Fair to middlin', ma'am, although my bats are still a plague. Have you got a roost for me?"

She smiled at him real kindly. It was funny. She could have been his daughter, what with the age difference between them, but he acted like she was his mother. She fell right in with it, too. "We always have a place for you at the Russ House," she replied. "And the special tonight is your favorite, the pounded-steak dinner." She looked over at me and Miss Justice and smiled sweet. "Are you ladies friends of Mr. Beldon?"

"He was good enough to show us into town, ma'am," I replied. "I'm Geneva Kincaid, Gini for short, and my friend here is Miss Elma Justice. We'd like a room, too, if it's not too dear."

She quoted a fair price with meals included. I paid her a week in advance, and she showed me and Miss Justice to a small, tidy corner room that looked out on Tough Nut Street and the vacant lot next door. Gingham curtains hung in the windows and a vase with some sage sat on the dresser. There were no bugs or other vermin. After, I went to the livery with Jingles and got my horses grained and settled, instructing that they not be turned out to mill with strange horses. Jingles rented a box for his team, too, and after he pulled the cotton out of their ears and tucked it in his pocket, he turned them in together. Right away, Gracie got busy with her feed bucket, but Comanche was not in there two minutes before he locked his knees and commenced to snore.

"Confidentially," Jingles said to the stableman, "I'd not rent out this stall next to them if I was you. My Comanche may look peaceful now, but he is ever on the alert and will savage any horse he can reach. I tell you this because I won't be held liable for damages."

The stableman said he would keep it in mind.

The Russ House began dishing up supper about a half hour after we got back. The food was better than fine, and the dining room was packed with rough customers. For the way they acted, though, you would have thought they were at Sunday Meeting, and all on account of their having so much respect for Miss Nellie Cashman. There was not one head in that place with a hat on it.

The next day we set out to look for work. Miss Justice went in search of the City Hall, and I walked over to Allen Street to have another gander at the town and pick up a copy of the *Epitaph*. There were no jobs of real interest in the paper, but as I wandered down the sidewalk, I saw a little sign in the front window of the Striped Garter Saloon. It said:

SINGER WANTED

BETTER BE GOOD

I walked in the door.

The place was sure not jammed, but there was more crowd than you would expect for nine-thirty of a Thursday morning. It was a good-sized bar, about the same as the Thirsty Buzzard back home, but a whole lot tonier. Gilt lamps hung on chains from the ceiling, and the walls sported gas jets between paintings of naked ladies and photographs of mustachioed men. I took the latter to be local celebrities. Some of the pictures had slug holes in them. There were maybe twenty tables altogether, each set with six or eight chairs. A handsome brass-railed service bar, near thirty feet long, ran down one side of the place; a staircase hugged the other. Along the back wall was a little stage, draped with gold-tasseled, green-velvet curtains. Next to red, green is my favorite color, especially that dark, piney green. I thought it was real beautiful.

Over by the stage, a poker game was in progress: an all-nighter, by the looks of the players. One woman, a fancy dresser, was sitting in, and when she saw me she got up and walked over.

"You bin lost, *Liebchen*?" she said. She was tall, blonde, and on the healthy side, and she wore the kind of half-smile that made you think she had secrets. It put me a little in mind of Tuck. One of her eyes was light agate brown. I cannot say for the other one, as she wore a turquoise-colored eye patch over it to match her dress. The patch was stitched with silver threads in the pattern of a spider's web, and had tiny rhinestones added for dewdrops. I had a hard time of it not to stare.

"No, ma'am," I said, "I am not lost. You advertised for a

singer, and I'm a good one, no brag. But singing's where I draw the line, so if the job includes other activities, I am not interested."

She tapped a finger on her lips. They were rouged bright coral. "Maybe it be held to dat," she said, "though for dis 'stablishment dat be a first." She looked me up and down. "Dis is costume?"

"I have a dress," I replied, "but it's not fancy. I'll buy a better one out of my wages if the pay is decent."

"I tink ve best to hear you sing before in vardrobe ve invest." She didn't look to be taking me very serious, but she called over her shoulder, "Hector, put down cards und to piano sit. Dis *mädchen* vants for us to sing."

A chubby, bald-headed fella shoved away from the poker game, but before he got all the way up, one of the other players, a thin blond man with a mean scowl, snarled, "Chrissake, Inga, it's the middle of a goddamn hand!"

Hector started to sit down again, but she said, "Da game vaits, Doc."

The blond man swore and slapped his cards facedown on the table. The other players put their cards down, too, and Hector got up again, though he threw in a lot of chair-scraping for effect. He sauntered over to the upright, and I went to stand beside him.

"Got music?" he asked.

"No, but I can sing most anything you can play."

"Pick a short one," he whispered. "You don't wanta get Doc mad."

"Da longer da better, *Liebchen*," Inga said with that funny little smile. She was watching Doc, who poured himself a shot of Who-Hit-John and tossed it straight back. He looked real irritated.

"Ballad or lively?" I asked.

She still gazed toward the poker game. "Somet'ing slow, mit notes drawn out. Test voice better dat vay."

"All right," I replied. "Mr. Hector, do you know 'The Cavalry Widow's Lament'?"

Well, I sang it out just as sweet and sorrowful as I could, and by the time Hector had played the last mournful chord, the counterman was rubbing his eyes with a bar towel and even that surly Doc was blowing his honker. "The Cavalry Widow's Lament" is the best tune I know for getting people all emotional, though "Don't Let Mama See Me Hang" is a good one for bringing up tears, too.

Inga lifted her eye patch just enough to daub the edge of her hankie underneath. "I give you borrow of dress," she sniffed.

She quoted me a wage near double the most I would have asked, and took me back to her office, where she loaned me two glittery dresses out of a wardrobe trunk. They almost fit, and I told her I could alter them myself. After she gave me ten dollars cash money as a goodwill advance and we traded names, I confided that I didn't want my true name on the sign. I was thinking about that Malone Bros. Mercantile. It was bad enough to be so close to those dang Malones—who were still mad for all I knew—without advertising "Geneva Kincaid" in ten-inch poster letters.

She must have been used to such things, for she didn't question me on it. Instead, she said, "You could use maiden name of your mama."

"It was LeFleur," I said, "but I don't think I'd better use that, either."

She pursed up her lips for a few seconds, then said, "LeFleur. Das ist French flowers, but you be looking more Irish, like da Kincaid, und you got such pretty red hair . . . Ach! I got it! How 'bout Irish Gini Rose? You like?"

I said it was as good as any, and she wrote it on the back of a liquor bill so she wouldn't forget. Then she shook my hand, told me to be back by eight-thirty, and showed me out the side door.

And that was how I came to work for Spider Eye Inga von Kopf, take the name Irish Gini Rose, and be a headline singer at the Striped Garter Saloon.

I suppose it goes without saying that Miss Elma Justice was not one bit pleased about my employment, but I was not so happy about hers, either. She said she had been told there was no need for a schoolteacher, thank you, and had ended by taking employment as a day clerk at the Malone Bros. Mercantile. We were each so mad about the other's job that we didn't speak during dinner or even afterwards, and when I came back from my first night at the Striped Garter, Miss Justice kicked me all night, though she later said it was just bad dreams.

Miss Justice's new job did not turn out to be much threat to me, after all. First off, the printers spelled my name wrong on the advertising posters, so they came out *Irish Jenny Rose*. That was even better, to my mind, for Jenny is a more common name and would not attract the Malones' curiosity. Even if it did, I doubted any of them would have known me, anyhow, what with all the face paint Inga had me wear and the fancy hairdo and spangled dresses. Of course, it helped that not one of the Malone boys seemed to be in town right then. The store was run by a tall, dark-haired, fine-looking man named Will Fowler. By the time Miss Justice had worked there a week, I could tell she was sweet on him.

"He is an excellent commercial manager," she told me over dinner one night, "and keeps a tidy ledger. But he is better than that. He has studied the law, and plans to return to the East to complete his degree, once he has saved the funds. It is my firm belief that he will make a fine and upstanding attorney."

"I don't know how he will be at readin' the law, Miss Justice," I replied, "but he's sure got the blue eyes to fox any jury."

We still shared quarters at the Russ House, but Malachi was not rooming with us. To let him have his winter sleep in some sort of natural peace, I put him in a wood crate with a lid to keep out dogs, and set the whole business under the hotel porch. Miss Cashman said he would not be bothered there, and the warmth from the building would keep him from freezing.

As for me, I guess the Striped Garter was all right, and I found out quick that I was not the only one with a made-up name. It seemed like all the ladies up and down the street, be they singers, dancers, whores, or all three, had taken on (or been stuck with) monikers to go with their trade. Right there at the Striped Garter we had Gopher Toe Peg, Red-Deuce Marie, Bonnie Scotland, the Viking, and Two Apples Annie. They all worked upstairs, though right before my first and last shows Bonnie Scotland and Two Apples Annie did a sort of squealy, high-kicking dance that was brand-new from Paris, France, and called the Can-Can. I don't think they were very good at it, since Bonnie sometimes fell down and they were as apt to kick each other as the air, but the boys liked it.

I had my days free. Most afternoons I'd take Jigsaw or Jelly out for some exercise. I'd canter out of town thinking to do some sight-seeing over the countryside, but most times I'd find myself heading north, paralleling the road to Tucson. I got in the habit of visiting the same little hill.

Sometimes I'd sit there for a whole hour, scanning the horizon, watching for Tuck and the Danahoes and Tyrone. I always came back alone, though.

Besides seeing to the horses, I spent my days reading and keeping my ears open for news of Tuck and puzzling over that *Spirit Kettle* business. I went on stage three times a night—at nine, ten-thirty and midnight, with a fourth show at one-thirty on Fridays. The crowds seemed to like me; at least the place quieted down and gunplay was held to a minimum while I did my numbers, and most times the boys tossed coins on the stage. They did this because I gave them a good entertainment, and also because they wanted me to bend over so they could look up my dress. My Gam did not raise me to be a fool, though, and I always waited till the curtain pulled closed to gather my spoils.

I usually made four or five dollars cash on a weeknight, seventeen or twenty of a Friday or Saturday, and I had to split it with the "house." Spider Eye Inga told me this outdid any singer she'd ever had, and I felt kind of proud of myself. The most I ever made in tossed coins in one night was forty-three dollars and four cents, of which I got half.

I do not know who pitched the four cents, but if that is all a person is going to throw, he should just keep his money.

The first night I sang, a drunk cowboy followed me to the dressing room and made advances toward me. I tried to be polite, but he would not take no for an answer, and in the end I was forced to break a cane-back chair over his head. The story got around town, and after that I had little trouble.

Jingles Beldon left Miss Nellie's after about a week, and when he went, all those gunnysacks from the back of his rig were filled up with empty bottles—whiskey, beer, and soda pop—that he had collected around town. It made near half a load and was about all Gracie and Comanche could pull, and made me certain he must be running a still out at his claim. He did not get out of town, however, before his Comanche horse chewed up a half-blooded Plantation Walker that was stalled next to him. The Walker was owned by a preacher, to whom Jingles paid seven dollars and four bits in doctoring bills.

The mean blond cardplayer who'd been so rude the day I got hired turned out to be none other than the famous Dodge City and New Mexico gambler, Doc Holliday. He frequented most of the gaming halls on Allen and Fremont Streets, and spent a good bit of time at the Striped Garter. He was a surly customer when sober and meaner when he was drunk, which was most of the time. I suppose some of it could be excused on account of he had the consumption and had to cough up blood. A thing like that cannot leave a man in a cheery mood. Anyway, after that first day he was always polite while I "trod the boards," and once he pulled a pocket gun on a man that tried to sing along with me during "O Martyred Sons of Georgia." Doc was from the South, and that one always got him stirred up.

He had a friend who sometimes played cards at the Striped Garter, too, and that friend was one Wyatt Earp, brother to Deputy U.S. Marshal Virgil Earp. Wyatt was famous, too. Both he and Doc had made their reputations up in Dodge City, Kansas, where they ran with a couple other gamblers named Bat Masterson and Luke Short. Having read stories about them, I was impressed, even though they were third-rate celebrities compared to Tuck Brennan. Wyatt had been a sometimes peace officer in Kansas and he was one here, too, though his title of deputy was only from the county and he was mostly a tax collector. Like his brother, Virgil, he took his job serious and had aspirations. This was made clear one night not more than two weeks after I started at the Striped Garter.

After my first show, I had gone out to the alley to get away from the cigar smoke and noise—and also to practice walking in my high-heeled shoes, which were still giving me trouble—when I heard enough gunplay to pass for the Fourth of July. Now, shots were not all that uncommon in Tombstone, though the Earps had cracked down on raucous gunplay and fewer people were getting winged by accident. Generally, you paid the shots no mind unless they were fired so close you had to duck, but this night was another matter entirely. Most everybody had heard that Curly Bill Brocius was in town, and that U.S. Marshal Fred White was out to arrest him. In a town of two thousand and some souls, none of which can keep his lips from flapping, it is hard to have a secret.

Curly Bill was a real bad character, and he ran with a trashy outfit that was made up of the Clanton and McLaury boys, plus a few others like Frank Stillwell, John Ringgold (more often called Johnny Ringo), and the Aztec Kid. They were dangerous men, being cattle rustlers, stagecoach robbers, and killers. They headquartered both on Babocamari Creek and the mosquito sinks of Soldier Holes, and ran stolen Mex cattle and horses out of the Sulphur Springs Valley. It was said they would plug a man for two dollars; less, if they were liquored up.

When I heard the shots, I ran to the street to see what the trouble was. Sure enough, there was Curly Bill and his bunch. Marshal White was just crumpling to the ground, gut-shot. Curly Bill stood beside him, gun in hand. The blast had been fired at such close range that it had set Marshal White's clothes on fire. This happened right across the road from me, so I could see real good when, a half-second later, Wyatt Earp leaned out of the shadows and came down hard with his pistol barrel to knock Curly Bill cold.

Wyatt grabbed hold of Bill with one hand and fired a few rounds over the heads of the gang before he dragged his prisoner off. Those Clantons and McLaurys were so shocked to see their buddy buffaloed that they just stood there blinking. Now, I have said they were dangerous, but I will add here that they were also cocky and not very bright, for none of them had the smarts to leave town afterwards. I saw Phin Clanton and the Aztec Kid in the crowd when I did my next show. They were at the bar, bragging it up like usual.

The tips were good that night. I had picked up my coins off the stage and started down the darkened back hall toward the dressing room when somebody took hold of my arm. It gave me a fright, and I swung a fist.

It landed against his chest, but I believe it did me more harm than him, for I punched his lawman's badge square on and bruised my knuckle.

"I've heard about you, Irish Jenny Rose," he said. "It's a good thing there are no cane-back chairs in this hall, or I might find myself buffaloed as sure as I have buffaloed half of Curly Bill's boys tonight, and will surely buffalo the rest."

Well, right then I knew him to be Wyatt Earp. "I'm sorry," I said, "but you should not grab people in the dark without expectin' a fight."

He was some handsomer than his brother, Virgil, but he was just as serious. "Is Doc Holliday out front?" he asked.

"He is."

"Go out and get him for me."

"I can't do that," I said. "He's playin' stud with Buckskin Frank Leslie and the Rio brothers, and he's winnin'. He'll most likely shoot any fool who disturbs him."

Wyatt scratched at the back of his head. "I don't believe Doc would shoot you, but he will make a commotion. I cannot have a commotion right now. I don't suppose you know Phin Clanton when you see him?"

"I do," I said. "He's out front with the Aztec Kid. They're both gettin' skunked. And I'd appreciate it if you'd leave go of my arm."

He did, and said, "Then, Irish Jenny, I hereby deputize you to go out there and advise Phin Clanton that someone wants to see him. Tell him it is a lady. He'll come for that."

"How can you deputize me? You're only a deputy yourself."

"All right, then," he said, "I deputize you in the name of my brother, Virgil. The heinous murder of Marshal White earlier this evening puts Virgil in charge of Tombstone."

"I can't see how that gives you any authority. And where is your brother, anyhow? I didn't see him racin' to help Fred White."

"You are wasting time. Just go out there and do as I say. Walk him right past this storeroom."

Well, I figured I ought to do my civic duty. Phin was well in his cups when I gave him the message, and he staggered right along after me. I led him down the hall, and about three steps past the storeroom I heard a creak, a thud, and then a thump. I spun round to find Phin Clanton heaped on the floor. Deputy Earp stood beside the storeroom door, pistol in hand.

"You have knocked him senseless!" I said. "I saw you do the same to Curly Bill Brocius."

"And four others since then," he replied, a little smug. "They presently reside in jail with their friend Bill. Now go get the Kid." He holstered his gun and began to haul Phin out of the way.

The Aztec Kid was dispatched just as tidy as his friend, and then I was sent to fetch Doc Holliday. He put up a ruckus, all right; but once he stopped shouting long enough to let me whisper the reason, he came along quick enough. He and Wyatt dragged Phin and the Kid out the back door and off to jail, but not before Wyatt tipped his hat to me. "I owe you one, Irish Jenny Rose," he said.

I told him I would hold him to it.

8

'Tis the Season

About every other Wednesday, the Malone Bros. Mercantile got a freight load of inventory from Tucson. Sometimes there were dime novels in the shipment, and Miss Justice would bring me the new titles. I had plenty of time to read and, as I was making good money, I could afford the luxury. When I'd finish with a book, I'd give it to Miss Nellie, and she started a little lending library for the other boarders. They were mostly hard-rock miners, but a good many already knew their ABC's (or were learning them, of an evening, from Miss Justice), and near all were hungry for a good yarn. You would be surprised at the way people will wait for two or three weeks to read a book for free that they could have read right away—and without smeared grease or preserves on the pages—for five or ten cents.

Anyhow, about a week before Thanksgiving, Miss Justice came home with three whole books for me. There was a new *Panhandle Slim* and a couple half-dimers: *Iron Hand O'Rourke; Blood Will Tell, or Courage on the High Plains,* and *Buffalo Bill and the Dakota Gambler.* I was always glad for new stories, as they helped to take my mind off Tuck and the boys. That and the gold, just sitting out there, waiting for us.

I settled on the Buffalo Bill, and took it with me to the Striped Garter. I didn't get started reading till after the first show, but when I came to page 11, boy howdy, did I get a start, for the "Dakota Gambler" of the title was none other than Tyrone O'Neill!

Well, you can bet it was near all I could do to keep from carrying that book onstage with me for the second show, and by the time the third set came round, I was most of the way through chapter 5. The story told all about Buffalo Bill and how he struck up a friendship with Ty (the "gallant Gaelic gamesman," the author called him) and how the two of them had all these adventures rescuing a girl named Wild Horse Alyssa and running some ruffians out of the Black Hills. Of course, after hearing all of Zack's complaints about his Ghost Ruggles book, I realized that this story probably wasn't wholly factual, either. But it was real exciting all the same, and after my last show, I took it along when I went out front.

Now, I have said that I was just a singer there, period, and did not go upstairs with men. That is the Lord's Truth, no matter what you may have heard or read in the recent scribblings about me. But the Spider Eye still appreciated it if I "socialized" after my shows, even if only for a half hour or so and just to talk. I did not mind so much. The fellas who had been in Tombstone a spell had heard about that business with the cane-back chair, and were real polite. Of course, every once in a while a new one would come in and try to get familiar, but if one of the boys didn't set him wise first, a good kick or punch from me would settle his hash.

I usually stood at the bar and drank tea or sarsaparilla and jawed with the fellas about their claims or their mothers or their girls back home, but that night I was too full of Tyrone O'Neill to do much talking. We had a big crowd for midweek. About all the chairs were filled with customers, but I could see Doc Holliday sitting all by himself, dealing out face-up poker hands. When he sat alone like that, folks tended to leave him be; but I figured I would not be much bother to him if all I did was read.

"Doc," I said, once I'd elbowed my way over there, "it looks like you're in no mood for company, but—"

"You're right about that, Irish. Go away." He started in to cough. He was having a bad night. Blood spotted his handkerchief, and a half-gone bottle of whiskey sat on the table in front of him.

"I won't bother you, Doc," I said. "Inga likes for me to be out front a while, but I am at a real excitin' part of this book and want to keep going. Nobody'll come near me if I'm with you."

He stared at me for a minute, and then he said, "That's the hell of it, Irish." He reached over and yanked out a chair. "Well, sit down."

He went back to his bottle and cards and I went back to my pages. But he must have been awful bored, because after about five minutes he said, "What's that you're readin'?"

I held up the cover.

"I can see that," he said, kind of nasty. "I mean, what's it about? Man doesn't like to see a woman that fixed on anything, 'less it's him."

I must have looked at him funny, because he added, "Don't take it personal. You're too goddamn skinny for me. Besides, I think I have a wife somewhere." Then he poured himself a shot and tossed it back. He smacked the glass down on the table. "Well? I asked you a question."

He was in a black mood, and you did not mess with Doc at a time like that. I said, "It's about Buffalo Bill Cody and a famous, handsome gambler named Tyrone O'Neill and how they—"

"Ty O'Neill's got himself in a book?" he said, and barked out a laugh. I had never once seen Doc smile: not when he was winning, not even when he laughed. And when he was drunk, that laugh was plain evil. It always made you think that the next thing he might do would be to pull a knife.

"You know him?" I asked. I still felt pretty safe, for even though he was a famous killer, he had never murdered a female to my knowledge.

"Know him?" he snarled. "That slippery, back-stabbin' Black Irish bastard owes me seven hundred dollars!"

Well, I couldn't let that pass. "I don't know about any seven hundred dollars," I said, "but I'll have you know that I am personally acquainted with Tyrone O'Neill, and he is not any of those things. He is a fine man with a good way about him. He is true to his friends and knows how to treat a lady with respect."

Doc snorted like he was real disgusted, and that got him to coughing. When he was finished, he said, "I don't know where you met Tyrone, but I tell you true, Irish—he's all sizzle and no steak. He'd sell his mother for dice money and never miss her till he needed more cash."

I stood right up on that last one. "Go ahead and shoot me for it, Doc," I said, "but I won't have you castin' aspersions on his character. Tyrone O'Neill is a gentleman, which is more than I can say for the likes of a drunkard like you."

He reared back in his chair and glared at me down his long nose, and for a couple of seconds there, his face got real dark. I had talked out pretty brave, and pretty foolish, too, considering; but it was too late to do more than stand my ground and hope for the best.

Finally he slouched down in his chair again and poured out another shot. "Whatever you say, Irish," he muttered, and swallowed his whiskey.

He started in coughing again. I could still hear him over the crowd noise when I was halfway across the room.

• • •

Thanksgiving came and went, and still no sign of Tuck or the others. I had learned to walk in my high heels real good by then, and could strut all over the Striped Garter's stage without one stumble. I could swish my skirts with the best of them, too, and sometimes gave the boys a quick look at my knees if I was singing a saucy number. I never hiked it higher, though, as I kept in mind that I was a lady. For that same reason, I always scrubbed my face and changed back into my bucks before I left the saloon. If Gam had ever seen me on the street in glitter and paint, she would have skinned me for sure.

The newspaper made frequent mention of Apache raids to the west of us. Though the citizenry of Tombstone had no cause for alarm, the folks over by Gold Flush and parts south were having a nervous time of it. A couple of times the paper said that a band led by the "infamous Manuelito" was involved, along with some other groups, and once they even mentioned Sees Silver. They didn't call him that, of course. They referred to him as Asesino Pequeño, which he had told me was the name the Mexicans called him by. The *Epitaph* proclaimed him a stealthy and dangerous killer, and said he had come by his moniker by perpetrating the murders of six men, two of them white, before he reached the age of ten. Boy howdy, that sure sent a prickle up my back! It was the first and only time I was glad Gam was gone. If she had not been dead already, such vile news of her only son would surely have killed her.

Due to crooked politics, Deputy Wyatt Earp had got put out of his job after the November elections. I heard that there were quite a number of fellas that got paid to vote against him, some as many as six or eight times. As he still owned part of the Oriental Saloon, he was not at loose ends; but he got to spending more time down at the Oriental, so we didn't see much of him at Inga's place anymore.

Tombstone politics were a shabby thing. Even after all the hubbub over Marshal White's murder, the pettifoggers ruled the killing accidental, which put Curly Bill's boys back on the street and up to more mischief. Since I'd helped Wyatt Earp corral two of them, I was some nervous about this. Phin Clanton had me the most concerned, as he had brothers and they were just as crazy as he was. But I guess Phin didn't think I was worth the bother. The Aztec Kid was another story.

About a week after he got out, he came in the Striped Garter with Johnny Ringo. They had been drinking heavy and were swaggering around and playing the big shots like usual. While I sang on stage, Ringo made some rude noises he thought were funny, and the Kid hollered out, "Why cain't this dump get a singer with some decent tits on her?"

Now, if Doc had been there, he would have put a stop to the catcalls with bullet or blade; not just because I was singing, but because he didn't like his poker disturbed. But Doc wasn't around that night, and the rest of the regulars were too scared of the Kid and Ringo to say boo.

I ignored them and just kept on singing. I saw Inga send over Red-Deuce Marie and Bonnie Scotland to distract them. Bonnie had some luck. She was on Ringo like taffy on an apple, and they disappeared up the stairs before I got past the eighth bar of "Go Whitewash Grandma's Picket Fence Before She Leaves for Heaven."

Now, the Aztec Kid was half Yaqui Indian and half Italian. Both of these handsome races have countless noble qualities (which persons of either ancestry will tell you at the drop of a hat), but the Kid had not inherited a one of them. He was ugly and mean and stupid, and half-crazy even when he wasn't liquored up; and it was said he once made his money as a scalp hunter. They said he wasn't too fussy who he took the scalps off, either.

Anyhow, all little Red-Deuce got for her trouble was a curse and a rough shove. She landed against the hard edge of a table, grabbed her arm, and started to cry. The Kid didn't even look to see where she had lit. He was too busy calling vulgar things at me, like, "Why doncha go someplace and learn how to sing!" and "If I was an ugly bitch like you, I'd never leave my room for fear of gettin' shot for an egg-sucker!" Then he laughed. He had a kind of giddy, off-kilter laugh, all the stranger for coming from such a big, dark man.

I guess I could have stood his lame comments and kept up the song, which was what the Spider Eye was motioning me to do, but when the Kid sent Red-Deuce sailing and not one coward went to defend her, I just plain quit. Hector, the piano man, went on for a couple bars without me, then he stopped, too. Boy howdy, did that place get quiet.

Then the Kid said, real loud, "What's a'matter? You forget the words, Miss Irish Jenny Stinkweed?"

"No," I said, "but you have forgot your manners. I think you had best take your leave and get on home to Soldier Holes, for if you don't stop shoving defenseless women and shouting unpoetic insults when a lady is trying to sing, I'll have to take measures."

You'd think that would've shamed some of the regulars into action, but it did not. It only got the Kid to laughing again. I tell you, that titter of his sent ice right through your bones.

"Measures!" he snorted, once he got hold of himself. "That's a good 'un! What you gonna do, have your yeller-belly pal Wyatt the Burp sneak up on me in the dark?"

"There is no sneak in this, Kid. You are makin' me mad, and that is not a smart thing to do." I looked down to Dennis

Clarkson, he being near me at the foot of the stage. "Dennis," I said, "give me the loan of your pistol."

I was lucky it was Dennis. For one reason, he carried an old Colt .44 Army pistol, the kind that shoots with black powder and ball and is a scary weapon to face. For the other reason, Dennis was the fella I'd cracked over the head with a cane-back chair when I first started at the Striped Garter, so he was more scared of me than he was of the Aztec Kid. He handed his pistol right over, no questions.

That dang .44 felt like it weighed fifty pounds, but I aimed it out at the Aztec Kid with both hands. "You had better say you're sorry, then say good-bye," I said, "or, so help me Hannah, I will shoot."

Well, you have never seen a floor clear faster. Fellas scattered like flies off a porch screen. Bodies jumped the bar, ducked under tables. Hector dove behind the piano and dragged the stool in after him.

That dang Kid just started in laughing again. "You stupid skinny-assed lawman's bitch," he tittered. "I ain't got no 'punctions 'bout shootin' vermin, male nor female."

I had figured it would take a pure fool to draw on somebody who already had him in their sights, and that was the only reason I had aimed that Colt in the first place. But "Fool" must have been the Kid's middle name. He went for his gun.

I didn't think twice. I pulled the trigger and shot him square in the foot. The kick knocked me off my high heels, and I sat down hard.

His gun, which had barely cleared leather, went flying, ricocheted off the wall, dropped behind the spinet, and knocked Hector cold. I guessed that would teach him to hide behind pianos when there's work to be done.

The Kid was whooping and screeching something terrible, and using cusswords I had never heard, part in Italian and part in Yaqui. The rest of the boys stayed froze under the furniture till he hopped and hollered his way out the door. I got back to my feet, tossed Dennis Clarkson his gun, and said, "One'a you boys throw some water on my piano player."

Spider Eye Inga announced a round on the house, Hector was resuscitated and went back to his keyboard, and I finished my song. I got an extra-long round of applause with a good measure of whistles and hat-waving thrown in, and picked up over twelve dollars in tossed coins. I guess cowardice makes men generous.

Wyatt and Virgil Earp came round later that night. "I hear you're the one who shot the Aztec Kid in the foot," Virgil said. He did not look real mad.

"Yes, I am," I replied, "though his foot wasn't the part I was aimin' for."

I guess he didn't care to know my real target, because all he said was, "Those old forty-fours can be a trick to aim."

Wyatt took a swallow of his beer before he spoke up. "You worked quite a bit of damage, Miss Irish Jenny Rose. Doc Dutton says the Kid came within a hair of losing his foot. He'll be bedridden for a good month or two, on crutches for some time after that, and will always have a limp."

I had a draw on my sarsaparilla. "Then I guess that'll make one less rustler for you Earps to chase."

About a week later, the Aztec Kid got somebody to shove his sickbed to the window of his second-story room at the Lucky Cuss Hotel, from which he proceeded to take a couple shots at me as I walked to work. He missed me wide, though he shot out the display window at Myrna Maguire's House of Fortune *(Palms Deciphered, Mysteries of the Stars Revealed, Gentlemen Welcome)* and had to pay her damages.

His pals came and hauled him off to Soldier Holes the

next day, and as they loaded him in the buckboard he told everybody who would listen as how he planned to get his vengeance on me. I did not pay those threats much mind, as I hoped to be long gone from Tombstone by the time he got mended good enough to take any action.

Pretty soon it got to be Christmas. I had been full of thoughts of the gold map and Harlan Wilbeck and Burl LaFouche and Tuck and the Danahoes and especially Tyrone, but as we neared the holidays I could hardly keep anything in my mind except Gam, and how it was my first Christmas without her dear presence. Back home in Hanged Dog, Fats McFadden always freighted in a wagonload of fresh-cut pines from the mountains, and Doc Ben Winslow would get us one to set up by the front window. Pearl Scrimm would come over, too, and we'd string popcorn and cranberries for the tree. We'd light candles and sing carols and have eggnog or hot cider and open our presents, and Gam would always look out the window and say, "I do miss the snow."

Well, that Christmas Eve, Tombstone had enough snow to make up for any and all that Gam had ever missed. You may think it odd that a place like Goose Flats in the Arizona Territory can have snow, but it does. It is scrub desert, all right; but it's up a ways in altitude, and when it gets cold it does not joke around. The snow hadn't piled up deep, but there was still enough to cake your shoes and dust your hair good if you walked more than a block in it.

We were busy at the Striped Garter, though some of our regulars were missing. The Earps had families, and were home with them. Doc Holliday had not been in for two days. The Spider Eye said he was probably off somewhere with Big Nose Kate Elder. Big Nose Kate was the woman he was married to, or not married to, according to who was talking.

Even Doc would tell you a different story every time, if you were brave enough to ask him.

Inga let me go home after the ten-thirty show. I gave her a hand-sewed eye patch, with a spiderweb stitched in gold thread and the spider's body made of a teensy polished turquoise with silver-wire legs. She liked it fine, and showed it off to everybody. She gave me a pair of red shoes to go with the new costume I had just had made, then she locked up and went upstairs to celebrate with her girls. Inga was real sentimental about Christmas, and I think it was the only day of the year the Striped Garter closed its doors.

Miss Justice and Mr. Will Fowler were a pretty serious "item" by then, and being as his place of residence was the back room at the Malone Bros. Mercantile, he spent Christmas Eve with us at the Russ House. It was kind of cozy, though there were a bunch of people. Besides us, there was Miss Nellie Cashman and the rest of her boarders; Francine and Consuelo, the kitchen helpers; the Widow Stillwell, who set type over at the *Epitaph*; and the Reverend Hiram Kehoe. He was the traveling preacher whose Plantation Walker had got chewed up so bad by Jingles's swayback.

"My faithful Deuteronomy is well recovered, Sister," he said, "and bless you for asking." He was of medium height and skinny and wore a serious black frock coat just like the Earp brothers favored, though for a Baptist he was a real understanding man and never tried to dunk anybody against their will.

A couple regular boarders, Earl "Quartz-Sniffer" Breen and his son, Lucky Marvin, had managed to find a good bushy cypress, just the right shape and almost seven feet tall, and it was set up in the dining room and fully decorated. As Miss Nellie was leery of fires, it had no candles; but all the shiny tin and copper and glass ornaments picked up the gas jets' lights so that it fairly sparkled. It was pure beauty, and it made me awful sad.

By midnight, folks were having a high time. Miss Nellie had just sunk a hot poker into a pitcher of spiced cider when we heard the clamor.

"Jumpin' Jerusalem!" said one of the miners before he remembered himself. "Beggin' your pardon, Reverend. But it do sound like Saint Nick has just whoaed his sleigh on Miss Nellie's porch."

I knew who it was, all right, but before I could race to the front door, in Jingles came, stomping caked snow off his boots and swatting his floppy, snowy hat against his thigh. The little round scarred place on his scalp was red from the cold.

"Felicitations, folks!" he grinned. "I have brought my cussed team down for the festivities, not that their behavior of late has been deservin' of the treat. I hope to pick up a goodly load of bottles, too, what with the holidays."

"How's it go with you, Jingles?" I asked, and took his hat. It was getting soggy, now that the snow had melted.

"Not too bad, Miss Geneva-Kincaid-Gini-for-Short. I am needing feed, flour, beans, and lard. I hardly knew you, as you have pulled on a dress."

"I have got two new ones," I said, "not counting my work clothes. They are not so fashionable, but they are sturdy and I wear them on Sundays and holidays. I still ride in my bucks, though."

"A dress is a good thing for town," he replied. "Course, it'd be a magnet for bats."

Miss Nellie led him off toward the punch bowl. Everybody gathered round him, and I was left standing alone. I tell you, I don't think I had ever felt so lonely as I did that night. But I have always found the best thing to do when I am feeling low is keep busy, so I went over to Lucky

Marvin, he being on the edge of the crowd, and said, "Tell Jingles I'll take his team to the livery. He's been long on the road, and should stay in the warm."

It was snowing harder by then, big clumpy soft flakes that floated down like feathers. There stood Comanche: head drooped, fast asleep. A little drift was building up in his sway. The pony Grace was awake, but sitting down.

"Gracie," I said, after I tugged the cotton from her ears, "I am too dang cold to pry you up or argue. Gain your feet right now or, the Lord Jesus' birthday or no, I will have to boot you in the haunches."

Well, she rolled her eyes and snaked her head at me like she might bite, but in the end I guess she knew I meant business, for she gave out a groan and hauled herself up. I put her cotton back in, woke up Comanche, and headed for the livery.

Considering all the bottles Jingles had hauled out of town on his last visit, I expected the wagon to be heavy with homemade cactus whiskey, but once again, the only thing back there was a plank and some empty burlap sacks. I decided that Jingles must be practicing to be an expert marksman, and used them all for target-shooting. Either that, or he was throwing them at his bats.

Willis Stephens, the night man, had gone home early for the holiday, so I settled Comanche and Grace myself. After that, I went up one side of the aisle and down the other, breaking the ice in each horse's bucket with a curry comb handle. You'd think that dang Willis would have checked them before he left.

I was glad he was gone, though, as I had wanted my solitude. I was also glad there were no corpses in residence. Right next door to the stable is Clapman & Hodge Undertakers, and they advertise "Night Orders May Be Left at the Livery." The first time I saw that ad in the *Epitaph*, I figured they meant you should leave them a note: "Pick up my uncle in the morning as he is dead, Yours Truly, etc.," or something like that. But it seemed folks around town took advertising at its word, for several times I had stopped down after my last show to find a deceased person stretched out and blanketed over in a vacant stall. I thought it was nice the Grim Reaper had stayed clear of us for the holiday.

I always kept a few sweets in my coat pocket for Jelly, and after I finished up the water buckets, I gave him and Jigsaw a couple butterscotch drops. Despite the teasing I'd got from Willis and the other stablemen, I had tied a big red holiday ribbon on the front of each of their stalls. Gam had always done that at home for Christmas. Seeing those bows made me miss her that much more.

I went into Jigsaw's box and threw my arms around his winter-shaggy neck, and tears commenced to spill down my cheeks. "What if Tuck doesn't come, Jigsaw?" I whispered. "What if Ty and Mace don't come either and we never get the gold and I have to spend the whole dang rest of my life getting kicked awake by Miss Elma Justice?"

Jigsaw swung his old spotted head around and pushed his face up against my shoulder, like he was telling me it was all right and that he still loved me. It made me bawl all the harder, and I was just working myself up to a real pitch when the stable doors creaked open. I hoped it wasn't some mourner dropping off his dead grandpa for Clapman & Hodge; that would have been just about the end of me. I made myself stop crying, gave my face a quick rub on my coat sleeve, and turned round.

It was only a fella leading a horse. The mare was pretty snowed up, and the fella was bundled in a heavy jacket. His hat sat low on his forehead, and as I had only lit one lantern when I came in, I couldn't see his face. When he was almost up to me, he said, "I'll be needin' to . . . Geneva?"

At the first sound of his voice, I shot out of that stall and locked my arms round his waist. That will show you what a state I was in. I am not usually one to go hugging people or hanging on to them, but I practically had Tyrone O'Neill in a death grip. And as hard as I tried, I couldn't stop blubbering.

He was real nice about it. He gave me his handkerchief and said, "I'm past flattered, darlin'. Nobody but me own lovely horse has been this gladdened at the sight of me in ages." He made me blow my nose, then he said, "Vain I may be, but I'm not so self-admirin' as t'think that's the entirety of it. What's this dire burden you're laborin' under? Are times so hard that ye and Zachary are havin' Christmas with the livestock?"

Well, that got me to leaking all the more, but I managed to tell him about Zack and how he had been murdered by that bowlegged Apache north of Tucson, and how Sees Silver had avenged him.

"Poor, poor darlin'," he whispered, and stroked my hair. I fell apart all over again.

When I finally got hold of myself, I told him about the Russ House and Miss Justice and Jingles. We bedded his mare down, and he said he would come back to the hotel for the night.

"I'll be findin' a new roof tomorrow," he added, "if one can be had on Christmas Day. It's hard to tell how long a wait we'll have for Tucker. I'll need to be plyin' me trade in the meantime, love, and 'tis best if I lodge near me livelihood."

"You only said Tuck. What about Mace and Pete?"

"Aye, them as well if they're able. 'Twere neither of them in such fine fettle when I bade Tucker and Queenie good-bye."

We walked back to Miss Nellie's. There were no more

vacant rooms, but Jingles said he'd share. Ty shook hands with everybody and gave them "Season's Greetings," and everybody liked him right off. The Widow Stillwell, who is sixty-five if she is a day, got all blushy and giggled when she shook his hand, and Miss Justice sent me a real curious look when she learned he was my friend.

Before the party broke up, we had time for a toast and all four verses of "Angels, From the Realms of Glory," with Quartz-Sniffer Breen on the ocarina, Jingles on harmonica, and Lucky Marvin tapping the spoons. Ty stood with his arm round my shoulders for the entire thing. He knew all the words, and he had a good, clear voice.

The next morning, the Reverend Kehoe held a Christmas service in Miss Nellie's dining room. He was a popular sermonizer, so we had quite a crowd, and afterwards Miss Nellie did a landslide business for late breakfast. As she was so busy, I offered to lend a hand in the kitchen, and therefore missed out on the Reverend's second sermon. That one was held at the Striped Garter. Spider Eye Inga opened up the place for services, and the meeting was heavily attended by the "ladies" of Allen Street, and not a few of their clients.

I did not have much chance to talk to Ty before he set out to find himself a room, as me and Miss Justice were real busy helping Miss Nellie, Francine, and Consuelo get the holiday baskets ready. We had almost forty of them lined up on the big oak worktable, and into each one went baked ham and applesauce, scalloped potatoes, candied yams, biscuits, and a pot of honey; pickled beets and cukes, creamed corn, mincemeat pie, and plum pudding; and all the plates and silver to go with it. There were supposed to be green beans with bacon, too, except that Francine accidentally tipped over the pot and dumped it all on the floor. That Francine was about the clumsiest woman I ever met. Miss Nellie kept her on out of sympathy, as her no-account husband had run off to Bisbee with a low woman from Madame Bouvier's Palace d'Amour, and Francine had no other way to make money.

Anyway, we split up the load and set off with deliveries around three in the afternoon. Quartz-Sniffer Breen drove Miss Nellie's buckboard, Miss Justice had Will Fowler to squire her around in a rented buggy, and Jingles volunteered to take me. We had a real good time, what with Jingles's rig making all that bell-noise and him crying out "Ho, ho, ho!" every time we reined up in front of the next shack or tent. Even Gracie had the Holiday Spirit, as she only had to be levered out of a sit two times; and when we passed Acting Marshal Virgil Earp, he just smiled and tipped his hat and made no threats about disturbing the peace.

In between stops, I thought to ask Jingles why he had collected all those bottles on his last trip to town.

"Because by day's end I am sick of rocks," he said. "Besides which, rocks do not let the light in."

Well, that stopped me short. I did not ask any more about bottles, and didn't even bring up the bats. To my mind, every person is entitled to his or her own craziness, but it is not my duty to fathom it.

That night the Striped Garter reopened, and after a good feast at the Russ House I was back at work. I wore my new red dress. It was sewn all over with spangles and sequins and was better than fine, except that Miss Janet Beatty, over at Janet's Fine Fashions and Stitchery, had cut it lower in front than what I'd expected. Miss Janet stitched a clever seam, but she was used to dressmaking for ladies who sold a whole different product than me, and I guess habit got the best of her.

Anyhow, I didn't fill it out so good, but Inga showed me how to put wadded-up tissue paper under my chests so they bulged out at the top real impressive. I had my new red shoes and scarlet feathers for my hair, and Inga loaned me her brightest red lip rouge. If Miss Elma Justice had ever seen me like that, the shock would have likely given her apoplexy, but I thought I looked pretty dang good, and pretty dang grown-up. A lot of boys had come into town for Christmas so we had a big crowd, and from all the whooping and hollering, I guess they liked my outfit fine, too.

I hadn't seen Ty since he left the Russ House, and I'd been too busy to think much about him. But I was real glad when, about halfway through my second show and right in the middle of "If Love Is the Sickness, Whiskey's the Cure," he walked right in the Striped Garter's front doors. He ordered at the bar, and then eased back against it, elbows propped, to watch the show.

Now, I thought it odd that he didn't wave or give me a sign of hello, especially since every time I caught him from the corner of my eye he was staring straight at me. For my last song of the set, I did "Sweet Lucinda Link." It is real melodic and has a lot of "range," and makes the most of my voice. I sang part of the first verse right to Tyrone. I guess I was showing off for him.

I finished up and the boys tossed their coins, and after the curtain closed and I picked up the five dollars and two bits that had been thrown, I went out front.

The crowd was pretty thick. It took me a while to get near Ty, what with all the howdys that had to be said along the way and the one fella I had to punch in the belly. I hated to do that, it being Christmas and all, but he just wouldn't hear "no." Anyhow, I had almost made my way over to Tyrone when Red-Deuce Marie took my elbow.

"Here," she said, and stuck a little piece of paper in my hand. "Saved me a trip."

"What is it?"

Red-Deuce shrugged, "It's from that flashy number standin' down betwixt Curt and Kenny Ames."

It was Ty, all right. I figured maybe he wanted to apologize for being so rude and leering like that and not even waving how-do. I opened the note. The handwriting was real elaborate, and it said:

My Dear Miss Irish Jenny Rose,
    Loveliest nightingale, you are an unexpected delight to these beauty-starved eyes and ears. It would be my honor and privilege to share a bottle of this establishment's finest with you, should you deign to favor this humble servant with your company after the show.
    Yours in fervid but respectful hope,
        T. O'Neill

Well, I read that dang note three times over. I knew Tyrone was a slick customer, but I had never imagined him to be such a one for flowery speech. I couldn't decide if he meant it true, or if he was just making fun of me for having the sand to stand up on the stage all rouged and powdered and high-heeled and pretend I was fancy. Finally I folded the paper back up, stuck it down the front of my new red dress, and went over to him.

He had seen me coming, and a silver-bucketed bottle of French champagne waited by his elbow. The look on his face put me a little in mind of Frank Malone, except on Ty it was not at all disagreeable.

He took off his hat and made a gallant bow. "Dearest Jenny Rose," he said, "I'm thrilled beyond measure. Had ye not accepted, I surely would've suffered the agonies of Christ."

I felt my face go all hot, but I said, "Tyrone, I'll bet you have paid ten dollars for that bottle. If you wanted to drink with me so bad, we could have had sweet cider at Miss Nellie's for a dime."

Well, that handsome jaw dropped practically to his chest, and he said, "Geneva?"

I said, "If you are feeling pukish, there's a cot in the back."

By then, though, he'd collected himself. "Geneva pet," he said, his smile back in place so firm you never would have known it had slipped, "let's the two of us find a table and have ourselves a wee chat."

Well, we had that champagne, and he swore up and down that he'd known all along it was me underneath the fancy hairdo and paint, though he did admit he had never guessed I was a "natural songbird." He sure treated me different than before: just like I was a lady that he might take out to an elegant supper or the theater, if there'd been such a place in Tombstone. I liked it fine.

I was a little tipsy for my next show, but the crowd was six times drunker and nobody noticed, even when I forgot and left out the middle verse of *Three Cheers for Billy*, so that he only got two cheers.

After I got off work and scrubbed up and changed my clothes, Ty took my arm and walked me home. We were halfway down the street when I remembered about the Dakota Gambler book.

"You never mentioned to me that you knew Buffalo Bill," I said.

"Who, darlin'?"

"Buffalo Bill Cody. I didn't know you knew him. I read about your adventures with him, the ones you had in the Black Hills when you saved that girl named Alyssa. It was real excitin'. It's the one book I kept for myself and didn't give Miss Nellie for the miner's library."

Now, that was about the longest speech I'd made all evening, since I'd mostly been listening to Tyrone wax poetic about this and that. So I was pretty disappointed when he said, "Geneva love, I've not the faintest notion what you're talkin' about. I've played a hand or two with Bill Cody, but I'd scarcely call it an adventure. 'Twas a small pot and, as I'm recallin', neither of us won it."

"Holy Hannah, Ty! Between you and Zack, you have just about destroyed my faith in literature." You may think it odd, but I honestly did not remember till just then about Doc Holliday being so murderous nasty on the subject of Ty O'Neill. "Tyrone," I began, "there is somethin' you ought to know."

He smiled, too dang charming for words. "Something else ye read in that book of yours, love?"

I never got to say, because just then Doc himself came reeling out of Big Jim Harold's Bar and bumped smack into us. It was pretty confused for a few seconds, what with it being dark and the two of them trying to pick each other up. I took advantage of the fluster to slide Ty's pistol from its holster and hide it behind my back. It was not that I wanted to leave Tyrone unarmed. I just figured that if Doc was after mischief, he'd be watching Ty's hand, not mine. Besides, having shot the Aztec Kid in the foot (and got away with it) probably made me feel braver than I had a right to.

Doc was the first one to recognize the situation. "O'Neill!" he thundered. He was pretty skunked. "Where's that nine hundred you owe me, you sonofabitch!"

"'Twas six," said Ty.

"He told me seven," I said.

Doc shook himself off and wiped at his coat front. That worried me, for he sometimes carried a pig-sticker just inside his lapel. "Well, it was a lot," he said to Ty, real nasty.

"I was prob'ly closer to sober when I told her seven, so that's what I'll settle for."

Tyrone didn't even look nervous. "And I'm supposin' ye want it here and now, in this dark, cold, inhospitable street?"

"If not sooner," Doc said, and made to reach inside his coat.

I brought up Ty's Peacemaker. "Stop right there!" I was awful scared, as any person has a right to be when they are holding a gun on a known killer like Doc, but I had that pistol in both hands, and I kept the barrel level.

Both of them looked pretty startled. Ty slapped his holster, like he couldn't believe I'd lifted his gun without him knowing. "Geneva!" he said. "What in the blessed name of—"

I held the gun steady. "He called you a back-stabbin' bastard," I said. "Doc, I hate to tell on you like this, but you practically said Ty was not fit company for snakes. Tyrone, I think he means to murder you."

"I thought—" Doc began before he was seized by a coughing fit. He opened his jacket to show me there was no weapon, then pulled out a big stained handkerchief. He was near doubled over and hacking bad. Ty grabbed his arm and sat him down on the bench in front of Big Jim Harold's window, which left me pointing that pearl-handled Peacemaker at nothing in particular.

When Doc finally got quieted down, he waved a hand at the pistol and croaked, "You're chock-full of surprises, Irish. I heard about the Aztec Kid, but I still would have laid money that a cane-back chair was more your weapon."

Tyrone leaned against the building and thumbed his hat back. "Ye sound a misery in the chest, Doc. I thought Arizona was good for the lungs."

Doc wadded up his kerchief and tucked it away. "Couldn't say one way or the other. But whiskey's got a beneficial effect. Not that I can afford much of it, what with carryin' so many goddamn debtors on my books."

Tyrone chuckled. "Ye never do so terrible bad, Doc."

"I never do so terrible good, either."

"Hold on just a dang minute," I said, and wiggled the gun to get their attention. "Doc, does all this cordial talk mean you are not goin' to kill Tyrone?"

Doc looked up at me, real disgusted-like. "Irish, what the hell makes you think I'd kill a man who owes me twelve hundred dollars?"

"Five," said Tyrone.

"Seven," I said, and handed Ty back his Peacemaker.

We went inside Big Jim Harold's. After Doc called for a bottle and they both had a drink, Ty reached into his pocket and brought out a fat roll of bills. He thumbed off seven hundred dollars, in hundreds and fifties, and pushed it across the table to Doc. There was still plenty left in his roll. He said, "Count it out, Doc darlin', and from now on I'll have ye stop defamin' the good name of O'Neill."

Doc tidied up the bills and put his glass on them. "Goddamn it, Tyrone," he scowled, "I don't know why you have to go round callin' everybody *darlin'*. Makes a fella nervous as hell."

Tyrone grinned. "Then I'm thinkin' that's as good a reason as any to continue. What do ye hear from Big Nose Kate?"

Doc poured himself another shot. "As little as possible," he grumbled, and tossed the whiskey back. "Deal the cards."

9

The Second Conflagration

We went all through January, and still no word from Tuck or the Danahoes. I saw Tyrone at the Striped Garter about every other day, though. He would play with anybody who had money, but he ·best liked a game with the other professionals like Doc or Wyatt or Johnny-behind-the-deuce O'Rourke. In the long run, I do not believe he did better than break even when he gamed with them, but I think he preferred their company.

Inga's girls fell all over him, and Two Apples Annie was so love-struck it was pathetic. He was always real gallant to any female, but anybody could tell it was me who was special to him. He even gave me a genuine topaz ring he won in a game. It was too big for my finger, but I wore it on a silver chain around my neck. I treasured it.

The Apache were still causing a hoorah to the west of us, according to the *Epitaph*, but they were not venturing quite so far north of the Mex border. Manuelito was mentioned again two times, Sees Silver once.

The Russ House limped along with just one kitchen helper. Consuelo's husband had taken her back home to Sonora, which left us stuck with Francine. We had a Chinese girl for a week, but after Francine accidentally dropped a cast-iron skillet on her foot, she quit and went to work

178

waiting tables for Deet Siddens over at Aunt Deet's Café. I can't say I blamed her.

At the Striped Garter, we got a new contraption Spider Eye Inga special-ordered through the Goldwater's down at Bisbee. It was like a great big music box. You put in a nickel and it would play whichever of the ten songs you picked. Inga had them put it against the wall beside Hector's piano, and it seemed like about every night there were at least two fistfights over somebody playing the same song too much or not enough. Machines are wonderful things, but they can sure cause trouble.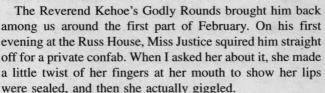

The Reverend Kehoe's Godly Rounds brought him back among us around the first part of February. On his first evening at the Russ House, Miss Justice squired him straight off for a private confab. When I asked her about it, she made a little twist of her fingers at her mouth to show her lips were sealed, and then she actually giggled.

Now, that was a strange thing indeed to be coming out of Miss Elma Justice, but as her behavior of the past couple weeks had been all-around odd, I let it pass. She had got real absentminded, and was always forgetting where she left things, or even what day it was. In addition, she had grown lax about her clothes-matching. One morning she waltzed off to work in a blue dress with pink shoes and a peach parasol. She went through the whole day like that, and did not even notice till I remarked on it at supper.

Anyway, the night after Reverend Kehoe's arrival, she didn't come home on time and I got worried. Miss Justice always walked a long and curious route to work and back so that her eyes would not be perverted by the sight of brothels, but the week before she had got immersed in her thoughts and forgot to turn the last corner to bring her back to Fifth. Since on that occasion she had walked near to the city limits before she remembered herself, I figured if I didn't run to fetch her, she might daydream herself all the way to down to Bisbee. I was just setting out when Miss Nellie waved me back.

"I'm just going to scout for Miss Justice," I said. "I think she has got herself misplaced again."

Miss Nellie smiled. I guess she had noticed the strangeness about Elma, too, but she was too sweet a lady to mention it outright. "She isn't lost," she said. "She will be working late at the mercantile all week, taking inventory. I doubt you will see her at all, except to sleep, until Sunday."

I had my dinner with Quartz-Sniffer Breen and Lucky Marvin. I kind of missed Miss Elma Justice and felt hurt she hadn't remembered to tell me she'd be gone, but Quartz-Sniffer told some funny stories and Lucky Marvin showed me a trick with three thimbles and a pea, and I had a good time.

Two nights later, Francine dumped the big sugar tin into the laundry tub, which was quite a trick even for her. It would have been a calamity for any other restaurant in town, but not for us at the Russ House. Since Miss Justice had a key to the mercantile, whenever tragedy, short supply, or Francine struck after business hours, Miss Nellie would just send me or Miss Justice or Lucky Marvin up to the store to get the item out of stock and put it on her bill.

I had an hour before I needed to be at the Striped Garter, so I volunteered to run the errand, thinking to say hello to Miss Justice and give her a break in her inventory work. I also hoped I might catch a glimpse of Ty on the way. He had not been in the saloon for the past couple days, and I missed him. Looking back on it, I guess I was pretty dang lovesick, even then.

I wasn't the only one shot by Cupid's arrow, though, for I hadn't gone far when I spied Miss Justice and Will Fowler.

They were sitting at a window table at Aunt Deet's Café and holding hands over a fried chicken dinner. I hated to bother them for the key, and decided to just go down to the store and take a chance on somebody else still being there to let me in.

A few blocks later, I ran into Ty. He was standing on the sidewalk out front of the telegraph office, rolling a cigarette. "Well, good evenin', darlin'," he said, just as creamy as could be. He pointed to my skirts. "I see the Reverend Kehoe's still in town. What's bringin' ye down this way in such a bustlin' hurry?"

"I am goin' to the mercantile," I replied. I thought it was real observant of Ty to notice I always wore a dress in honor of the Reverend. "Francine has ruined the sugar, and Miss Nellie needs a few pounds to tide her over. We have missed you at Spider Eye Inga's."

He smiled real warm, and if I'd been a cat, I would have purred. "I'll be by tonight. I've a grand surprise for ye."

"What kind?"

He waggled his finger. "The best yet, love."

When I tried to coax him to tell me more, he just winked and sent me on my way.

Down at the Malone Bros., lamps were lit but the front door was bolted. When nobody answered my knock, I went back to the storeroom door. It was standing open and I walked right in.

The gas line had not run this far up the street as yet, but there were plenty of lanterns set out on the shelves and packing crates, so it was good and bright. I thought it odd nobody answered my hello, but I went on up front, found a ten-pound bag of sugar, and plopped it on the counter next to the marble jar. Now, why the Malones would stock such a multitude of aggies and puries and steelies in a town with hardly any kids is a mystery to me. Every time I saw it I was puzzled, especially since they seemed to sell a lot of the dang things; leastwise, the level in the jar was always rising and falling. The only possibility I could figure was that Tombstone, A.T., had a whole contingent of miners and cattle rustlers who were secret marble shooters.

Anyway, I commenced to search out a scrap of paper. I found a pad on the bottom shelf, back behind the register, and I was just standing up with it when I heard bootsteps.

It was himself, Joe Malone. His coat was folded over his arm and he was straightening his suspenders, so he must have just come in from the outhouse.

He looked about as shocked to see me as I felt to see him, but right away his surprise turned to nasty. There is nothing meaner-looking than a Malone in a temper fit, especially a bushy-faced Malone like Joe. "Caught you red-handed, you thieving whore's whelp!" he hollered, one fist in the air.

Right then and there, I vowed to give Miss Justice a stern talking-to. I don't know how a person—even a moony-eyed one—could forget to mention a thing so important as a Malone being in town. I got hold of myself right away, though, and said, calm as I could, "You have sure changed your tune since we last met, Joe. And if you think I came down here to steal sugar, you're wrong. I was about to leave a note."

"Sure you were," he said, real sarcastic. "What have us Malones ever done to you, Gini Kincaid, to deserve the treatment you give us? First you burn down our warehouse, then you hire a gang of thugs to work over my poor brother Frank, and now you have the brass to come here a-thieving! Do you have a wagon outside? Do you want me to help you fill it up with stolen goods?"

"I guess you must have talked to Frank and Amos since the last time we met, Joe, but they have told you a fib. I never burned down anything that belonged to you."

"It almost did!" he shouted. His face was getting real red. "We have had to build a whole new facility, young woman. That was no cheap proposition!"

"It's no skin off me, Joe. Furthermore, I hired no 'gang of thugs.' They were two fellas I just happened to meet, and they were nicer to your possum's-butt brother than he deserved. And like I'm tryin' to tell you, I was about to leave a note to put this sugar on the Russ House bill."

He shoved himself into his suit coat. "There's no call to be writing any notes, Miss Gini Kincaid, for you will need no sugar in prison. Arson will be the charge! Arson, assault, and burglary! I am taking you to the marshal. The law in this town is poor indeed, but I intend to press charges. I will send to Virginia for Mr. Evert Fairbanks, too, and we will see some justice done, by God!"

I jumped up and swung myself over the counter, thinking to run, but my dang skirts caught on the marble jar and tipped it. Right there is another strong reason why a dress is no good when there's work to be done. Anyway, those marbles went everywhere, and I landed right in the thick of them. I skidded like a five-year-old on buttered skates and landed sharp on my hip.

"*Now* look what you've done!" Joe shouted as I scrambled to my feet. "What are you gonna do next, pour molasses in my flour barrels? Take a razor to my ready-to-wear?"

"I'd do either of those before I'd let you haul me to jail," I hollered, and took off for the back door.

That Joe was pretty quick for a fat man, especially one that's running on a floor full of marbles. We both did a lot of skittering and slipping and banging into things, but I made it to the back room just ahead of him. I was two jumps from the door when he grabbed my skirt and yanked it hard. I gave a yell and fell crosswise against a tall pile of bolted yardage.

Long, heavy rolls of calico and gingham went tumbling and knocked Joe's legs out from under him. He let go of me quick enough, but as he went down—arms flailing—he backhanded a lantern.

He must have whacked it pretty dang hard, for it flew a good fifteen feet to shatter against a stack of crates.

Excelsior and shavings popped into flame. Fire raced up fresh-painted walls, ran along floorboards, licked at windows. I scrambled fast, and I was clear through the door before I realized Joe was still inside, laid out cold.

Well, just because a man is rude and pigheaded doesn't mean he deserves to cook under his own yard goods.

It took quite a bit of grunting and straining to get him as far as the threshold, and by then we were both covered with soot. I was coughing pretty bad, and I'd had to pause twice already to beat out the flames on my hem. At the doorway, I stumbled and went down to my knees. I couldn't seem to get back up, and I remember thinking I'd heard that folks died from smoke before they had a chance to burn.

There came a hand on my shoulder, voices, the thud and pull of boots stomping on my skirts; somebody dragging, then carrying me.

The flames had spread like quicksilver. My eyes smarted so from the smoke that I could hardly open them, but as I was borne away I heard things crashing and breaking and exploding inside the mercantile. I heard people shouting, too, from far away, yelling for help and buckets and the pump wagon.

Whoever was toting me put me down. I felt water splash my face, and looked up through swollen and teary eyes. It was Ty, and it must have been he who'd brought me out and lugged me clear across the back lot to the water tank on Fremont Street. I tried to talk, but it turned into a raspy cough. He helped me into a sit, rubbed my back, and made me drink some water.

A goodly crowd had gathered on Allen Street. They were a distance from us, but I could see that some were forming a bucket line. Most were just watching the fire, though. The whole of the mercantile was engulfed by then, so most of the water was getting tossed on the places next door, just in case. It was a good thing there was no wind, or I guess it might have taken the whole dang town.

"Nosy firebug troublemaker! Mace sure had you pegged, girl. You set one'a these damn things in every other town you visit?" It was Stinky Pete, healed up fine and just as stupid as ever, and arranging Joe Malone on the ground. He didn't look any too clean, and I guessed that if my nose hadn't been so full of the stench of scorched cloth and hair, I probably could have sniffed him from where I sat. He and Ty were almost as sooted up as me and Joe, and part of Joe's beard was singed away. Joe's eyes were closed, but I could tell he was alive by his chest moving up and down.

"When I told ye there'd be a surprise," said Ty with a grin, "I didn't conceive ye'd be tryin' t'top it. 'Tis lucky I remembered ye were headin' this way."

Joe Malone started to moan a little and twitch his hands. Pete dumped some water on him, and he came round. "Call the law!" was the first raspy thing out of his mouth. He pointed straight at me. "I want her jailed! I want her whipped! Hanged!"

"Aw, cripes!" Pete said. "This fella's almost more trouble than you, Miss Gini Smart Alec."

I was about to tell him that up till a minute ago I would've been pleased to hear he was not deceased, but Joe Malone cut me off.

"Destruction of private property!" Joe croaked, louder than you would've thought he could after having all that smoke in his lungs. "Theft! Arson! My store, my new store!" He was making so much commotion that we didn't notice Wyatt Earp until he had walked right up on us.

"Evening, O'Neill," he said, and lit a skinny cigar. He stood between us and the inferno, in silhouette; and he was so cool that when something else exploded inside and the street crowd made a sound like three hundred people all-at-once telling a horse to whoa, he didn't even glance round. "I believe that dress of yours is beyond repair, Miss Irish Jenny Rose," he said after a pause. "You do not look too fit, either, Malone. Just exactly who is it you want us to hang this time?"

Joe's eyes were fair bugging out of his head. One of his brows was singed clear off. "That brat!" he croaked. "She did this! Arson! Assault! Attempted murder!"

Ty helped me up to my feet. "Murder's a gruesome thing to go round shoutin', Mr. Malone. Why, the poor brave lass nearly got herself asphyxiated, and her all the while tryin' t'pull your ungrateful carcass out of the conflagration."

Wyatt took a slow puff on his cigar. "Is that the truth, Irish Jenny?"

"Yes sir, it is. Though it was Tyrone and Pete, here, that pulled us the rest of the way clear of the building." My throat was awful scratchy and it was hard to catch my breath, but I kept going. "That fire was an accident. I'll witness that. But it was his accident, not mine."

"Lies!" Joe shouted, all crackly. "She's a born falsifier, bred and raised by whores, drunkards, and Apache lovers! I want her locked away from decent people! I want her locked away from my property! And why aren't you up there putting out my fire, Earp?" He stopped on account of a coughing fit.

"The Volunteers are hard at work on the pumps, and my brothers Virgil and James have organized a bucket brigade,"

Wyatt remarked as he tapped away his cigar ash. "I don't believe it is doing much good, though."

"What're you folks doing all the way down here?" Doc Holliday stood over Joe Malone, who was still doubled up, hacking. Doc must have walked down from the Fremont Street side, and I don't know how long he'd been there, listening. He tipped his hat. "Best show'd appear to be down on Allen. Evenin', Wyatt, Tyrone."

Ty nodded and Wyatt said, "Evening, Doc."

"This is sure one loudmouthed sonofabitch you got here on the ground," Doc went on. "I'm not at all in favor of the tone he was taking with our little Irish." He looked over at Stinky Pete. "You with this noisy fool, or you just standin' around?"

Pete actually took his hat clear off, and I guess he was so overwhelmed that he forgot all about his being a wanted man worth forty whole dollars and said, "Pete Danahoe, Mr. Holliday . . . Doc. Friend of Ty's."

Doc grunted. "Don't rightly know if that's a recommendation." He studied on me for a minute, then said, "Irish, you are sure one unholy mess." He looked back down at Joe, who was just getting over his fit. "Fella coughs worse than me. Suppose I'm catchin'?"

"Do your dad-busted duty!" Joe wheezed, and tried to get up, without much luck. "You Earps are worthless! Gamblers and scofflaws the lot of you, running this town for the pleasure of your depraved associates instead of for law-abiding businessmen!"

Doc growled, "You're beginnin' to wear on my nerves, mister."

But Joe didn't know when to shut up. "Riffraff!" he croaked. "Spend your time consorting with scum!"

Doc eased out his pistol.

Joe paid no mind. "Gambling and swilling liquor with

trash! I'm not surprised you'd take the side of this fire-starting hellcat!"

Doc said "That does it," and cracked Joe over the head. Joe went thump on the ground.

"Obliged," said Wyatt.

"No bother," said Doc.

Wyatt turned to me. "Is there truth in what Malone says? Did you have a hand in setting this fire?"

I heard Pete give a snort, but at least he had the smarts to hold his comment. "I was inside when it flowered," I replied. "But the actual blaze was started by Joe. He knocked a lantern over when he was chasin' me."

"And why was he after you?"

I squared up my shoulders. "I'd rather not say."

"Don't press her, Wyatt," Doc muttered around the cigar he was lighting. "She's liable to pull Tyrone's gun on you."

The mercantile roof caved in with a thunderous crash. Sparks whooshed up in the air, and the crowd tossed their hats and cheered at the pure splendor of it.

"It'll be his word against yours, Irish Jenny," Wyatt said after the noise died down. "If he swears out a complaint, Virgil will have to lock you up. The law is the law."

Joe was coming round again, though he was not all the way with us. "Arson," he mumbled, "murder . . . Theft and mischief . . ."

Doc looked real disgusted. He said, "This the same fella that was in Virgil's office the other day, raisin' hell because the city hadn't shoveled up the road apples out front of his store?"

"Locked away for a hundred years . . . ," mumbled Joe, who was feeling some better.

"He's the one," said Wyatt. "The day before that he was in to harp about Chinese Willie sleepin' it off in his alley, and the day before that——"

"What if I was gone?" I broke in. "What if I was out of town before Joe filed his complaint? Made out the papers, I mean."

Deputy Earp twisted his cigar, studied on the lit end. "If I were you, I don't believe I'd head toward Soldier Holes or Sulphur Springs. I hear your friend the Aztec Kid's up and around again, and those are his haunts."

"All right, then," I said. "West. Across the river."

"Somebody help me," said Joe, who was up on his knees and partway back to his senses. "My head! What happened?"

Wyatt rolled his cigar betwixt two fingers. "You fainted."

"Delayed reaction, most like," said Doc. "From the smoke. I'm a medical man, and I know these things."

"Shut up, Holliday," Joe croaked. "You're nothing but a has-been tooth-yanker, and you're as bad as the Earps! And you, you little hooligan, you're going away for a long time, I'll see to that! I am a personal friend of Judge Billy Ray Patterson, and he will hand you out a stiff penalty, all right!" He doubled over and launched into another coughing fit.

I don't mind saying I was kind of scared. I crossed my fingers for luck, and said, "Wyatt, you remember the night Marshal White got killed and you came to the Striped Garter looking for Phin Clanton and the Aztec Kid?"

"I do."

"And do you remember as how you allowed you owed me a favor?"

"I do, indeed."

Joe had got his hacking under some control. "Damn you, Earp," he growled, "stop your jawing and arrest this girl. Clap her in irons! Or is hauling in one scraggly bar-rat too big a job for you?"

Wyatt heaved a weary sigh. He looked me in the eye and said, "Across the San Pedro?" When I nodded a quick yes, he looked down at Joe, then over at Doc. "Oh, hell," he said. "You're closest."

"My pleasure," replied Doc, and whacked Joe Malone upside the skull again. As Joe folded, Doc remarked, "I hope a half hour's long enough for you, Irish. I don't believe I hit him harder than thirty minutes' worth."

When we got down to Allen Street, we stopped so I could catch my breath. Ty tipped his hat, said he'd be right back, and left me with Pete, who seemed less interested in the fire and the mob than in the back lot we had just come from. Doc and Wyatt were still up by the water tank, standing over Joe Malone and smoking cheroots.

"Was that the honest-to-God Wyatt Earp and Doc Holliday?" he asked. His jaw hung down some, and I was kind of embarrassed for him.

My breathing still troubled me, but I said, "No. They are fake ones we hired to fool you. The whole dang town's in on it, and we are goin' to have a good laugh on you just as soon as we get this fire put out."

He shot me a mean look. "You'd better watch that lip, gal."

"Dad-blast you, Pete Danahoe! You're gettin' me plain exasperated. How come you don't see a person for months and the first thing out of your mouth is smart talk? Don't you even have the simple manners to say hello? I bet you don't take such a reckless attitude with that girlfriend of yours."

"Don't you be talkin' about my Loula!"

He gave my arm a little jerk and raised his hand up like he might smack me, but just then Ty popped out of the crowd. "I see the two'a ye are gettin' along famous," he said, and aimed us up the road.

We had barely crossed the street when I dug in my heels.

"Holy Hannah, Ty, we can't *all* leave town! Somebody's got to wait for Tuck."

"Geneva m'love," he said as he started me walking again, "that's t'other half of your surprise. Himself and both Danahoes rode in this afternoon and checked into me own hotel. We were goin' to descend upon ye at the Striped Garter tonight for a grand reunion party. They're not up here watchin' the show, so they're bound to be at Deet's Café waitin' on young Pete and m'self for dinner."

It turned out that nobody was in the café. They were all outside, Aunt Deet included, watching the flames from a distance while their dinners got cold. Tuck saw us first, and he broke out in a big grin that changed quick to concern.

"Miss Gini!" he said. "What in the blessed name of Hera has happened to you?"

I guess I had never been so glad to see anybody as I was to lay eyes on Tuck's old face, and I was about to say so when Mace Danahoe stepped up on the walk. He had a checkered napkin tucked in his collar and he was clutching a mostly eaten chicken leg in one hand. "It figures," he said, real disgusted. "The minute we heard them yell 'fire,' I told Tuck I'd bet my horse and saddle—"

Tuck said, "Hush, boy." He crossed his arms over his chest and looked down at me. "All this hoopla your doing, Miss Gini?"

"No sir, it is not. It's Joe Malone's doin'. I just happened to be on the premises. And hello to you, too, Mace. I suppose I'm happy to see you're not dead."

He made a snorting sound, and Ty said, "In the interest of time, mayhaps we could be discussin' this on the trail? We've got less than a half hour before the constabulary's activated."

Mace ripped the napkin off his shirtfront, shoved it and the chicken leg at Aunt Deet, and stomped off toward the hotel to collect their things and settle the bill. Pete went up to the OK Corral to fetch their horses, and Ty went down to the livery to saddle Jigsaw and his mare. Tuck said he'd walk me back to the Russ House. As luck would have it, Miss Justice and Will Fowler were watching the fire not fifteen feet from where we stood.

"Wait a second, Tuck," I said, and waved toward my friend. "Miss Justice! Over here!"

She appeared plenty shocked to see me so disheveled. She made a big fuss and insisted on going back to the Russ House with us.

A glance in the mirror told why everybody had stared at me so funny. Most of my skirts were burned down to the petticoat and there were sooty smudges all over my face and arms. But that wasn't the worst of it, for that dang fire had burnt away about a half-foot of my hair on the right side. I had thought I was mad at the Malones before, but boy howdy, this was a new mad altogether!

Miss Justice got some scissors and started to even it up as quick as she could. While she snipped away, I told her about Joe and the fire.

"I will be grieved for you to go," she said. "Besides everything else, you will not be here for my wedding, and I had planned to ask you to be maid of honor."

I wheeled round so fast I nearly ran my face into her shears. "Well, that sure explains a lot," I said.

"Hold still, Miss Kincaid. I am trying to hurry."

After she evened up my hair and tied back what was left with a ribbon, I changed clothes quick and launched into packing. As I stuffed my belongings inside my satchel, I said, "I'd like to give you a wedding present. I will make you a gift of Jelly, on condition that you promise he'll always have a kind home with you and not be sold to horse traders or questionable persons."

She had gone down on all fours to pull my squirrel gun out from under the bed, but she poked her head up to say, "That is most kind. We will take good care of him." She smiled.

I said, "When are you and Will Fowler plannin' to tie the knot?"

"It was to be three weeks from this coming Saturday, but what with the fire putting us both out of a job . . . I am not so certain now." Her lower lip commenced to quiver.

"I'm not done yet, Miss Justice." My money jar had been the last item to surface, and I dumped it on the bed. "I have made high wages and tips at the Striped Garter," I said. I scraped up about one hundred dollars in bills and coins, jammed them in my bag, and pointed at the rest.

"Since you and Will Fowler may be a while findin' employment, I want you to have that, too. It is probably about a hundred and fifty. Where I am goin', I won't have call for it. And after that, I'll have more than I can use. Besides, even though it was your forgetfulness that caused me to fall into an altercation with Joe Malone, I feel bad about havin' been part cause of you losin' your place of employment."

Well, I'll be danged if she didn't start in to cry.

"You stop that, Miss Justice," I said, and then, as if my eyes weren't still smarting enough from the smoke, I commenced to bawl right along with her. It was about then that Tuck knocked on the door.

"Miss Gini," he said real soft, "you had best be lighting a fire under it. I do not mean that literally."

"Comin'." I swept up my bag and squirrel gun.

"Your friend Mr. Brennan seems very nice," Miss Justice sniffed as I went to the door. "What would you like me to do with your tortoise?"

If I'd had a free hand, I would have slapped myself upside

the head. "Miss Justice, I had near forgot! I'll take him along with me, and I thank you for the reminder."

She followed me out to the lobby at a trot. Tuck was waiting by the desk. He had his hat off, and he was talking with Miss Cashman. Miss Elma Justice scouted out Lucky Marvin and sent him running to drag Malachi's crate from under the porch while I paid up my bill. I also bought a small ham, a round of cheese, and a big sack of biscuits for the trail. Miss Nellie tried to refuse the money, but I made her take it.

As Tuck and I hurried out the door, she gave me a little hug. "We will miss you, dear Gini," she said. "Please do come and visit."

"I will try, Miss Nellie," I said, though what with the Malone situation, I doubted I would ever again ride into Tombstone, A.T. "You'll say good-bye to Quartz-Sniffer and the others for me? And Jingles, too, when you see him?"

She said she would.

After I got Malachi squared away, me and Tuck did a quick walk to the livery. Pete and Mace were already there. Ty had Jigsaw and Jelly and his mare saddled and waiting. Up the street, the fire was still blazing away, but it did not look so energetic as before.

I explained about Jelly, led him back to his stall for the stableman to unsaddle, and gave him a good-bye lemon drop and a kiss on his old pink nose. Tuck called for me to hurry, and I hopped up on Jigsaw.

Miss Elma Justice had followed us up from the Russ House as far as the corner of Fifth and Allen, and she waved to me. I waved back, with a cry of "Good-bye, Miss Justice! Good-bye!" as me and the boys cantered west out of Tombstone.

•   •   •

It was not the brightest night, being clouded over, and we had a hard time seeing clear. We rode single file, me in the lead, and our conversation kept pretty much to *watch out for that bush* or *look where you're goin', you fool* until after we crossed the San Pedro River. About then, the moon slipped free of its cover and we all relaxed a little. I reined in Jigsaw to let Tuck come up even with me. We were moving at a rambling jog, and that old Zeus horse of Tuck's had such a smooth gait that Tuck could smoke his pipe and never clench down on the stem.

"Are we safe to go so slow?" I asked.

"Ty seems to think there won't be much effort spent at putting a posse together, what with everybody so busy admiring the blaze. I'm in agreement with him, though I'd like to push ahead for a few hours before we camp."

"I know we've been busy keepin' from falling into arroyos and the like," I said, "but you've been awful quiet, for all that. I hope you're not mad at me because we had to leave town so quick. When I said that fire was not my fault, I didn't lie."

He took a puff on his pipe. "I'm not angry with you, Miss Gini."

"That's good, Tuck, but I think I am maybe a little ticked at you."

He twisted toward me and scrunched his brows together. They looked black in the moonlight. "Why so?"

"You said everybody was goin' to part company as soon as you got the Danahoes up to Queenie's place and laid Bobby to rest. You said we'd be safer that way. Well, it was not so safe for me and Zack, Zack especially. He got to be a good friend to me, and he got killed on account of there being just the two of us when those Apache stole up. And now I see that you and Mace and Pete never split up at all. If we had all been together—"

"I suggest you start consulting your brain before you open your mouth, Miss Gini," he said, angry and bitter and weary all at once. "I did say good-bye to the Danahoes, once it was apparent they were both on the mend. And I had to travel nearly to Alamogordo, New Mexico, before I shook Wilbeck's boys. I only hooked back up with Mace two weeks ago up around Hargrove Wells, and that was by accident. We picked up Pete in Tucson three days ago."

"Oh. Well, you didn't say . . ."

"You only knew Zack Ruggles for a couple weeks, Miss Gini. I worked, slept, sweated, cussed, and commiserated with him through some of the hardest, most godforsaken years of my life. I know you miss him sorely, but compare your grief to mine. And remember that I have only this afternoon heard about Zack's departure from this earthly plane. You've had several months to get used to the idea."

Right about then, I was almost wishing I had got killed back there with Zack. "I'm sorry, Tuck," I said after a couple minutes. "I mean that."

"It's all right, Miss Gini," he replied, so soft I could barely hear him over the swish and crackle the horses' legs made in the brush. "I didn't intend to be so harsh. I suppose you're feeling bad that you couldn't save him, either; but honey, if Zack Ruggles didn't spot that ambush, no living man could have. No living redheaded girl, either. Not even the daughter of Perry LeFleur."

He smiled a little on that, and I tried to smile back. I said, "Me and Sees Silver made a big stone cairn over Zack's resting place. I can find it again, easy. I thought after we got the gold, I'd like to haul a nice marker out there for him."

"I suppose I should write Eudora."

"I already did."

Tuck nodded, though he had turned away and would not

look at me. "Sees Silver is the one Ty told me about? The son of your Gam and Cuchillo Rojo?"

"Yes."

His pipe had gone out, and he tamped it with his thumb before he lit it again. "A marker would be a good thing, Miss Gini."

He didn't say any more, so I didn't either. I rode alongside him, feeling lower than a well-digger's boot sole and wondering how to make up for being so dang thoughtless. I even went so far as to consider telling him about Cañon de los Espejos and Spirit Kettle and that "shave-tale" business, by way of showing my contrition, but just then Stinky Pete loped his mount up along Tuck's other shoulder.

"S'long's we're havin' to pick our way through half the Territory in the middle of the night," he said across Tuck, "you might at least tell me 'bout Doc and Wyatt."

I shrugged. "What you want me to tell you?" I thought he was pretty rude to disturb Tuck, though I was kind of relieved he had butted in and kept me from spilling the beans.

"Well, what're they like?" He tried to look like he was bored and only asking for something to say, but I could tell he was real eager. "I heard Doc can dead-center-shoot a silver cartwheel in midair with a pocket gun. I heard Wyatt is as good with a Peacemaker." He patted his holster and looked smug. Both he and Mace carried Colt Peacemakers, too. Course, probably better than a quarter of the hip-rigging population wore the same brand of firearm, in one form or another; but by the look on his face, Pete seemed to think it made him and Wyatt Earp practically twin brothers. I didn't have the heart to tell him that Wyatt carried a Smith & Wesson half the time.

"I have never seen them shoot at coins," I replied, "so I can't say. Doc has a bad reputation, but he was always good to me and I have never actually seen him shoot a person. He has pulled his gun or a knife in my presence a few times, though. To tell the truth, it seems to me that both he and Wyatt use their pistols more to break skulls than to put slugs in them. Plus which, I thought you wanted to buy a ranch and marry your Miss Loula and raise some horses. That has not got much to do with gunfighting. Pig-thieving, either, come to think of it."

"Why, you little—"

"Are we heading the right direction, Miss Gini?" Tuck said around his pipe stem, and Pete shut up.

"Yes sir, we are. We can keep goin' this way for about another—"

"I dinna think Doc's a man ye ought to be admirin', boy." Ty had pushed his mare up to join us, though Mace still trailed behind. I guess he was still mad about having to leave town so fast and miss out on the rest of his fried chicken dinner. "Doc's a black-hearted scoundrel of the first water," Ty went on. "I'm not entirely certain the Earps are terrible trustworthy, either."

Pete twisted toward him. "Well, I heard that one time in Dodge, Wyatt shot—"

Tuck raised up his hand. "Would somebody be kind enough to tell an old man just who in glory these two gents might be to cause the three of you to gossip like a flock of biddy-hens?"

Pete looked pure astonished. "Cripes, Tuck!" he said. "Doc Holliday? Wyatt Earp? They're famous! Famous gunfighters from up in Kansas! I heard that—"

"We didn't get the Kansas newspaper in Yuma Prison, boy," Tuck said, real weary. "And don't tell me what you heard. My cranium is already overflowing with the lore of countless fast guns and keen shootists. I don't need to go adding any wet-behind-the-ears Quick-Draw Johnnies to the list. Miss Gini, if we are indeed going the right direction, I will just ride out ahead of you tongue-waggers. I need some quiet."

He goosed his horse a little and loped out about ten yards in front of us. He rode that way, just smoking his pipe and never looking back, until we stopped four hours later to make camp.

10

Cañon de los Espejos

Over the next days, we took a jog to the north here or a crook to the south there, but mostly we moved west: across grassy flatlands gone to hills polka-dotted with cactus and creosote and manzanita and mesquite; over those pink-gray, green-splotched hills to rocky crags where nothing grew, and back down again. In turn, we passed the markers from Mescal Mort's map: Bear Bite Hill, Squaw Circle Rock, Granite Needle, Jaguar Hole, and other places that had no names, just little pictures Mort had drawn. We did not see one other person after we left Tombstone, but we were soon a pretty nervous bunch, for the map was leading us deeper into the wild and mostly unknown area where renegade Apache were thought to headquarter. I had already been past fortunate on the occasion of my one run-in with Apache. I didn't think I could count on doing so well if I were to bump into another batch of them.

It was warming up fast. Malachi roused from his torpor and seemed to enjoy riding on my lap of an afternoon. Mace borrowed my Buffalo Bill book (Tyrone having finished it back in Tombstone), and in the evenings he and Pete traded off reading it and razzing Ty about that "Dakota Gambler" business. I do not think Pete truly believed it was all made up, for he took to tagging after Tyrone and pestering him nonstop about Bill Cody as well as Doc Holliday and Wyatt Earp.

By the third day, the last of the smoke's ill effects had worked clear of my lungs and I could have talked nonstop without having to cough. However, nobody did much conversing that day, as it poured from mid-morning till past sunset. We rode right along in it, water running from our hat brims in thick, cool drizzles, coursing down our dusters, soaking the horses and turning the desert into gravelly mire.

The next day we came to the place Mort Scobie had called Cañon de los Espejos. It was right on the Mex border. You kind of rode down into the first part without expecting it to be there. The canyon snuck up on you, funneled you inside real gradual, and all of a sudden there were stone walls all around and you didn't remember leaving the flatlands. The main canyon was broad, maybe a quarter-mile across at its widest, and cut down the middle by a wide, shallow stream, still muddy from the rain. There were chunks of brush scattered out along the banks, where recent flooding had discarded them.

I could see why somebody had named this place Cañon de los Espejos: that meaning Canyon of the Mirrors. The high walls were patched, here and there, with broad sweeps of some material so shiny that when the sun caught them right, they practically blinded you. Tuck said they were probably heavy mica deposits. He had put his pipe away sometime back, and carried his Winchester across his lap. Ty and both Danahoes had eased out their rifles as well. All were keeping a tense watch on the rims above.

After about a half-mile, the canyon walls began to creep closer on both sides. By the time we'd gone in a mile it was like a maze, and I was pretty dang busy keeping track of that map in my head and making sure we took the right forks. Passages opened here and there to side' canyons or caves, and the main of Cañon de los Espejos split and twisted and turned back on itself: sometimes wide, sometimes so narrow that the roof of the passage was closed up. In the broad passes, there was an abundance of mesquite and creosote, cactus, a few paloverde or cottonwood trees, and plenty of critters and birds. Once we surprised a pair of coyotes that were just about to make short work of a jackrabbit. They ran one way, the jackrabbit took off another, and we rode on, right down the center.

In one middling-sized passage, the sandy banks were pocked with javelina tracks. I hoped we wouldn't run into the brutes that had made them. Javelina are big, long-snouted wild hogs that are always in a bad mood, and they can be murderous nasty.

In the narrowest places, the roof closed up altogether and left us in darkness. There was little room for anything but rock walls and water and the smell of wet stone, and we rode single file, our horses hock-deep in the muddy stream and us holding matches aloft.

After over two hours of twisting through the maze, I waved to Tuck that we were to dogleg into a side passage to the left. I waved to him because he was a bit off from me, the canyon being some wider there, and he had been real specific about nobody raising their voice or talking more than necessary. He held up his hand to signal a general stop, and cozied Zeus up next to Jigsaw. "Are you sure you're going to be able to get us out of here, Pathfinder Kincaid?" he whispered.

"I'm gettin' you in, aren't I?"

"That's what I'm worried about."

"If you ask me, Tuck Brennan, it's a little late in the game to question my map-rememberin' skills. Mr. Mort Scobie wrote some pretty picky instructions at the bottom of his map for this last part, and I am followin' them to the letter even though he did not spell so good. The map says to turn at the opening with the two fat streaks of white quartz cutting across, which this one's got. Inside is something called Spirit Kettle." To tell the truth, I couldn't wait to see just exactly what kind of place would have a name like that.

Stinky Pete came up abreast of Tuck. "We been at——" He had forgot to keep his voice to a whisper, and all of a sudden we were surrounded by what seemed like a thousand Pete Danahoes, all saying *been at* over and over and over. Tuck gave him an awful dirty look. Ty's mare reared and snorted at the ruckus, which made it even worse. Once the noise died down, Pete leaned over and, whispering this time, said, "We been at this an awful long time. I'll bet she's gone and got us lost."

"If you don't trust me," I said soft, but in a serious tone, "go ahead and turn back. I will be happy for my part of the extra share you leave behind."

His dull boy's face wadded up into a scowl, but he followed along with the others when I reined Jigsaw into the quartz-marked side passage. Fifty feet of twisty, single-file riding later, and just like Mescal Mort had written on his map, the passage opened out into the place called Spirit Kettle.

It was a box canyon, oval-shaped, maybe fifty yards deep and forty yards wide, and the only way out was the way we'd come in. The floor was mostly flat and scrubby, just turned green with spring, and still puddly here and there. The walls were sheer pink granite with a few of those shiny mica patches. They shone like odd-shaped sheets of window glass where the light struck them.

Part of the place was deep in purplish shadow, for the walls curved in at the top to make a smooth overhang most of the way around and a good forty feet up. It looked like the canyon had once been a huge cave, and that God had just lifted the lid off. Or maybe He had punched it in—in several places, at distances from the walls of from fifteen to twenty feet, I could see sharp, rocky rubble heaped in long lines so neat it looked like it had been piled there for a fence. It had crumbled from the overhang above and fallen in chunks as small as gravel and as large as billiard tables. You could not have paid me a million dollars to let out a sharp shout in there.

"We're here," I whispered, and swung down off Jigsaw.

For a minute, everybody was real quiet while we listened to the canyon music. Outside, going down the main of Cañon de los Espejos, the wind had whistled in the narrow places and gusted in the wide. Inside Spirit Kettle, something about the way the desert breeze breathed over the rim made a soft drone, a little like the way a jug or bottle will make a note when you blow across the hole. But this was real subtle, and you felt it in your spine and the roots of your hair as much as heard it. It was scary and beautiful all at once.

"Well, we're someplace, all right," Mace said finally. He had spoken soft, but we could all hear his words echo gently, mixed in with the wind music.

"Cripes," whispered Pete. He rubbed at his arms.

Ty dismounted and patted his mare's neck. "Spirit Kettle," he whispered. He was smiling.

"How'd you know that?" I asked.

"Ye forget Sam Gonzales," Ty said softly. "Sam remembered Spirit Kettle fine enough, love. Said 'twas a place crowded with specters. A place even the Apache wouldn't enter." He paused a second and smiled, like he was imagining the wind's drone to be the voices of the dead, and I felt my arms break out in goose bumps. "I believe Sam had about the same reaction to the place as our young Pete here," he continued at last. "He just couldn't recall the gettin' back to it. Or Cañon de los Espejos."

"What now, Miss Gini?" Tuck's head was tilted up. He was watching the rims above.

"This way." I left Jigsaw ground-tied behind me and walked toward the north wall. Except for Tuck, who was still keeping an eye to the rims, the others followed.

Other than that "shave-tale" business and a general sort of direction toward the north, Mescal Mort Scobie had not been real clear as to exactly where the gold was. I did not know if it was buried or maybe jammed in one of the low fissures in the canyon wall, and to tell the truth, I did not know if we were searching for a sack or a strongbox or three of each. When we got near the rock face, I said, "We'd best spread out."

Mace whispered, "What are we lookin' for?"

"Danged if I know," I replied. "The only other thing on the map says 'shave-tale.' Maybe there's some rocks shaped like a lieutenant's bars. Somethin' military, maybe. But since Mort Scobie could not spell for spit, I am not goin' to stake my reputation on it."

"Seems to me you haven't got much reputation to *stake*," Mace muttered.

"Can't you hold off being spiteful for even five—"

"Here!" Tyrone hissed. He was about twenty feet from us, and he was pointing down at something in the brush. "Would ye be settlin' for a shavetail mule? Or what's left of one."

We were all with him by then. There at his feet, the weeds grown up through it, lay the skeleton of a mule. The bones had long since been picked clean, but there were still brittle scraps of leather halter draped around the sun-bleached skull. Crackled straps ending in dusty brass fittings drooped down through the white bars of its rib cage and trailed out into the brush.

Ty turned the skull over with the toe of his boot, then picked it up. His finger traced a line up its center to a small, round hole over one eye socket. "Where Mort Scobie's bullet went in," he said.

"Mescal Mort shot him?"

"Dinna be lookin' so appalled, Geneva m'love," he said. "'Twas only a mule."

I was kind of surprised to hear that come out of him. I whispered, "If I ever have a mule, Tyrone, remind me not to leave him in your charge."

"Fits with the story," said Tuck, who had come to stand behind us.

Since nobody had ever bothered to tell me the story, except for somebody stealing gold off somebody else and then losing it to Apaches, I felt kind of left out. I was about to demand a plain explanation for how this poor critter had got here in the first place when Mace snapped his fingers to get our attention. He was not more than ten or twelve feet away, near the canyon wall. Grinning, he pointed down into the weeds. Half under a mesquite bush was a broken wood crate, its short, splintery boards bleached to the same color as the desert floor. Something glinted dully between the cracks. Ty dropped the mule's skull and we all started over.

Pete got there first, a smile splitting his face. "This is it!" he said, and you could tell it was all he could do to keep his voice to a whisper. "Oh Jesus! Oh Lordy!"

Before Mace could stop him, he bent down and tore at the boards with his hands.

There was a short sharp hiss.

Pete jumped back, swung his arm to the side. The rattler was still hooked into his wrist by its fangs. Its dull, diamondbacked body whipped out to the side and slapped Mace across the face.

Pete screamed high and thin. The echoes were drowned by the groan of rock separating from the rim above and the crash as it hit the canyon floor. Mace grabbed for the snake, ripped it free, hurled it away. Tuck seized Pete by the shoulder and shouted, "Center! Get to the center!"

I grabbed Jigsaw and Zeus and ran. Ty caught his mare and Pete's gelding. Bucking wildly, reins flapping, Mace's horse skittered out of reach. Mace and Tuck, dragging Pete, just missed being clipped by a sheer wedge of granite.

Even with my hands over my ears, it sounded like the inside of an army cannon. All around, the rim broke away in curtains of rock that plummeted forty feet to crash and break on the canyon floor. Mace's horse ran too near a rockfall, got hit by a hunk of rock, fell, struggled back up. I could not hear Pete, but I could see his mouth opening again and again as he screamed. Tuck hit him hard in the jaw, and he went limp.

It may have been only a few minutes before the worst of the rockfall stopped, but it seemed like forever. By the time I got Jigsaw and Zeus quieted, Tuck had already tied a tourniquet around Pete's arm and cut a slash where the snake had struck. He sucked out blood and poison, spat red on the pale green weeds.

Mace held Pete's other hand, and even though Pete was still out, he said things like, "Hang in there, Pety. You're gonna be fine, just fine, you wait and see. You got your ranch money now, Pety." He just kept talking, even though you could tell by his face that he knew it was bad. Pete's wrist was bright red, and his hand and forearm had already turned purple and all mottled. His arm was swelling fast.

The air hung heavy, like it had absorbed part of the weight of those rocks, and the ground seemed unsteady under my feet. The low hum of wind music we'd heard when we first came in was a different pitch now, more jagged and raw and less sure, as if the earth had been wounded and was weeping over it. Mace's horse was cut bad across the croup. It stood about fifteen feet from me, head down, nostrils wide, eyes ringed with white.

Tyrone was not fazed. He thrust the rest of the horses' reins at me with a "Here, darlin'" and trotted past Tuck and the Danahoes. A goodly pile of rubble was laid in a high rocky hedge between us and the opening by which we'd entered Spirit Kettle, and Ty disappeared behind it. He was back in two minutes, and he was smiling.

"Is it clear?" I had tried to whisper, but the walls caught up the last part of it, and sighed *clear* over and over. A few more rocks, small ones this time, showered down over the long, piled rows of raw stone.

Ty nodded, held his finger to his lips, then made for the dead mule and the gold. I didn't know how he could be so cool. My legs were still shaking and I had a taste in my mouth like metal. I made myself close my eyes and take two deep breaths. The horses were still a little spooky but they had settled down enough to be left alone, so I dropped their reins and followed after Ty. Tuck and Mace did not need my help with Pete, and I thought if I stayed still much longer, I might throw up.

The mule's skeleton was gone, buried under huge hunks of granite. But the line of rockfall from above had been narrow, and the gold and its broken crate were untouched. Ty had already kicked away a few stray rocks and the rest of the broken boards. He stood over the prize he'd uncovered. There was a whole different kind of smile on his face than I'd seen there before. In his hand was a thick bar of solid gold. In the weeds at his feet, dusted by what was left of the sun-rotted crates, lay a pile of maybe forty bars just like it. He turned the single bar in his hands like it was the only thing in the world. He stroked it like a lover.

"Tyrone?"

I jumped. I had not heard Tuck come up. Neither had Ty, for he whipped around fast and his hand went to his gun. He remembered himself right away, though, for he relaxed just as quick as he had stiffened. He held the bar up so Tuck could see. "A lovely sight, isn't it, Tucker darlin'?"

Tuck nodded, kind of curt. I thought he'd be more excited, but all he said was, "Let's get packed up. Doubt I got enough venom out to save him, but either way the boy's liable to be off his head for a while, and that means noisy." He looked up at the remaining stone overhang, high above. "This is no place for fever dreams. I want to be well shed of this whole canyon by nightfall."

It turned out there were thirty-six bars in all. They were heavy, and we split them out between us so as not to wear down any one horse more than necessary. Mace's horse was not hurt too bad after all, though he was still awful jumpy. I told Mace that once we were clear of Cañon de los Espejos, I'd see what I could do about a poultice for the wound, though it looked to me like I would likely have to lay in a few stitches, too.

Pete was still unconscious, and after we got the gold divvied out, we tied him across his saddle. It fell to me to lead him. He rode the buckskin Bashful Ben Lamar had traded for his sorrel back in Horsethief Basin, and it was a good, steady pony. A cautious one, too, for as we wove, single file, through the passage from Spirit Kettle to the main of Cañon de los Espejos, that horse was real careful not to scrape Pete's bobbing head against the walls.

Tuck seemed even more watchful on the way out than he had been on the way in, if that were possible. "In canyon

like this, Miss Gini, night can come as quickly as blowing
out a lamp."

"I don't see what difference that makes, Tuck," I said.
"Apache never attack at night, anyhow."

His eyes flickered between the rims and the path ahead,
never rested on me. He said, "Your Gam tell you that?"

"No, but—"

"You read too many dime novels, Miss Gini."

As we traveled the winding canyon path, both Tuck and
Ty kept their heads twisting like nervous birds. Where the
width of the canyon permitted it, me and Mace rode on
either side of Pete. He already had some fever, and though
he was out cold and therefore quiet, beads of sweat glistened
across his forehead and the back of his shirt was soaked.

It took the better part of two hours to thread our way
through the worst of the maze, me in the lead, remembering
the map in reverse. At last we entered a wide, brushy bell in
the canyon. It was maybe two hundred and fifty yards long
and half as wide, with thick brush on both sides of the rocky
stream banks and a big stand of ironwood at the far end. I
was relieved to realize there would be only one more narrow
passage after this before we were on our way out of Cañon
de los Espejos. Those skinny places made me awful
nervous. I kept imagining Apache in every shadow and
crevice.

We had gone about halfway across when Tuck held up his
hand. We all reined in and waited. He sat real still, as if he
were sniffing for something almost as much as looking, and
then he wheeled his horse and shouted, "Go!"

He pointed toward the ironwood trees. We kicked our
horses into a gallop. I reached over and lashed Pete's horse
across the rump. Jigsaw was fast, and that buckskin of
Pete's was no slouch. We jumped to the lead right off, but
we hadn't gone two strides before the shooting began.

The first thin cracks of rifle fire turned into a barrage that echoed into a blanket of sound. I was almost to the ironwoods when I saw a glint of sun on steel in their midst. I hauled Jigsaw sharp to the right. The others saw, too, and followed suit.

Tuck and Ty fired up toward the rim, pumping their guns almost faster than I could see. Just as Mace twisted in his saddle to fire back toward the passage, his horse stumbled and went to its knees. He pitched forward, rifle sailing; landed in the stream; nearly got trampled when his horse leapt up and ran past him, all fast as a wink. Tuck shouted "Here, boy!" and raced toward him, arm out.

I kept heading for the brush, for a stand of paloverde. Ty had the same idea, and he was going to beat us all there. His mare galloped full out. She was two leaps from green cover when she screamed and went down. Ty vaulted clear, scrambled into the brush.

I wheeled Jigsaw again. He swung so fast his rump slammed into Pete's buckskin, and Pete's lead rope was ripped from my hand. At a lope, the buckskin splashed across the steam, Pete's head banging against the stirrup. I reined Jigsaw after him. As he spun, half-rearing, I felt a sting above my ear, and then I was falling.

I didn't open my eyes right away. I could tell that I was leaned up against a rock and that we must be back in the brush, for I could feel bushes stickering my arm and one side of my face. I knew the sun must be in my eyes, too, for the inside of my lids were reddish orange. My head pounded something fierce. I didn't know how long I had been on the ground. There were scuffling sounds, like nervous horse hooves skittering in gravel. Far-off voices spoke in Mex. One said, "That one, get that one."

Something heavy landed on me. I slitted open my eyes at

the jolt and found Pete across my lap. He was coming
round, though he didn't seem to know where he was. His
arm was so swollen it was about to split his sleeve, his eyes
were heavy-lidded and unfocused, and his breath came in
thin wheezes. His lips moved and he tried to say "Mama?"
but not much sound came out.

Careful not to move my head or body and therefore give
sign I was awake, I looked up. I must have been out for
some time and Tuck and the others must have put up a
lengthy fight, for the sun had mostly disappeared over the
far rim of the canyon. Deep shadow had overtaken most of
it and nearly reached us at the far wall. I figured it'd be
completely dark inside a half hour, but right then, the last
rays were blasting into my eyeballs and casting an orange
haze over everything around me. I heard voices, gruff and
low, talking in Mex.

I had expected to find Apache ripping their way through
our possessions. Instead, against the glare of the sun, I saw
five *bandidos*. One, dressed in a black shirt and black pants
with conchos all down the legs, was busy tying Mace
back-to-back with Tyrone under a paloverde. Tyrone was
unconscious, and both he and Mace were gagged. A large
bloodstain darkened Mace's pants leg, and he sagged
against his ropes. Tyrone's head was down, but what I could
see of it was bloody. Both of them looked beat to squash.

A second *bandido* stacked kindling on the rocky stream
bank, about fifteen feet back from the water. He had a fire
started. It was smoking like crazy because of the wood
being so damp.

The third bandit stood over Pete and me. He was armed
like there was a war on, with two pistols that I could see, a
bowie knife strapped to his leg, and a rifle slung across his
back. He leaned on a second rifle, which I recognized as
Tuck's Winchester. He was paying less attention to us than

to the fourth and fifth of his ambushing pals. One was in white. The other, who wore a dirty blue shirt, had a long scar down one side of his face. They, like the others, had ammunition belts strapped across each shoulder and pistols stuck in their belts and holsters. They had Tuck down on the ground in a little clearing in the undergrowth about twenty feet from us. His hands were tied behind him, and they were beating on him without mercy. They were laughing.

Without moving or opening my eyes any wider than I had to, I glanced out over the canyon. In the shadows across the stream, I could just make out three more of the bandits as they rounded up Jigsaw and Mace's horse. I could not see our other mounts, but noises to the right told me they were tethered not too far away.

Scarface and White Shirt were still pounding on Tuck, except now they weren't laughing. I think they were mad because he wouldn't cry out. White Shirt stood up and started to kick him in the ribs. I glanced up at the guard over Pete and me. He was still watching the beating. They had not bothered to tie either Pete or me, thinking we were either dead or no threat. Scarface kicked Tuck again. That time, Tuck grunted loud with the pain. Our guard laughed and called, in Mex, "The old rooster is not such a tough bird." He leaned Tuck's Winchester up against a rock and unclipped a canteen from his belt.

Slow, so as not to draw attention, I ran my hand down Pete's back. I couldn't turn my head without the movement giving me away, and I prayed real hard that they had neglected to disarm him.

My hand crawled down Pete's sweat-sodden shirt, crept over the small of his back to his gunbelt, inched along the nubs of cartridge loops. But when my fingers curved round his hip to meet his holster, that old Peacemaker of his was long gone.

I froze when the bandit in the black shirt stood up from where he had tied Mace and Ty.

"Leave the old man," he shouted, in Mex, at Tuck's tormentors. "Help Vasquez with the fire."

I risked a quick turn of my head to get my bearings. The east wall of the canyon was maybe sixty feet behind me. The brush grew dense enough that I thought I might be able to hide and get off a few shots if I could skinny round our guard and grab the Winchester. The sun was leaving us fast, too. The other side of the canyon was already shadowed thick enough to be night. Darkness had pushed across the stream and overtaken Vasquez and his smoky fire, and likely wouldn't take more than a few minutes to creep over us, too. The night would be my friend if I could get to cover.

But Pete lay across my lap, heavy as a rock. I knew I couldn't squirm from under him unnoticed. For just a minute I got kind of mad at Pete: not because he'd been tossed across me, which he couldn't help, but because he didn't carry a concealed knife or pocket gun like his big hero, Doc Holliday.

White Shirt and Scarface walked off toward their buddy and left Tuck, unconscious, sprawled in the dirt. Black Shirt, who looked to be the leader, called to our guard. After a glance at me and Pete, during which I held my breath, he walked off, clipping his canteen back in place. He forgot the Winchester entirely and left it leaned up, about ten feet from me. He and Black Shirt dragged Tuck over by Mace and Tyrone and gagged him.

Just then I heard another man call out. I chanced a quick head-turn to the right, and saw him and another villain over where I'd heard horse noises. The rest of their mounts and ours were picketed there, all right, and there were two more *bandidos* with them. That brought it to ten all together. They were going through Mace's saddlebags.

The hombre that had shouted held something in the air: one glistening gold bar.

Well, they all ran right over and commenced ripping through our things. They were crowing and congratulating themselves and tossing gold bars into a sack on the ground.

Night fairly raced toward us. One minute I could see Tuck and the others, the next there was nothing but their purplish outlines. Nobody was paying me any mind. I began to worm my way out from under Pete. He was burning up, drifting in and out of consciousness and still mumbling, but so soft and thin and breathless that nobody but me had heard. I had seen folks who were snake-bit before, but I had never seen one taken so fast by it. I figured that even if Pete lived, he'd more than likely lose his arm. His fingers were as fat and tight as sausages and had turned purple. They'd turn black next.

I got him slid down as far as my knees. The bandits went through Tyrone's saddlebags, pulled out the gold bars, dropped his clean clothes in the dirt. I slithered my left leg free. Atop me, Pete started to cry.

Scarface yanked my satchel off Jigsaw and ripped it open. I freed my right leg down to the knee. My boot top caught on Pete's gunbelt, and I began to rock him, to get him the rest of the way off. The movement brought him round a little more. His throat must have been closed up awful bad, because when he gasped for air he made a loud whistling sound that started my heart practically pounding through my chest. I clamped a hand over his mouth and held myself still. One bandit twisted round and stared at Mace and Tyrone for a second, then went back to crowing over the gold along with the others.

The sun was almost gone. Like an indigo blanket, shadow moved up me and Pete, washed blue-black murk up the bandit's legs, edged toward the canyon wall behind us.

Scarface held up Malachi, said something I couldn't quite catch. They all laughed, and he threw Malachi into the darkening brush, just like he was a rock and not a critter who could get hurt. Then he turned my satchel upside down and dumped it out.

My right leg came free all of a sudden. I scrambled to my feet and jumped toward Tuck's Winchester. At the same instant, Pete sucked in air again, so loud that it sounded like a scream going backwards.

They all wheeled, guns raised. I grabbed the Winchester and hurled myself back into the bushes as their first volley exploded. From the corner of my eye I saw Pete jerk and spasm as their bullets took him, and knew I had just the same as killed him. I scrambled as fast as I could. Lead spatted into the gravelly dirt all around me, sang off the boulders and canyon wall, sliced chunks off the bushes, filled my nose and eyes with dust and the stench of creosote. I stayed on my belly, worked my way deeper into the undergrowth and prayed Jesus I wouldn't come face-to-face with a rattler or scorpion. I felt my calf jerk and burn, and knew I'd been shot. I kept crawling.

All of a sudden, they stopped. The last echo faded just as the last rays of sun failed. It was just the way Tuck had said: like somebody blowing out a lantern.

I waited.

They seemed in no hurry.

Some of them had torches, all of them had guns. A few of them were smiling. They spaced themselves out to form a big U, with the canyon wall closing the top, and me trapped in the center. Then, their legs swishing the undergrowth, they began to close in.

I knew I was bleeding bad. My bucks were sticky on my calf and getting stiff, and I was feeling weaker all the time.

I had heard stories about the things *bandidos* did. Some were more cruel than an Apache or Yaqui, and judging by the way I'd seen them treat Tuck, these boys fell into that category. If they did not torture and kill us tonight, they would do it in the morning. Either that, or they'd slit our eyelids and leave us staked out for the sun and the coyotes and the ants.

I was not going to die that way.

I eased my bad leg up under me, gathered myself, and popped straight up, firing.

My first shot took out Scarface. He went down with a whoop, torch flying, as I cranked another cartridge into the chamber. I took a slug in the shoulder just as I got off my second shot. The impact knocked me off-balance, and I missed. The Winchester gave me no more than a click when I pulled the trigger the third time.

Black Shirt waved his men to put their weapons down. He was grinning. He said, "Maybe we have a little sport, *compadres*."

They all started toward me.

I flipped Tuck's Winchester around and took the barrel in both hands, thinking to use the stock like a club. When they closed in near enough, I made myself ignore the fire in my shoulder and leg. I started swinging. I missed more than I hit and I didn't have much strength in that one arm, but before they wrenched the rifle away, I had got one fella a good blow to the head, and butted another in the belly hard enough that he grunted and went to his knees.

They dragged me, kicking and hollering, toward the stream and their fire. It smoked a thick white plume straight up, and threw a circle of light big enough to just reach the paloverde where Tuck, Ty, and Mace were bound.

I stumbled and fell next to the fire. My shoulder burned as bright as the flames, and I could feel something grating around in there. I didn't want to cry, but I couldn't stop my eyes from watering.

Black Shirt reached down, grabbed a handful of my hair, and hauled me up by it. I swung at him with my good arm. He twisted away from the blow, laughing, and kicked my legs out from under me so that I dangled by my hair.

Behind me, I heard somebody shout that Rodriguez was dead. I guessed he was the one I'd shot.

I got my feet under me again. Black Shirt yanked me hard to one side and I screamed. I half-expected to see his hand come away all full of red hair and blood. He said, in American, "I am a good-natured man, señorita, and up to now I have had a fortunate day. Why do you wish to cause me such trouble?"

"I will cause you more if you don't let us go."

He laughed, and I spat at him.

That earned me a slap across the face. To tell the truth, I was hurting so much everyplace else that I barely felt it, but I remember tasting blood in my mouth.

Black Shirt said, "I give you first to Castillo, because you have killed his cousin. After that, we share."

As the others laughed, he gave me a shove and I fell backwards into the arms of the one called Castillo. He grabbed my bad shoulder, spun me around so hard I cried out, then gave me a good stare. He was sunbaked and squat, with lank, dirty hair and mossy teeth. He didn't look like he was mourning his cousin one little bit.

He dug thick hard fingers into my shoulder. I beat at him with one hand, tried to twist away, cursed and yelled.

Somebody grabbed my legs. I felt them jerk off my boots, tear at the laces on my britches, yank them down over my knees and feet.

I remember crying out "Gam! Gam!" in a voice hoarse with screaming, and then Castillo hauled me to my feet again. When he realized my leather shirt wouldn't come off except over my head, he pulled out his knife and held it to my throat. Hands grabbed me from behind, and he began to slice open my blood-soaked shirtfront.

I felt the tip of his blade skitter down over my collarbones, between my breasts. I tried to throw myself forward on it, to die right there without any more hurt or humiliation. But the hands from behind restrained me, and I didn't do more than scratch myself on the point of his blade.

He sawed his way through the rest of the buckskin with a fast, sick, tearing sound, and then he held the sides of it open and looked at me.

"Scrawny," he said in Mex. "But better than nothing."

Of what happened next, the clearest picture I have is of that devil Castillo: Castillo laughing with his gray-moss teeth while the others shoved me down to lie in the hard, sharp gravel; Castillo ripping off his gunbelt and tugging at the buttons on the front of his pants; and then the arrow.

I will remember that till the day I die, the way he was leering one minute and dead the next, with his willie in his hand and that arrow through his throat and the blood spurting.

The others dropped me and scattered. It got real confusing about then. Shots were fired. I heard screams. I grabbed Castillo's knife, and crawled, bare-naked except for the flapping top half of my bucks, toward Tuck and the others.

I reached Tuck first and pulled off his gag. His old eyes were wet with tears. As I sawed through his bonds, he said, "Oh Gini, Miss Gini."

The shots came faster. I could see the far-off explosions of rifle fire, like quick flurries of fireflies. I cut Mace free. He had a terrible look on his face—hurt and scared and shamed and mad as hell, all at once. Somebody else screamed, and then the scream was cut short. A stray slug sang into the paloverde, and a broom handle–thick branch fell down across us. We heard the horses scrambling, then the sound of galloping hoofbeats: three, maybe four horses. Tuck and Mace ran toward the fire and grabbed weapons off dead or dying *bandidos*. There were three in the firelight circle by then, counting Castillo.

Another scream echoed through the darkness before galloping hoofbeats drowned the sound. Tuck yanked a serape off one of the dead and flung it at me. I dropped it over my head, finished cutting Tyrone's bonds.

Ty jumped up. He ran to a wounded Mex who was making for the bushes, booted him in the ribs, grabbed his rifle, then darted off into the brush without so much as a look or word.

I heard a thud, two more shots, the sound of another horse galloping away; and then Jigsaw, trailing a picket line with three more horses attached, came thundering into the light. They swerved around the fire, headed right at us. Tuck and Mace dove one way, I dove the other and curled myself into a ball. Jigsaw jumped and cleared me. The next two horses swung out to the side, but the last one came straight for me. I rolled, but a hind hoof dealt a sharp blow to my bad arm.

They disappeared into the dark. I heard them splash through the stream, and then it was quiet.

I sat up, wrapped in that dirty serape and holding my arm. Tuck looked at Mace, then they both looked at me.

Mace breathed, "Sweet Jesus."

Tuck came right over and put his arm round me, careful not to hurt my shoulder. He flinched when he moved. I swallowed hard and said, "They have broke your ribs. I can bind them for you."

A soft chuckle came from deep inside him. He said, "Yes,

I imagine you can, Miss Gini," and then he kissed my forehead.

Mace crawled over to us. A fresh flow of blood from his thigh wound blossomed dark over his already stained pants leg. "What the hell happened?" He peered out into the black. "Where's Ty?"

"Trying to get his gold back, if I know Tyrone O'Neill," Tuck said. We all looked up at the sound of rifle fire, distant and thinly echoed. "Let's take ourselves into some cover. We're not out of this yet." Grunting, he helped me stand, and we started hobbling back into the brush, me and Tuck half-carrying each other. Mace limped after us, and when we passed his brother's body, he paused to lean down and cross poor Pete's arms over his chest and close his eyes. It seemed an odd thing to do, what with so much danger all around; but I understood, and I pretended not to see.

He had caught us up and we were well past the firelight when a voice called out, "Kin-Kay! Neva Kin-Kay! Do you live, my sister?"

I had stopped crying before, but that started me all over again. Mace's mouth dropped open at what he must have thought was my genuine stupidity, but I called right back, "I live, my brother!"

Tuck fought me on it some, but I made him take me back toward the fire. I was dizzy and I had to concentrate hard on getting one foot put in front of the other. But we made it, and just as we stepped into the circle of light, Sees Silver entered from the other side. It might have been because my vision was some blurred, but he seemed bigger and rougher than when I'd last met him. He was stripped and greased for battle, but Gam's garnet and gold-filigree necklace still glittered round his throat. In one hand he carried Zack's Henry rifle. In the other, he clutched Malachi, who snaked his head out to blink at the fire.

He held Malachi forward and said, "I have found the not-for-eating animal of Glows Like Sun."

"I thank you, my brother," I said at just about the exact moment the fire started to spin and my legs wobbled out from under me.

11

For Love of Ty

It was still dark when I woke.

Someone had fed the fire, and it cast a wide pool of light, of which we were at the edge. The *bandidos'* bodies had been dragged off, and several Apache braves dozed by the fire. One of them was snoring. I recognized him as Roberto, the one who had almost made dinner out of Malachi the day Zack died.

I was wrapped to the chin in blankets, and my leg and shoulder thudded and burned something fierce. Mace was to my left, sound asleep on his back, mouth open. His features had gone soft with sleep, and with the firelight washing gently over him, he looked real sweet, just like a kid.

Tuck was to my right, nearest the fire. He had one arm cocked back to pillow his head as he stared up at the stars. I wondered if he was going over their names in his head. When I stirred, he said, "It'll be another half hour till dawn, Miss Gini. Why don't you get a little more rest?"

I fingered the chain at my neck and found the topaz ring strung on it. From what I could feel, it was the only thing I had on under those blankets. "Where's Ty? Is he back? Who bound up my shoulder? And where are my clothes?"

Tuck smiled. "Well, Miss Pandora, I guess you're feeling better." With a grunt and a grimace, he hauled himself up into a sit. His shirt and vest were off and the top half of his union suit was unbuttoned. His ribs had been bound with cloth strips.

He saw me looking, and said, "Mace wrapped me. And he did a fine job, Doctor Kincaid, so don't go making faces."

"What about his leg?"

Tuck rooted out his pipe and match tin. "Clean wound, not much to it."

"And Pete?" My head filled with the image of him, agonized with rattler venom, spasming as the bullets took him. "I killed him, didn't I?"

He took hold of my arm, through the blanket. "Don't ever say that again."

"But I—"

"You did what you did. We all do what we do."

He puffed on his pipe, and the bowl glowed red. Sweet homely smoke, smelling like Tuck and safety, curled up white against the night sky. "They think awfully high of you, Miss Gini. Sees Silver and his bunch, I mean. Unusual."

I tried to shrug, but my shoulder wouldn't let me. "Apache honor the woman's clan. Gam said so."

He puffed again. "Clan, yes. Women, no. Most times, *Shis-Inday* don't bother to—"

"What's *Shis-Inday*?" I didn't say it as good as him.

"That's what the nations call themselves. Means Men of the Forest. Long ago, the Zuni named them Apache. It means Enemy."

Gam had never told me that. I said, "What don't they bother with?"

He tried for a smoke ring, but there was too much breeze and it fluttered into tatters. "Naming females. They call them things like Daughter of Smiling Coyote or Bold Spear's Woman. Treat them like slaves and barely mourn their passing after they're worked to death. 'It was only a woman that died,' I've heard them say. No, he thinks high of you. They all thought high of your Gam."

"How would you know that?"

He rubbed at his knee, studied it. "Honey, I knew her when she lived with Cuchillo Rojo. He and I were old acquaintances. I wouldn't call us friends, but I had a steadfast respect for him."

I tried to sit up, but my shoulder pounded so bad I sagged back down. Tears welled out of my eyes, ran hot down my temples. "Tuck Brennan, you are making me pretty dang sore at you!"

He daubed my face with his long-john sleeve. "Don't go fidgeting, Miss Gini, or you'll tear yourself open again. I did some pretty fancy backwoods doctoring on you, and I'd hate to see it go to waste."

The pain eased off some and so did my waterworks, during which time another Apache appeared by the fire and poked the sleeping braves to wake them. He must have been out in the brush, on guard, and he came up so silent that I didn't realize he was there till Roberto stopped snoring with a grunt.

The guard pointed at me and said something to Tuck that sounded like, *"Neva Kin-Kay to-tats-an see-dah, Brennan."* Tuck nodded at him, and he stepped back into the darkness.

"That was Thistle Rope. You'll be comforted to know he says you're not dead."

"Thistle Rope? You know, Tuck, for somebody who is always sayin' as how nobody remembers him, you sure get recollected by a lot of people." I stared straight up, at the stars. I found a constellation Tuck had showed me once before, and fixed my eyes on it. "How good did you know her? Gam, I mean."

"Enough to admire her. They all admired her. She walked proud, with her head held up and all that flaxen hair flowing down her back like Godiva's cloak. Cuchillo Rojo's people would always part to let her pass. He gave away his other wives to honor her. She was a great woman."

I gave up on the stars and turned my head to stare at him. "If you were so all-fired admirin' of her, why didn't you get her out of there?"

He held my gaze for a long minute before he said, real soft, "You're very young, Miss Gini."

Mace sat up and leaned across me. The sleep gone, he looked grown-up again. His gaze went to Pete's body, wrapped in blankets near the edge of the brush. For a second I thought he was about to cry, his eyes went that soft, but then he caught me looking at him. Quick, his features went hard and he scowled at me before he turned to Tuck. "Where's Tyrone?" he whispered. "Where's the gold?"

I said, "How long have you been awake, listenin' to other people's private conversations?"

They ignored me. Around his pipe stem, Tuck said, "Might be halfway to the California Gulf. Might be dead. As for the gold, it's either with Tyrone or gone. Maybe both. How's your leg?"

"Like the wrong end of a branding iron."

There was a cry I took at first to be some night-hunting bird. Then I realized it was a human, screaming far off, shrill and high. The scream came again and I shivered. Over by the fire, one Apache chuckled and elbowed his pal.

Tuck's pipe had gone out, and he tapped the bowl against his palm to empty it. "Our friends caught themselves some *bandidos* a few canyons over." The sound repeated, a short strangled burst of human pain; then again, long and drawn out. "It was worse earlier," he said, without looking at me.

I tried to haul myself up again, but my shoulder didn't let me get far. "Got to stop them."

Mace shook his head, and a shock of dark hair fell down

in his eyes. "You want to help those bandits after what they were gonna do to you? After what they did to Pete?"

It came again, thin and horrible, but this time the sound was cut off at its height.

Tuck said, "I imagine that's the last of it."

Dawn was coming. Our side of the canyon was still pitch dark, but a soft orange-pink haze had begun to tease the far rim. Then, with a suddenness you could almost hear, the sun connected with those mica patches. I had never witnessed such blinding brightness in all my born days.

Mace blinked and rubbed at his eyes. I guessed, like me, he was seeing yellow-white glare spots on the inside of his lids. Tuck, who was the only one of us smart enough to look away before it happened, threw back his blanket and put his pipe away. He said, "You think you can stand up, son?"

Mace and Tuck buried Pete while I looked on from my blankets. They piled the site high with rocks, just the way me and Sees Silver had done for Zack's grave; and then, voice cracking, Tuck spoke some words. Mace turned his back and cried into his sleeve. I bawled pretty good, too, though I admit it was as much guilt and pain as mourning. Tuck's eyes were bright with wet, but he didn't weep tears: at least, none that he let me see.

A few more Apache wandered back, some of them leading strayed horses. Another group straggled in with a half-dozen jackrabbits and some doves, which they proceeded to dress out and rig on spits over the fire. By about ten o'clock, it was the three of us and a dozen braves, but still no sign of Sees Silver or Tyrone. I took to hanging on to that topaz ring all the time, like it was a talisman that would make Ty come back safe.

Tuck found my satchel and stuffed my belongings back in it, and if he was shocked at my red saloon dress, he didn't say anything. The clothes were some trampled, but nothing was ruined except for a pair of drawers. Tuck ripped them into bandages when he changed my shoulder dressing. He also found a half-full bottle of some *bandido*'s mescal, and made me drink some of it. It helped some, though I had to close my eyes lest the sight of the worm in the bottle make me gag.

The last three braves, Sees Silver and Manuelito included, rode into the canyon around noon. Tyrone was with them. He looked dog-tired and dirty, and there was still dried blood on his face from the beating he'd taken the day before. He was riding a Mex horse. After he tied it to the new picket line, he fetched himself some leftover rabbit from the sticks near the fire and sat down with us under the paloverde. Well, the rest of them were sitting. I was still down flat and wrapped in blankets. Tuck said I was to stay still, which was why he had so far refused to give over my britches and a shirt. "To insure your compliance, Miss Gad-About Kincaid," he said. I was kind of mad at him, but I kept my trap shut.

Anyhow, I was so glad to see Tyrone that I could have kissed him. I might have, too, if my shoulder hadn't hurt so bad and Mace and Tuck hadn't been looking on. Mace was full of questions, but Ty didn't even say hello till he'd eaten. He licked at the last rabbit leg bone, tossed it over his shoulder, and said, "'Twas tasty, but the heathen have got nothin' on ye in the culinary arts, Geneva."

Tuck shook his head, and Mace said, "What were you doin' out there all night, anyhow? You didn't seem real burdened down with our gold when you rode in."

Tyrone pulled out a handkerchief and wiped the rabbit grease from his mouth. Some dried blood came off, too, and he scowled at the stain on his linen. "I'm in dire want of a bath. And you're right, Mason. The pirates eluded me. By

me own tally, from countin' the bodies—and pieces there-
of—on the way back, I'd say three of the blackguards
scooted free. That bullion's likely deep into Sonora by
now."

Mace glared at him, like it was his fault the *bandidos*
robbed us in the first place. "You don't seem real upset,
Tyrone, 'specially for a fella who risked his hide for it."

"Dame Fortune's whim, boy-o," Tyrone said with a
shrug. Mace's nasty tone, like most everything else, just
rolled off his back. "Sometimes ye win the pot, sometimes
ye walk out with nothin' but the pants ye wore in. You're
lookin' chipper, Geneva darlin'."

He smiled, bright as sun on canyon mica.

The Apache pulled out mid-afternoon. They took the
bandidos' horses and all their possessions, but they left our
things untouched. Tuck told me this was a sign of great
respect, since most Apache he'd known would steal their
own brothers blind and brag on it. As the others rode out,
Sees Silver squatted next to me and pressed something into
my hand: Gam's garnet earrings.

"These are for woman to wear," he said. "You keep, to
remember our mother. And me."

I thanked him for the earrings, and I thanked him for my
life, too. For all our lives.

He made a guttural sound, then jabbed a finger at the string
of horses Roberto was leading along the stream bank. "We
see smoke, we come. Now we have new horses—*host-kon-
ay*." He held up his fingers to show six. "Also guns. You
were brave, Neva Kin-Kay. I saw you kill. I saw you wounded
in battle, with honor. I saw you spit in the black-shirted
dog's face."

He leaned toward me, and his face got extra serious. He
said, "I tell you now that all will know of you. All will hear

of my sister with hair the color of red rock after rain. All
will hear how you fought, and all will honor you. If you
were bigger, you could come with us."

"And be *Shis-Inday*?"

I think he almost smiled.

I closed my hand over the earrings. "I will never forget
you."

He looked around quickly, like he was making sure no
one could overhear, then added, "You should know this,
Neva Kin-Kay. Your friend in the black coat, who rode
through the canyon last night? I think he is crazy."

"Tyrone? Crazy?"

"I think so, my sister. He shoots at ghosts and makes the
spirits angry. I think he has a bad spirit in him."

"But—"

He stood up. "I go now. Guard yourself, my sister."

He hopped up on his pony and splashed down the middle
of the stream to join the others. They disappeared into the
ironwoods. It was the last time I ever saw him.

Ty had been down at the water washing up and, as Sees
Silver cantered out of sight, he walked over to me. "Havin'
a bit of a so-long pow-wow with the redskinned side of the
family, m'love?"

"I guess. Tyrone, do you believe in ghosts?"

He grinned and ran his fingers through wet hair, black as
patent leather. "Of course, darlin'. The Irish *invented* ghosts
and fairies. We require 'em. And what a question for ye to
be askin'! I'm thinkin' Tucker's been givin' ye a wee drop
too much of the mescal."

Tuck and the others built a pyre over Ty's poor mare and
burnt her up to keep her from the scavengers. It took more
than a whole day, and it was awful. There is nothing worse

than the smell of cooking horse, especially a horse you knew and admired.

It was four days before Tuck thought I was healed up enough to try riding, and even then, he held us all down to a walk. I didn't ask where we were going. I didn't much care. My calf, which had been shot straight through (although shallow and toward the outside), was on the mend, but my poor shoulder still pained me awful with every move. Tuck gave me the ball he dug out, for a souvenir.

Traveling slow like that, and slower the next day on account of a downpour, it was four days of plodding before we got anywhere near civilization; and even that was not so civilized.

Around nightfall we came to an abandoned adobe. Tuck said he knew it from a long time ago. He called the place Joshua Tree, after the big one growing out front of it, and said the building had been tumbledown ever since he could remember. Judging from its condition—roofless, one mud brick wall busted down to chair level, and the rest going slow to crumble and melt—it might have been there a couple hundred years, left over from some Spanish or Mex pioneer. But it gave some shelter and was free of snakes and centipedes and the like.

We kindled a small fire on the floor of the adobe. After a dinner Tuck cooked under my direction, Mace put away his knife (with which he'd been picking his teeth) and said, "I'll be goin' off in the morning."

I set aside the little piece of prickly pear I'd been hand-feeding Malachi. "Goin' off where?"

"Mendacity, I'd hazard." It was Tuck. Pipe in hand, he sat on what was left of the caved-in wall. In the night behind him, the full moon—immense and soft yellow—barely cleared the horizon. Before it was Tyrone's silhouette, a black shape wandering between that big old Joshua tree and the horses. He was whistling, low and soft; I think it was "The Poacher's Wake." I remembered what Sees Silver had said about bad spirits, and rubbed down the gooseflesh on my arms.

"Got to go home, tell Ma about Pete," Mace was saying. "Loula, too." He dug into his pocket, pulled out Pete's watch, flipped open the case, and peered at it. He'd been fiddling with that watch, or Pete's pocketknife, most all the time since Pete got killed. "They're both gonna take it terrible hard." He passed me the watch. It was the first time he'd let it out of his hands. "That's Loula Mahoney," he said.

To be honest, I was not much interested in Loula right then. I took a look anyhow, to be polite, since Mace had been nearly civil to me since his brother got killed. Also because it seemed like he meant it as an honor.

Loula was light-haired, like Pete, and had a soft face. She didn't look more than thirteen or fourteen. She didn't appear real bright around the eyes, either, and I figured she and Pete had likely been well matched. "She looks real nice," I said, and handed it back. "I will be proud to meet her."

"You're going with Mace, Miss Gini?" Tuck said.

Mace jammed the watch back in his pants and snarled "The hell she is!" like he'd got his finger caught in a spring trap.

So much for polite. "Well, excuse me for livin', Mace Danahoe. I only thought . . . Well, where *you* goin', Tuck?"

He studied on his pipe. "Not quite certain, for the long run. Losing that gold put a crimp in my retirement plan. Mayhaps I'll take myself up to Prescott. Visit Queenie Caulfield and cogitate a spell. Be pleased to ride with you as far as your hometown, Mace."

Ty joined us, smoking pouch and papers in hand. He

stepped over the half-wall, sat down a couple feet from Tuck, bent a paper into a long V, and shook in a little tobacco. "Then we'll all be sayin' farewell come mornin'," he said as he rolled it up. "I'm headin' west for the Colorado River. I'm after doin' a little gamin' along the California border."

"Not much over there," said Tuck.

"Except Yuma Prison," Mace added.

Tuck chewed on his pipe stem, and Ty said, "I was thinkin' a bit north'a there. Ehrenberg, or Half Moon Crossin'. Maybe all the way up to Mohave City."

Mace scowled. "Even those aren't much. I would'a thought you'd be off for someplace fancier."

Ty gave his cigarette a last lick, stuck it between his lips, and lit it. The match light played over his face something wonderful. No evil spirits there. "I daresay that would'a been the plot and plan of it, Mason. But me San Francisco stake went the same way as your and Pete's ranch money." He shook out the match. "South, and in considerable haste."

After a minute of quiet, Tuck said, "I believe Queenie Caulfield would be glad to put you up for a spell, Miss Gini. Until you settle on a plan."

Mace slouched down on his bedroll and tipped his hat over his eyes. "Reckon you could find yourself good employment memorizing poems, Red. Or maybe you could get a job with the U.S. Army, torchin' smallpox houses."

I stuck my leg out and gave his boot a good kick, but he only grinned and folded his arms over his chest.

"You'll be riding with me then?" Tuck asked.

I gave up revenging myself on Mace, mainly because he was too far away to punch without paining my shoulder. I said, "I don't know, Tuck. I don't like to split with you, but I've already seen Prescott. Maybe . . ." I had a grip on that topaz ring with one hand. The other, fingers crossed, was behind my back. I fixed my gaze on Tyrone, hoping like crazy.

He had finished up his cigarette and ground the butt under his heel. When he looked up, he said, "I suppose ye could be ridin' to the river with me, love. I imagine ye could find a roost singin'."

It was all I could do to keep from letting out a big happy sigh, even when Tuck said, "Wouldn't you rather come north, honey?"

I as much as ignored him. "Thank you, Ty," I said. "I'd admire to see the river."

We broke camp at dawn. I could tell that Tuck wasn't exactly joyous over my plans, but I was so tickled to be going off with Tyrone and have him all to myself that I barely heard a word Tuck said to me. He finally gave up, saying, "Well, Miss Gini, I suppose you're grown-up enough to choose your own course. But if you change your mind or find yourself in need, I'll be at Queenie's. And if I'm not, she'll know where to find me."

"I'll be fine, Tuck. And me and Tyrone will see you again real soon, I know it." I hoped that wasn't a lie.

He gave me a big bear hug that was a tad too hard on my shoulder, but I didn't mind. Then he stepped up on Zeus.

Mace said, "Keep her away from the matches, Ty," and him and Tuck rode off at a lope.

"Let's be on our way, love," Tyrone said. He didn't seem to notice that I was misty-eyed from the good-byes, and boosted me up on Jigsaw real businesslike, saying, "I'm thinkin' we can make it in a couple'a days if we refrain from dawdle."

He was right. He was riding Pete's buckskin, which he had paid Mace forty dollars for. Though it was not nearly so pretty as his poor black mare and not so good-trained, it was a quick horse as well as sound. We made good time, arriving at the river's edge late on the second day.

Tyrone wasn't happy with the first little town we came to. Neither was I, as there were probably fewer than fifty people in the whole place, and they were all low-class types. After a short night there, we moved on upstream to Ehrenberg. It was not much nicer, its permanent population being mostly dead-ended pilgrims and Mexicans, the majority of which did not really want to be there but couldn't decide where a better place might be, and therefore never quite got around to leaving. But it was some bigger than the last town and had a decent port business with lots of river folk coming and going, which Ty said was good for gambling. We stayed.

He got us rooms in the hotel and announced right off that he'd take me over to a saloon where the owner owed him a favor and would hire me. I thought that was kind of rude, since I knew I could sing good enough to find a job without the help of favors; but he looked so handsome when he said it that the mad went out of me real quick.

I sang at Bud's Yellowjacket Bar every night but Wednesday, and it was a sorry place. The customers talked loud all during my numbers and tried to pinch me, and it seemed I had to wallop somebody about every night. If I had to choose between the Tombstone crowds and those along the Colorado, I would have taken miners and cowboys and horse rustlers over river rats and water-trash every time.

I think Tyrone might have agreed with me, for we had not been in town one week when I found him in the alley behind Bud's Yellowjacket, practically beat to pulp and robbed blind. He could barely walk, and though the doctor said he had no broken bones except for a cracked rib or two, he was in bed for five days and it was almost a week before his face looked even halfway normal. It was a miracle he hadn't got his nose caved in or an eye put out.

"'Twas a bad-tempered loser," was all he'd say, with his face all blue and purple and turning yellow-green. "Hazard'a me profession."

I fed him soup and tended his bruises, prayed his face would heal up to look like before, and wondered how anybody who had been so mistreated could seem so dang cheerful.

I was not making one-fifth the money I had cleared at Spider Eye Inga's, and could not stand the town. It was nothing but dust and boats going by and black widow spiders that wouldn't stop webbing in the corner of my room, no matter how many I killed. But even brass-knuckled and blackjacked, Tyrone acted like Ehrenberg was the Prince of Cities. Just seeing him smile or hearing him talk pretty made it bearable.

I kept Jigsaw at the livery, but about the first thing Tyrone did when he hit town was to sell off his buckskin. I told him it was a good horse and he ought to hold on to it, but he said, "Boardin' a beast I've no need for is a capricious expense, Geneva darlin'. If ye were wise, ye'd divest yourself of that paint horse and save the upkeep money. Ye can always buy another if ye have a need."

But I wouldn't sell, and between Jigsaw's board and my hotel bill and feeding myself (and Tyrone, too, for the time he was laid up), I was barely breaking even with my salary. I kept the hundred dollars I had brought from Tombstone sewn in the lining of my carpetbag, in case of dire emergency.

Dire emergency arose after we'd been in Ehrenberg about a month. I was in the hotel dining room and trying to eat the bad breakfast they'd served me when Tyrone strode in and pulled up a chair. Flesh mended perfect, he was grinning all over, as handsome and good-smelling as a new day.

"Well, I'm off," he said.

I just about dropped my fork. "What?"

"North, to Half Moon Crossin'. The steamer *Halcyon* is in port, and I'm ridin' her upriver this very afternoon."

Well, I would have jumped right up and told him what-for, but the dining room was crowded and I didn't want to make a scene. Instead, I leaned across the table and whispered, "Tyrone O'Neill, do you mean to tell me you have brought me all the way to Ehrenberg, A.T., taken me a-walking three nights a week and kissed my hand good night at the door every time, talked to me sweet and called me pet names; and now you are just going to up and leave me stranded in this godforsaken hole with no place to work except the worst saloon north of Yuma?"

He tugged at his mustache and grinned at me. "Those weren't the precise words I would've employed. . . ."

I must have glared at him something fierce, because after a few seconds, he said, "I suppose ye could come along, sweet."

I smiled and stood up. "You're some kind of tease, Tyrone O'Neill. You had me goin' for a minute. I'll pack my bag and fetch Jigsaw."

His fingers curled about my wrist. "Ye can't take him on the barge, darlin'. The *Halcyon*'s loaded solid already with a troupe of idiot pilgrims and their worldly goods. And I'll not have ye ridin' alone along the river."

I sat back down.

"I suppose there's no chance'a ye sellin' the brute?"

I shook my head.

"Well then. I was talkin' to a fella the other day, Weevil Jukes by name, who boards a few horses on the side. I believe ye might leave your Jigsaw there for five dollars a month. I'm doubtin' he grains for that price, though."

I didn't mind about the grain. It was spring, there was plenty of green fodder growing, and Jigsaw was an easy keeper. We went on up to the livery. After the owner said he would not store my saddle, I sold it to him for six dollars and four bits. That was not a fair price, but it was the best it looked like I was going to get. I pulled Jigsaw's shoes, and then we rented a beat-up buggy and set off for Weevil Jukes's place.

It was about seven miles out of town, and dilapidated was too fine a word for it. The sign by the road said:

WEEVIL JUKES

HORSES & CATTEL BOT & SOLD

HIDES

The house was a pile of sun-rotted gray boards that looked to have been thrown together by a blind drunkard on a building spree, and the barn had fallen clear in on itself. Off in the weeds by the smokehouse, a pack of mangy dogs growled and snarled and fought over something on the ground. It might have been beef guts, as a fresh hide, black flies buzzing thick on it, was nailed to the side of the house and Weevil Jukes had bloody smears on his arms and clothes. He must have done a lot of slaughtering. I saw three more hides, two black and one speckled, rolled up on a workbench in the yard.

There were several steers in a dirt lot, and a billy goat was busy eating the fence. Five half-grown spotted shoats rooted at the brambled base of a rusty pump, and another lay up by the stoop, chewing at a rope of what looked like cow intestine. But despite the ramshackle condition of the place and the man himself, his steers and hogs were fat and sleek, as were the half-dozen horses and twice as many cattle we passed on the way up.

"Be rightly pleased t'see to him for ya, missy," he said. He was a little man, bony, with a pruny face and no front teeth. Hair the color of scrubbed carrots stuck out from under his floppy hat. He walked all round Jigsaw and patted him and felt his legs. He remarked on his sleek coat and the fact that he had no blemishes.

"Yes," I said with some pride. "The only mark he carries is that Crown P brand, which he came to us with. I have never let him be where he could scar himself, and I trust you will do the same."

He was busy looking in Jigsaw's mouth. "Got some age on him."

I was about to remark that a little age was good on a horse, but Ty put his hand on my shoulder. It was all healed up by then, though it still grated a tad when I moved it certain ways.

Ty said, "And what'd be the goin' rate, Mr. Jukes?"

"Hold up there, pig!" Jukes shouted, and took off toward the pump. Right next to it was a well I hadn't seen before—just a hole in the ground with a few boards thrown across it and some sticks poked around in imitation of a fence. One of the shoats had knocked over the stakes and got a leg stuck between the boards. The poor thing was squealing something awful. Jukes got to it before it broke the rest of the way through, and hauled it out by its front feet.

It skittered away, and Jukes walked back, dusting his hands on his shirt. "Keep meanin' to cover that proper. Only about fifteen foot deep, but that's a long drop for a hog. Be a waste of bacon." He patted Jigsaw on the neck and said, "Now let's see. The keepin' fee. What'd ya hear it'd be?"

Tyrone said, "I heard five dollars a month for good pasture."

"Ya heared rightly, Mr. O'Neill. That's in advance."

On Tyrone's advice, I handed over twenty dollars of my Tombstone money for four months' board, and told Weevil Jukes that if I had to be away longer, I would send him more. I gave Jigsaw a good-bye hug and a kiss on his soft old nose, and we turned him out with the other horses. Before we climbed in our buggy and started for town, Ty and Weevil had a few words.

"What were you talkin' to him about?" I said after we'd put some distance between us and the Jukes place. I was twisted round on the seat with my head craned out, watching Jigsaw get smaller and smaller.

"I pressed another five on him," Ty said. "For special care."

Since Tyrone had been hurting bad for living money ever since he got rolled in back of Bud's Yellowjacket Bar, I thought that was about the sweetest thing I'd ever heard.

Half Moon Crossing was no bigger that Ehrenberg, but it was livelier. There were better saloons to pick from, and though the pay was still bad, I got a job in one where the boys listened to me sing at least some of the time.

We checked into the Half Moon Hotel the same way we'd registered in Ehrenberg: as Mr. Tyrone O'Neill and his sister, Mary. It was hard getting used to people calling me that, but Ty had thought it best to change both first and last names in case the Malones were after me. I was right to do it, for it was in Half Moon Crossing that I saw my wanted poster.

The paper, tacked up with a raft of others outside the post office, said that Geneva Kincaid (also known as Gini Kincaid, also known as Irish Jenny Rose) was wanted for arson, assault, malicious mischief, and destruction of private property. A reward of two hundred and fifty dollars was offered by the Malone brothers. There was a drawing, too, but it was so poor I was sure nobody'd know me from it. They also described me two inches taller than I stand.

The bill said I was usually attired in buckskins and rode a paint horse. Since Jigsaw was with Weevil Jukes and I had taken to wearing dresses, I felt safe. However, I kept to flat shoes and started wearing my hair braided or pulled into a knot (instead of loose, like in the picture), just in case.

The Half Moon Hotel had been built by a miser. None of the walls were more than one plank thick and all the rooms were just alike: a skinny, hard bed, one chest of drawers, and one chair. The quarters were so tiny there was just enough room for the door to open without hitting the bed. If Malachi had been a bigger tortoise, I don't think the two of us would have fit in there.

My room was next to Tyrone's, and I could hear him plain. I was so crazy for him by then that the sound of him humming while he dressed or shaved, or the creak of his bed when he rolled over at night, was like food for the starved. Knotholes and cracks pocked the walls, and I suppose I could have spied on him. I do confess to having watched him trim his mustache on one occasion, but otherwise, I didn't peek. A person has a right to his privacy.

Ty played mostly in the Pole Barge Saloon, where I worked, and though he won some hands I fear he lost as often. Now, back in Tombstone I had watched him game a good bit, and I knew he was possessed of the best memory for cards I have seen on a person outside myself. But lately, it was like he just didn't care. I wondered if it was me, bringing him bad luck and making him lose his concentration; but when I said something, he just laughed. He did not seem upset by his losses. In fact, he acted real happy, almost expectant. I hoped that was because maybe he was falling in love with me. I know I was awful stuck on him.

I do not mean to say that me and Tyrone had any "funny business" going on. He acted too much the gent for that sort of rambunctiousness, and my Gam had raised me to be a lady. But sometimes, of an evening, he'd walk me down by the river and curl his arm round my shoulders and talk about when he was a little boy in the Old Country; and twice he even kissed my cheek. I tell you, I just about melted right into the river gravel.

We were into our fifth week in Half Moon Crossing when the bad thing happened.

Ty being in the midst of a rare winning streak, I had walked myself home from the saloon and gone to bed. I remember, I was dreaming about Ty. I will not describe what the dream was about—except to say it was a pretty good one—but all of a sudden I realized Ty wasn't talking in my dream anymore. He was talking for real, and in the next room. And the lady talking to him sure wasn't me.

"Pansy, me love," he was saying, "I'm not in the mood to be discussin' business just at the moment."

She laughed: a soft, grown woman's laugh with knowing in it. "If we don't discuss it now, Ty-boy, we won't get back around to it for hours."

He chuckled low, and said, "'Twas just what I had in mind."

I have heard people say as how, in some real extreme circumstances, their blood turned to ice. Well, right at that moment I knew what they meant. Real careful, so as not to creak my bed, I got up and went to the knothole I'd peered through to watch Ty trim his mustache.

He had his tie and jacket off, and was loosening his collar. The woman was perched right on his bed, bold as you please. She was dark-haired and so pretty I hated her right off, with eyes so big and so blue it seemed they took up most of her face. She crossed her legs at the ankle, just like she thought somebody with her face and her voice could be prim, and said, "Cicero doesn't trust you, dear. I don't think he'll come."

Ty took off his vest, tossed it over a chair; unbuckled his gunbelt and laid it on the dresser. Then, though I could hardly believe it, he got down on his knees in front of that woman, took hold of her foot, and unbuttoned her shoe.

"He'll come," he said, "when ye tell him the prize." He slid her shoe clear off and kissed the top of her stockinged foot. I was so mad I about bit a hole in my lip, but I couldn't stop staring.

"And what's the prize this time, Ty? Another pot of gold at the end of the rainbow?"

He ran his hand up her leg, under her skirt, and before I knew what had happened, he was rolling her stocking down and off her leg. He said, "Pansy, I believe you're a witch. Ye've hit it precisely." He stopped to kiss her bare foot. I wanted to kill him.

"A fortune," he said as he slipped off her other shoe. "Gold bullion, bright and perfect. And all Black Ear Cicero and his bunch need do for their share is ride along and help me fetch it."

He rolled down the other stocking and kissed that foot, too.

She made a little hissing sound before she said, "And just how did you happen to run across all this free gold, Tyrone?"

He ran one hand up each of her legs, pushing her skirt as he went till it was over her knees. He said, "'Tis a tangled tale, me darlin'."

She touched his hair. "Say it anyway."

"You're a terrible tease, Pansy," he whispered. "First you're a month late arrivin', and now all ye want is talk."

"Tell it," she purred, slit-eyed as a tabby full of cream.

He sighed. "Yes, m'love. On behalf of me previous employer, I went after it with a few unsuspectin' acquaintances. And things were workin' like the insides of a water clock till foul fate interfered. But ye know me, darlin'."

She soothed his brow. "Would that I didn't, Ty-boy. Is your brogue getting thicker?"

He pressed lips to her palm. "Mercy, beloved! I'm about to make ye wealthy. I left the fortune exactly where 'twas found, where no bandit will look and no Indian will go." He kissed each finger, one at a time.

She curled her hand—kissed with lips meant for me— round the back of his neck. "What about your friends?"

"They're thinkin' it's lost, gone to the wilds of Mexico in the saddlebags of wanton desperadoes. And me former employers believe the same, though I nearly paid me looks to convince 'em."

"Always playing both ends against the middle, aren't you, Ty? But even if Cicero takes the bait, what makes you think he and his outfit will settle for a sixty-forty split? There's five of them and one of you."

He pushed her skirts up to the middle of her thighs and ran his fingers under the ruffled edge of her pantalets. She cooed at him. I wished those river rats back in Ehrenberg— some of Wilbeck's outfit, from what he'd just said—had gone ahead and finished beating him to death.

He said, "Those odds won't last for long, Pansy me dearest. Not once the plunder's carried clear of the wild country."

She leaned forward and fingered the top button on his shirt. "Cicero's boys are a wicked bunch, Ty-boy. How will you do it?"

He pushed his hands up under her skirts to her hips. "The same as I would'a done my previous associates, had we got the gold out. They have to sleep sometime, me love. And 'tis better odds than I had before. Now I'm free of Wilbeck's dastardly mob, too; and them offerin' me only a twenty percent finder's fee, and that after hagglin'!"

So soft I could barely hear, she said, "And just what can your little Pansy expect out of all this, Tyrone O'Neill?"

"I'll buy ye the stars themselves, darlin'! We'll hie ourselves east, or to Europe if ye fancy. All ye have to do is convince Cicero, and we'll live like kings."

She began to unbutton his shirt. "A king and a *queen*." She ran her fingers through the dark fur I hadn't known was on his chest. She whispered, "I'm not going to let you double-cross me like you did in Silver City. You're a black-hearted bastard, Tyrone."

"I'll not argue it," he said, and pushed a bit closer to her. "But dinna take me for a total reprobate. I've got me limits. That's why I let the gold lay. 'Twas one in me party I would'a felt terrible sorrowed for killin'."

Women are fools. There I was, peeping at him while he undressed some other female and sweet-talked her and confessed what foul things he had done—and would have done if he'd had a chance. And as het up as I was, I was actually touched that he would have felt regret to murder me in my sleep.

And then he said, "'Twould have been a distressin' thing indeed to take the life from a fine man like Tucker Brennan."

I stepped back from the knothole, shivering so fierce I could scarce control my limbs. I made myself take two deep breaths, and then, as stealthy and as fast as I could, I slipped into my britches and boots, stuffed clothes and Malachi inside my satchel, and slid my squirrel gun out from behind the dresser.

I was still quaking when I stepped into the hall, still sore as a frog on a stove lid when I tiptoed past his room. And just as I got to the landing, I heard that woman giggle.

Something took hold of me, something powerful and vile. Blind fury, they call it, and they are right. Like somebody else had moved in and taken me over, I set down my satchel and gun and went back to Ty's door. I tried the latch. They had been in such a hurry to get at each other they hadn't bothered to lock it.

Bold as you please, I pushed on the door and stepped into that tiny room, blood pounding hot at my temples.

They were both half-naked, her more than him, and twined together on the bed with him on top. He raised up on his elbows and looked me square in the eye.

He smiled like he'd just bumped into me on the board-walk in broad daylight. "Ye should always knock, Geneva sweet."

That vile thing in me went *pop*. I reached across his dresser, grabbed his fancy, pearl-handled pistol, and pointed it at him as steady as I had aimed it at Doc Holliday out front of Big Jim Harold's Bar.

"I loved you, you sorry snake turd!" I took hold of that topaz ring he'd given me and yanked it hard. The neck chain broke and I threw the whole business at him. "Stand up. I am goin' to shoot your willie off."

"Let's not be hasty, pet," he said, and reached for the gun. He didn't even bother to get off that Pansy woman, that's how casual he was. He grabbed the barrel. I pulled away, but he gave a hard yank and I stumbled.

Pansy screamed when the bullet took him, but he fell across her and muffled all but the first note of it.

I dropped the gun, turned and ran; grabbed my things,

took the stairs downhill three at a time. A man in a long black duster had just come into the dark lobby. I didn't see him till too late, crashed into him, and knocked him into the desk. I scrambled up and kept going. There was one horse tied on the rail out front. I grabbed that bangtail and showed it my heels.

Pansy must have rolled Tyrone's body off her by then, because she started screaming.

The black-coated man stumbled out and thundered, "Stop! Stop, you!"

I galloped into the night, his shouts and Pansy's shrieks of "Murder! Help!" fading behind me.

12

On the Run

Now you have really done it, Geneva Kincaid.

That's what I kept telling myself as I galloped south: *You have really gone and done it this time.* I was so deep in regret and loathing and grief that I went near five miles before it dawned on me that, on top of everything else, I'd thieved a horse. I reined that poor stolen pony down to a walk. He was lathered and winded, and he was grateful.

The wind had about whipped the last tears and panic out of me, and I set myself to thinking what to do next. The smart thing would likely be to ride another fifteen miles downriver to Brewster's Ferry and cross over into California, where an Arizona posse wouldn't follow. That in mind, I rode on through the night, staying within earshot of the river and switching back and forth between mourning Tyrone and hating him.

Brewster's Ferry is not a real town. A man named Lemuel Brewster had a shack there back in the fifties, where he did some trading with Mex and American pilgrims till the Yuma Indians burnt him out and peeled the skin off his living body. Somebody else built on his site later on, but kept the name out of respect.

There are two buildings at Brewster's Ferry: a general store that doubles as a trading post, saloon, and post office; and a squat adobe called Colorado Kate's that rents a couple rooms, cooks meals, and provides the private services of Colorado Kate herself.

It was just coming dawn when I rode in. Soft silvery fog was heavy over the water and the banks. Things smelled wet and crisp and fresh, and there was no sound but the river's thick burble and my pony's hooves crunching wet gravel.

The sky was dark gray—no color, no stars, just a blurry glow on the eastern horizon—and because of the mist you couldn't see where the banks stopped and the water began. It was like being in a cloud but on solid ground at the same time. Maybe that's what Heaven's like. I figured it was likely as close as I'd get, having done a murder. Of course, I'd shot down that *bandido* in the canyon, but he had a gun and was going to kill me, and I think the Lord understands about self-defense. But Tyrone, scum that he turned out to be, hadn't held any knife to my throat; and accident or no, there was hate in my heart when the gun went off. Hell-bound for certain-sure, I was determined to live a real long life and put off the Lake of Fire as long as possible.

I could not see or hear the ferry, so I guessed it was across on the California side. I rode down to the landing, dismounted, and waited, wondering what the Golden State would hold for me.

I was about ten minutes into a good daydream about singing on a stage someplace fancy, maybe San Francisco, with rich gents even better-looking than Tyrone O'Neill giving me diamond bracelets and red roses and begging for my hand in holy wedlock, when I heard men's voices and what sounded like a passel of horses. I was scared near to death for the two seconds it took to realize they were coming from the wrong direction to be a posse.

A minute later I could see blurry shapes through the mist and half-light. As they came closer, I made out a string of horses and four long-coated men: dealers, most like. Fog swirling lazy round their legs, they whoaed up by the store. One commenced to bang on the door to wake somebody up.

I tied my mount by the landing and hiked over to the friendliest-looking fella. He was big-bellied and red-cheeked, and had a long droopy gray-blond mustache, raggedy at the corners where cigarettes had burnt too close and sizzled it.

"These horses for sale?"

He tugged on his earlobe, which was part gone, maybe bit off in a fight. "Reckon. You in need?"

"Not dire," I said, not wanting to drive the price up. "Wouldn't mind lookin', though."

We went down the line as the sun crept higher, fast burning out the ground vapor. I was sorry for its going, but at least I could see how the ponies moved when he trotted them up and down for me.

"This one's calf-kneed," I said when he brought out a bald-faced chestnut. "Sickle-hocked," to the little copper bay. "Tendon on this one'll pop on the first hard canter," to a dishwater palomino. A dark chestnut with white feet moved more like an eggbeater than a horse, and the sorrel was too close-coupled. "He'd jolt me clean out of the saddle after twenty feet," I said.

By the time we got near the end of the string, the fella was tuckered and surly from trotting out all those ponies. "You are plain exasperatin' me, girl!" he panted. "I don't think you want to buy a horse at all."

I told him I might if he'd show me one.

The sun being clear of the horizon by that time and warming the morning in a hurry, he took off his duster and threw it over the rail. "All right," he said. "I only got these two left to show you, thank God. And to tell the truth, I don't know a durn thing 'bout 'em. Bought 'em forty mile down the pike from a widder woman what was packin' up to go back east. Ain't had a chance to throw a saddle on neither one, so I ain't vouchin' for bridlewise."

One was a blood-bay colt, pretty in the head and neck but narrow in the shoulder and not more than two years old. The other was a gruello gelding. He looked to be about five years, and was a tad shorter than Jigsaw but still of good size. He was built solid if not fancy, and had a kind eye.

"How much?" I asked, after I'd seen him move and looked in his mouth and sacked him out with the horse trader's duster.

"Don't go flappin' my coat all over that cayuse, girl," he said, and grabbed it back. "I could'a told you he weren't no spook if you'd asked. He's seventy-five dollars."

I just about keeled over. "You got some nerve, mister. I don't even know that this horse is broke to ride decent. I will give you twenty."

"Twenty's an insult. And as to broke, get on him and we'll both see."

He boosted me up and I took a turn around the yard, bareback and with a halter for a bridle, all the time keeping an eye to the north. I had visions of an irate mob from Half Moon Crossing thundering in at any minute. I wished the ferry would hurry.

"He reins fair to middlin'," I said after I jogged the gruello back and jumped down. "Trot's choppy." In truth, he handled real nice and owned a smooth gait, but when you are dealing, you have to say the worst.

"Didn't look so choppy to me, missy. He's dollar-sound, you can see that yourself, and the widder swore he was sweet as rock candy with no bad habits. Raised him from a colt and named him Filibuster. Said he answers to it. Name alone's worth the price. Sixty-five, and you're robbin' me blind."

I folded my arms. "Widows can lie, same's anybody else.

Plus, you will have a hard time selling a horse of this unwholesome color. Thirty."

"There are those as likes a mole-colored horse. Sixty."

"Not many. I do not like it much myself, but I'm in a hurry. Thirty-five is my last offer. For that money I can buy a sound horse of a decent color and name it any fancy thing I like."

I let him chew on that for a couple minutes. Now, gruello is a sort of bluish, washed-out, mouse-gray shade, with the horse having black "points" like a bay or buckskin. I had said the truth about some folks not caring for it, but I had lied about myself—I thought he was real handsome. Besides, Gam always said the best color for a horse was fat, and Filibuster was that, all right.

The dealer heaved a sigh. "Forty," he said. "Rock bottom."

"Thirty-seven fifty."

"Done."

As I was getting out my money, he asked, "What about that little mud-brown jughead you got tied by the dock? Want to sell him?"

It having been dark when I swiped him and foggy when I rode in, I had not noticed he was mud-colored—or jugheaded—till just then. I said, "No, he's not mine to sell."

I asked if they were heading toward Half Moon Crossing, thinking to send the brown pony back with them, but he said they were cutting northeast after they picked up provisions. By the time I paid for my own things—a badly used saddle and hackamore, assorted provisions, and two greasy bacon and biscuit sandwiches—they were gone and the ferry was just docking.

I was more antsy by the minute about the law coming down on me. I saddled Filibuster quick and led him down by the dock. I wondered if that brown pony would just wander on home if I set him free.

I had barely reached the landing and commenced to pull my bag off the stolen pony when a young, curly-haired fella stepped off the ferry. He was amazing tall, with eyes the color of sage in spring, and he was leading a big dapple-gray horse with a roached mane. He walked right up to me like he was my best friend and said, "Why, howdy! Good to see you! Pastor Middleton down here? That's his Soapy horse you've got there, ain't it?"

It figured it *would* turn out to be a preacher's pony. Right then I just knew the Devil must already be making me up a brass nameplate and a welcome sign. I couldn't think of a dang thing to say, so I just smiled up at the cowhand and patted the jughead's neck.

"You down here with him?" he asked.

I took a deep breath and crossed my fingers, for all of a sudden I had a sterling idea. "The pastor's not here," I said, grinning right back like I owned the world and had never had a secret. "My name's Mary O'Neill, and I sing at the Pole Barge up in Half Moon Crossing."

"Yes'm, I know," he said, and blushed. He wasn't more than eighteen. "I heard you sing, 'bout three weeks back. Name's Danny Sloan."

I didn't recognize him, but I said, "Sure, I think I remember you. Well now, Danny, I have got a sort of family emergency, and Pastor Middleton let me borrow Soapy as far as Brewster's Ferry. If you're goin' up toward Half Moon, I would sure appreciate it if you'd return him. It'd save the parson a trip, and I'd count it as a personal favor."

My heart was pounding double time, but I held a steady smile.

"Be an honor," he said. "Soapy has carried the pastor on the Lord's work up and down most all this river. He must think awful high of you, indeed, Mary O'Neill, lettin' you borrow his Soapy horse!"

"I think high of him, too," I said, though I had never before heard his name or met him, unless you counted knocking him flat in the Half Moon Hotel lobby. "You be sure and tell him I said thanks again, and I'll see him just as soon as my cousin Jane is well."

"I reckon he's prayin' for you right this minute."

I reckoned he was, too, though it was more likely he was praying for me to get caught so he could have his horse back.

I pulled my carpetbag and rifle down, and he took Soapy's reins. He said, "You crossin' over to California?"

"Fast as I can. Cousin Jane's ailin' something awful. Oh, and Soapy hasn't had breakfast. He could use some restin' up, too."

He jabbed a thumb over his shoulder at his friends, who had got off the ferry before him. They were hollering at him to get a move on. He said, "We figure to stop and feed a couple miles upstream. Good luck to you, miss, and your cousin, too." He tipped his hat, mounted up, and rode out.

I waited by the dock till he was out of sight, and then I climbed on Filibuster, reined him away from the dock, and headed south, toward Ehrenberg.

I had made myself some time, for once Danny Sloan spread the word I'd crossed the river, they'd likely give up looking for me. Even if they checked at Brewster's Ferry and found out I hadn't crossed there, they'd calculate I did it farther downstream; they'd have to figure only a fool wouldn't jump the territorial line when it was that close. Oh, there'd probably be new posters printed up on the off chance I'd show up in Arizona again, but those would take a while to get around: a month, maybe longer. By which time I could pick up Jigsaw, get over to Mendacity, find Mace, wire Tuck, and maybe even retrieve the gold.

Out of the Territory was the safest place to be, but I was newly bound and determined to leave with bright metal— and a bright future—in my saddlebags.

A day later, I bypassed Ehrenberg and headed straight for Weevil Jukes's place. By then, it had dawned on me that riding the same paint horse mentioned on my Malone Bros. poster wasn't the smartest idea in the world, but I didn't much care. I missed Jigsaw terrible bad.

Weevil Jukes was in the yard, shouting at his hounds and pigs and loading a buckboard with big, twine-bound rolls of hides. He didn't notice me till I practically rode right up on top of him.

"Mornin', Mr. Jukes," I said, and hopped off Filibuster. "I have come to fetch my paint horse that I left with you. Thought maybe you'd like to buy this one off me, long's I'm here. He's a handy mount and I hate to part with him, but I don't need two."

I guessed I had given him a start, for he opened his mouth like he was going to say something, then closed it again.

"Well, maybe you aren't buyin' right now. But I need to collect Jigsaw and get on my way. Where's he pastured?"

His mouth moved again, like a beached sunfish.

"Mr. Jukes?"

"Didn't expect to . . . That is, your brother, Mr. O'Neill," he said . . ."

"Where's my horse, Mr. Jukes?"

He threw back his skinny shoulders and stuck out his chin. "Ain't here. That brother a'yourn said you wasn't comin' back. I give him over the money you give me, plus seven dollars American money, no Mex. Told me in town three days before, said if he brought you out we was to work it that way. Said he wanted shed of the fool critter, but he was humorin' you and I was to do the same. It were a strange deal."

Now, after I'd killed Tyrone, all the mad I'd felt toward him had got turned to grief; but all of a sudden that mad was back worse than before. He'd betrayed me again, but this was worse than kissing on that Pansy woman and lower than hiding the gold: he'd sent my poor Jigsaw off to get spurred bloody by some drunk cowboy or ridden into the ground by some fool, and all for the board money plus seven dollars cash. If I could have shot Tyrone all over again I would not have hesitated, and this time I would have done it a-purpose.

"You tell me where you sold that horse to, Weevil Jukes, or so help me Hannah, you are goin' off to meet Christ Jesus by the force of my bare hands."

I must have looked barbarous enough to do it, for he took a step away. He mopped his brow with a dirty bandanna. "He ain't, that is, he ain't exactly—"

"Where's my horse!"

He jumped at that, and yelped, "Look at my sign, dammit! Critters bought and sold and hides! That spotted horse was old, nobody'd want him!"

My stomach turned over. "Just fifteen," I said, and it seemed my legs were melting into jelly. "Just a little younger than me."

"Too old! What work's he got left in him, *real* work, I mean? A year? Two, maybe? Couldn't'a got my money back. Spotted hide's worth four times as much as the horse, shipped back east. Not a blemish on him, 'cept that brand, nice and clean. Adds character, they say. De-luxe goods. I got me a business, and I—"

I remember running at him with my hands out, reaching for his scrawny neck. I don't know if he fell back or I pushed him, but either way he crashed through the boards that covered that old well. Muddy water splashed up and spattered my bucks.

He was neither dead nor busted up, more's the pity, but at least he was knee-deep in water and fifteen feet down. "Ain't my fault!" he hollered up at me. "Your brother said you was too dern silly over that old horse, and he was right, 'cept he didn't tell me you was plain loco on top of it! Fertilizer and chicken feed, mucilage and hides, that's all most'a these nags is worth once they gets to me, and yours weren't no different. It were a fair deal!"

He kept hollering while I untied and searched every bundle on that wagon, and he was still yelling when I headed for the house.

Weevil Jukes might have looked like a poor man, but I think he was doing pretty dang good if his inventory was any indication. He had hides aplenty: some cow, some goat, and a few coyotes and puma he must have trapped or shot on the side, but mostly it was pony skins. He had them stacked and rolled and bundled all over the place, waiting to be loaded on the wagon with the rest. It must have been a whole year's worth of slaughter, packed up and labeled for the big shipment.

I found my Jigsaw in the front room, in a bundle tagged, *For Phillips & Son, Miniapolis/St. Paul. Grade Exselent to Prime.*

I didn't cry. I was too bone-deep mad and wounded to my soul and filled with righteous purpose.

I shooed Weevil Jukes's steers and horses out of the lot and pasture and headed them for open country at a dead run. Filibuster must have sensed what was up, for he worked those cattle and ponies like he knew he was saving their lives. If those critters were smart, they wouldn't stop till they passed Phoenix.

When I got back to the yard, Weevil was still down the

well shaft and cussing a blue streak. I ignored him. I had a
mission. I picked up a short plank and a shovel and tied
them behind Filibuster's saddle. I found a jar of red paint in
the kitchen, and that went into my satchel next to Malachi.
I rolled up Jigsaw's pelt and secured it underneath.

"Help me outta here, you crazy bitch!" Jukes hollered
from the shaft. I walked on by.

Working fast, I toted every hide and skin—every bundle,
every stack—out of that rickety house and piled them on
the wagon. Weevil Jukes smelled the lamp oil and kerosene
I poured on next. There was a lot of it. He cried, "What you
doin' up there? You want another horse? Want your money
back? I'll give you a horse, any horse you want!"

I said, "Shut up," and popped a match with my thumbnail.
I tossed it on the wagon. The whole miserable, filthy
business whooshed up into flame, and I said amen.

Then I dropped a rope down to that horse-murdering
sonofabitch. I told him if he kept trying, he might be able to
lasso the pump and haul himself clear by nightfall, but that
I didn't give a good spit if he never got out.

He snarled a curse and shook his fist. "You'll suffer for
this! I'll have the law on you!"

"Get in line, horse-killer."

It wasn't till after I'd put Weevil Jukes far behind me, not
till I'd ridden away the miles and the afternoon, that the
tears came.

It was dark by then. I didn't care. Far out in the
wasteland, I dug a grave by firelight, then sat beside it for a
long time: Malachi next to me, Jigsaw's skin across my lap.

I remembered the way Gam had healed and gentled him
when he first came to us, and how, back in Hanged Dog, I
used to ride the desert on his bare back, my cheek to his
neck, his mane and my hair billowing together in the dry
night air. I remembered his speed and heart and fire, and

how he'd always nicker soft when he heard my voice or saw me coming. I stroked the place on his back that, if you scratched it just right and long enough, made him doze off. I combed out his mane so it lay smooth and flawless. I gave a last kiss to the place on his neck where white like milk and chestnut like polished cherrywood met in the shape of a tiny prickly pear; and then I buried him.

At first light, my eyes near swollen shut with mourning, I took paint and board and made his marker, my finger for the brush.

I wrote, *Here Lies Jigsaw Kincaid, What Is Left of a Good Horse*. There was not much more room, so under that I put a cross, and then the shortest Bible verse I know. It said, *Jesus Wept*.

So did I.

It took four days to reach Mendacity. It should have taken only two and a half or three, but the first day after laying Jigsaw to rest I was not thinking very straight and got kind of turned around. But me and Filibuster and Malachi finally found the town and made straight for the saloon.

"How do I get to the Danahoe place?"

"Five mile nor'west, more west than north," said the bartender, once he got over the shock of me walking in the front door. "Won't find nobody out there, though."

"Has to be somebody," I said. "It's Mace Danahoe I'm lookin' for."

He polished a glass. "Gone."

"His ma?"

"De-ceased."

That stopped me. After a minute, I said, "Where'd Mace get off to?"

He picked up a new glass and shrugged. "Suppose they

might know at Mahoney's." He gave the glass a last twist in his rag and held it up to the light.

"Would that be Loula Mahoney?"

He sent me down the street to a two-story frame house with a sign out front that said, *Boardinghouse, M. Mahoney, Prop. No Spitters.* The front door was screened with cheesecloth, stretched tight to keep the flies out. I knocked.

A green-eyed, gray-haired fat woman, wiping floury hands on her apron, answered. "Yes?"

"Mornin', ma'am. My name's Gini Kincaid, and I am lookin' for Miss Loula Mahoney. I was told—"

She turned her broad back on me and shouted up the stairs, "Loooo-*lah*!" It near fractured my ear bones.

Somebody sang back, "Coming, Mommy."

The fat woman said, "You'll pardon me, I got goods bakin'." Then she clumped away down the hall.

A couple minutes later, Loula skipped down the stairs. Her picture hadn't lied, except maybe she was chubbier in person. She looked about fourteen, and acted like ten. She stared at me from the other side of the screen door, then twisted to peer down the hall behind her. "Mommy?"

"It was me she called you for, Miss Loula. I'm lookin' for Mace Danahoe. I thought you might—"

"Danahoe?" she said, and burst straight into tears. "My Pete's dead," she wept, grinding fists against her eyes. "Mace said he got murdered. And my dog died the very same week. Cinders. Cinders and Pete, both gone." She stopped crying all of a sudden. "Do you think dogs go to Heaven?"

I said, "I'd like to think so. Horses, too."

She stuck her nose in the air. "I don't like horses. They step on you. Will you have cider?"

She opened the screen, grabbed my sleeve, and pulled me

inside. She was short, but she had me outweighed by a good forty pounds.

I said, "Thank you, but I have got no time for refreshments. I'm lookin' for Mace. You know where he went?"

"Away someplace. What you got against cider? It's bottled, ain't no bugs in it."

"What happened to his ma?"

Loula plopped down in a faded red parlor chair. "Pete's granddaddy."

"What about him?"

"I don't know. Something about their granddaddy. Pete and Mace's mommy died. Do you have a dog?"

"No. Did Mace go there? To where their granddaddy is?"

"Pete's dead. Can't go nowhere. Can't have a ranch with lots of smelly horses and nice shaggy black dogs." She started blubbering again.

I grabbed her by the shoulders and gave her a little shake. "Not Pete, Loula. Mace. Did he go down to Oro Tiempo? Down where his granddaddy is?"

Loula shrank back like that tiny shake was an attempt on her life. She opened her mouth wide and cried, "Mommy! Mommy!"

The fat woman appeared in the parlor door, a hard frown line between her beetley brows. "What you doin' to my Loula?"

"Tryin' to get a straight answer. I'm lookin' for Mace Danahoe, ma'am. And to tell you the truth, I'm gettin' real tired of sayin' so. You know where he went?"

She parked doughy hands on wide hips and sighed. "I see. Stop cryin', Loula. Go get yourself a cookie." Loula's tears gave quick way to a grin and she skipped out, humming.

"He talked 'bout a couple places," Loula's mother said. "You a friend?"

I wasn't quite sure if that was the right word for what Mace Danahoe was to me, but I said, "Yes'm."

"His mama, that'd be Opal, she got real poorly about four, five months back. Had a growth on her neck. Went from pea-sized to billiard ball to baker potato between new moons and turned blue-black. Couldn't swallow hardly nothin'. Doctor here said it was a goiter, then said it wasn't, then said he wouldn't touch it. Opal didn't know where her boys was. It finally got so bad she wrote that rich father of hers for help to see a specialist. You'll pardon my language, but that old Harlan Wilbeck is one low bastard. I know, 'cause I nursed Opal at the end, right here in my house, and I seen the one and only reply she got after she'd writ him four times. Was just one sheet of paper with no 'Dear Daughter' or 'Love, Father' or nothin'. Just said, 'I have no daughter named Opal,' and that was it, period. She died on me two days after, weighin' less than eighty pounds, and that tumor big as a sugar melon."

Without being asked, I slumped down in the chair Loula had just got out of. "Oh," was all I could think to say.

"Mace took it real bad. Raved about the whole family bein' dead, and it all bein' the old man's fault. Talked about goin' to Oro Tiempo to give his granddaddy what-for. Think I convinced him out of it, though. Been enough bad blood and bad business with that old devil already. He was talkin' about Tombstone 'fore he left, said it was a sproutin' town where a young fella could get in business on the ground floor. Mace always had a head for business. I'd say he went there."

From the back of the house, Loula called out, "Mommy, can I have some cider?"

"Yes, honey. Careful you don't spill and draw ants." She turned back to me, and melancholy overtook her face. "I was awful sad about Pete. I can't live forever, and I thought

Pete'd take care of her after I'm gone. He never seemed to mind, never seemed to notice the . . . the way my Loula is."

I stood up. "Thank you, Mrs. Mahoney. I appreciate your talkin' to me so frank. I'll try Tombstone."

Tombstone was only a two-day journey and I neared it late the second afternoon, but I waited till the dark hard center of the night to ride in. Though it was May, the nights were still chilly and I had my duster pulled round me with the collar turned up. I bypassed Allen Street, went round the back way to the Russ House, and reined Filibuster right up under the window of my old room. There was somebody sleeping in there, all right, and I could just make out the shape of one of Miss Justice's parasols, leaned up by the door. I tapped on the glass.

There was a grunt and the bedcovers shifted, but that was it. I tapped again.

The body on the bed sat up.

"What's that?" said Will Fowler, all grouchy. He had on a floppy nightcap and looked so silly I had a hard time not to giggle.

Then I heard Elma. "It was nothing. Go back to sleep, Mr. Fowler."

"It's me," I said low, "Gini Kincaid."

"Who?" said Will, still groggy and rubbing at his head.

"Miss Kincaid?" Elma Justice Fowler was there in a wink. She pushed the window the rest of the way up and clasped my hand across the sill. "How I've missed you! Are you well? Mr. Fowler and I have seen those awful handbills Joe Malone printed up. Do you think it wise to be in Tombstone?"

"More like necessary, Miss Justice. I mean, Mrs. Fowler. I'm tryin' to locate a man called Mace Danahoe."

Neither of them had seen or heard a thing, but they both promised to ask around. They agreed it was not smart for me to stay in Tombstone. "My husband will guide you to sanctuary," she said. "Get your pants on, Mr. Fowler."

He hauled on his britches and climbed out the window, then boosted me inside so I could chat with Miss Justice while we waited.

Ten minutes later he was back, mounted on Jelly and making "hurry up" motions with his hand. I hugged Elma Justice Fowler good-bye, reminded her about sending the wire I'd just written out to Tuck, and crawled straight from the sill to Filibuster's back. We were out of Tombstone in no time.

I had never spent much time with Will Fowler, but I liked him. He was a sizable man, square-jawed and wide-browed, with a solid, honest-to-the-bone look. I pegged him for the sort who'd end up mayor and always keep nickels in his pockets for the kids. "Where you takin' me, Mr. Fowler?"

"To a friend. And call me Will." He cleared his throat. "I never had a chance to thank you for Jelly. He is a fine animal, and Elma and I are proud to own him. I'd also like you to know how deeply we appreciated the, uh, other. It enabled us to start a small business here in town, and I believe within two years' time, my projections being correct, we'll have the resources to return east so that I might conclude my legal education." He shifted in his saddle a tad. I supposed it was pretty embarrassing for a man like him to thank a female for a gift of money.

I said, "You are welcome on both counts. We don't need to talk of it again."

From what I could see through the dark, he looked relieved.

I said, "There's been more trouble since I left. I don't want to talk too much about it for fear of causing you and

Miss Justice—I mean, Mrs. Fowler—grief. But you got a right to know I'm in worse straits than just what it says on that Malone poster."

He nodded. "I see. Then it's best you don't tell me, Miss Kincaid. Complicity, you know."

"Call me Gini."

We were just a few miles out of town near a stand of evergreen oak when a voice called, "Halt up, there!"

I near jumped out of my skin. I made to wheel Filibuster and take off, but Will Fowler reached across and stayed me.

"Who is that skulking in the night?" he called. "Come out from behind those trees!"

Two dark shapes, mounted men, emerged from the oak grove's shadows. One carried a rifle across his lap. One of them, I couldn't tell which, said, "Would that be Will Fowler?"

"It would."

The riders approached us. One said, "What sort of business have you got out here at three in the morning, Mr. Fowler?"

I was on the alert, for any of that Clanton and McLaury bunch would just as soon rob and shoot a body as shake hands, and they were known to lurk in desolate places. I wished I had a revolver. My squirrel gun was not a good weapon for close-in fighting, and Will Fowler was not armed, though you would not have known it by the courageous way he spoke.

"My business is my own," he said, just like it was the center of town at midday. "Who might I be addressing?"

The man with the rifle reached us first, and I knew I had gone from the skillet and straight into the cook fire when I recognized him.

"Didn't mean to offend," said Wyatt Earp. "By Christmas! Is that Irish Jenny Rose you've got there with you?"

"It's me, all right," I said, trying not to sound as nervous as I felt. "I'm aware I've used up my favor with you, Wyatt, but I want you to know I won't be taken in."

The man with him laughed and said, "This skinny little thing is the infamous fire-setting Terror of Tombstone?"

Will Fowler said, "Evening, Morgan," and the man, still laughing, nodded.

"You'll excuse my brother," Wyatt said. "He has had dealings with the Malones, too."

"Seems to me you've got an awful lot of brothers."

"I'm fortunate for it, Irish Jenny. And although up until a few hours ago I was part of a sworn posse, I am no longer even a temporary officer of the law." He had taken a cigar out of his pocket, and he paused to light up. "I am still in the saloon business, however. If you hadn't got into the habit of ticking off Joe Malone, I would have hired you away from Spider Eye Inga and set you on our stage at the Oriental." He shook out his match and flicked it away. "I have not given up politics entirely, though. I'm of a mind to run for county sheriff. Do you plan to stop in Tombstone?"

"Not unless you intend to win votes by force."

"You are too young and the wrong gender to do me much good at the polls. I take it that if I was to arrest you in my brother Virgil's stead, you'd put up a heated resistance?"

"Heated is too tame a word."

He sighed. "To tell the truth, Irish Jenny, I have been out after rustlers all night with no results, and am not much in the mood for a skirmish. On top of which, I don't believe Virgil needs his jail cluttered up. Unless, of course, you have got in more Dutch since you left here, and added a bank job or murder to your list."

He had meant it for a joke. I tried to return his smile, but I think mine was kind of thin.

"You running out on your wife, Fowler, or are you just escorting Irish Jenny?"

Will looked a little flustered, but he said, "I'm taking her to Jingles."

Wyatt tugged his mustache. "A fine choice. I trust you'll stay clear of town and away from combustible goods, Irish Jenny."

Just after the sun cleared the horizon, me and Will rode down into a winding little gorge and followed it along for about a half-mile until we came to a campsite.

A mine entrance yawned in the far bluff, and a lean-to and corral were jury-rigged a little farther down. The hind end of a swaybacked sorrel horse stuck out of the lean-to, tail swishing. In the corral, back turned, ears pinned, her black and white rump planted in the dirt, sat the pony Grace. The rest of the site was mostly dirt and rock with hardly a touch of color, except for the strangest building I have ever seen. It was little, maybe ten or twelve feet square, and glinted green and amber and blue and garnet like jewels.

Will cupped his hands round his mouth and called, "This is Will Fowler! Anybody alive in there?"

"Sufferin' miseries!" came the reply. "There be none so wicked as those who will come callin' unannounced."

And out of the sparkling house made of whiskey bottles and beer bottles and glass that had held soda pop and stomach bitters and croup tonic and hair oil, stepped Jingles Beldon.

"Morning," said Will. "Sorry to drop in without invitation."

Jingles held his hands high in the air, then grabbed his head and let out a whoop. "Why, if it isn't Attorney William B. Fowler and Geneva-Gini-for-Short-Kincaid!"

"I'm no lawyer yet," said Will, not that Jingles paid him any mind.

"Get down off that mouse-colored horse, Gini-for-Short! You too, counselor. It ain't often I get to entertain folks on such opposite sides of the law in one sitting. What happened to that old red and white firebrand pony you used to ride?"

Jingles's one-room house was a pure marvel. Mortared with just enough adobe clay to hold them together, the walls changed with the day, sparkled like treasure on the outside, made rainbows on the inside.

"Be hot as Hades in there come full summer," Jingles said after Will fed Jelly a butterscotch drop, mounted up, and bade us good-bye, "but ain't it a beaut? Well, make yourself to home, but watch that gruello horse around my Comanche. Don't suppose you'd want to go down the old shaft and fetch some breakfast, would you?"

The mine that opened near his camp was played out, and he used it for storage. His wagon was in there, along with mining equipment, boxes of explosives, and foodstuffs hung on ropes from the rafters. It was an odd place to store things, for that old shaft was also the source of his famous bat problem.

Hundreds, maybe thousands, roosted in the tunnel. They swarmed out at dusk and back in just before dawn. The floor was always slippery and the whole place reeked. Guano spattered the tinned goods and crates and the tarps Jingles used to blanket his rig. I followed his example and always took cover in the bottle house during their flying times. We'd watch through the clear bottles till they were either all in or all out, and only then would we open the door. They were not the kind that bite, but every time I had to go in there after supplies I got the collywobbles.

Having given over his old digs to the bats, Jingles was

working a mine another quarter-mile down the gorge. He wasn't having much luck with it yet.

"There's a vein, Gini-for-Short, there's a vein, all right. Comes out up yonder." He pointed high on the bluff. "But that's just the baby-finger tip of her. The rest's hidin' inside the rock, waitin' for me to tickle-tease her out."

The way he teased was to set a charge on an extra-long fuse, holler "Fire in the hole!" and then run at me fast as he could and shove me in the dirt. Since I was nobody's fool (except maybe Tyrone's) and always kept well back, I thought this was kind of silly. Also, Jingles was a born blaster, and could place a charge careful enough to gauge within a couple inches either way what would stay put and what would get vaporized. But he'd lope over and shove me down every dang time, regardless. To tell the truth, I don't believe Jingles really expected to make a rich strike. I think he just enjoyed the excuse for blasting.

Will Fowler paid us a call the next week, and brought the sorry news that Mace Danahoe was nowhere in Tombstone. I guess it just wasn't a day for good tidings, for he also brought out a few recent copies of the *Epitaph*, one of which carried an article about the capture, five weeks prior, of renegade Apache. Some had escaped, but the army had delivered Manuelito and Sees Silver and six others back to the reservation in chains. It made me feel ashamed, thinking of them treating such proud men that way.

Will said, "I ran into a friend of yours on the way out, Gini."

"Who was that?"

He smiled, reached into his coat, and pulled out a little paper package bound with a skinny green ribbon, tied real precise. Inside was a new deck of playing cards. There was a note that said, *The Spider Eye's new singer can't hold a candle to you, Irish. These are to help you pass the time. Regards, John Holliday.*

"I guess Wyatt must have told him," I said.

Will nodded. "Not much gets past any of the Earps' crowd these days. They have eyes in the night, what with that murderous Clanton outfit shoving them one direction, the Citizens·Safety Committee pushing the other, and the County Ring Democrats kicking the legs out from under honest men. We're having bad times in Cochise County, I fear."

He talked on for a while about local politics and who was doing right and who was doing wrong and who was being plain stupid. Being a staunch Republican, he backed the Citizens Safety Committee and the Earps, and explained his reasons in more two-dollar words than I knew existed. Miss Elma Justice had met and married her match for oration, all right.

He stayed for some midday tortillas and beans, and just before he left, he patted his pockets and said, "Almost forgot!"

He gave me a telegram, addressed to Elma Justice Fowler and dated three days earlier. It simply said, *WILL COMPLY,* and was signed T. Brennan.

Jingles went back to moving the rock his latest explosion had brought down, and I buried my nose in *Epitaphs*. I guess those papers must have inspired Jingles, for after I'd exhausted them, he brought me up to date on the news too stale to print, including the cave-in of a Tombstone street.

"Fools tunneled smack underneath it," he said, "and the timbers gave out. Whole buggy, team and all, there one minute, gone the next. Boom! Straight down." He scratched the bald circle on his scalp. "Miracle nobody was killed. Had to shoot one of the horses, but they led the other out safe, a mile west of town. Heard the buggy was a wreck.

Good thing they were not carrying bottles. Or nitroglycerin." His head snapped toward the lean-to. He hollered, "Hi there, Comanche! Mind your manners, you villain, or I will have to take measures!"

As far as I could see, that poor swayback wasn't doing more than drooping his head down, but Jingles added, "I mean it, you murderous rascal!"

He turned back to me like there'd been no interruption and said, "Nitro. Now, there's something might discourage a bat. You blast a mine, they just wait a few days and move back in. Pigheaded, bats are. But with nitro, a feller could flick it at them, a drop at a time, individual-like. . . ."

"That happened back home, too," I said. "In Hanged Dog."

"You hurl fireballs at your bats there?"

"No, I mean the cave-in part. Except it wasn't a buggy. The old Busted Flush Mine starts a half-mile out of town, and the C shaft runs under Pinkerton's Café and the Malone Bros. Mercantile. Goes all the way past Juan Marcos's cantina on Solana Row before it turns back out of town. But that one's pretty deep and supposed to be shored up good. What gave out was a branch that ran under the old cemetery. Coffins kept droppin' through the tunnel roof. Had to seal it off and move the graveyard. My Gam's in the new one."

"Good for her," he said. "A wise woman."

I would have remarked that she didn't really have much say in the matter, but sometimes there was no talking to Jingles.

One morning I woke first and lay quiet, watching the colors slide across us. A little beam of blue ended in a sky-colored circle on his face. I watched the sun move it over his head, across the bald spot. His lids fluttered and he sat up so quick it startled me.

"Your eyeballs woke me," he growled. "You think it's

polite, starin' at a sleeping person? If I am gonna be on display, maybe I should just take a job with the circus and get paid for it! I saw an elephant once, I tell you that? Touched it, too. They got the prickliest little hairs. . . ."

"I was lookin' at your head, Jingles. What happened to it? That's not a normal place for a man to start his balding."

He stretched his arms. "Ain't a normal place for a man to be scalped, neither, but there you are." He stood up and I followed him outside.

"I never heard of such a thing. How can you be scalped and still be alive?"

"Easy, if you ain't dead when they scalp you. Same fella with the elephant had him an ostrich bird. I'm not talkin' camels here, no ma'am. I've had a gulletful of camels. Had camels coming out my ears. But an elephant and an ostrich? Now, *there's* a pair!"

"Holy Hannah, Jingles! You talk more sideways than anybody I ever knew!"

He gave out with a sigh, pulled up his suspenders, and lowered himself on a rock by the cook site. "You know why I got all those bells on my wagon?"

"I thought you liked 'em."

"Used to 'em, I guess. But Apache, they hate 'em. Too much noise, callin' up spirits or somethin'. I don't like Apache, nosiree. Got tangled up with a few Coyotero Apache about ten or twelve years back, 'fore they got reservationized. I have heard there's some scholar feller says the Indians are the lost tribes of Israel, but I don't believe it for a slap second. No kin of Moses or Abraham would have tied me to a wagon wheel and made ready to set me afire for a party game."

"What happened?"

"Well, he says they come over on boats or rafts or

some-such, got off in Brazil or Mexico or maybe it was the Yucatan, and—"

"I mean the Apache!"

"Oh. Well, a scouting party of troopers happened on us, and the red devils grabbed up all they could carry and hopped on their ponies. But before the last heathen galloped out, he diddled quick on my head with the tip of his knife and took a little chunk of me for a good-bye gesture. That just ain't a Hebrew thing to do, and I'll not be convinced otherwise."

"I have a hard time with that, Jingles."

"So do I. I bet you never knew any Israelite to carve a man's head, did you?"

"No, I mean . . . The Apache may take a lot of things, but they don't lift scalps."

"This one did, even if it was just a token. Trooper what caught up with that knife-happy skunk brought my hair back to me, but it was too late to stick 'er back on. Kept it for a watch fob, but I lost it a couple years back in a card game. I got a few other scars from that day I could show you if I was an immodest man, which I am not. Subject closed. Now, let's talk ostrich."

13

Oro Tiempo

Two weeks to the day after I'd moved in with Jingles, Tuck came for me. After I gave him a big squeeze hello, he held me at arm's length and looked me up and down. "Well, you're doing fine, Miss Gini. Just fine."

I looked him over, too. I said, "Tuck, I believe you have grown some stomach back."

He patted his belly and grinned wide. "I suppose you'll run it off me again, now that we're setting out on an errand of mercy."

I couldn't for the life of me figure out what mercy had to do with stolen gold. I was about to say so when he added, "I'd have hustled old Zeus a tad faster if your wire'd been more specific. As it was, I had to read the sad tidings in a Tucson newspaper."

"It was in the paper?" I went all cold, thinking for sure the whole dang world already knew about Tyrone being murdered and me doing it.

Tuck dipped fingers into his pocket, brought out a folded clipping, and handed it to me.

There was a picture of Mace Danahoe and another of an old, white-haired man with a waxed mustache and eyes like frost. The caption said he was Harlan Wilbeck, and the big print under that read, *Oro Tiempo Mine King Slain by Grandson*. The story began:

Late on the evening of April 19th, gunshots emanated from the home of wealthy Oro Tiempo citizen and founder, Harlan Wilbeck, aged 79 years. Alarm was immediately raised, and Wilbeck's housekeeper, Verleen Hitchcock, rushed downstairs to find the home's front door standing open and papers rifled in Wilbeck's study. A rapid search of the house, conducted by Mrs. Hitchcock and two other servants, revealed a grisly tableau on the second floor, where Mr. Wilbeck's blood-soaked and lifeless body lay sprawled across his own bed.

Suspicion immediately fell upon Wilbeck's grandson, Mason Danahoe of Mendacity, with whom Wilbeck was known to be on poor terms. On a visit to the house three days prior, Danahoe quarreled openly with his grandfather and was forcibly removed from the premises by Wilbeck employees.

The suspect was hastily apprehended by Pima County Deputy Sheriff "Cotton" Carnahan in nearby Becerro Suelto, and brought to swift trial before Judge Ray Dean Mountjoy's court. Danahoe pleaded his innocence, insisting he had been thirty miles away en route to Leona Springs at the time of the killing. Jury members were not convinced, and did not need to leave the courtroom to return a verdict of "guilty as charged."

Wilbeck's surviving partner and son-in-law, prominent businessman Burl LaFouche, commented that he was well satisfied with the law's handling of his nephew. He told this reporter, "They cannot hang the murdering (expletive) soon enough for me."

The story went on about how Wilbeck had come out to the Territory in the olden days and struck it rich, and told what a sterling citizen he'd been and how he'd boosted the territorial economy and how everybody loved him. I didn't much care about that part (since from what I'd heard it was practically all lies), and skipped down to the end. Execution was scheduled for May 22 at ten A.M. I had lost track of exact dates the last few weeks, but I didn't think we were too far from Mace's last day.

Tuck pointed to the bottle house. "There's a marvel."

"You should see it at sunup," said Will Fowler, who had guided Tuck out from Tombstone and was currently standing by, holding Zeus and Jelly.

I meant to tell Tuck about Tyrone, but instead my mouth said, "Sees Silver got caught and taken back to San Carlos."

"Bound to happen," he replied. He looked past the bottle house, down the gorge. Jingles had just come into sight, whistling and talking to himself and Gracie as she plodded beside him, pulling the little rock cart.

Gaze still fixed on Jingles, Tuck said, "When did they take him? Sees Silver, that is."

"Near two months back, according to the *Epitaph*."

"Then I imagine you're celebrated among the Apache Nations by now, Miss Gini. How's it feel to be famous?"

"Beg pardon?"

"There's been lots of time for talk around the fires, honey, and tales get stretched with the telling. Likely both you and Ghost Ruggles are fabled characters by now. I believe that man's about to lose a piece of his thigh to that pony."

Jingles was still a ways off, but close enough that we could hear him jabbering to Gracie. Her neck snaked out every few steps, her yellow pony teeth clicking close to his pants leg, never quite catching cloth. There was a kind of rhythm to it.

Tuck turned to Will Fowler. "That the gentleman you told me has been taking care of Miss Gini? Jingles Beldon?"

Will nodded.

Tuck said, "Wouldn't be the same as Horatio Beldon, would it?"

Will said he believed so.

Tuck muttered, "My goodness," then said to me, "Where's Tyrone? I had an idea he'd be with you."

"He's not, I mean, he's . . ." I'd been practicing in my head for weeks, but all of a sudden I couldn't muster the grit to fess up to the killing. Instead, I told him about visiting Loula Mahoney's mother. "She said Mace was awful mad when he left there," I said at the end of the telling. "Maybe he really did kill his granddaddy. Maybe we got no right to break him free, if that's what you're of a mind to do."

Will Fowler said "May I?" and took the clipping from my hand.

Tuck didn't notice. He stared straight at me, and his face was hard. He said, "Miss Gini, I know you and Mace have scrapped like terriers since the dawn of your acquaintance-ship. But I'll tell you this once, and only once: that boy may be a hothead a good measure of the time and a fool on occasion, but he's got no murder in him. If you didn't believe that, why did you wire me in the first place?"

"Excuse me," said Will Fowler. He had finished reading. "Am I to understand you plan to aid and abet a jailbreak?"

Tuck took the clipping from him, folded it careful, and stuck it in his pocket. "This is a grievous miscarriage, friend Fowler. I can't say who really killed Harlan Wilbeck, though I've got my suspicions; but I can tell you it wasn't young Danahoe. This hanging will be a murder if there ever was one, plotted and planned by Burl LaFouche to clear the last heir out of the way. From what I have lately heard of Tombstone shenanigans, legal high jinks should be no news to you."

Will nodded thoughtfully. "I see your point, Mr. Brennan."

Just then Jingles reached us. He was whistling "Rowena Said She Didn't, But Katie Said She Did" with added gusto now that he figured to be within earshot of an audience. When he stopped, Gracie made one last try for his trousers, then closed her eyes and plopped into a splay-legged sit.

Will Fowler did the introductions.

Tuck shook Jingles's hand. "Pleased," he said. "That's quite the pony you've got there. Do you get chomped on much?"

Jingles lifted up his hat and rubbed at his bald spot. "Only by gnats and spiders, though I once got raked bad by a javelina sow. My Gracie is an even-tempered puss-cat. It's only by her calming influence that I am able to handle my devil-horse, Comanche." He pointed toward the swayback dozing in the corral. "He is treachery incarnate."

Tuck nodded as serious as if he'd seen Satan's own horns growing right out of that horse's head. He said, "I thank you for keeping Miss Gini safe. You wouldn't be the Horatio Beldon that raised the Stars and Stripes over the Presidio at El Cedro in fifty-six and told the Mexican Army to go to hell, would you?"

"Guilty," Jingles said. "And I'm pleased to make your acquaintanceship. I had heard you were dead in Yuma Prison. How do you feel about bats?"

"I feel they keep the bugs down to a tolerable level, friend Beldon. And as much as I'd admire to discuss this further, I'm afraid Miss Gini and I have no time to spare. That is, if she is not too high-minded to come along."

I looked him right in the eye. "Try to stop me, Tuck Brennan."

He laughed, head back. "Perhaps another day, Beldon?"

"Like to tag along and confabulate," Jingles said, "but somebody's got to stay here and hold the place down. These past years I have not had much in the way of escapades. I miss the old days. Gonna miss Gini-for-Short, too."

Will Fowler took his leave. Tuck shook his hand and so did I. "Say good-bye to Miss Jus—I mean Mrs. Fowler," I said. "Give her my best."

He said he would, then untied a sack from his saddle horn and handed it over. Inside was a five-pound ham, a bag of boiled eggs and another of biscuits, some dried apples, tinned peaches, honey, cactus jelly, and what looked to be a whole chicken, cut up and fried perfect. "Miss Nellie and my Elma pressed this on me as I went out the door," he said. "They send apologies that it was not a richer parcel."

It was more and better food than I had seen in some time, since Jingles preferred to live solely on beans, tortillas, and game. I am a good cook, but there is only so much a person can do with jackrabbit and snake.

I said, "Thank them for me, Will. This is treasure." And then, even though he turned a little red and made a harrumphing sound in the back of his throat, I hugged him.

As we watched Will and Jelly lope out of sight, Jingles announced that he had some blasting to do and had best get back to the shaft. I went to hug him, but he stepped away. I believe his eyes were wet. He said, "You get moving, Gini-for-Short, and get out of what's left of my hair. I'm a man who has urgent chores."

He gave Gracie a tug, and he must have caught her off guard because she stood right up without being levered. They ambled on down the gorge, Jingles all kind of slumped over, Gracie nipping at his trousers every couple steps. Just before he rounded the bend and left our sight, he turned and hollered, "You take good care of that girl, Tuck Brennan, or you'll have Horatio Beldon to answer to!"

Tuck was in such a toot to get us gone that he didn't give me any chance to tell him about Tyrone. It was just as well.

Between learning Mace's troubles and saying good-bye to Jingles and Will, I had lost both the heart and the courage to confess. When I tacked up Filibuster, he said, "Why, what's happened to your Jigsaw horse, Miss Gini?"

"Murdered," I said, and snugged up the girth. "Everybody's murdered."

He boosted me up. "There sounds to be a sad tale in this, honey, but you'll have to tell me on the trail. You got your tortoise?"

I patted my satchel.

"Then let's get cracking. We've got just five days to get ourselves to Oro Tiempo, and it's bad country. I wish Tyrone was here."

I said, "No, you don't," and galloped out ahead of him.

After a long day and more hot and dusty miles than I cared to count, we camped on the northwest edge of the Santa Rita Mountains. It was a clear, warm night, but there was no moon and I was glad for the light of our cook fire. We were both beat out from riding so hard all day, and neither of us said much till after we'd had our supper. Tuck fished the last chunk of peach from the tin and gave it to Malachi before he poured himself another cup of coffee and settled back. "That was a fine hen your friends sent, Miss Gini," he said with a yawn. "I believe we have got some catching up to do."

I was in no mood for it. I hadn't got round to mentioning the gold, mainly because I'd have to mention Tyrone in the process. Advising a man like Tuck that you have murdered his longtime friend is not an easy thing, even when there is a fortune at the end of the telling.

"For my part," he went on, "I've been up at Queenie's." He began to fiddle with his pipe. "She was kind enough to give me over her extra room, and I have been doing some gardening and hog-slopping and pie-eating and fattening up, and that's about it."

His bedroll was already laid out, with his saddle rigged for a pillow at one end. He stretched out and cocked an arm over it. "All I have wanted these past years, apart from living long enough to get out of Yuma Prison, was to retire in tranquillity and grow myself a nice, comfortable belly. Now Mace goes and gets himself in trouble, likely for no other reason than to work some fat off me. Take no offense, Miss Gini. You are a camp cook extraordinaire. But your meals get mixed in with a good deal of outdoor work, such as vacating the scene of infernos and getting shot at by Mexican bandits. Those things tend to take the weight off a man. What have you and that rascal Tyrone been up to?"

I opened my mouth, but no words came out.

"Miss Gini?"

I took a deep breath. "Tuck, I have fretted on this and thought up about sixteen ways to slip it into the conversation casual-like, but right now I can't think of a blamed one of them. Tyrone's dead."

He sat up with a jerk, pipe snatched from his mouth and gripped tight in his hand.

My legs were too shaky to hold me. I sat down on the other side of the fire. "He's dead, Tuck. He was in cahoots with Harlan Wilbeck and he stole our gold and behaved low with a hussy and murdered my horse, and I killed him."

Tuck looked awful serious, which did not make me feel any better, or any less scared. He said, "I think you had best start from the beginning, Miss Gini."

I did, from Tyrone getting beat up at Ehrenberg to what I'd overheard at the Half Moon Hotel about Ty's double-crossing us—and Wilbeck, too—and leaving the gold back at Cañon de los Espejos; to me walking in on him and Pansy and then pulling the trigger; and right on through to Weevil

Jukes slaughtering my poor Jigsaw. I think I got everything in, though I was terrible nervous during the telling. And in the end I broke down and bawled.

Tuck got up and came over to me. I jerked away when he sat, thinking maybe he was going to give me a smack and rightfully so, but instead he put one arm round me and got out his handkerchief. He held it up to my face, and said, "Blow."

I did. And then I started crying worse because he was being so nice.

"Hush," he whispered. "It's been a bad time for you, hasn't it? I'm sorry for your hurt, child. I never should have let you ride out with him in the first place."

I snuffled into the kerchief a last time and handed it back. "I would'a gone anyway."

"I suppose you would." His pipe had gone out. He relit it one-handed and gave me a soft squeeze. "In my life, I have had the great pleasure to know four genuinely strong-headed women. One was a long time ago, when I was young and cocky and didn't have the sense to value such a rara avis. The second was Miss Perry LeFleur, whom you resemble more every day, honey, and that's a compliment. The third was your Gam, and the fourth is this little brown-eyed bit of nothin' under my arm."

I rubbed at my eyes. "Who was the first lady? What happened to her?"

"Her name was Edith Brown, and she married my best friend. He was the boy I told you about, the boy with the memory like yours. By Hera, that was a long time ago. A world away." He smiled. "Well, better than half a continent, anyway." He pointed out into the night, toward the heavens; jabbing with his pipe stem, drawing from star to star. "There, in the sky. Can you find Arcturas? Do you see the North Star?"

We sat quiet for a few minutes, and then, soft, he said, "I met Tyrone when he was just seventeen. First shook his hand after a cantina fistfight in a godforsaken little hamlet called Tres Arroyos, New Mexico. Bravado, that's what Ty had. In Yavapai City, I watched him run through a barrage of lead to pick up the moneybags after Elroy Chavez went down. Ty got hit four times and kept running. Any sane man would have just laid down and bled to death, but not Tyrone O'Neill. Not when there was cash involved."

I knew my history. I said, "Elroy Chavez died there."

"He did indeed. He wasn't dead just yet, though, and when Ty went racing out there, we thought he was going for Elroy, and the hell with the money. Turned out it was the hell with Elroy, instead. Of course, Elroy was shot up even more after all that lead came flying at Tyrone. Ty said he could tell he was a goner, so we just let the subject alone. But after that, I knew about Tyrone. Do you know what I mean, Miss Gini? I *knew* about him."

He picked up a stick and poked at the fire. Sparks flurried up, caught in the breeze. "I tell you truly, I always liked him despite the way he was, and I believe I understand why you were so fixed on him. Ty was like that. Men admired him. He melted women. There was none better in a scrape. I'd have trusted him with my immortal soul so long as I was sure I had something he wanted. Outside of that, well . . . I guess it doesn't surprise me about his having hid that bullion all over again. It was lucky you overheard. You can take some solace in that."

"But I don't understand, Tuck. I don't understand how he could be so nice and so mean all at once, and . . ."

"And not know the difference?"

I nodded.

"It was just something missing in him, honey, something the rest of us are born with. And he couldn't be changed, not any more than you can make a blind man see by reading him a list of colors."

A chill traveled through me. I pulled my knees up under my chin and hugged my legs. "Doc warned me. He said Ty would sell his own mother for dice money."

"Who?"

"A gambler in Tombstone. The one Pete admired."

"Then Pete finally admired a wise man." He took a puff on his pipe. His tobacco smelled sweet and homey. "I'm truly sorry about your Jigsaw horse, Miss Gini."

"I still dream about him. I dream him so real that I'm shocked when I go to saddle up and Filibuster's there instead. I don't even dream about Gam anymore, but I dream Jigsaw most every night. Seems wrong, but I can't help it."

"You can't blame yourself." Malachi had wandered toward us, and Tuck scooped him up. "Outside of your old hard-shelled friend here, Jigsaw was all you had left of your growing up. It'll get better. Always does."

He put Malachi down, then chuckled low.

"What?"

"I fear you're going to have a hard time of teasing when Mace hears you set the match to Weevil Jukes's hides. I believe I would've enjoyed seeing that myself."

A coyote gave voice in the distance. We both fell silent and listened as another joined in. Tuck still had his arm round me and was rubbing my shoulder, comforting and strong, and for a little while it was just the coyotes' song, the pop and snap of our fire, and the thin far-off whine of wind lacing through the mountains. It wasn't till the coyotes broke off their music that I mustered the courage to ask the question that had gnawed at me since that first day in the Thirsty Buzzard Saloon.

"Tuck," I began, staring at my knees because it was too

important a thing to ask eye-to-eye, "when was the last time you were in Hanged Dog? Before you were sent away to prison, I mean."

He rubbed his chin. "I believe it would have been the fall of sixty-four, Miss Gini."

"Maybe around September?"

"Sounds to be on the mark."

I took a deep breath. "Tuck, you ever notice that your hair is about the same color as mine? Except for the gray, I mean." I was going to add in about our noses, both straight and narrow, and us both having dimpled chins; but my throat closed up on me.

He waited a minute before he said, "Honey, if you're asking what I think you're asking, I plain don't know. It's a hard thing to say, but I doubt Perry herself could have told you for sure. I'll say this for certain, though: if I ever had a daughter, I'd be proud to have her half the girl you are."

Three days of rugged country later, we were in the Black Tank Mountains. It was just coming sunset when me and Tuck rode down into a little valley, about fifty yards off the road and well hid. We tied our horses in the brush and climbed to the top of a ridge. Flat on our bellies and taking turns with a spyglass, we peered down on Oro Tiempo.

The town nestled in a flat, boat-shaped cup in the land. Hills or rock ridges rose up on every side. It was not a very big place, but a town hall, a steepled church, and some stores and houses and such were strewn over the valley floor. The middle part of Oro Tiempo was mostly businesses and storefronts, with the dwellings at the edges. At the far end, where the valley narrowed and the hills pressed in hard, were rows of lean-tos and shacks. I guess even as small a place as Oro Tiempo has got its poor.

Most curious was the biggest, grandest, three-story wood

house I had ever seen. It had turrets and geegaws and gingerbread aplenty and was painted mostly green, with blue and orange trim. Genuine stained glass glittered in some of the windows. It centered the town like a big bright jewel, and looked all the stranger for being just about the only all-wood structure in the whole place. A yellow-haired woman stood on the front porch, by the swing. She was pulling the cover over a birdcage.

I handed Tuck back his spyglass and said, "That's sure a fancy whorehouse they got down there. You reckon that's the madam?"

He chuckled. "You'll find no soiled doves there, Miss Gini, and I believe the lady is Mace's Aunt Ruby. That's the former home of his late granddaddy, Harlan Wilbeck. By the way Ruby's making herself to home, I'd wager Burl LaFouche is long settled in."

He waved a hand toward the northern hills. "Black Tank Creek runs, according to season, in the next valley over. Mining operation's over there." Next he pointed down toward the main street, to a place about three blocks past the Wilbeck house. "There's the jail."

I could see it plain. A scaffold was rigged up in the vacant lot next to it. Two men were testing the trapdoor lever, which looked to be sticking.

Tuck pulled at my sleeve. "Come on, honey."

We camped two valleys over. When Tuck woke me, it was still dark. He had on a rumpled black suit and wire-rimmed glasses, and there was a beat-up *Book of Mormon* in his hand.

"Tuck?" I pulled myself up on one elbow and rubbed my eyes. "What are you doin'?"

"Rouse yourself from the arms of Morpheus, Miss Gini, and help me break camp."

He didn't even give me time to make coffee, just got busy saddling the horses. I started rolling up our blankets. By his bed was an opened paper parcel, fluttering in the breeze. When I picked it up, a dress fell out.

I held it up. It was not very stylish, and our fire had burnt down so low that there wasn't enough light to tell what color it was. "Is this mine?"

Tuck gave his horse a gentle poke in the belly and tugged again at his girth strap. "Was going to be," he said, "but the plans have changed since I bought the gear."

"Changed how?"

The girth was tight enough to suit him, because he let the stirrup drop and moved on to saddle Filibuster. "When I first concocted this plot and bought the getups, I figured on you and me and Tyrone. Then it got to be just us two, and I figured it might still work. But now it's just me, Miss Gini."

"But—"

"Hush, child. It's been fourteen, fifteen years since there were posters with my face on them, and I've changed a good bit since then, even if Methuselah's brother is down there to recognize me. But there's fresh paper out on you from your Malone fire. That shooting in Half Moon Crossing's likely been added on by now, too. I won't take the chance of you being recognized."

I stuck the dress under my arm and rolled up his blankets. "How they goin' to recognize me if I'm disguised?"

He finished tacking Filibuster and patted him on the neck before he came to help me with the blankets. "They might not. But what if something goes wrong? They catch me, I'm charged with aiding a jailbreak. They catch you, it's murder. Besides, that whole town is populated with Harlan Wilbeck's henchmen—Burl LaFouche's, now—and their kin. They'll go doubly hard on anybody who has the tiniest sympathy with Mace Danahoe. Now give me that dress."

I jumped back, the dress clamped under my elbow. "No sir, Tuck Brennan. I have come this far, and I'm not backin' out now."

He kicked out the fire. "Why, Miss Gini!" he said with a laugh. "You act like you've got a choice! Now get cracking and climb up on your horse."

Being as there was only the light of the stars and a skinny crescent moon to see by, it took us almost an hour to pick our way to the road, follow it two miles, then cut off into the valley below the ridge we'd spied from the day before. All the while, Tuck would not hear a word about me riding in with him, and by the time he called a halt in the valley, he was so annoyed that all he said was, "Get off your horse. Now."

By then the sun was on its way up, so we could see what we were doing. He took a blanket and rigged it over my saddle, pulling up the stirrups first; then tied it round with twine that he fixed in a tear-away knot like you use to tether an animal. When he was finished, Filibuster appeared to be a well-loaded packhorse.

I couldn't stand being quiet anymore. I said, "How am I supposed to ride him now?"

"You aren't. I'm taking him for Mace."

"Well, how's *he* goin' to—"

Tuck pointed to the rope end hanging down from the knot. "When we come out, all he'll have to do is jerk that and the whole thing will fall apart."

I folded my arms across my chest. "Seems to me like a lot of trouble for no reason."

He let out a big sigh. "Don't you think it might be just a tad suspicious leading an extra saddle horse up to the jail twenty-four hours before the scheduled execution of a notorious outlaw, even if it is a humble servant of the Lord doing the leading? Don't you think that might make somebody wonder just a little bit?"

I looked at my feet. I felt pretty stupid, all right.

Tuck came over and put his hand on my shoulder. "I'm sorry, Miss Gini. I didn't mean to snap. It's been a while since I attempted a show like this." He put his spyglass into my hand, curled my fingers round it. "You watch through this. When you see us coming, you quickstep yourself over to the road. I'll try to snag another horse on the way out of town, but be prepared to be snatched up on the fly, regardless. Understand?"

"You make me pretty mad sometimes, Tuck Brennan."

He held up his *Book of Mormon* and, grinning, said, "That's Brother Brennan to you, Sister Gini." Then he kissed me on the forehead, said, "Don't worry, honey," and took off toward the road. I climbed to the crest of the ridge and stretched out, spyglass to my eye.

He went in slow, Zeus and Filibuster plodding. The sun was clear up by then, and it had brought the wind with it. It sang and whistled through the rocks around me; and though it came from behind and was not blowing into my face or eyes, it pelted the back of my head with grit. Down below, it raised a white blanket of blowing dust, thick as fog along the Colorado, that clouded the ground knee-high on Tuck's horses and made their long, blue shadows float and wave. Tuck had his *Book of Mormon* out and open, like he was studying on it real serious. He was traveling so leisurely that I got kind of bored and had myself a look at the rest of the town.

Oro Tiempo was coming awake. Ruby LaFouche must have been a real early riser, as she was already in her backyard, overseeing two maids who were beating Persian rugs, adding more dust to the breeze. A stage was out front of the Wells Fargo office, and two fellas were loading on trunks and bags. Over in the churchyard, a couple Mex kids threw sticks for a brown and white dog to fetch.

It looked like there'd be plenty of time before the festivities, and the ground under me was iron-hard. I still had that dress, which had turned out to be an ugly shade of brown, and which I had carried all the way from camp in hope that Tuck would change his mind. I rolled it up for a chin pillow. By the time I got it fixed, the wind had picked up some. Ruby LaFouche was helping her maids take down the rugs, Tuck was about a block away from the sheriff's office, and the stage, kicking up billows of alkali dust, barreled out of town and toward me. It rumbled past, down on the road, but I kept my glass trained on the jail.

Tuck went inside. Two minutes went by, then five. The wind cried through the rocks, burned the back of my head, whipped at my hair. I clamped my hat to my head with one hand.

It wasn't real hot yet, but sweat started to bead on my brow, where the wind didn't catch it, and run down to blur the looking end of the spyglass. I was wiping the lens when the first shots sounded.

I got the glass back to my eye in time to see Tuck, already on Zeus, pull his gun and fire toward the jail. Mace yanked the rope on Filibuster's camouflaged saddle. Wind snatched the blanket, sailing it up the street. The stirrups flopped down and banged Filibuster in the ribs. He spooked and jumped away just as Mace tried to climb on.

Somebody was shooting from inside the jail. Tuck's hat flew forward before the wind took it the other way. Zeus reared, then bucked out in back. Tuck almost went off him. Mace got a foot in Filibuster's stirrup and hopped up.

People stuck their heads out windows and doors, pulled them back in like startled tortoises. Somebody started ringing the business out of the church bell. Two fellas, rifles flashing, came running up the street behind Tuck and Mace as they galloped toward me. Gun barrels poked from second-story windows. Men dashed out of buildings, threw themselves behind wagons and water troughs, raised rifles and handguns.

Tuck and Mace weren't shooting at all then, but the gunfire sounded like string after string of firecrackers. Hunched in their saddles, wind in their faces, dust streaming behind them, they passed the scaffold, the hotel, two blocks of storefronts. They were just coming up to the Wilbeck mansion when Tuck got hit.

He fell straight back and disappeared into the blowing roil of dust. Mace wheeled Filibuster and went back. I saw him lean down, his arm stretched out, but it was too late.

Armed men were all around, closing in, tightening the circle. Tuck lay on the ground; at least I figured he did, as I could not see him for the dust. Mace's hands rose over his head. A man in a tan shirt, badge glinting on his chest, motioned to him to dismount. He did, and no sooner had his boots touched earth than that lawman swung his rifle butt and smashed it into the side of his head. Mace dropped to his knees. I could just see his head and shoulders. Then the man kicked him over into the dirt and I couldn't see him at all.

A good-sized crowd had gathered. Even Ruby LaFouche came out on her front porch. Handkerchief held to her face, she stood beside her caged canary and watched. A big-stomached man in a suit came out and stood next to her, thumbs hooked behind his lapels.

Somebody caught Zeus and led him back. They picked up Mace and threw him across Filibuster's saddle, then put Tuck over Zeus. I did not know if he was dead or alive until they walked the horses past the undertaker's office and carried him into the jail.

During the next hour the wind died down some, and the jailhouse was busy with comings and goings. A doctor was there, for I saw him tote in his black bag. I watched when they led the horses away and took them to the livery, which turned out to be across the weedy lot in back of the jail.

I lay there all morning and afternoon, watching and thinking, and saying a few prayers, too. It was dusk before I realized how hungry and thirsty I was. I didn't have food or water, or even Malachi to talk to. All I had was an ugly, wrinkled brown dress. I skidded my way off the ridge and back into the little valley, spread out the dress for a poor mattress, and tried to sleep.

14

Race for the Gold

It was not yet dawn when I entered Oro Tiempo, and as I walked down the center of the main street, most buildings were still dark-windowed. I had on the dress, which was so big that it bagged over my clothes. I don't know what Tuck could have been thinking when he bought it.

Now, when I was about nine, Gam told me how Apache boys steel themselves by making a hard run of four miles with a mouthful of water, which they are not allowed to swallow or spit out. I didn't run any four miles, but I got myself a mouthful of water and I dog-trotted up and down Solana Row for the whole of an August afternoon. I did not swallow one drop till it came dinnertime, and Gam made me. I figured that if I could do that when I was just a kid, a little drymouthed march down into Oro Tiempo couldn't be all that tough. My lips were cracked from thirst, and my stomach, having been deprived of vittles since dinner two days before, had gone from noisy to hurting. I tried not to think about it, or about the light-headed way I felt. I told myself it was almost a True Apache Test, and even though I stumbled a few times and fell once, I made it to the sheriff's office.

The lobby was small and lantern-lit, with a central aisle and a desk on each side. A thick door with a barred window was set in the back wall. The cells were beyond.

I guess they figured they'd already locked up every genuine desperado in the county, since there was only one man on duty. He was middle-aged, lanky, and wore a deputy's badge. Feet propped up, he sat behind the left-hand desk, and he was reading a Monkey-Ward catalog. He was not the lawman who had busted Mace with his rifle butt, but that did not make me like him any better.

At my boot step, he put down his catalog, tugged open the top desk drawer, and pulled out a pistol. I swallowed, hard and dry. "Don't shoot me, mister," I whispered, voice cracking. "I just want to report a thieved horse."

He put his gun away, then got me a chair and some water, for which I was wholly grateful. After I drank the first cup, I told him I had been riding along toward town the day before when a big man in a black suit jumped out from behind some rocks and took my horse at gunpoint.

"He is a round-muscled horse," I said, after another drink. My voice was coming back toward normal. "Gruello-colored, five years of age, with a snip of white on his nose. He is the only horse my papa and I have got, and I want you to find him and arrest the culprit."

The deputy scratched his sunburnt neck. He had a skinny, narrow-eyed face and a nose like an axe blade. "And might I ask why a little thing like you is out ridin' the desert all by her lonesome? Ain't safe out there, what with highwaymen and unsavory characters and more Apache vermin bustin' out of San Carlos last week."

I was real tempted to pursue the Apache part of that and ask if he knew the names of the men who had got free, but instead I said, "If it's any of your business, my papa is breakin' rock at a location I am not inclined to divulge, on account of he thinks it's a rich vein. I was comin' in to see the town and pick up some flour and salt. Plus, I heard you were goin' to have a hangin'. I never saw a hangin' before."

The deputy stood up and went to his file cabinet. He was smiling. He said, "You stick around long enough, it might get to be two. And I think we have already got your gruello horse. The wheels of justice turn fast in Oro Tiempo. I'll need you to sign a complaint."

"If you have got my horse, sir, I'd admire to see him before I do any sort of paperwork. I have been terrible worried."

He said he supposed it was all right and led me outside, then round back and across the lot to the livery. The sun was more than halfway clear of the horizon by then. Roosters were crowing, and the town was just waking. There was nobody on duty at the livery, though. It was not a very nice one, being dark and rank, like they were too cheap to lime down the stalls. We walked toward the back, and he pointed at Filibuster.

"That him?"

"It is. Where's my saddle and such? I had a pet tortoise in my bag when that highwayman stole it. I need to make sure he's all right."

Malachi was fine, but there was a bullet hole right through my satchel. I did not have time to see what had got ruined, though. I told the deputy that I wanted to spend a little time with my critters, but that I would be up directly to sign the complaint. He walked out, whistling.

I found our vittles bag and hacked off a chunk of leftover ham, just to shut my stomach up. While I gnawed on it I tacked Filibuster, then found Tuck's gear and saddled Zeus. I saw right away why he had bucked so bad out front of the jail. A long gash ran across his neck where he had been grazed by a slug. Somebody had cleaned it up and salved it. They had also been lazy enough to leave the salve jar in the stall. I stuck it in Tuck's saddlebags.

Mace's horse was there, too. He had not been taken good

care of, as he was awful dirty and his mane and tail were matted. I curried him quick (just on his back where the saddle would go, so he would not get sores), and tacked him up, too. I filled all the canteens and water bags, then grabbed an empty grain sack, scooped about twenty pounds of oats into it, and tied the sack behind Mace's saddle. I did all this in about ten minutes, and then I led all three horses out of the livery, tied them by the outhouse in back of the jail, and walked round to the front door.

Inside, I dipped myself another cupful of water and drank it down. "I'll sign those papers now."

"You shouldn't ought to be drinkin' like that after goin' without for so long. Make yourself sick." The deputy went over to his files again, turned his back while he sorted through them. "You check your belongin's? They was all still there?"

"Yes," I said, "except for my squirrel gun. I see it there with the others." Watching him all the time, I stepped to the side of the desk.

"I'll get that for you in a minute. Have to unlock the rack. Hangin' is in about four hours. If you're wantin' a place to rest while you wait, you might go up the street to Miz Sanders's boardin' house. Can't miss it. It's right next to Kreitinger's Household Goods. You been in town before, ain't you? I'm thinkin' I recognize you."

"Been in once before. You might have seen me on the street." I leaned over, hooked my finger inside the drawer, and nudged it open an inch before it caught.

"That's it then. You best try the boardin' house. Hotel's booked full. Folks in for the hangin'."

"Oh." Praying Jesus I'd make no noise, I gave the drawer a little jerk. It slid out another two inches before it caught again.

"Can't figure where them gol-dang forms got to. . . ."

I moved behind the desk. I could just see the tip of the gun barrel. I grabbed that balky drawer with both hands.

"Sam?" A woman's voice, from the doorway. "Sam McKay?"

Cussing under my breath, I stood straight and eased the drawer closed with my lip.

"Why, Mrs. LaFouche, ma'am!" He took off his hat, which was more than he'd done for me. "What you doin' down here, and so early of a mornin'?"

Her dark eyes flicked over to me, then back to him. Up close, she was a real elegant lady, with a sad and regal face. "I have come to have a last word with my nephew. I have no intention of attending the . . . I won't be present later."

"Yes ma'am, I sure do understand." He forgot all about me. He took a big iron key ring off the top of the file cabinet and went to the barred back room door. He unlocked it, banged it open, and ushered her through, hollering, "Heads up, boys. Lady visitor!"

Quick, I yanked open the drawer, grabbed the pistol, and followed, gun behind my back.

Mace was in the nearest cell on the left. He was standing by his little window, like he'd been looking out at the scaffold. Tuck was in the next cell over. He lay on his cot and there were bloody bandages strapped across his chest, but his eyes were open. He gave a start when he saw me.

I walked right up to the deputy.

"I'm sorry, miss, but you ain't authorized to—"

"Open it."

"What?"

I brought the pistol up and jabbed it in his side. "Mace's cell. Open it."

He just stood there.

Mace put hands on his hips and laughed like a loon. "You

better do it, Sam. If she don't shoot, she's bound to set you on fire."

Deputy Sam McKay jammed the key in the lock, and I said, "Boy howdy, Mace Danahoe! If all you can do is talk smart, I have half a mind to just let you—"

The deputy whirled round and slapped the gun from my hand. I went sprawling. The pistol skidded along the floorboards and stopped against Ruby LaFouche's shoe.

Deputy McKay relocked the cell and parked hands on his hips. "By Jingo!" he smirked. "I knew I'd seen you before, and it wasn't on no street, neither. I'll bet anything I got paper on you."

He grabbed my wrist and jerked me up. I kicked him in the leg and punched him a couple of times, but he was pretty tough and hung on tight.

"Leave me go!" I hollered, and took another swing at him.

He flung me back against the bars. My head hit hard, and everything went to twos and threes and fours. Like triplets, he said, "Sorry you had to see that, Mrs. LaFouche. Would you be s'kind as to hand me that pistol?"

Ruby LaFouche picked up the gun and, calm as anything, smacked him over the head with it.

She didn't hit him very good. All three of him wobbled and staggered and stared at me like *I'd* done it. I got the pistol out of Ruby LaFouche's hand, aimed for the deputy in the middle, and whacked him again. This time he went all the way down. I slid to the floor next to him.

Ruby got busy unlocking Mace's cell, then Tuck's. I sat on the floor, shaking my head and trying to settle my brain back to just one picture of everything. I watched her throw her arms round Mace and hug him. I heard her say, "I'm so sorry, I'm so sorry."

Mace dragged the deputy into a cell, found rope to bind

him, and used his neck scarf for a gag. Ruby took the deputy's pistol from me and gave it to Tuck. She said, "I didn't know what to do, Tucker. When you came for him yesterday, I thought my prayers had been answered. I'm so sorry. . . ."

"Hush now, Ruby girl. I think we'd best lock you in over here, make it appear you were overpowered, too."

"I don't care anymore."

"I care," Tuck said, and made her go inside. He turned the key. "Jinx and Opal would have cared."

She gripped the bars. "Tucker, something else . . ."

Tuck leaned toward her just as Mace grabbed me by the shoulder and hauled me up to my feet. "C'mon, Miss Bonfire. Help me get the guns. Sheriff comes on duty at seven. I want to be long gone by then."

We locked the front door, unlocked the rifle rack, and emptied it. Mace scooped them all up and had me grab the gunbelts that were hanging on pegs behind the far desk. He sorted out his and Tuck's arms and I rescued my squirrel gun. We tossed the rest in a third cell and locked it, and then Mace went back to the office. He came back carrying his saddlebags and a lumpy white cloth sack.

Tuck had finished his confab with Ruby LaFouche. Mace unlocked the back door and said his good-byes to his aunt. Tuck took her hand through the bars and kissed it, saying, "You're a good woman, Ruby."

He was in bad shape, but he said he could ride. "Doesn't look like I've got much alternative, does it?" he said, and smiled kind of thin. We got him outside. Mace helped him mount up, and then he opened the outhouse door and tossed the jail keys down the hole.

Tuck lifted his reins. "All right, ladies and gentlemen. This time, we try the back way. Slow and easy till I tell you different."

He moved Zeus into a jog and we followed. I hoped the
Lord had his eye on us, for even at that easy pace Tuck was
having to hang on to the saddle horn, and his face was
white.

We slid slow past the livery, then over another block and
down that street—the main of the town spread out to our
right, and a row of shacks and houses butting against the
steep hill to our left. Outside of a young girl chasing a
chicken and a runty white dog that barked at us till I shook
my finger and said "No!" we did not see a soul, though we
heard snatches of sleepy talk floating from this house or
that. Another block later, we were at the edge of town and
passing squat, blue- and green-doored adobes that sat right
up at the street. We were almost to the last one when a door
opened and a grizzled Mex stepped out.

I jumped and Mace's hand went to his gun. As the man
held his hands out to show they were empty, his eye settled
on Tuck. Suddenly, his wrinkled face was flooded with
satisfaction and he crossed himself quick. He started to keep
pace with us. He might have looked about three hundred
years old, but he sure could trot. Just loud enough for us to
hear, he said, "The Lady of Guadalupe, she answers all
prayers! I know you from the old times, Señor Brennan! I
am Paco Lopez, from Santo Gregario. You and your friends
go through Cañon de Negro."

We heard two shots, close-spaced, then somebody yelling.

"Judas!" breathed Mace. "C'mon, Tuck!"

But Paco Lopez grabbed Tuck's reins. "Cañon de Negro,"
he said quickly. "There is much stone there. You will not
leave track. Cut south just past this hill, then west after one
mile. They will not see. I will say I saw you go toward
Rabask Springs. I will pray the Holy Virgin to see you
safe!"

Blocks away, at the center of town, somebody started ringing the church bell like they planned never to stop.

Tuck nodded. *"Muchas gracias, amigo."*

As we galloped away, Tuck gripped tight to his saddle horn, Paco Lopez called, *"Vaya con Dios, Señor!"*

Like the man had said, Cañon de Negro was a trackless place. The whole of that wide, shallow canyon was dull black rock and lots of it, sometimes in buckled sheets and sometimes in loose stone and gravel. Not much grew there except lonely clumps of scraggly grass, and I saw no wild critters except lizards and bugs.

I had a bad side-ache from drinking too much water too fast, and a headache from getting slammed into the jail bars, but Tuck was a lot worse off than me. Even though we had to stop and tie him to his saddle, he insisted we keep as fast a pace as the bad footing would allow. Mace rode on one side of him and I kept close to the other, pacing him all the time, sometimes putting out a hand to steady him.

We passed through the canyon and came out the other end and onto the flats around noon. There had been no sign of a posse, so Tuck allowed that we might take a short stop to rest the horses and eat.

As soon as I set Malachi out for his first fresh air in a day and a half, I checked Tuck's bandages. He had not started to bleed again, but his face was like ashes and what few words he had to say were spoken through clenched teeth. There were some weeds and bushes around, so while Mace saw to the horses I scouted through the brush, hoping to find some herb or plant that would ease Tuck's pain. I did not have any luck, but when I got back, he seemed to have enjoyed a miracle cure. He was sitting up, eating the last of the ham and joking with Mace. To tell you the truth, it made me kind of mad.

"How come I leave you almost dead and come back to find you ready to dance at a hoedown?"

He chuckled. "Serendipity, Miss Gini."

"Sarah who?"

Mace held up the sack he'd brought along with his saddlebags, and reached inside. "Stuff Mama took along with her when she . . . when she went to the Widow Mahoney's to die." He pawed around in the bag. I could hear things rustling and clinking. "The widow packed them for me; guess she threw in everything in the room. Old pictures, a music box, letters . . ."

His hand came out, a pint bottle in it. "And this. Laudanum. I kept it. Figured it might come in handy someday."

Tuck nodded. "We've got some riding to do, and there'll be no time for bed rest."

"Why?" I said. "Seems to me we shook that posse. We got all the time in the world to get to that gold. You told Mace about the gold, didn't you? And . . . and the other?"

"He did," Mace said. He didn't sound mad, but he didn't look at me, either.

"You children best eat something," Tuck said, and waved a hand toward the vittles bag. "No time for cooking, but there's still a tin of peaches and some leftover biscuits. I suppose those boiled eggs are too far gone to eat, Miss Gini?"

I thought it might be my imagination, but Tuck seemed to have gone a lot more relaxed than a person would expect, under the circumstances.

"I apologize," he said, almost courtly, in sort of a slurred way. "I seem to have eaten the last of the ham. Awfully rude. Eat quick. We needs must be off and away."

"You're sure talkin' funny, old man. You all right?"

Mace found the peaches and stabbed the tin with his pocketknife. "It's the painkiller," he said, real matter-of-fact, and began to saw off the lid.

"Holy Hannah, Mace, he can't ride like that!"

Tuck reached for his canteen, missed it the first time, found it the next. "Ride I must, ride I will. Queen Ruby has spoken. The king's horde is on the march, and we race them for the Fleece."

"What! What kind of a dang thing is that to say? Mace, what's he—"

"Leave him alone." He shoved the peaches at me. "You want some?"

I stuck a chunk in my mouth and gave a fat slice to Malachi, who snapped it up in a hurry. "I'm tellin' you, Mace, we're not movin' another step till he's right in the head. That gold's not goin' anyplace. We can wait for him to heal up. We can wait days, weeks, months. We can put it off till fall if we have to. Next year, even!"

"Malingerers!" Tuck roared.

I jumped and spilled peach juice on my arm.

"You two have dawdled long enough!" He staggered over to the horses, snugged up Zeus's girth, and tried to mount. He wasn't doing too good, and Mace went to help him. I scooped up the vittles bag and Malachi, and ran after. Mace had him up on his horse by the time I got there.

"We ride to Joshua Tree tonight. Mason, my boy, tie me in. This opiate of yours has more kick than I anticipated."

Mace got to work on the ropes.

"But Tuck," I said, thick peach juice dripping off my fingers, "that's got to be at least thirty miles, and—"

He shouted, "No excuses, Argonauts!" and, weaving in the saddle, cantered away.

I handed Mace his bag and checked Filibuster's saddle. "I

think you've poisoned him with that stuff, Mace Danahoe. I think he's gone clear crazy."

He swung up on his horse. "I think you think too much."

Tuck was acting normal by mid-afternoon. By sunset he looked like Death and took a short swig of laudanum, but he wouldn't let us stop. We made Joshua Tree about an hour after nightfall, though the horses were the worse for it.

We camped in the ruin. Mace gave Tuck another dose of medicine, and left the bottle with him while he settled the horses and I scrounged us up some dinner. By the time we finished eating, Tuck's painkiller had kicked in and he felt good enough to take out his pipe. He puffed on it while I checked his wound and daubed it with salve.

"This is only horse medicine, Tuck, but it's the best I've got. Does that hurt?"

"Miss Gini, my sweet, I am so tanked on poppy juice, I imagine somebody could shoot me again and I wouldn't feel it. Don't take that for an invitation. Did you tend my Zeus?"

I tore up my next-to-the-last pair of underdrawers for a fresh bandage, and started wrapping him. "I did. He looks to be healing up faster than you, old man. You need to lie still for a few days, lest you rip open again. Did they dig that slug out, or is it still in there?"

"It's out. And we've no time for lounging."

Mace was across the fire, watching Malachi wolf down a june bug. Bugs are not a normal food for a tortoise, but I guess Malachi had gone so long without sustenance that he would eat about anything.

Mace said, "She's right, Tuck. You're too stove up to be going like this."

I had finished Tuck's chest, and helped him back into his sleeves. Wincing, he said, "Nonsense and folderol. I'll be better tomorrow. Better yet the day after."

"Boy howdy, Tuck Brennan! I think you have drunk too much of that opium mash again. You keep doin' that, you will not only embarrass me by talkin' crazy, you will most likely die. What put the burr under your blanket?"

He eased back onto his bedding. "Ruby LaFouche."

A fat locust crawled up the ruined half-wall. Mace swatted it with his hat, then fed the remains to Malachi. That tortoise was making up for lost time and was so greedy for vittles that he near took Mace's finger along with the bug. Mace didn't seem to mind. He jerked his thumb free of Malachi's jaws, gave his hand a shake, and said, "What's Aunt Ruby got to do with killin' yourself?"

"You underestimate me. I wouldn't have lived to be such an old man as sits before you now if I didn't move quick and heal fast." He puffed at his pipe. "Now. According to Ruby, Burl LaFouche had a visitor the other day. Ruby didn't hear the conversation, but she saw the lady leave and heard Burl call her by name. It was Ty's friend Pansy. Pansy Foyle, to be precise. And she was tucking a fat roll of bills into her purse as she went out the door."

I sat straight up. "What? Why would she be goin' to see Burl LaFouche?"

Tuck didn't look at me. He said, "Right after that, Burl had two more visitors. A couple of Wilbeck and LaFouche's best boys. Ruby was at the top of the stairs, listening. Said she couldn't make out too much, but she heard Burl mention my name—in an unfriendly tone, I might add—and Tyrone's. And gold."

"But she couldn't! How would she know where—"

"Let me finish. About an hour later, those boys and a few others rode out of town, and they haven't been back since. Now you can talk."

I opened my mouth, but Mace beat me to it. He said, "I thought Tyrone was dead." He jabbed a finger toward me.

"And *she* said he didn't tell that woman where anything was."

They both looked at me. "He didn't tell her, Tuck. He only said he put it back where he found it. I swear!"

"I don't doubt you, Miss Gini," he replied, and took another sip of laudanum. "But for all we know, he didn't die right off. It's entirely possible he lingered long enough to tell your friend Pansy where that canyon was and how to find Spirit Kettle. For all I know, he drew her a map in his own blood. Tyrone always had a flair for the dramatic."

I looked out over the half-wall toward the horses. I remembered the last time we were here, remembered Tyrone's silhouette and the way just watching him had made me feel. And then I remembered that last night in Half Moon Crossing, and the way I'd felt when the gun went off.

Mace poked the fire with a stick. Sparks gusted up. Real quiet, he said, "How much head start have they got?"

"Three days."

I said, "Pansy sure took her time goin' to tell him."

Tuck shrugged, one-shouldered. "Maybe she tried to put together a bunch and go after it herself, and couldn't. Maybe she didn't figure there was much rush. A lot more maybes, which I won't waste any time in listing. The point is, she did what she did, and Burl LaFouche did what *he* did. And now we are going to hope his boys have a hard time finding the place and we can beat them there, or—second best—run into them on their way back."

He took another pull on the laudanum. I started to reach for it, but Mace caught my eye and mouthed, "No." I sat back.

"And there's another situation you two ought to keep in mind. Things were confused in town this morning, and my old friend Paco Lopez—who I have been trying to place all day to no avail—likely succeeded in setting them out on the wrong track. But Burl LaFouche is no fool. He'll figure where we're going, and sooner or later we're going to have his thugs pressing us from both sides. Moving fast and moving tricky is the only way. Unless, of course, you want to plain give up on that gold. I suppose we could all just cross over to California and take up ditchdigging or dishwashing."

"All right," I said. "You're set on this. But there's somethin' I don't understand. No offense to Mace, but if Ruby LaFouche was filled with family love to the point where she helped break you boys out of the hoosegow, where was she when her only sister was dyin' of a black tumor?"

Tuck tapped his pipe bowl against his boot to empty it, then stretched out on his blankets. "She didn't know. Simple as that." He pulled his hat down over his eyes and crossed his arms over his chest. "You children best get some rest."

He was snoring in two minutes, which left me and Mace with nothing to do but be uncomfortable. Mace made a big deal out of being real interested in feeding Malachi a cricket. I cleaned up the supper things. Finally, I couldn't stand it anymore. I said, "That is the first time you ever agreed with me, I think."

"What?"

"About Tuck restin' up. I do believe that if I live long enough, you might even call me by my name."

"Don't go conjurin' up hearts and flowers. I only agreed because you were right."

"Well, that's sure a stupid thing to say! Why would anybody agree with me if I was wrong?"

"Which is why I usually don't. But the law of averages was on your side. Sooner or later, you had to be right."

I kicked him in the leg, but not real hard, as I did not want him to holler and wake up Tuck. "You are a mean person, Mace Danahoe."

"And you are a walking catastrophe. And don't go trying

to kick me again. I see you cockin' your boot, and don't think I don't."

I put my foot back down. "I think I'm too tired to be mad at you, anyway." I sat down on my blankets, cross-legged. "What you goin' to do with your share, Mace? You still want to raise horses like you and Pete— Sorry."

"Shouldn't be sorry to talk about him. Just because a man's dead don't mean he never was alive. The dead ought to be spoken of." He stirred the fire again, then laid his stick aside. "I don't know what I'll do with it. I was gonna take Ma away from the Territory. Someplace green. Hire her a maid and set her up in a house where she'd never have to fight the wind or the dust again. I don't know, now. I never had much heart for ranching. Maybe I'll go into business. I've got a head for figures. Got a good sense of what folks want and how much they're likely to pay for it."

Tuck mumbled in his sleep. The mutter got louder until it turned into words. He spoke a sentence or two before he rolled onto his side and went silent again.

I whispered, "What in tarnation was that?"

Mace shrugged. "Latin or Greek or somethin', most like."

I stared at Tuck's broad back and watched his side move as he breathed. "How's it happen, Mace?"

"What?"

"How's it happen that a man who knows about stars and long-ago heroes and books the way he does . . . how's it happen that he ends up in Yuma Prison? I mean, how's he end up in the Territory in the first place? To be real honest, I don't think Tuck's from around here."

That dang Mace laughed so loud he almost woke Tuck, and that time I did kick him. He clapped a hand over his mouth, and when he finally finished snickering, he said, "Judas Priest, girl, you just figure that out?"

"If all you're goin' to do is make fun of people, you can

just talk to yourself. I am goin' to sleep." I stretched out and turned my back on him.

"Seems a person who claims to read and remember as many books as you ought to know those facts."

I pulled up my blanket. "I don't claim anything but the truth. For your information, none of my books ever said. And I thought I told you I was goin' to sleep."

There was a long pause before Mace said, "Delaware."

I rolled right over and stared him in the eye. "Delaware! What kind of a place is *that* to be from?"

"Man can't help where he gets born. He came west in the fifties. He was a schoolteacher back east. Massachusetts, I think."

I got up on one elbow. "You are makin' this up to tease me. I have known some schoolteachers—the Widow McBride back in Hanged Dog and Miss Elma Justice who is now Mrs. Will Fowler—and Tuck's not like either of those people."

"Have it your way."

I could only bear the quiet for about five minutes. "A man does not get in Dutch with the legal system for bein' a knuckle-rapper."

Mace moved onto his back and looked up at the night sky. "I don't know the whole of it, only what I remember Daddy saying, and that was a long time ago. Tuck got into it with some fella, down around where Monkey Springs is now. The fella had got his hands on a Mexican woman and, well, Daddy made me cover my ears for that part, but I guess it was pretty bad. Word came round to Tuck, and—"

"Did he know her? The Mex lady, I mean?"

"I don't know. Anyway, he got into it with the fella and they got to shouting and then shooting, and the fella got killed. Turned out he was second cousin to the Territorial

Governor. That's all I know of it. You want more, you can ask him yourself."

We had sweated all afternoon, but the night was pretty cool. I snugged my blanket up under my chin. "I guess that's enough. But what about this 'schoolteacher' business? And what's an Argonaut, anyhow?"

He turned away from me again, then rolled back long enough to hand me Malachi. "Judas, girl, you're wearin' me out. Take your critter and go to sleep."

It was not yet light when we left Joshua Tree behind. I was surprised at how much better Tuck was doing, but he was not healed yet. He had a swig of laudanum with his breakfast, and kept the bottle with him. We traveled pretty much the same route back to Cañon de los Espejos as we had left it by, but we made twice the time. Tuck figured to make it in another day and a half.

We were jogging through a little cluster of low, rocky hills when I saw the rock sign. I was so excited that I didn't think to holler at Tuck or Mace. I just hopped off Filibuster and ran right over to it.

Now, I think I can be excused for that. Gam had spent a lot of time teaching me about Apache rock signals, but this was the first time I had ever seen one someplace other than our own back garden.

I was all hunkered over, trying to cipher it out, when a shadow fell across me. I jumped, having nothing on my mind right then but Apache, but it turned out to be Mace.

"What you doin' back here?" He looked kind of mad, but since that was normal for him I did not take it personal. "You're lucky Tuck noticed you missing."

"Where is he?"

Mace tipped his head back and to the side. Tuck was maybe a hundred yards off. He had ground-tied Zeus halfway up one of the last, low hills. Spyglass to his eye, he was sprawled at the crest and peering out over the flats beyond.

Mace rubbed his sleeve across his face, then pointed at the pile of rocks. "What's that?"

"Apache sign."

"I know that," he scowled. "Man don't live in the Territory his whole life without recognizin' Apache markers. I mean, what's it say? You're supposed to be the big expert, aren't you, Little Miss Sister to the *Shis-Inday?*"

I didn't reply. I was too busy trying to figure out those rocks and, to tell the truth, I was having a hard time of it. Apache signals are a real complicated system. It has to do with how many rocks there are and what shapes and patterns they're laid in, but also how they're piled, and whether some stones are earth-side down or earth-side up or resting at an angle. I went through all the configurations Gam had taught me: the different ways of piling rocks to say who had passed by and when, or where the nearest water was, or where the trail led, or if something important had happened nearby; but this was different than anything she'd shown me.

Mace shifted from foot to foot. "Well?"

I stood up. "Tuck wants us."

"You expect me to believe those rocks say—"

"No, stupid. Over there." I pointed toward the top of the little hill. Tuck was waving at us to join him.

Mace got back on his horse. "You didn't say what it meant."

I climbed on Filibuster and pushed him into a trot. "It means there were Apache here."

Mace kept up with me. "Well, *I* could'a told you that! What's the big message, Red?"

"Can't you ever say my name?"

He didn't answer, because right about then we reached Tuck's hill. We dismounted and joined him at the crest.

"Get down!" he hissed, and we flopped on our bellies on either side of him. He pointed out across the brush-dotted flats. "Company."

I could see them: six riders, maybe a quarter-mile out and moving toward the south. I reached for the spyglass, but Mace got it first. He squinted into it, twisted at it, and then he got real still. Soft, he said, "I'll be a ring-tailed sonofabitch."

Tuck took the glass from him and handed it to me. I spotted the riders, moved the lens from one to the next. I gasped and looked again. "Holy Hannah, Tuck! Is it a ghost?"

Chuckling, he took back the spyglass and collapsed it. "No hauntings on the desert today, Miss Gini. I swear, that Tyrone's got more lives than the Buddha's barn cat."

"But how? I shot him! It was practically point-blank!"

"Well, that's pretty damn simple to figure, isn't it?" Mace snapped. "You missed him. Can't you do anything right? Can't shoot straight, can't read rock sign, can't—"

"Hush!" With a grimace, Tuck rolled over on his back and slid a few feet down the hill before he sat up. "Keep your bickering down to a roar, if you please. What rock sign?"

Mace pointed. "She can't read it."

"You don't need to act so satisfied, Mr. Mason Smarty-Pants Danahoe. I noticed you couldn't cipher it, either."

"Never claimed I could."

"I can't help it if it wasn't one of the ones Gam showed me."

Tuck took hold of my boot and yanked hard. I skittered and bounced down the slope on my backside, little rocks showering down with me, till I was even with him.

He took out his handkerchief and wiped the sweat off his forehead and the back of his neck. "Might one ask if you kenned anything of interest from it, Miss Gini?"

I shook my head. "'Bout the only thing I can say is that it was tampered with, no longer than three, four days back, outside. I figured the way it was before it got moved. It was just a signpost, kind of. Showed where there's a spring a day's march away. But the last ones through changed the message on the top. I couldn't read it." I twisted so as to rub my backside and move a stone out from under me. "If I missed Tyrone entirely, how come it took him almost three months to get round to fetchin' the gold?"

"You just answered yourself. You didn't miss him. He's likely been laid up all this time. Explains why Pansy was so tardy with her little double cross, too." Tuck took a short sip of laudanum and made a face. "Nasty stuff."

"Those men with him. I'll bet one of them is that Cicero fella Ty and Pansy were talkin' about."

Tuck nodded. "Black Ear Cicero. He's down there, all right. Bad business, that one. Our Tyrone is scraping the bottom to consort with that trash."

"Tuck?"

He slid the bottle into his pocket and brought out his tobacco pouch and pipe. "Yes, Miss Gini?"

"In spite of . . . in spite of everything, I'm kind of glad Tyrone's alive."

He patted my knee. "So am I, honey."

Mace skidded down next to us in a flurry of pebbles. "Well, *I'm* not. Shouldn't we get after him?"

"Not yet. You're forgetting something."

I said, "Burl LaFouche's boys."

Tuck lit his pipe. "Right you are, Miss Gini. I believe we had best just sit here for a time and let Tyrone get on with what he's doing. We know where he's headed. Mason, why don't you see if you can't find some shade for those horses. Miss Gini, you take my glass and skinny back up top and keep an eye on Ty and his friends. Let me know when they're out of sight."

I took the spyglass. "What are you goin' to do?"

He leaned back and pulled his hat over his eyes. "I believe I'll have myself a smoke."

15

Cãnon de los Espejos Revisited

The plain ran from horizon to horizon, and since Tyrone and his pals weren't traveling fast, it took them almost an hour to get halfway across. Mace spelled me about then, and I climbed down the hill to join Tuck for a nap in the shade.

It was maybe another hour later when Mace chucked a few rocks to wake us.

"What is it?" Tuck said as we climbed to meet him. "Tyrone out of sight?"

"He is." Mace moved over to make room. "It's something else." He handed Tuck the spyglass and pointed in the direction Ty's party had come from.

Tuck took a look. "Seems somebody stole our idea." He passed the glass to me.

There were five riders, too far off to make out their faces. "Tuck, you reckon those are LaFouche's men? The ones he sent out after Pansy called on him?"

"That's my guess."

Mace was sweating worse than us, having been out in the sun, and when he shook his head no, a drop flew off his nose and hit me in the cheek. He said, "That don't make sense. Why would they be comin' from over there?"

I wiped his sweat off me. "Boy howdy, Mace! If you can't figure that out, you had better not go round callin' other folks stupid."

He scowled, which made another bead trickle down into his eye. He rubbed at it and growled, "All right, Miss Know-It-All. If you're so damn smart, you tell me why they're way over there when Oro Tiempo is the other direction."

I looked at Tuck, but he just grinned and said, "Go ahead, honey. I'm fascinated."

That made me kind of nervous, but I took a deep breath and said, "Now, I've been thinkin' on this, and I figure that if Pansy knew where the gold was, she would've left Tyrone earlier and gone to sell what she knew to Burl LaFouche. But she didn't, so that means she was likely hangin' round Tyrone while he healed up from my bullet, hopin' the whole time he'd let somethin' slip."

Mace picked up a rock and skipped it down the hill. "It was probably nothing like that. You read too many of those cheap shoot-'em-ups."

Tuck smiled. "Let her finish."

I said, "I am glad there is somebody here that recognizes my natural smarts." Mace rolled his eyes, but I ignored him. "I figure they probably stayed right in Half Moon while Ty mended and gathered a gang together, and I also figure Pansy didn't waste much time lightin' out for Oro Tiempo once she saw which way they headed. I think Burl LaFouche sent his boys on a hard gallop to the Colorado River to track Ty. I think that's what they're doin' now, except now they're takin' it easier, just followin' along and stayin' out of sight, waitin' for Ty to lead 'em to it." I stopped, and when neither one of them said anything for a minute, I added, "Well, that's how I see it."

Because he had been so quiet, I half-expected Tuck to pat me on the knee and then explain just where I was wrong, but instead he said, "I tend to concur, Miss Gini."

Mace scooted a few feet down the hill before he stood up.

"Well, whoever they are—and I'm not saying I agree with you—they're gonna make this whole deal twice as hard."

By dusk, LaFouche's men had crossed the plain, and we set out after them—slow, and well to the east. They made no fire when they camped, and neither did we. It was a nervous time. We chewed hardtack for our dinner, spoke little, and slept light.

The next day was spent in slow, hot travel. A couple times we were able to take higher ground, and Tuck peered through his spyglass from a ridge or hilltop.

That afternoon, we managed to get a bit ahead of them by swinging to the east, and were waiting when they passed only two hundred yards from the rocks where we were hid. When it was my turn with the spyglass, I recognized two of them: that ugly Vince and his mule-lipped friend, Ronnie, who I told them Ty said he "took care of" in Prescott.

"More like Tyrone shook his hand and gave him drink money and a message for Burl LaFouche," I added.

"Undoubtedly correct," said Tuck. He was feeling better every day, and though he still took a sip of laudanum from time to time, he was needing less of it.

That night, we camped once more with no fire and no coffee and nothing for our dinner but hardtack and jerky. I was getting pretty dang sick of dried beef, I can tell you. Though the days were terrible hot, the nights were crisp and I would have admired the comfort of a little fire and a hot dinner.

Tuck figured we'd catch sight of the canyon's wide mouth early the next afternoon, and he was right. We watched, peeking over the crest of a rise, as Vince and Ronnie and their friends started into Cañon de los Espejos. It looked some different than the last time we were there. The stream down its center had dried up to a trickle, and by the time it reached the flats it was nothing more than a few dirty puddles. Except for scattered paloverde and some buckhorn cholla and prickly pear, the vegetation on the canyon floor had gone from fresh green to baked-out yellows and grays, even though it was barely June.

One thing was the same, though: those mica patches in the canyon walls still glinted blinding bright. Burl LaFouche's men seemed struck by the effect. Through the telescope, I watched them crane their heads and twist round in their saddles as they pointed up at the glassy places.

We waited till they had traveled the length of the first wide canyon and disappeared into a narrow passage at the end before we walked down the back of the rise, to the horses. Mace grumbled, "Isn't it about time we went down there and got after them?"

Tuck pulled down his canteen and unscrewed the top. "Why? Sooner or later, they'll be coming out, and likely quite a few less than went in. No, I believe we'd best hold our ground and let Tyrone and his monkeys do the work for us."

I said, "Tuck, as much as it pains me, I have got to side with Mace. They could pick up the gold, hightail it out the other end of the canyon, and get clean away to Mexico." From the corner of my eye, I saw Mace smirk. I tried not to look at him.

"I doubt they'll do that, Miss Gini," Tuck said after he took a long drink. "Besides, we can't exactly afford to take the chance of bumping into them. All together, there are eleven of those boys, and not a one of them would be overjoyed to see us. That's eleven to three, and I refuse to fly in the face of odds like that. However, I predict that when the first six bump into the last five, they'll whittle down the odds for us all on their own."

I stuck my boot in the stirrup and climbed up on

Filibuster. "I didn't say I wanted to shoot it out. I just want to keep in spyin' range."

Tuck grabbed my reins. "Step down, Miss Gini. You are not riding down the canyon."

I heard leather creak behind me, and knew that Mace had mounted up, too. I said, "I have got no intention of ridin' down along their path. I'm goin' to stay up top, keep track of 'em that way."

Mace moved his horse up next to Filibuster. "She's right, Tuck."

I said, "That's twice we agreed. Either I'm gettin' smarter or you are."

He shot me a dirty look and smacked me across the thigh with his reins, though he didn't do it hard.

Tuck rubbed the back of his neck and stared at the ground. Finally, he looked up at me. "I must be getting softheaded in my old age," he muttered, and climbed on Zeus.

At a gallop, we cut out on an angle that put us, after a gentle climb, on the eastern rim. We kept well back from the edge and slowed to a jog to hold kicked-up dust to a minimum. There were ragged hills to the northeast and the south, but the land above that part of the canyon was flat, sere desert that didn't support more than isolated clumps of sage or sunburnt creosote.

The canyon twisted through the desert like a lunatic snake. In some places, the walls winged out and away from the floor below and a person might have climbed or skidded down if they were afoot. In others, the opening at the floor was wider than up top, so a passage broad enough to ride two abreast might narrow to just a couple inches at the surface, if it made the surface at all. When we'd been at Spirit Kettle, it had looked to me like a cave with the roof gone. Seeing it from the top side, I wondered if maybe most of Cañon de los Espejos hadn't been a whole monster of a cave system long ago. I bet that when it was, about eighty million bats lived in there. Jingles wouldn't have liked it one bit.

We passed the main canyon, then the twisting crevice above the narrow course that linked it with the canyon where the ironwood stood, and where we'd had our bad luck. I noticed Mace didn't try to peer down into that one, and kept his eyes straight ahead till we were past it. I looked, but we were too far from the rim and on the wrong angle for me to see Pete's grave site.

We caught up with the LaFouche bunch a half hour later. We didn't see them, but we heard them. They were traveling one of the narrow places again. I got off Filibuster, crawled to the edge of one of those slits in the desert floor, and peeked down. Far below, the canyon belled just wide enough for riders to travel single file, and Burl LaFouche's men were passing beneath me in the shadows. Because it was narrowed down, the stream was healthier here, and came up over their horses' fetlocks. Vince was in front, a rifle across his lap. I knew it was him, as he was the only one with a gray hat. I couldn't tell which one was Ronnie.

I pulled back from the rim, lest they should look up and spy me, and waited till the last one passed out of hearing. Then I ran back to Tuck and Mace.

"I recollect that passage," I said as I climbed into my saddle. I closed my eyes and brought the picture of Mescal Mort's map into my head. "They've got a turn to the right, a long corridor wide enough for three horses . . . Maybe you remember. The one where we saw javelina track."

Mace scowled. "Just get on with it, will you?"

I reached to slug him in the arm, but he twisted out of the way and I missed. I said, "I think maybe Tuck ought to give you some of that poppy juice. It might sweeten up your temperament."

"Keep your voices down!" Tuck snapped.

I said, "Sorry." Mace just looked away.

It was plain that Tuck was in pain, but he had not drunk any laudanum since early morning. I guessed he wanted to keep his head clear, even if it meant he'd hurt. He said, "Then what, Miss Gini?"

"After the place we saw the javelina track, they'll swing left and come out in a middlin'-sized canyon, the one with the rock slide at the far end. Then another narrow passage, a left, a right, a twist-back, and—at the place with the white quartz streaks—Spirit Kettle. Hold my legs."

I got my knees up on the saddle, then my boots, and stood up slow. Mace hung on to me, though he wasn't too careful about it and I wobbled some. I looked out over the land, calculating in my head just where each slash and gap in the ground figured—or didn't figure—in the map. It was harder to trace the route from up top. Side canyons twisted out every which way: some broad, some so skinny they were hardly more than cracks in the ground. In a couple places I could see where a passage had looped back on itself to leave nothing but an island of desert sticking up in the middle, with a moat of sheer cliff all around. About a mile or so to the south, the land rose up in craggy rock.

I slid back down in the saddle and pointed. "There's the next wide place they'll come to. See it? Kind of squarish-shaped? We can make it to there if you don't mind jumpin' over a couple cracks, but I don't think we can get as far as Spirit Kettle. It's either in those rocks to the south or just past 'em. They appear too rough to travel, and we don't have time to go round. I don't know if I could find it then, anyhow."

Mace mopped a bandanna over his throat. "What? Something you admit you can't do? Better wire the papers, Tuck. This calls for an extra edition."

"I could say somethin' real clever to you, Mace Danahoe, but I don't believe I will waste my breath."

"You waste it every time you open your—"

"Shut up!"

We did, as Tuck looked real mad. After a minute he calmed down some and said, real clipped, "If you think you can control your bickering, I suggest we cut over to the last canyon and wait there." He put his knees to Zeus without waiting for an answer. Me and Mace followed.

We shortcutted across the desert at a lope, and I was real proud of the way Filibuster jumped those crevices. One was narrow, just a couple feet wide; but the other was almost four, which is a pretty long hop when you figure it's maybe thirty feet straight down if you don't make it. I walked him up to that one first, so as to let him appreciate the seriousness of it, then went back about twenty yards and gave him my heels. He was a game pony, all right. He launched into the air, sailed the chasm, and landed on the far side with a yard to spare. I don't believe even Jigsaw could have done better.

What with the shortcut, we beat LaFouche's boys to the canyon. We ground-tied our horses well back from the rim and sat in their shade.

I opened my canteen and took a drink. I only had a couple swallows left. I said, "What if we see Ronnie and Vince and the others go in, but nobody comes out? What if they go out the back way, to Mexico?"

"Well, we'll just have to go after them, won't we?" Mace smirked.

Tuck ignored him. "They won't go south, Miss Gini. Tyrone has no love for Mexico, and the Mexican authorities have even less admiration for him. The same goes for Black

Ear Cicero. No, they'll come back this way, all right—if the LaFouche mob doesn't get them first."

I said, "I can't see anything from here but rocks," and made to move closer to the rim.

Tuck made a grab for my pants leg, but I was too fast for him. He whispered, "We're here to listen, not look. You stay off that rim or they'll see you!"

I waved my hand. "I'll keep low."

I crawled to within five feet of the lip, then got down on my belly and inched forward. There was a stunted Mormon Tea bush right at the edge, and I aimed for it, thinking it could shield me from view. I heard Mace hiss "Not so close, stupid!" but I ignored him and slithered my way right up to it till I was nose to shrub. It was pretty good cover, all right. It sure wouldn't have hid me if I were to stand or sit, but lying down it was just fine.

A low branch jutted right into my line of sight. I grabbed it to break it off and give myself a better view. I also figured to save the branch for later. You can make good medicine from a Mormon Tea bush.

It was stubborn, though, so I reached into the shrub, got a grip on the main trunk for leverage, and yanked again. This time the branch came free, but the whole dang bush kind of lurched to the side.

Before I thought to scramble away, it tilted forward. Roots popped out of the ground in a spray of gravelly dirt, and the ground under my front half caved in.

You can bet I let go of that bush quick and jabbed my toes into the dirt, but gravity got the better of me, and the canyon rim, too.

I slid over the edge, blinded by dust, stones pelting me everywhere.

Now, I was sure I'd go straight down, land on my head, and meet Jesus directly, but that wasn't the case. There had been slides here before, and the ground took a sharp slope. It was not a pleasant angle, especially face first, but I got myself rolled up into a ball, fell the last half that way, and ended with my back against a big boulder. Pebbles were still spattering down on me when I heard Tuck.

"Miss Gini!" he called, soft, from above. "Honey, can you hear me?"

I couldn't see him. I hissed "I'm all right! Stay back!" and hoped he'd heard. It wasn't safe to talk louder, for I could already make out echoing hoofbeats coming toward me.

Quick, I scrambled off the flow of avalanched dirt and rock and skidded down behind some half-dead creosotes next to the canyon wall. That put me in a little box: the canyon wall hard behind me and to my right, the rock slide sloping high on my left. I couldn't see the main of the canyon, just the end of it straight ahead of me.

I pressed my back against the canyon wall, slid down slow, and hugged my knees, for right then I realized the horse sounds were coming from the wrong direction.

It was Tyrone and Black Ear Cicero and the others on their way back from Spirit Kettle. Black Ear Cicero was in the lead and, being as they emerged only twenty feet from where I was hid, I could see him clear. One of his ears and the skin around it was purple-black, and he wore two gunbelts slung over his shoulders, Mex style. He looked like a nasty piece of work.

Tyrone rode in next. I put a hand to the canyon wall to steady myself. I don't remember anything that ever affected me so strange as did seeing him again. I wanted to hug him and throttle him, all at the same time.

Dust was still rising from the rock slide, and Black Ear and Tyrone had a good look at it and the rim above before they waved the others in.

There were four more men. One had long light brown hair

that hung almost to his waist in oily waves. There was a big knife strapped to his thigh, and he looked like he'd scalp a preacher for a nickel. As mean as he appeared, the next one put such fear into my bones that I had to bite my tongue to keep from gasping out loud. It was none other than the Aztec Kid, the same gun-happy killer I had shot in the foot in the Striped Garter Saloon. I tried to make myself as small as possible, wishing I was invisible or maybe in New Mexico.

I held my breath as they rode past. The next-to-the-last one was just even with me when I heard a little rustling sound at my feet, like pebbles shifting. The first thing I thought was *snake*, and if my bladder had been full it would have emptied right then and there. Real slow, I leaned forward and peeked over my knees.

It was a big fat tarantula, brown and hairy, and he was climbing up on top of my boot toe. I guess the rock slide had disturbed him. Now, tarantulas are fearful-looking critters, but they are not so poisonous as some people think. Most times the bite of one is no worse than a bee sting. But still, when you have got one sitting on your boot and he may or may not decide to take a stroll up your pants leg, it is a pretty disturbing thing.

I was staring at that spider when I heard the plod of horse hooves turn into a scramble. I looked up to see Cicero's bunch riding straight for my hiding place. I almost stood up, thinking that if they'd already found me out, I could at least kick that spider out of the way.

They didn't come for me, though. Without a word, they jumped off their horses and shooed them into the little bushy corner between the rock slide and the canyon wall, which meant right on top of me. Then they scattered.

Through the cover of brush and milling horses' legs, I saw three of them light out across the stream and dive into

ground cover near the fat canyon wall. Another ducked back
into the passage they'd just ridden out of. Rifles in their
hands, Tyrone and the one with the long oily hair climbed
about fifteen feet up the back slope of the rock slide and
ended up above me, kicking down a shower of stones in the
process.

Everything got real quiet again. One of their horses
snaked his neck down on my side of the creosote and tried
to grab my hat. I flicked his muzzle with my fingers. The
tarantula moved to my other boot, which was a lot better
than up my pants.

Then I realized what had sent them to cover. Riders were
coming into the canyon, coming toward us. Above me, I
saw Tyrone lift a hand to signal his boys to wait. The
hoofbeats came slowly closer, splashing water, crunching
gravel. I could hear the creak of saddle leather. I dug
fingernails into my palms.

Ty's hand dropped. His boys opened fire with a gusto that
fair shook the canyon. I jumped at the noise, and the
tarantula skittered up my boot.

I leapt up and commenced to whack my pants leg, which
spooked the horses. They bolted out into the canyon. One,
a loud-colored Appaloosa, didn't get far. A stray slug caught
it as it crossed the stream. It screamed, bucked out, went
down on its side, and died.

I felt terrible about the Appaloosa horse, but I was still
busy shaking the spider out of my pants. I finally hit the
right place hard enough and half-squished it between my
boot top and pants. It fell out, furry legs twitching, and I
stomped on it to put it out of its misery.

The canyon boomed with gunfire, vibrated with echoes. I
was out of the line of fire, being behind the slide; but I was
standing straight up, which is a stupid thing to do if a person
is trying not to be seen. I hunkered down quick and glanced

round to where Ty's boys were shooting from. They were still busy and, by the sound of it, the LaFouche men were putting up a good fight. But when I peered up to where Ty and his friend were perched, that long-haired man was staring straight down at me. He smiled.

You know how a rabbit, if it's scared bad enough, will just freeze up and let the coyote take it? That's how his eyes made me feel, like I was dead or worse, no matter what. I couldn't do anything but squat there and stare back, my knees shaking.

Tyrone was busy with his rifle, and hadn't noticed me. The long-haired man reached over and put a hand on Ty's shoulder, like he was going to say, "Lookee what I found," but as he did it he raised up too high.

The side of his head exploded. Blood and matter sprayed out, rained onto my hat and face, spattered the granite wall; and even as he slumped, he kept looking at me. Tyrone saw he was dead, pried the rifle from his hands, shoved him aside, and went on shooting. The body started a slow slide toward me, boots first.

There was no place to get out of the way. I hugged the canyon wall as best I could, but he came down square on top of me: blood soaking his shirt and what was left of his head, ear dangling by a thread of skin, open eyes staring.

His weight pushed me down into a cramped crouch. His head lolled against my chest, bloody side down. There was just a tiny hold in the other side, where the bullet had gone in. Just a trickle of blood, nothing to really remark on. But underneath, I could feel his blood and brains soaking through my shirt. I was glad for the gunfire. It covered the sound when I threw up the hardtack I'd had for lunch.

I went all the way to the ground. Once down, I was able to roll him partway off me and into the creosotes. Bullets glancing off the wall above sent down a shower of granite chips and powdered mica that stuck to my sopping shirt. Spent but still-hot cartridge casings from Tyrone's rifle pelted down over me and the corpse.

I was really getting to hate those canyons. It seemed like every time I was in them, I ended up laying in the dirt with a body sprawled across me and lead flying every which way. I clamped hands over my ears and waited.

I don't know how long it was before the shooting stopped, but it quit pretty sudden. I heard someone, who I took to be Black Ear Cicero, call out, "Whit?"

A voice from just inside the passage answered, "Still here."

"Kid?"

Much to my disappointment, the Aztec Kid rose up out of the brush across the canyon. He hollered, "Breathin'!"

"Callahan?"

There was a pause, then Ty announced, "Deceased." He stood up and looked down at Callahan. And right straight at me.

Our eyes locked for a second, and I'll be danged if he didn't wink at me. Grinning, he turned back toward Cicero and said, "Deceased and in the arms a'Gentle Mercy." And then, rifles held out for balance, he skidded down the slide to the canyon floor like he'd never heard of Gini Kincaid.

Black Ear Cicero finished the roll. "Biggs?"

There was no answer. Across the way, the Aztec Kid started poking the bushes. He had no blood on him, but he had a bad limp. I guessed he had my bullet, back in Tombstone, to thank for that. After a minute or two of gimping through the brush, he said, "Found him." He leaned down and I lost sight of him, but I heard him say, "Belly-shot."

Cicero said, "Will he make it?"

The Kid stood up, aimed his pistol, and fired one round down into the scrub. "Nope."

Black Ear Cicero emerged from his cover and pointed out over the canyon. He yelled, "Whit, you and the Kid get those horses. Make sure them fellers is all the way dead, too."

Ty joined Cicero, and they walked out of my line of vision. About three minutes later I heard a man cry out, "Sweet Jesus, please! No!" I remembered that voice. It was Ronnie. There was another shot, and he didn't speak again.

I was shaking pretty bad. I figured any second Ty would tell them I was there. Either that or he was playing some kind of game. Maybe he wanted to let them find me on their own when they got round to burying their dead. Maybe he thought that would be real amusing. Aside from being scared, I was pretty dang perplexed, but I had long since given up trying to make sense of anything that Tyrone O'Neill did.

Flies settled on Callahan; my sticky shirt, too. I tried to reach his pistol. It took me several minutes, what with having to push him in a way his body did not want to go and do it quiet, but I managed. The only extra cartridges on him were for his rifle, and his pistol had just three rounds left in it. I wondered what Mace and Tuck were doing up top. I wondered if they thought I was dead.

A stick snapped, and Ty and Black Ear Cicero walked into view. I huddled down as best I could behind the part of Callahan that wasn't sprawled on me. Cicero went to the dead Appaloosa, and as he tugged its saddlebags free, Ty took a quick look in my direction, like he was just making certain I was still trapped and waiting. I know he saw the gun in my hand. I know he saw it pointed at him. But when Black Ear Cicero stood up with the saddlebags, Ty turned his back on me like a dare, and stood talking quiet with the other man.

After a minute he turned slightly, and I heard his next words plain. He said, "We'd best be after gettin' these lads under ground. Night'll soon be on us."

"Bury 'em if you want," said Black Ear Cicero, "but I ain't wastin' the time nor energy, and the gold's goin' with me. Kid! Bring my horse!"

Ty twisted toward my hiding place again. Looking me square in the eye, he smiled and said, "As ye will, Blackie darlin'."

I waited till the sound of their hoofbeats faded before I commenced squirming out from under Callahan. More than anything, I wanted to be away from the stench of blood and dust and gunpowder and death. From above, I heard Tuck call soft, "Miss Gini!"

I was afraid to answer him, lest once I opened my mouth I'd be able to do nothing but scream. My legs were still trapped, but I picked up a rock and chucked it, hard as I could, up and over the rim. There was a thud and I heard Mace cuss.

My legs came free with a jolt. I scrambled up and tripped over Callahan as I shoved myself through the bushes, not minding that they scratched my face and arms. My shirt stuck to my skin. Flecks of bone and tissue, granite chips, creosote twigs, and secondhand hardtack fell away as I stumbled toward the stream.

I crouched down next to the dead Appaloosa and scooped up handfuls of water, splashed them on my face and shirt. It only made a worse mess. Across the stream, the bushes shivered. A horse groaned in agony.

That dying pony was what finally did me in. I started

bawling—one fist jammed against my teeth to hold the sound in, the other pounding my leg.

A hand touched my shoulder. I twisted up swinging before I realized it was Mace. Behind him, dust still clouded a stripe along the rock slide to mark the path he'd skidded down. Tuck was at the rim. He was standing back several feet, but I could see his head and shoulders. He waved with one wide sweep of his arm.

Mace stared at my ruined shirt, his mouth partway open. He breathed, "Jesus. Where are you shot?"

"I'm not shot," I said, though it came out punctuated by sobs. "Callahan is shot."

Back in the brush, the horse groaned again, rattly and hopeless. Mace said, "Who the hell is Callahan?"

I felt like my insides had been scooped out and thrown away. I don't remember it clear, but I know I went back to washing my front in the stream. Later, Mace said that when he tried to get my attention, I told him to go to the pantry and get me some blueing for the stain, and as long as he was there, to set out a jar of Gam's home-canned peas for dinner.

The next thing I knew I was up on my feet and Mace was shaking me hard. "Gini!" he barked. "Gini Kincaid!" He slapped me across the face, and then he laughed.

"What's so dang funny?"

"I guess you're all right if you're hittin' back." He rubbed the red mark blooming on his cheek.

I stood there, wobbling. "Did I do that?" I didn't recollect it at all, though my right palm buzzed.

"No need to apologize."

"I got no intention of beggin' your pardon. I only—" The horse groaned again, louder this time, and we both turned toward it.

Mace began to unbutton his shirt. "Get out of that," he said.

"If you think I am goin' to change my shirt with you standin' here, you have got another think comin', Mace Danahoe."

He shrugged out of his sleeves and handed over the shirt. "Calm down, you little hellion. I won't jump your skinny bones." He slipped the knife from his belt and started off across the stream.

"What are you doin'?"

"Gunshot would bring that bunch back."

"What?"

"Judas Priest! Just shut up and change!"

I glanced up at Tuck. He had guessed what was going on, and, like a true gent, turned his back. Mace wasn't the gentleman type, though. I ripped off my shirt, washed fast, and rinsed out my hair quick as I could. The creek turned pink with blood. I turned round before I put on the shirt. It was way too big and sweated up, but at least it didn't have Callahan all over it. I was rolling up the sleeves when I heard that poor horse groan again, then Mace's voice.

"Ho, son; ho, son," he said, real soft. "Ho, son; easy, son . . ." The horse groaned once more, a long, sad sound, and then it stopped.

I started crying again, but this time in silence. As I tucked in my shirttails, tears dripping off my cheeks, Mace splashed through the stream and came up behind me. When I looked round, he was bent over the water, washing blood from his hands and knife.

I said, "Did you . . ."

He stood up and slid the knife back in its sheath. "You've got one hell of a bruise coming up on your neck, Red."

"I landed against a boulder when I— Dang you, Mace Danahoe! You looked!"

He was so smug I would have slapped him again if he'd been in range, but at least it snapped me out of crying. He

said, "Don't get your drawers in a knot. And quit stampin'
your foot. Think you can manage to climb back up that
slide?"

He took my arm, but I shook free. "Somebody's got to
bury these men," I said. "We can't just leave them for the
coyotes and javelina!"

"You can have a funeral or you can have the gold."

When I didn't reply, he grabbed my arm again and led
me over to the foot of the slide. Tuck threw down a rope. We
started to climb, and though we both slipped a few times, we
finally made it to the top.

Tuck got down off Zeus, who'd been pulling us up, and
put his arms round me. "All that blood, child! Are you all
right?"

I hugged him back. He made me feel solid again. "I'm
fine now, Tuck. Honest." Soft, so only he heard, I said,
"Tyrone saw me, Tuck. He looked me square in the face. I
think he would've let those others kill me if they'd found
me, but he didn't point me out."

He smoothed wet hair from my face. "I'm not surprised,
honey."

Mace coiled Tuck's rope and hooked it back on his
saddle. "The fire-setter wants us to dig some graves."

Tuck stepped back from me and shook his head. "Sorry,
Miss Gini. There's no time. I'll say a few words over them
from up here, though, if it would ease your mind."

"It would. Do you want my Bible?"

While I fetched it, I said, "If it's not too much trouble,
Mace, I think you could at least put on another shirt. A
half-naked man at a funeral doesn't seem real reverent."

He grinned. "What's the matter? Is it excitin' you?"

Now, the truth was that he cut a fine figure, but I was not
about to give him the satisfaction. I said, "I'm sure I don't
know what you're talkin' about. I am only worried you'll

offend the Lord. Plus, you'll get yourself a burn and I'll be the one to end up doctorin' it."

He got a spare shirt out of his saddlebags, but he didn't stop smirking till Tuck opened Gam's Good Book and read the Thirty-sixth Psalm. That is the one that ends: *Let not the foot of pride come against me, and let not the hand of the wicked remove me. There are the workers of iniquity fallen: they are cast down, and shall not be able to rise.*

We left behind us the bodies of three horses and six men: two of Black Ear Cicero's and all but one of Burl LaFouche's. The rest were long gone by the time we reached the mouth of the main canyon. We stopped there to water the horses and refill our canteens and water bags, but we didn't pause long.

"Keep yourselves on the alert, children," Tuck announced as we followed the trail. "In case you have forgotten, it's likely there's a posse from Oro Tiempo roaming around out here. If that man of Burl's—the one that got away—hooks up with them, they'll pick up this trail to track Ty and the others and run straight over us in the process. The gold in our future could change mighty quick to a rope for Mace and jail for you and me, Miss Gini. Personally, I have had enough of incarceration to last me several lifetimes."

"I'll bet you said that just to cheer us up," said Mace. "And I wish you'd quit calling me and this walking disaster 'children.' Well, me, anyway. You can call *her* any damn thing you please."

"I meant no offense, Mason. Everybody under the age of forty seems like . . . Miss Gini? What are you up to?"

I was off Filibuster and walking along slow, head down, about ten yards to the east. I said, "Well, for bein' out in the bull's-eye center of nowhere, we have sure got a lot of company. And Ty's gang and the posse aren't the only ones to worry about. Come look."

They did. Tuck crossed his wrists on his saddle horn and leaned forward. He said, "How many do you figure, Miss Gini?"

"Hard to tell, with them keepin' a line like that. I'd say at least fifteen. Likely the same bunch that fiddled with that marker we saw a few days back."

"Sounds reasonable. I concur on the number, too."

Mace shook his head and scowled. "Perfect. Apache."

I said, "They're a couple days ahead of us, and they're veering off toward the northeast."

"That don't mean a damn thing and you know it," Mace growled. "They skipped the reservation, and they're moving just to be moving. They could be anywhere."

Tuck pushed back his hat and wiped his brow. "Might work in our favor. I'll bet a nice Oro Tiempo posse would appeal to them more than we do. We've only got three horses, and that's what they'll be looking for. Extra horses and guns."

Mace said, "They might not see that posse at all. They might just see us."

"And they might be in the next county, boy."

Mace thumped a fist on his saddle. "Hell," he said, real sarcastic, "I don't know why any of us should worry at all. Last time we ran into an Apache, Little Miss Sister to the *Shis-Inday* turned out to be related to the whole damn Apache Nation. Judas Priest, why don't we send up some smoke and invite 'em to a party? Why don't we just bake 'em a goddamn cake?"

"Sees Silver is gone," I said, surprised when my eyes burned with tears. "They caught him. They took him away in chains. He saved your nasty hide. You ought to be grateful to be alive and free when a brave man like that is shackled in Hell's Forty Acres."

Tuck said, "That's enough. For the present, keep your eyes open and let me know if you see even the tiniest thing out of the ordinary. Mount up, Miss Gini."

We rode until it got too dark to see, and once again camped without a fire. Ty and Black Ear Cicero weren't so careful, though. The glow of their fire made a dim halo in the rocky hills on the horizon. I guess they hadn't noticed the pony tracks.

Mace was all for riding right in. "They're cocky now, Tuck. They think they're all alone out here. And now they're only four to our three."

"Ty O'Neill is worth any two," Tuck said. "And Black Ear's worth three, if you take sheer meanness into consideration. No, I believe we'll wait a little longer. Let's let Tyrone do the work for us."

"But Tuck!"

"What was it you heard Ty say back in Half Moon Crossing, Miss Gini?"

"He said a lot of things."

"I mean when he was talking to his friend Pansy about the Cicero gang."

I stared out over the distance, toward the dim light of Ty's fire. "He said they'd have to sleep sometime. Tuck, you think that means he's goin' to try to slip out tonight?"

Shielding the match with his hand, Tuck lit his pipe. "Maybe." He didn't look like he thought that at all.

I took the first watch. Mace went to sleep right off, but Tuck's wound was bothering him and he stayed awake with me for a bit. We sat in silence, watching that faint glow between the distant hills for almost an hour, before I said, "Tuck?"

"Yes, honey?"

"I know there's no understandin' what Tyrone does. But I can't help tryin' to puzzle out what he did today. I mean, when he spied me and didn't say beans."

"I'll tell you something about Ty, Miss Gini. He's an observer. He watches and he waits. He doesn't act so much as *re*act. Unless he's got something important at stake, that is."

"But I had a gun on him! That's pretty dang important."

He wagged his head. "He knew that if you were going to pull the trigger, you'd have done it already. No, he was just watching to see if the others would notice. I don't want to sound callous, honey, but don't believe for a second that Tyrone was trying to help you. His motives are wholly selfish."

I studied my knees. "I know," I said, though part of me wished I didn't. I lifted my head and looked at Tuck's strong, proud profile. He looked near regal in the moonlight, like some displaced king. "Mace told me you used to be a schoolteacher. Is that the truth, or was he tryin' to flimflam me?"

He chuckled. "No flimflam, Miss Gini."

"Dang it! I don't mean to say you're not smart, Tuck. You're for sure the smartest man I ever met in my whole life. But a knuckle-rapper like Miss Justice?"

He smiled. "Oh, much worse than that, Miss Gini. I was a professor." He turned his head and relit his pipe, careful to let none of the match-light filter through his cupped hands. "I was building up tenure, stuffing Latin and Greek and Ancient Literature into resistant, indifferent skulls. I used to dream about the West: the glorious, perfect, romantic adventure of it. I suppose that allure is hard for you to understand, honey, for you've lived here your whole life. But when you're a young man from a family of what is called High Social Standing, all that freedom and space and,

well, *newness*—not a fish fork or potted fern in sight—
well, it called to me as seductively as any siren ever
beckoned Ulysses."

He cupped the pipe bowl in his hand, studying it. "I
wanted to *be* like those heroes, not just read about them. I
suppose I was tired of dust. Dusty books, dusty minds. Dust
and cobwebs. That's how it seemed to me at the time." He
picked up a handful of dirt and let it sift through his fingers,
then smiled at me. "I just traded the figurative for the literal.
Somebody should have shot Horace Greeley."

"But—"

"Subject closed. I'll take over the watch, and Mace can
spell me. Get some sleep, honey. You've had a hard day."

Three hours before dawn, Mace shook us awake in time
to hear a distant crack of gunfire. Tuck was on his feet and
rolling up his blankets before I was clear awake. He said,
"How many shots all together, boy?"

"Three. Maybe four. The first ones were close together.
Hard to count."

I saddled Filibuster fast, then located Malachi. He didn't
want to go in the satchel and kept sticking his legs in the
way; but after I had a few sharp words with him, he gave up
and ducked inside his shell.

Tuck tossed me my bedroll. I said, "Is it Apache?"

He frowned. "Not enough shots."

I don't know why, but I felt relieved. "Then the others
must'a caught him tryin' to slip out. You think he's . . .
You reckon he's dead?"

Tuck was already on Zeus. He said, "Stick by me, you
two," and took off at a gallop.

16

The Gold Reclaimed!

We crossed the plain in slap time, riding full out till Tuck swung wide and eased us down to a jog. Slow, we circled to the west and crept into the low hills. Soon we could hear thin snatches of talk and, every once in a while, shouting or laughter.

I whispered, "They don't sound mad, Tuck. Maybe they were only whoopin' it up."

He didn't answer, just held a finger to his lips to shush me.

There must have been good water nearby and therefore underground, for the vegetation was almost lush compared to the flats we'd been traveling over. We left our horses near a small grove of half-grown cottonwoods and started up the back of a little rise. We moved as quiet and stealthy as Indians, and at the top we found ourselves peering over the edge of a brambled bluff.

They were down there, all right: all four of them, about twenty-feet below us, camped in a little clearing surrounded by weedy brush and boulders. On the far side, their horses were picketed at the edge of a thick, dark stand of live oak and hackberry.

The fire was going strong and looked to be newly fed. All round, bedding was tossed every which way, like a twister had gone through. The man called Whit was propped up against some rocks to the left of the blaze. There was a bandanna tied round his thigh for a tourniquet, and he fussed at it, twisting it with a stick to make it tighter, then looser, then tighter again. Fresh blood darkened his pants leg.

Black Ear Cicero and the Aztec Kid were on their feet, their backs to us. The Kid had a knife in his hand. They stood over Tyrone.

He sat on the ground, tied to a boulder. His legs were stretched out before him and his arms were pulled to the sides. His hat was gone. A thin line of blood started at the corner of his mouth and ended at his jawline. His right sleeve was soaked with blood, and I could see the tear made by a bullet or knife blade. Red splotches bloomed on his face, like he'd been beat up bad.

Black Ear Cicero hauled back with one foot and booted him in the ribs.

I gasped, and Tuck covered my mouth with his hand.

Ty sagged against his ropes. Cicero bent down and grabbed Ty's hair, jerked his head back. He barked, "Water."

The Kid limped to a jumble of gear, picked up a canteen, and dumped it out over Ty's face. He came to with a sputter.

Mace reached across me and tapped Tuck's shoulder. He whispered, "Look," and pointed past Tyrone, toward the ground near the horses.

"Must have been admiring it before they went to bed," Tuck whispered.

I saw it, too, when the light breeze tickled the fire higher for a half-second. It was our gold—or Mescal Mort's gold, or the Apache's gold, or Wilbeck & LaFouche's gold, or whoever's gold it rightfully was—half-hidden by weeds, but stacked prim and neat beside an old oak stump.

Below, Ty shook the water from his face and hair.

Cicero said, "Next time you try to murder men in their

sleep, O'Neill, you might try stranglin'. It's quieter. And you might make sure they're really sleepin'."

"I'd no reason not to trust ye," Tyrone said. You had to hand it to Ty. Even hog-tied and at the mercy of characters like that, he could smile. "How could I know ye'd be so treacherous as t'feign snorin'?"

Cicero slapped him across the face. From the side of the clearing, Whit looked up from his tourniquet and said, "Whack him again for me."

Black Ear Cicero obliged him by knocking Ty's head the other way. Whit laughed like crazy.

When Ty lifted his head and smiled again, blood smeared his teeth. He said, "Ye can't be blamin' a man for tryin' to better himself, Blackie darlin'."

I guess I will never understand the human heart. Tyrone had done me bad in countless ways, but there I was, admiring his pluck and feeling sorry for him, all at once. I nudged Tuck and whispered, "Maybe we should just draw down on those boys and put them out of business."

He frowned. "That's murder you're talking about, Miss Gini."

"We could just wound 'em. It'd be kinder than what they did to LaFouche's men. And what they're likely goin' to do to Tyrone."

"Ty knew what game he was sitting down to. Mace, get the— Mace?"

Mace was gone. Tuck grumbled, "Looks like you might get your wish, Miss Gini. I had hoped for better."

Below, Cicero walked away from Ty, sat down by the fire, and poured himself a cup of coffee. He said, "Somethin' I been meanin' to ask, O'Neill. I can figure why you kilt that Meskin back to Spirit Kettle. Hell, I kill me a Meskin ever chance I git, just on general principle. But how come you shot that horse? Seems to me you could'a just jumped on him and got clean away. Not had to bother with all this waitin' round. Not had to bother with us. Seems to me shootin' that horse all them months ago is what's about to git you kilt."

Ty's head lolled back to rest against the rock. He managed a smile. Even banged up like that, he was still so handsome it made my knees quiver. "'Twas this way, Blackie me love: the Mexican gentleman met his end because he happened to be on the horse. The gold also happened to be on the horse, which was runnin' loose and wouldn't be caught. Which is why that unfortunate beast came to be deceased. There were riders comin' upon me fast. Might have been *bandidos*, might have been Apache. 'Twas the quickest way of makin' certain the booty stayed put. I was figurin' I had a fifty-fifty chance of savin' it that way, since the natives think the place is brimmin' with spooks and banshees."

The Aztec Kid was still standing beside Ty. He threw back his head and burst out in that high, silly laugh of his. "Guess it didn't work out too good, huh, O'Neill? Guess you made a mess!"

That dang Kid had not got any smarter since his days of shooting at me from Tombstone hotel windows. Ty looked up at him and smiled. "Me darlin' boy, you're perspicacity incarnate."

The Kid turned quick to Cicero. "What's that mean? He insultin' me?"

Ty said, "Giuseppe me boy-o, I dinna believe that's possible."

"I told you not to call me that, you mick bastard! Blackie, make him quit it."

Black Ear Cicero leaned back and sipped his coffee. "You make him."

The Kid kicked Tyrone in the arm, where he was

bleeding. Ty screamed; Whit and the Kid both laughed. Tuck clapped a hand over my mouth at the same second. It was a good thing, for I was about to cry out.

Just then, Mace crawled up beside us. He was grinning like a fool.

Tuck let go of me and hissed, "Where you been, boy?"

Mace brought up his arm. His fingers were curled round a gold bar. He whispered, "I can get the rest. Four, maybe five more trips. It's heavy, and I've only got so many pockets big enough."

I said, "I didn't see you! How'd you do that?"

He ignored me. Tuck said, "Then the both of us can do it in two. Miss Gini, you stay put. Those boys spy us, you get on your pony and hightail it, understand? Just hop on Filibuster and head straight for California."

"But Tuck!"

"No buts." ·

He and Mace slid away and disappeared into the dark.

Down by the fire, Ty had passed out again. The Aztec Kid had to throw water on him twice to bring him round.

I didn't catch sight or sound of Tuck or Mace, but once, when the flames flickered higher for a heartbeat, I glimpsed a hand as it snaked out of the weeds and snatched up a gold bar. The pile had shrunk a good bit by then.

The Aztec Kid held his knife to Ty's throat. He said something to Tyrone, too low for me to make out, and then he snickered and so did Cicero.

Ty grinned at him, cocky as if he was holding four aces, and said, "Why, Giuseppe me love, I'd no idea ye were so inclined. If only I'd known, I could'a set ye up with a lad in Ehrenberg whom I've heard is keen on it."

"Goddamn it! I didn't mean I— And quit callin' me that!" I was sure the Kid was going to slit Tyrone open then and there, but instead he threw down the knife and pulled his pistol. "That's about enough, Mr. Candy-Ass O'Neill," he snarled, and put the barrel to Ty's temple.

Tyrone didn't flinch. He looked right past the Kid and up at Cicero. His mouth opened like he was going to say something. Then it snapped shut.

I guess it must have been a combination of my having crept forward a couple inches when the Aztec Kid started getting out of hand; that, and the wind teasing the fire higher at just the right moment. But Ty saw me plain.

He could have given me away easy. Instead, his eyes flicked back to Cicero, just like nothing had happened. He said, "Blackie darlin', are ye goin' to leave this gimp-legged blitherin' idiot murder me when I'm the only one who can lead ye to the gold?"

"Who's the idiot?" the Kid snorted. He still had that pistol jammed against Ty's head. "Any man of us could find it blindfolded!"

To Cicero, Ty said, "I wouldn't be so terrible certain of that." He was grinning pretty wide. "In fact, I'll hazard that if ye were to take a look for the booty, ye'd find it vanished."

Nobody said anything for a few seconds, and then Cicero waved his hand. "Take a look."

As the Kid reholstered his gun and stepped toward the picket line, every muscle in my body went into unmitigated cramp. I prayed Tuck and Mace had their guns ready.

The Kid limped over to the gold stash. His legs were in the way, and I couldn't see the ground. He kicked at the grass. He bent down and swished the weeds with his hands. He went round back of the stump. Then he kicked it, hard.

"Gone!" he hollered. "Gone!"

Whit yanked his tourniquet tight and hopped to his feet. "Cain't be gone! Let me look!" He hobbled toward the Kid.

Cicero shook a fist in Ty's face. "O'Neill! Where'd you—"

"If ye'll remember, Blackie darlin', 'twas there when ye trussed me. I can say, with all humility, that I'm a man of many skills. But prestidigitation—at least with objects as cumbersome as those bars—isn't among me gifts."

Whit and the Aztec Kid were back. I shoved myself away from the cliff's edge. I could still see them, but now it was through a web of twigs and leaves. It was a good thing, because they all started twisting their noggins like hoot owls.

The Kid was madder than a shaved bear. He shouted, "Well, if you ain't got it, who does? And don't say ghosts or banshees!"

"Hardly spirits, boy-o. Get to untyin' me, and I believe I can lead ye to it on the straightaway."

Cicero looked like he might be thinking it over, but the Kid was too steamed for logic. He pulled his pistol again, pressed the barrel above Ty's right eye. He cocked it. "I've took enough shit from this shanty Irishman!"

I squeezed my eyes shut, waiting for the shot. Instead, somebody shouted, "Drop it now, by Gaw!"

I opened one eye.

Cicero, the Aztec Kid, and Whit snapped straight. They stared past Tyrone, past the picket line, toward the wood.

The voice, which sounded some familiar to me, said, "Now! Or you're dead where you stand."

Ty looked surprised for just a half-second, and then he grinned real big. Being tied up, he couldn't turn round toward the voice. Instead, he looked up toward me. I don't think he could have seen me, but he winked anyway. And then he called out, "Vincent-me-darlin'-Conway! Would that be your charmin' and dulcet voice I'm hearin'?"

Suddenly, the woods were filled with sounds, the kind a

bunch of men make when they've had to be quiet and careful for too long, and are enjoying stirring up as much commotion as is possible by tramping through wood and brush.

"It is, by Gaw," said old broke-nosed Vince as he stepped out into the light, his pistol drawn and pointed straight at Black Ear Cicero. "If I was you, Tyrone, I wouldn't look so goddamn glad to see me."

More men came up out of the trees. Cicero and his boys had their hands up over their heads. They looked pretty nervous.

"'Tis glad I am, though. Ye see before ye an unfortunate victim of tragic circumstance. I can't begin to be communicatin' the travesties I've suffered while a prisoner of these foul ruffians."

Cicero said, "You son of a—"

That was as far as he got, because one of Vince's men hit him upside the skull with a rifle butt. There were at least a dozen of them in the clearing by then. A couple wore badges. One was Deputy Sam McKay, who both me and Ruby LaFouche had buffaloed back in the Oro Tiempo jail. He was over by the picket line. He called out, "This is Davey James's mare. Steve Moore's gelding, too."

Vince nodded without looking over at him. He tipped his head toward Ty and said, "Get his ropes off."

"'Tis a wise man who—"

"Shut up, O'Neill."

Ty got to his feet. He was holding his hurt arm. He shrugged and said, "Fine. I'll be pleased to be keepin' me peace. But ye might be interested to know that even now, as I'm closin' me mouth—on your orders, mind—your employer's gold is on its way out of the—"

I didn't hear the rest, because right then a hand grabbed

my boot and dragged me back out of the bushes and halfway down the slope toward the horses.

"Come *on*!" Mace hissed.

I got up and brushed myself off. "I can walk, you know."

He got a grip on my arm and pulled me over to Filibuster. Tuck was already there, mounted up and waiting. "Well, you sure can't hear," Mace whispered. He practically threw me on my horse. "I've been tryin' to get your attention for five minutes."

He handed up my reins, and I snatched them from him. "There's a whole mob down there," I pointed out. "The posse from Oro Tiempo."

Mace jumped up on his horse. "No fooling," he said with a sneer, and took off for the flats at a lope, me and Tuck close behind.

It was lucky that dawn was on its way. We went full out, our horses' necks stretched straight, their nostrils wide. After a half hour the sky had gone from purple-gray to pink to early-morning blue. I reined Filibuster in a little. It was not a fair pace for the horses, who were lathered and blowing. Besides, I couldn't see anybody chasing us. But Tuck dropped back and without a word reached over and quirted Filibuster across the rump. That made me pretty mad, but there was too much wind in my face to shout at him.

It was near another twenty minutes before he finally let us slow down to a jog. Poor Filibuster was all in. The others didn't look too fit, either.

Tuck said, "I'm sorry, Miss Gini. About slapping your horse, that is. But you were lagging."

"I don't see any point in torturin' these animals, Tuck. Nobody's after us."

He took a drink from his canteen. "Oh, they're on the

march, Miss Gini, have no doubt. You just haven't seen them yet."

"You should've heard Tyrone, Tuck! He was changin' his story about every five seconds, tryin' to boondoggle those boys, first one bunch, then the other!"

"Did he appear to be succeeding?"

"Mace grabbed me before I could tell. But the posse untied him. And that ugly old Vince fella was with them. He looked to be runnin' the show, even with all those badges around."

Tuck nodded. "He's Burl LaFouche's head muscle man. In Oro Tiempo, that takes precedence over the law."

With the flat of his hand, Mace skimmed lather from his horse's neck, then shook it from his fingers. "Ponies can't stand up under this, Tuck. Not carryin' us and the gold, too. We need to find a safe place to hole up."

Tuck slowed us down to a walk. "No such thing with that bunch after us. Not in this part of the country. Those boys are local, and they can out-nook-and-cranny me. We'll have to take our chances. We'll walk these horses another ten minutes before we water them, then walk another ten or fifteen before we start to build up speed again. The last thing we need is a horse with a twisted gut. Miss Gini, if you happen to have any prayers memorized which would fit this occasion, I'd appreciate it if you'd recite them now."

The horses cooled out some, were watered light and walked out some more. By then, the sun was up good, the sky was bleached to almost white, and the day was warming up in a hurry. I stuffed all my hair up under my hat, which helped a little. The land, gravelly desert with a bush here or there, had started to roll a bit; and as we came to higher ground, Tuck pulled out his spyglass and had a look behind us.

He swept the horizon from right to left, then halfway back again before he stopped and squinted. "There they are," he said. "Son of a goddamn bitch." He parked the glass in his pocket. "Excuse me, Miss Gini."

He wheeled round and we pushed into a gallop again, though our horses could not manage their earlier speed and it was more like a tired lope.

I guess that posse did not care if they killed their mounts. No matter how hard we went, they kept closing on us. Within another half hour, they had shortened the gap enough that, when we breasted a rise, the little dots of their forms could be seen with the naked eye.

I was plenty scared. Our ponies were in bad shape, Mace's the worst. The day had already gone from warm to cookstove-hot, and that was not helping either.

We pushed ahead, making worse time with every step. Ten minutes later we were down to a trot and nearing another rise. I was almost afraid to ride up it and look back. I knew the posse had gained on us considerable since the last time we'd checked. I wished I had a real repeater, and not just Gam's old squirrel gun.

As we started up the slope's low grade, me and Tuck riding even, Mace lagging behind, I turned my head and shouted, "Filibuster is half-dead! We have got to stand and fight. They're goin' to kill us anyway. At least we can let the horses live!"

Tuck reined in Zeus so fast the horse half-reared. I whoaed up Filibuster, too, which didn't take much effort. "Holy Hannah, I didn't mean right here! Don't you think we ought to get on the other side of the ridge?"

Real soft, he said, "I believe that position is already occupied, Miss Gini." He pointed. I followed his finger to where Mace was already staring.

Fifteen or sixteen mounted Apache braves lined the crest of the rise. Most carried rifles. A few had lances.

I whispered, "Why don't they do something?"

Mace hissed, "Look at our horses. I don't think they're real worried about us getting away."

Tuck's eye moved up and down the line, like he was searching for a familiar face. I did the same. They were all strangers to me.

Tuck gestured to the one in the middle, then held up one hand, palm out, and said something in Apache. The brave ignored him. Gam told me once that most Apache think it dirties their language to speak it with folks they do not know and respect. I took this to be one of those times.

Tuck tried again. In Mex, he said, "Perhaps you do not remember me, friend, but I know you from the old days when you were in the camp of Cochise. I am Tuck Brennan, who Cochise once called He Watches Stars. I ask you to let us pass, in the memory of friendlier times."

The brave he addressed was wizened and dark-skinned, with eyes as sharp and black as flint. A bright orange sash was tied across his brow. His expression didn't shift one jot. In Mex, he replied, "I do not know your face. Cochise was long ago. You are not my friend. A friend would know my name."

Tuck was just as sober as that brave. He said, "I only waited for an invitation to use it, as might be made to a friend. I hoped you would remember me in such a manner, Geronimo."

Now, despite the fact that we were about to get squished between a lynch-minded posse and a line of murderous Apache, I was pretty dang impressed. I guess if you are going to get massacred, you might as well get massacred by somebody famous. And it looked like that was just what was going to happen, for Geronimo didn't seem the least little bit persuaded by Tuck's fine speech. He just sat his pony like a statue. The only move he made was to tilt his rifle barrel a couple inches forward.

With that, four braves, two from each end of the line, started down toward us. I sure wished Sees Silver was there, or Manuelito, or any of those boys who had helped us with the bandits in Cañon de los Espejos and would therefore remember us. And then, just like the Good Lord had shot it into my head with a heavenly bullet, I had an idea.

I nudged Filibuster forward a couple steps, and then I dismounted, real slow. I heard Mace whisper, "What the hell do you think you're doing?"

Terse, Tuck said, "Let her be."

Shaking inside, I walked about twenty feet forward, which put me halfway between Tuck and the Apache. I looked Geronimo square in the eye and hoped to Jesus he hadn't been too long away from the San Carlos campfires. Then I put one hand over my heart and thumped my chest. I said *"Shis-Inday!"* real serious-like. And then I took off my hat. All my hair fell down in a red tumble. I pushed it out of my eyes. I pounded my chest once more. *"Shis-Inday!"*

Geronimo still stared at me, just as flat and no more lively than a rock.

Well, that was the one and only trick I had. I was about to back my way down to Tuck when I heard the first whisper. It started as a blurred murmur, but then another brave took it up and another and another, and pretty soon it was a buzzing hum: *Neva Kin-Kay, Neva Kin-Kay, Neva Kin-Kay* . . .

Geronimo was the only one who did not take up the chant. A long-faced warrior to his left, who had been busy watching the horizon, leaned toward him and spoke soft into his ear. Even that didn't change his expression. He stared at me a moment longer, then backed his pony to the side and away.

The one who had whispered to him did the same, making a hole in the line of braves. Then he said to me, "Pass, Neva Kin-Kay."

We moved on: slowly, for Tuck said there was no more need to hurry. It was about ten minutes before we heard the first distant gunfire and whoops. By then, we were off our horses and leading them. I stopped and turned toward the sound.

Tuck put his hand on my shoulder. "Come along, Miss Gini."

"But they're goin' to kill Tyrone!"

Mace gave me a dirty look. "Judas Priest! You beat everything!"

Tuck said, "Don't worry about Ty, honey. He's pretty hard to kill. Even when a body does manage to murder him," he added with a grin, "he doesn't stay dead very long."

Now, I knew he was only saying that to make me feel better, and that he was worried, too. Tyrone was just one of those people you couldn't help but worry about, even while you were busy hating him. There is likely something wrong with feeling that way, but a person can't help their heart.

After a while the sounds faded, though I don't know if it was because one side had killed off all the other or if we had just got too far away to hear the battle. A little after that, we mounted up and started off at a jog. I asked Tuck where we were headed.

"I was thinking north," he said. "Colorado is a nice place, or so they tell me. I'd be delighted to have you youngsters tag along, if you think you can keep your fussing down to a roar."

"I'd admire it," I said. "The stayin'-with-you part, that is."

Mace frowned, but he kept on riding along beside us.

"I believe," Tuck said, "that we ought to address the question of the split. Now, it seems to me that the greatest share should go to Mason. It is, in a way, his inheritance, and Pete's. If it's all right with you, Miss Gini, I think it should go fifty percent to Mace and twenty-five each to you and me. That is, if Mace doesn't object."

"I object," said Mace.

If he'd been close enough, I would have slugged him. "Well, that's fine with me, Mace Danahoe! You can have all my share, if you're so greedy as to not appreciate folks who have about got themselves killed on your behalf. But Tuck gets his cut, just like he said. He is an old man and needs retirin' money."

Tuck looked at me kind of funny. "I'm not *that* old, Miss Gini! I'm barely sixty. My Uncle Thaddeus was still riding to the hounds at eighty-three!"

"That's not what I meant," said Mace. "I meant I think it ought to be an even split. Thirds. I been thinking on it. It don't matter whose gold it used to be. What matters is who worked to get it. We all worked even."

I felt pretty stupid. I said, "I'm sorry, Mace. That's real square." And then, because I had no wish to wallow in humility, I said, "Tuck, would you know what day this is?"

He smiled. "Day of the week?"

"Date. Are we in June yet?"

"I'd say we were just about in June, yes. Why?"

"I think my birthday's next week, if the ninth is in there somewhere. My sixteenth birthday."

"Why, heartfelt felicitations, Miss Gini! I regret there

isn't a mercantile in our path. I would have found just the right gift for such a momentous occasion."

I kept my eyes on Filibuster's mane. "There is one thing you can give me, Tuck. Something I'd like better than anything."

"What's that, honey?"

"A headstone for Zack." I turned toward him, hoping. "I know I can find the place if we swing over that way."

Mace rolled his eyes. "And just where the hell is he gonna find a headstone? In his back pocket?"

Tuck laughed and rubbed at his chin. "Maybe so, boy. Let's head on over toward Tucson. I'll do a little cogitating en route."

Four days later we found the place and Tuck left me and Mace there.

"Try not to kill each other while I'm gone," he said, and jogged away to the south.

We waited two days, and Mace was in such a surly mood that I did most of my talking to Malachi. He seemed to be the only one enjoying the delay, as he was out of the satchel and on the ground the whole time. Watching him plod around all carefree (and chomping down on anything that didn't outsize his jaws) made me feel awful guilty about having hauled him for so long. He was such a good-mannered tortoise that he would never complain, but I guessed that riding in a dark valise more than three-quarters of the time could not be nice for him.

Tuck came back on the third day, and he was not alone. The fella with him was driving a beat-up buckboard, and in the back of it, wrapped up in gunnysacks, was a real nice limestone marker: not too big, but not little, either. Mace helped the two of them unload it and set it up at the head of Zack's cairn. It said:

ZACHARY ZALMON "GHOST" RUGGLES
1814–1880
A BRAVE MAN
A TRUE FRIEND

I thought it was a fine sentiment.

Tuck did not introduce us to the buckboard's driver, who didn't speak one single word till the work was done and he climbed back up on his wagon. And what he said then was, "I trust this here's the last favor I'll be doin' for you, Brennan. I trust it brings me square."

"It does, Jimmy," Tuck replied. "You haven't seen us."

The man gathered his reins and clucked to his team. "Oh, I ain't see'd you. I ain't see'd nor heard a blessed thing. I didn't notice for one minute that feller yonder is the same boy in all the papers what crashed out of jail after he kilt his own granddaddy." He turned the wagon in a wide circle and started back south. "You ain't see'd me neither, if'n you gets caught. You fellers al'ays gets caught or ends bad, like that 'un 'neath yon rocks. No, I ain't see'd a thing. . . ."

For somebody who rode in so quiet, he sure rode out noisy. The only thing that quieted him down was distance.

Tuck said a few words over the grave to solemnize the placing of the stone. I have to admit that I shed a few tears. After he finished, Tuck put on his hat and said, "It's still early. I believe we should put some miles behind us before sunset."

We broke camp, but when it came time to put Malachi away in my satchel, I couldn't do it. His stubby old legs waved stiff in the air as I looked him in the eye. That wasn't easy, for he was swinging his head back and forth, but I finally got his attention. I said, "Malachi, you have been a fine pet and a loyal companion, but I think it's time you got on with the natural business of bein' a free critter and I got back to having underdrawers without tortoise mess on 'em. I'm goin' to leave you here with Zack. Maybe the two of you can look out for each other."

I put him on the ground by the cairn, ran my finger along the arrow-scar on his shell for the last time, and mounted up.

Tuck said, "You sure you want to do that, honey?"

I looked down at Malachi. He was already poking his way toward a small prickly pear. I said, "I'm sure."

Tuck said he was taking us to the home of a friend. "Gospel Joe Varney. You know him?"

"Heard of him but never met him," I said, kind of surprised. "He's a crazy old miner. He used to come into Hanged Dog every now and again for supplies."

Tuck nodded. He was busy trying to fill his pipe and hold his reins at the same time. "He's the one. He's halfway up in the White Mountains. There's rich grazing for the horses and cool evening breezes for us. I believe we might bide there for a few days and rest up before we head on north."

"We're goin' that close to Hanged Dog? Is that safe?"

"We'll ride a circuitous route. Getting that tombstone for Zack was about as much chance as I want to take with a town until we get clear of the Territory. And if I didn't say it before, happy birthday, honey. And, by Hera, I nearly forgot!" He reached behind, unbuckled one saddlebag, and pulled something out. "A present. How's it feel to be a celebrated individual?"

It was a dime novel, writ by somebody named Bartholomew Strump, and the title was *Outlaw Songbird: Gini Kincaid and the Tombstone Tragedy*.

I could scarce believe it. I shut my eyes tight, opened them, and looked again. It still read the same. The girl on the cover had red hair like me, but she looked about ten years

older and had on a lot of face paint. She wore a bright red
dress cut practically to her knees and she waved a smoking
pistol in each hand. Behind her was a town consumed by
flame.

I said, "Is that supposed to be me?"

Tuck chuckled. "Miss Gini, some say fabrication is the
price of fame. Personally, I believe it is the other way
around."

"But why would this Strump fella write me up? I never
even met him. And I sure never did anything brave!"

"I'd argue that," Tuck said with a smile. "And I imagine
Strump is some short-pants Tombstone hack who got tired
of writing up those Earp boys of yours and thought he'd
have a go at you for a change of pace. They turn those books
out fast and slapdash."

I opened it to the middle and read a couple paragraphs.
"This is lies! Terrible lies! Listen to this!" I held up the book
and commenced:

> It was at gunpoint that the flame-haired gamin—
> mistress of the deadly John "Doc" Holliday—switched
> her allegiance to the dashing Tyrone O'Neill, known to
> some as the Dakota Gambler.
>
> "Heartbreak or no, Doc, it's Tyrone I love," she
> cried, and aimed the pistol at his chest. "Set me free,
> or I will have to plug you." A coward to the core,
> Holliday demurred, plotting black vengeance all the
> while.
>
> By night, she still sang and strutted at the infamous
> Striped Garter Dance Hall, where cheap, spangled
> women welcome all comers with open arms. But for the
> handsome O'Neill, Gini gave up the lowly life to which
> she had sunk at Holliday's hands, and—

I snapped the book shut. "Holy dang-blasted Sufferin' Hannah! They make me sound like some kind of low floozy! And Doc Holliday? He never touched me, not once, and I only pulled a gun on him one time, and that was because I thought he was goin' to kill Tyrone, and . . . Holy Hannah!"

Dang that Tuck, anyway! Mace, too. All they did was laugh, and they kept it up till the tears fair rolled down their cheeks.

A few days later we bypassed Hanged Dog, cut up into the mountains, and wended our way through the trees to an old beaver meadow, divided down the center by a healthy stream. There had been rain the night before, and this vicinity looked to have been blessed with a new downpour. The weeds swished our horses' legs wet and the ground was still squish-muddy. The trees and grass were so green they nearly hurt your eyes. At the edge of the meadow was a dinky log cabin and, about ten yards past that, an even dinkier shed. As we rode up, a burro stuck its shaggy head out of the lean-to, and a skinny, gray-headed wire of a Negro man stepped out the cabin door. One hand held an old muzzle-loader. The other shaded his eyes.

All of a sudden he swung that muzzle-loader in a circle and busted out in a grin. One of his front teeth was gold and it gave off quite a glint. "By the Holy King James Version! Tucker, is that you? Is you risen from the dead? Is this Lazarus hisself come to call on an old sinner?"

Tuck laughed loud, called, "Not risen, only relocated," and jogged ahead. By the time me and Mace got up to the cabin and slid off our horses, Tuck and Gospel Joe were shaking hands and patting each other's backs and having a high old time.

"Joe, I'd like you to meet Miss Gini, who is currently

famous amongst the dime-novel crowd; and Mace, who isn't, at least insofar as we know. Children, shake hands with my old friend Joe Varney, the best Bible scholar and finest bee-through-a-blizzard tracker the U.S. Cavalry ever had the bad sense to retire."

"And nothin' left now but the shell of a crazy old rock-breaker. Praise Jesus! Pleased to meet you, Miss Gini, Mace."

I liked him right off. I said, "Pleased to be met."

"There's ground-tie stakes in the lean-to, if you want to tether them horses out to graze. Or you can just turn 'em free if you think they won't run off. Then come on in the house. I got me a couple fine jugs of O Be Joyful I'd be pleased to share. Ain't had no company since Hector was a pup. You still a whiskey-sippin' man, Tucker?"

I didn't try any of Gospel Joe's homemade rotgut, but I had a sniff, which was enough to nearly singe my nose hairs. I think he could have sold it for paint thinner. I knew he used it to fuel his lanterns, for they reeked of it. He sure had enough stockpiled: there must have been a dozen crockery jugs of the stuff and twice that many bottles, all stacked up against the far wall.

By late afternoon, Tuck and Gospel Joe were pretty well snookered, and Mace wasn't far behind. As for me, I leafed back through my dime novel and nursed a bottle of soda pop Joe had been using to block open the cabin's only window. From all the dust on that bottle, he must have had it a hundred years, but it sure tasted good to me.

Joe and Tuck got to telling all kinds of tall tales about the olden days, most of which I figured to be greatly exaggerated, since each was having a high time trying to outstory the other. They and Mace were out front, perched on barrels and telling whoppers, when the boy rode up.

I knew him right off. He was one of those Lawson kids

from down the mountain. Well, maybe not such a kid. Ambrose Lawson was older than me—about seventeen— though he was real scrawny and stunted, like he maybe had a tapeworm. Now, the Lawsons have got practically more kids than you can count, and they are for the most part real well behaved. But Ambrose was a bad apple. I had heard stories about him tying cans on dogs and doing mean things to cats, and the storekeepers always watched their wares if he was in town.

He was riding that same mare his daddy had loaned me the day Gam took sick, but he had not bothered to saddle or bridle her. He rode bareback, with just a halter and rope for a bridle and reins. There was a rifle slung over his shoulder. He whoaed up with a lot more yanking on the mare's rope than was necessary, and said, "Daddy sent me up here to warn y'all about a bear."

Mace must have thought that was the funniest thing he'd ever heard, for he commenced to double over with laughter. I guessed he was drunker than I'd thought.

Tuck and Gospel Joe didn't pay him any mind. Joe stood up, kind of weaving, and said, "Bear? What bear's that?"

"It's shot and it's crazy. Got a busted jaw. Ripped holy hell outta Corky Brown's place. Clawed Corky's leg up bad. He was hidin' under the bed at the time. Leg was all the sombitch could reach."

Tuck's head wobbled on his neck. He said, "Must not have been a very big bear if it couldn't even shove over a bed."

Gospel Joe wagged a finger and near put out his own eye in the process. "Corky's got hisself a bed made outta logs. Built right into the side of the cabin. Damnedest thing you ever seen. Take a full-growed grizzer to budge it. That Corky's a pious fella. Got hit in the head with a throwed sausage at the Methodist picnic back in seventy-and-seven and didn't even blast the fella what throwed it." When Tuck looked at him kind of funny, he added, "It were a big sausage."

Tuck shifted his attention to Ambrose, who had not bothered to dismount. He said, "How big's the bear in question, son? And how'd it happen to get shot and not killed?"

Ambrose had this real ugly face he made, where he curled his lip into a one-sided sneer and let it hang there. He was doing it right then. "Ain't a grizzer. Just a black bear, maybe two hundred pounds. You old coots're 'shined up good, ain't you?"

With a thud, Tuck leaned back against the cabin. "Would I be right to guess that maybe it was you who shot up that bear in the first place, and that's why your papa sent you round to warn the neighbors?"

Ambrose was studying Mace, who had stopped laughing and was passed out, flat on the ground. He looked up after a couple seconds, and said, "Well, I told you. I gotta go now." He glanced toward the window and I ducked back in a hurry.

Joe said, "Maybe you should stay the night, Ambrose. Take you till past sunset to get out of these trees. You don't want to be up here after dark with no roof."

"Gonna go down as far as Al Leonard's. Stay over there."

I waited till I was sure he was gone before I peeked out the window again. Tuck and Gospel Joe had picked up Mace and were dragging him back toward the cabin. I opened the door for them.

"That oughter do him," Joe said after they draped Mace across the table, it being closer than the bed. They weren't real careful about it. If I had not grabbed Mace's head, they would have slammed it into the doorframe.

Joe wiped his hands on his pants and looked out the door

at nothing in particular. "That Ambrose is a nasty piece of work and dumb as dirt to boot. I swan, I got real pity for Rose and Ike Lawson, for they is too nice'a folks to get stuck with that . . . Well, I ain't gonner say the words I want, on account of this young lady bein' present and also on account of I'm strugglin' constant to stay right with Jesus."

He stretched out his arms, then looked up at the sky. "*Devise not evil against thy neighbor, seeing he dwelleth securely by thee*. Proverbs Three, Twenty-nine. I s'pose I oughter get up the hill and tell Bill Forster 'bout the bear. That Ambrose didn't go up there, I'll lay money on it. He's in too much of a toot t'get down to Al's and cozy up with that purty Mary Ann gal of his. . . ."

"I'll ride on up with you, Joe," Tuck said. He looked no more able to ride a horse than walk a carnival tightrope. "We never got around to that discussion on Romans Nine."

Gospel Joe wagged his head, though it more waved and bobbed than shook. He said, "Best you stay here, Tucker, and sit with this Gini-gal. I 'magine I'll bide the night up there. 'Sides, I'm practical the only one in the county Bill Forster won't shoot on sight. Hell, he might even blast *me*—his eyes is goin'. Help yourselves to the jug whiskey."

He set out on foot, and he walked real good for a man as drunk as he was. Tuck stretched out on the bed. "If you don't mind, Miss Gini, I believe I'll take a short drift down Lethe's gentle waters."

"If that means you're goin' to sleep, old man, I don't think it much matters whether I mind or not."

I could have saved my breath as he was already snoring. I sat down at the table and propped my book up against Mace's rib cage. Not that I didn't have the story memorized the first time through, mind you: it was just such out-and-out folderol that I had trouble believing I'd remembered it right unless I was staring at it.

I puzzled over that dang story for a couple hours. The author, Mr. Bartholomew Strump, had made me into kind of a heroine, I guess, especially with the part he added in about me saving a couple orphans in a blizzard. In the end, he wrote that I burnt down half of Tombstone, killed three villains, and fled the county with Tyrone O'Neill and a fortune in banknotes. He also wrote that I was a crack shot. He said I could put out a catamount's eye at three hundred yards with a handgun. Now, that lie ticked me off more than most. First, there is no person living or dead who could fare near that lucky with a pistol. Second, it would be a mean thing. I wouldn't want a hungry cougar prowling my yard, mind you, but I think they are real handsome and I would never hurt one just to show off.

Finally, I put the stupid book away. Then I scraped together a bite of dinner and retired, but not before I went outside and closed up the window shutter real tight. I barred the door, lifted Mace's gun, and curled up by the cool stone hearth, the pistol in my hand.

I don't know when Mace and Tuck woke, but when I roused it was still the middle of the night and they were both sitting at the table. The glow of one lantern, turned low, washed gold up over their faces. The cabin door was standing open, and though the night had gone a tad chilly, Tuck had not lit the fire. I was glad, for after so many days of heat down on the flats, the breeze felt nice. They were talking soft. Tuck had his pipe out, but it wasn't lit. Mace was holding his head in both hands from the aftereffects of Gospel Joe's O Be Joyful. I realized why the door was open when he bolted off his chair and ran outside to upchuck.

When he came back in, I got to my feet. "How long you two been awake?"

Tuck said, "A while. Been busy."

I figured they'd mostly been busy being sick and com-
miserating, but I didn't mention it. Instead, I said, "Maybe
you'd like to play some cards. I've got a deck. Doc Holliday
gave it to me."

Mace appeared near green from the liquor, and he was in
a foul mood as well. He said, "A present from your *lover*?
And just what would we play, Miss Dime-Novel Heroine?
Go fish? Old maid?"

That made me pure mad, but I didn't let on. I was getting
pretty dang sick of him always riding me and making out
like I couldn't do anything right. I set his pistol up on the
mantel, seeing as how he was tempting me to use it. Then,
cool as I could, I said, "I don't like those. How about
blackjack? For money."

"You'd go flat broke in five minutes, girl!"

I smiled just a little. "I'd be willin' to take that chance,
Mace."

Tuck knew exactly where I was headed. He hiked up a
brow and said, "Matches will do, Miss Gini. With that
solid-gold memory of yours, you're in no position to be
gaming with friends for cash."

I leaned toward him and said, "I wouldn't have kept it,
Tuck. I just wanted to teach him a lesson."

"Go on, Geneva me love. Play the boy for filthy lucre."
Tyrone O'Neill stepped through the door and into the light.
"I'd admire to see what grand breed of stakes ye'd be
sportin' with."

17

A Bad Jail and a Worse Trial

"Ye'll be puttin' your firearms on the table, gentlemen," Ty said. Vince walked in right behind him. "And if ye wouldn't mind, I'd rather ye didn't touch them. Let's unbuckle and have the whole shebang. Slow."

Mace held out his hands and tilted back in his chair to show he wasn't armed. Tuck undid his gunbelt and slid it onto the tabletop. As Ty picked it up and tossed it out the door, Tuck said, "Evening, Tyrone. You seem to be a few men shy."

Vince barked, "Shut up, Brennan." He bulled his way past Ty and grabbed Mace by the collar. Mace swung at him, but Vince twisted out of the way and shoved a knee into Mace's midsection. Gasping, Mace doubled over. He sank, face first, onto the table.

"You got no call to bully an unarmed man like that!" I jumped toward Vince, but stopped quick when he swung his pistol toward me.

"I'll do what I damn well please, you little two-bit whore."

Tuck snapped, "You watch your mouth!"

Ty had spied Mace's gun atop the mantel. He tossed it out the door after Tuck's sidearms and said, "Ye'll be forgivin' Vincent, Tucker. He's nothin' if not single-minded."

Vince grunted. "LaFouche is offerin' a thousand each on

365

you and the girl, Brennan. And five thousand for this scum."
He tapped the back of Mace's neck with his pistol barrel.
Mace groaned.

"For me own part," Tyrone cut in, "I'm more interested in
the cargo ye lifted off Cicero."

"That, too," said Vince. Mace had caught his breath by
then, but he looked terrible green. Vince gripped him by the
shirt and slammed him back into a chair. "Where is it,
Brennan?"

"Cargo?" Tuck replied, eyebrows raised. He tilted his
chair back to balance on two legs.

I stared Ty in the face. "Me and Tuck don't parley with
horse-killers."

Ty cocked his head. "Beggin' your pardon, darlin'?"

"I think it's just a little too dang late to beg my pardon or
anybody else's, Tyrone O'Neill. You may have fooled the
whole of Arizona Territory with your handsome face and
smooth ways, but you're lower than a snake's belly in a
wagon rut and you have got the moral code of a tomcat."

He blinked a couple times, but his smile didn't waver.
"Why, Geneva me love! I didn't realize ye cared so deep."

"For Jigsaw. Not you."

Vince barked, "Shut up, dammit! Where's the gold,
Brennan?"

Tuck folded his arms across his chest and shrugged.

Vince pushed past Mace, seized my arm, and jerked me to
him. When I kicked him in the shin and tried to punch him,
he grabbed a fistful of my hair. As if that did not hurt
enough, he shook me till my teeth rattled.

Tuck jumped up and Mace twisted round to make a lunge
for him. They both froze when Vince pressed his gun barrel
to the side of my head.

That dang Tyrone was all teeth and dimples. "Now then,
Tucker. Where'd ye squirrel away the booty?"

Tuck sighed. His smile was gone. "All right, Tyrone. You win. But if I give you the gold, you have got to promise me you'll let these children go."

Ty pursed up his lips. "Seems a fair trade," he said after a moment. "Ye've me word."

I hollered "A lot *that's* worth!" and made to stomp down on Vince's foot.

Fast as a blink, he let go of my hair, grabbed me round the ribs, then hoisted me clear up off the ground and thumped my temple with his gun barrel. "Next time I'm gonna come down on your skull," he muttered before he looked toward Ty. "That's six thousand dollars of our money you're givin' away, Tyrone."

"What's six thousand compared to the other?"

"The other's LaFouche's. Ain't ours, except the finder's fee."

Tyrone shook his head, like he was real tired. "I know it's a strain for ye, Vincent darlin', but try usin' your head. Insofar as your esteemed employer is aware, you're long since deceased at the hands of heathen cutthroats. And as for it's bein' his gold, that's a lie he's told ye. 'Twas Wilbeck's once, then 'twas the desert's, and now there's no rightful owner except by possession. Ye and I are a sight closer to possessin' it than Burl LaFouche."

Vince didn't answer, but he eased up on my ribs some. I took a big swallow of air.

Ty smiled. He could not have been smoother if you had oiled him. "LaFouche is already livin' like a king. He's in no need of it. 'Twould do nothin' but get lost in his bookkeepin' system; and you, after all your fine work, goin' to your grave a pauper with nothin' to show for your loyalty and sacrifice but a handshake and forty dollars a month. That, and a paltry reward that he'll likely manage to cheat ye out of."

Behind me, I felt Vince shift his weight from foot to foot. "All right," he said at last. "All of 'em go free. The old man included. And that's no favor to you, Brennan. I just don't want the bother of you. Get the gold."

Through clenched teeth, Mace growled, "Don't do it!"

But Tuck said, "A deal," and stood up slow, like he had suddenly aged ten years. "Mace, help with this stone."

"What?"

"You heard me, boy." Tuck was already bending to the fireplace. "Get over here and lend me a hand. I know when I'm beat."

Vince shoved me down into a chair, grumbling, "Hands flat on the table, you."

I was looking around for a gun. I was also trying to figure why Tuck and Mace were pulling up a big stone in the hearth when I knew the gold was in our saddlebags, piled in the corner.

Vince growled, "Hurry up, dammit."

Tyrone leaned across the table and turned up the lamp. "Can ye see what you're doin' there, boys? Wouldn't want ye to miss any of it, now would we?"

"By Hera, this rock didn't seem this heavy when we pulled it up before," Tuck muttered. "Mason, fetch me something for a lever or we'll be here all night. That poker'll do. You mind, Tyrone?"

Ty took a step back and smiled. "So long as ye dinna go applyin' it to me head, Tucker."

Outside, a horse whinnied. Another started a ruckus, then another. "What the hell's goin' on?" Vince jabbed his gun against the back of my neck and stared out the doorway, into the night.

Gospel Joe's burro was braying and squealing to beat the band. I was hoping the source of the tumult was Gospel Joe coming back early, but then I heard hoofbeats pounding off into the distance, then wood splintering, more burro brays, more hoofbeats fading.

Even Tyrone's grin had faded to a nervous scowl. "What in the blessed name'a—"

Tuck twisted up, poker in hand, and knocked Ty's gun away. Ty yelped and grabbed his arm. Mace launched himself at Vince, shoved him away from me and down to the floor.

Vince's gun sailed toward the doorway. I dove for it, clapped a hand over it just before it could skitter across the threshold, just before something black crushed down on my hand.

Now, you may not think a black bear is very big, especially if you see one next to King Grizzly; but I can tell you, when you are trapped in a twelve-by-fifteen cabin with one who is in a bad mood, any bear, even a two-hundred pounder, is way too big.

It was a sow-bear, and she was up on her hind legs. Her stench flooded the cabin. Her full weight ground my fingers against the pistol and floor. My hand felt like it had been pounded full of spikes, but I couldn't get it free. I felt my fingers bend the wrong way, then snap. I screamed and beat at her leg with my other hand.

She didn't take notice. Her lower jaw was half-shot-away and she was crazy with pain. Her front was streaked with dried blood and pus. Tyrone was straight in front of her, and she charged him.

He jumped out of her way, rolled, landed in the corner on our saddlebags, and knocked Gospel Joe's stockpile of O Be Joyful tumbling in the process. The sow changed her target to Tuck. He struck out with the poker but she slapped it from his hands. He dove under the table. She dropped to all fours and went after him.

Ty picked up a jug and threw it at her. It thudded against

the hump of her back and she reared up again as the jug hit the mantel and exploded into shards. White lightning sprayed into the air, splashed across the floor, spattered into my face.

I rolled over and snatched up Vince's gun in my good hand, tried to aim it at the bear. Vince and Mace rolled into me just as I fired. The slug ricocheted off the fireplace and shattered the window.

Tuck was trapped beneath the table and kicking the sow-bear in the snout. She roared, pulled back, came at him again. I heard cloth rip as she raked his leg. He yelled, "Shoot, dammit! Shoot!"

Eyes stinging from bear-stink and rotgut fumes, I leapt to my feet, aimed again just as Vince pushed up beneath me and ripped the gun from my hand. He spun and fired.

The shot knocked her back a couple feet. As she staggered, Mace grabbed Vince round the legs and pulled him down again. They banged the table hard, and the lantern on it rocked and nearly tipped over. I snatched it away just as the she-bear flung the table across the room.

Tuck rolled to the side, out of her path, which left nothing between her and me but air. She went up on her hind legs again. Not five feet away, Mace and Vince were on the floor, battling for possession of the gun. She ignored them. Breath rattling up her throat in deep grunts, she looked me straight in the eye. I froze.

Then she roared. That little cabin fair shook with it. She stood there a couple seconds, like maybe she was thinking she'd got herself into too big a mess here, or like maybe she was so crazy with hurt she didn't know which of us to savage first.

I still couldn't move. Tyrone could, though. He bumped into me on his way out the door. He was lugging one of the gold saddlebags with both hands.

I grabbed at him just as the bear bellowed another cloud of foul breath and charged. This time she leapt past Mace and Vince and came straight for me and the door. I let go of Tyrone in a hurry.

Tuck yelled something. Vince came up off the floor and tried to get past. I jumped, lantern swinging. I felt the bear bowl into me. As I fell, I heard a shot, then another. I don't remember hitting the floor, just a terrible pain in my head. That, and the color orange.

The smell came first: smoke and scorch, burnt wood and heat-popped rock; underneath, the sickly stench of charred flesh.

Next was the sound of voices, of boots swishing grass, of shovels cutting and moving brittle things, of water hissing and turning to steam.

Then came the pain. My head pounded. I made to lift a hand to it and cried out, for my fingers felt three times their normal size and filled with sharp things.

I opened my eyes. It was light, and I was lying in the mud. It took a second or two for my vision to wobble into focus, that long again for me to realize that a smoldering heap was all that remained of Gospel Joe Varney's cabin. At the end where Joe had stored his O Be Joyful, debris had been blown back into the woods as far as I could see. Part of a chair tottered on a limb.

The meadow seemed unharmed except for a charred patch here and there, but the trees closest to the cabin were scorched where they overhung it. Men, bandannas tied over their noses and mouths, sorted through the rubble with sticks and shovels. A couple carried buckets, and went round dumping water on the places that still smoked. Another waved his arm.

"Got a body here, Sheriff, least what's left of one." I

recognized his voice. It was Clell Swinbourne, who owned the livery in Hanged Dog.

"Can you tell who it is, Clell?"

I jumped. Sheriff Cyrus P. Russell was standing right over me, and Frank Malone, Civic Leader, was at his side. There was a mean grin on Frank's face.

Before Clell could answer, another man, who I recognized as Deputy Riggs when he pulled down his face cloth, said, "Here's another." He kicked away more debris, said, "Aw, Jesus," then turned his back. I heard the sound of retching.

Somebody laughed. It was that Lawson kid, Ambrose. He was over by the lean-to, which had not been touched by fire. Beside him was Gospel Joe Varney. Joe was not laughing.

Clell bent over the second body, then looked away quick. "No way to tell. They're awful bad."

Sheriff Russell knelt down and handcuffed me. "Gini Kincaid, I hereby arrest you for three counts of arson—"

"Four, now," said Frank Malone.

"Four. Give me those papers."

Smirking, Frank handed him a thick sheaf. Sheriff Russell shuffled through and continued, "Also assault upon the persons of Frank Malone, Joe Malone. Assault upon the person of Weevil Jukes. Attempted murder of one Tyrone O'Neill. Horse theft. Destruction of private property. Aiding and abetting jailbreak, also assault upon a sworn officer of the law. And it looks like we got two murders right here, well past the 'attempted' phase." He folded up the papers and stuck them in his back pocket. "You been busy since you left us, Gini."

"I didn't— I mean, there was a bear and Vince and Tyrone came, and—"

He hauled me to my feet, and when I swayed he caught me and felt the back of my head. "Got a goose egg there. We'll get Doc Ben for you once we get back to the jail."

I tried to talk, to tell him I didn't kill anybody, but then I realized that it was likely Tuck and Mace who were burned up in that shack, and all I could do was cry.

Ambrose hollered, "When do I get my five thousand dollars for that Danahoe fella? That poster says dead or alive."

"When you prove it was Mason Danahoe."

Gospel Joe had ambled toward what was left of his home. He bent down next to Clell. Gingerly, he poked at one of the bodies with a stick. Clell stood up and turned away, but Joe peered closer, studying. "Lord, Lord," he muttered finally. "I'd have to say it's them, Sheriff. The Danahoe boy and Tuck Brennan. I didn't know they was wanted when I took 'em in. I'll swear to that part on the Holy Bible, if you like."

The sheriff nodded. "I'll take your word, Joe. And I guess that means you'll get your money, Ambrose. I got to wire Oro Tiempo to tell 'em. Harley, bring me up a couple horses. Clell, will those bodies hang together good enough to cart 'em back to town?"

Clell, whose face had gone greenish, didn't look at them again. "Doubt we can even lift 'em out in one piece. Big one's still mostly buried, just got some rib cage clear is all. Got to move a beam and some rock. If it was my say-so, I'd just leave 'em where they lie and pile some dirt and stones over."

The sheriff pondered that for a minute, then said, "So long as we've got an identification, I guess it don't matter. Up to you, Joe. Your place."

Gospel Joe stood up, blew his nose, and said, "Don't violate 'em no more. I'd druther we just built a mound up and left 'em in peace. I'd like to see it done now, if you don't mind, and get some sanctifyin' words said. There's a crazy bear loose in these parts, likely on the trail of my burro, Wilma. I need to get her rounded up."

Clell Swinbourne (as well as Deputy Riggs, who was just coming out of the trees and wiping at his mouth) looked plenty relieved.

Somebody led up three horses. Frank Malone took one. As the sheriff boosted me up on another, he said, "You may have set some bad fires in your day, Gini Kincaid, but this is one you won't escape."

Nights, I dreamt about Tuck and Mace up at Joe Varney's cabin. Tyrone and Vince would come into the dream, and then the bear. I'd wake up frantic and sobbing, exhaust myself back to sleep with tears, then bolt awake again. Days, I continued to mourn, and in between jags of crying I was besieged by visitors.

It seemed like everybody who had ever been mad at me in my whole life was out there, and they were still mad. The Malones gathered in town, like vultures waiting for the carcass to quit walking. Fat Nell came down on the Prescott stage to identify me for inciting a riot at the Quartz Strike Saloon. Weevil Jukes showed up and pointed a bony finger at me through the bars. Even Mr. Evert Fairbanks, the Virginia lawyer, traveled all the way from back east to get his piece of me. Angry citizens popped out of the woodwork so fast and furious that I gave up keeping track of them. What with all the threats against me, Sheriff Cyrus P. Russell hired on three extra deputies to keep a round-the-clock guard for my protection.

I asked, just once, to be taken to church, but they would have none of it. I was not surprised, and I guess it was all right. Without standing on my cot, about the only thing I could see of the town was the old Mission's weathered bell tower. Its bell's deep tone of a Sunday morning and the way it stood, tall and solid against the hot white sky during day and the stars at night, reminded me of Tuck. Just its being there outside my window, to look at any time, was likely more comfort to me than being inside and getting stared at.

I had expected to be hauled up to Prescott for trial, but I guess the Malones had more "high-places" friends than I thought, for the capital city came to us.

The famous prosecutor and stalwart Democrat, Mr. Ignatius Starch, traveled down from Prescott with the intention of convicting me to further his own career. I guess he had not bargained on everybody in Arizona Territory laying blame for their troubles at the feet of Gini Kincaid, though. So many folks, each hoping to hang a stray complaint of killing or barn-burning or petty thievery on me, wandered or barreled into town that it was clear into July before he began to get the charges straightened out.

One thing they decided not to try me for was the attempted murder of Tyrone, as he refused to come to Hanged Dog. Now, I had been sort of holding out secret hope that maybe, just maybe, it had been Tyrone and Vince in that fire instead of Mace and Tuck. Sometimes I'd stare out my cell window and imagine that Tuck and Mace were on their way to bust me free. Sometimes I could almost swear I'd caught a glimpse of one or the other. That's how hard I was wishing. But when the wire came from San Francisco saying Mr. Tyrone O'Neill declined to press charges, well, something inside me went all the way flat.

After that, I didn't much care what happened.

Besides Tyrone, about the only one who did not show up to take a legal punch at me was the Reverend Middleton, whose Soapy horse I had thieved back in Half Moon Crossing the night I shot Tyrone. Of course, the pastor's complaint was on the list to begin with: I guess he must have filed it right after I took off on his horse. I would have, if I'd been in his shoes. But he wrote a letter to Sheriff Russell, saying that his horse had been returned to him promptly and unharmed and better for the exercise. He declined to press charges, and said he had come to think of the incident as "an unexpected loan to an unmet friend." Now, there is a Christian Gentleman for you!

They set a trial date for the middle of August, which meant I had to bide the worst kind of weather in an airless jail cell. I had visitors, though, while I waited. Pearl Scrimm came regular, as did Doc Ben Winslow. I guess he had taken up with Pearl sometime after I left town, but he still missed Gam. He and I got to crying over it one day, and I hugged him tight and told him I hadn't truly understood his grief before, and that I was sorry. He was still drinking bad; but, for a drunkard, he fixed my hand up pretty good, though he said the breaks were bad and I would likely always have trouble with my two middle fingers being stiff. I figured that in my case, *always* meant about two more months.

The newspaper scribblers arrived, and a day didn't pass but what at least one reporter came to hunker down outside my cell and ask me silly questions, some of which were mean and got me to crying. Even Mr. Bartholomew Strump, who had writ my Tombstone book, came to call. I gave him a piece of my mind about that "Doc Holliday's girlfriend" business, but he was real nice about it. He turned out to be a young, clean-shaved fella with an eager face. He came near every day for two weeks before he had to leave town, and he brought flowers for my cell each time, just like I was a real fancy lady. I kind of missed him when he went.

The week the trial was to start, Deputy Riggs rattled his keys in the big door that connected the cells to the front office. He called out, "More company for you, Gini. Don't look like reporters this time."

After he led them down to my cell, I reached straight through the door and hugged Elma Justice Fowler so hard I nearly squished her against the bars. She was weeping and Will looked awful solemn. Deputy Riggs brought them a couple straight-back chairs so they could sit in some comfort outside my cell, and then he let us be.

Elma daubed at her eyes with the corner of her hankie. It was periwinkle blue, like her dress and shoes. "Oh, Miss Kincaid," she sniffed, "I cannot bear to see you in such surroundings."

"I suppose they could be worse, Mrs. Fowler," I said, "but just seeing you again with your clothes all matched up makes me feel a good bit cheerier. I am also glad to see you, Will. Maybe you could represent me in this trial."

His eyebrows bunched together. "Do you mean to tell me you haven't availed yourself of counsel?"

"If you're askin' do I have a lawyer, the answer is yes. His name is Mr. C. E. O'Day. He is down from Prescott to defend me, though I think he's doin' it more for the publicity it will bring him than for the forty-three dollars and fifty cents I offered as a fee." When Will made a face at that, I added, "Oh, he gave it back. He said I am 'pro bono,' whatever that means."

Will nodded. "C. E. O'Day is purported to be a square man, Gini. You must stick with him. I am not licensed to practice the law."

"You will be someday. I think you should work with Mr. C. E. O'Day, Will. I'd feel better, for you know me and he doesn't. He's only been to see me twice, and that was just for me to sign things. He hasn't even bothered to ask if I did it on purpose. Plus which, he rode down from Prescott on the same stage with the prosecutor, Mr. Ignatius Starch, and I have heard they are chummy on the street. If I thought I had you on my side, I'd sleep better. I cannot pay you much, of course, but . . ."

Will's hands were folded in his lap, and he tapped his

forefingers together. After a minute, he said, "Ignatius Starch for the People and C. E. O'Day at the defense . . . My goodness, my goodness. Gini, this is bad trouble."

"Of course it's bad trouble, Will! Don't I know it more than most?"

"It's worse than you think. I do not mean that C. E. O'Day is not a skilled attorney. He is a clever lawyer indeed and will plead your case with genuine fervor. But Ignatius Starch is just as cunning, and they are friendly rivals of long standing. They both have political expectations, and like you I suspect they mean to use this case more to their own respective advantages than yours. I believe," he said, rubbing his hands together slowly, "that perhaps I *should* have a word or two with Mr. O'Day."

Elma reached over and took his arm, saying, "Thank you, Mr. Fowler," before she sniffled into her blue hankie again.

He asked me to tell him the whole story with nothing left out, which I did. I think Elma was shocked by parts of it, but she was not too offended to stay till the finish, and for the most part she sat right on the edge of her chair.

"I am surprised that Gospel Joe Varney has not been to see me," I said at the end, "even if only to toss some biblical curses my way. I hope that bear didn't do him harm."

Will and Elma stood up. Will said, "I will look into it. I will also go and see your Mr. O'Day."

It turned out that Gospel Joe would not be coming into town ever again. About a week and a half after my arrest, he was felling trees for a new cabin when he was struck down by a falling timber. By the time a neighbor found him, he had been trapped for a whole day, and died shortly thereafter. Nobody had bothered to tell me. That night, when I said my prayers (having got real conscientious about speaking with Jesus on a regular basis), I added his name in after Tuck's and Mace's.

Will Fowler was "hired' as assistant to C. E. O'Day, though I don't believe he was paid a cent for his trouble and hard work. He said he didn't mind, though, as it was the least he could do for the girl who had brought the woman he loved to Tombstone. Also, he said it was experience for his future career. Truth be told, I think he did it mostly because he was a plain good man.

But even with Will Fowler and C. E. O'Day on my side, it was a bad trial.

They held it in the main barroom at the Thirsty Buzzard, which had been newly painted for the occasion. Even though it was the worst sort of hot and stuffy weather, the spectators packed in tight. Commemorative fans, my face pictured on them, fluttered in every hand. The Malones were present daily: sitting in a row right up front, righteous smirks on their faces.

There was always a mob outside, too. Pearl Scrimm might have been my friend, but she was not stupid: she had benches built out on the sidewalk and charged two bits an hour to sit and look through the windows.

Attorneys Starch and O'Day took turns talking circles round each other and the court. Since they were both popular orators and the trial had drawn a record crowd, Judge Patterson didn't do much in the way of reprimanding them. He sometimes had to hammer down the throng, though. They were a rowdy bunch.

Mr. Starch brought in witness after witness to attest to my being a low person indeed. Even the Aztec Kid showed up, using his real name, which turned out to be Giuseppe Cicero. When he limped down the aisle and took the stand, he was dressed in a store-bought suit: likely supplied by the Malones. His hair was slicked and trimmed and he walked with a fancy cane. He told a long sad story about how I had, for no reason, shot him in the foot and crippled him for life, and later sicced vicious Indians on him and his half-brother, Antonio "Black Ear" Cicero, resulting in the death of the latter. I had not known till then that they were brothers.

Weevil Jukes, who still looked like vermin even though he was dressed up and washed, attested to my having assaulted him and then destroyed his inventory, also for no reason other than my "natural meanness."

Deputy Sam McKay came up from Oro Tiempo to tell how I'd murderously banged him over the head and set free a convicted killer. He also backed up the Aztec Kid's story about how I had set my "pet Apache warriors" on them and got nine men killed or wounded.

Some fella I had never seen nor heard of testified as to how I had shot his pet dog and laid a torch to his place of business down in Gypsum Wells. When I pointed out that I had never in my life been to Gypsum Wells and would never shoot a dog in any case, Judge Patterson threatened me with contempt.

To tell the truth, I would not have been surprised if one or two of those *bandidos* from down at Cañon de los Espejos had shown up to claim I'd bushwacked them at a prayer meeting and called their mothers bad names.

The Malones each took the stand. None of them had a kind word for me. They said I had been "bad business" since the day I was born. Frank told a long tale about how I had hired outlaws to beat him half to death and then desert him in the wilderness. He was pretty theatrical, but he didn't have a patch on his brother, Joe. To hear Joe Malone tell it, I had burnt up his Tombstone store with malicious intent, and would have torched all of Allen Street with a smile on my face if he hadn't bravely stopped me at risk of his own life.

Well, I got up and casually mentioned that in the time since I'd left Tombstone, some bartender with a lit cigar in his mouth had got too close to a cask of John Barleycorn and managed to burn down practically the whole dang town, and that I didn't see the Malones hounding *him*. I also mentioned, while I was at it, that it was pretty dang stupid to build a whole town out of wood when the nearest aboveground water was practically a dozen miles away at the San Pedro River, and that I hoped that this time they were building it back up out of adobe.

Judge Patterson remarked that if I said one more word, he would have me gagged.

Anyhow, in near every case, Mr. C. E. O'Day tore each witness's story into little pieces, then Mr. Ignatius Starch put it back together again, neater than before. By the time the prosecution rested, I did not know myself whether I was guilty or innocent.

The press had its mind made up, though. Even when it got to be the defense's turn and Mr. O'Day brought in all kinds of upstanding folks—including Miss Nellie Cashman, who came all the way from Tombstone at her own expense—to testify to my sterling character and kind nature, the newspapers continued to paint me as a murdering hussy.

But I had friends, even ones I did not know. For two days running, some ladies marched up and down across the street from the Thirsty Buzzard. They carried signs that said, *Downtrodden Females Unite!* and *Gini an Innocent Puppet of Men!* and chanted "Free Gini now! Free Gini now!" Actually, it was sort of embarrassing. I was glad when Judge Patterson made them stop.

Much to my surprise, Doc Holliday rolled into town one Thursday afternoon with the intent to volunteer as a character witness. He visited me that night in the jail; and after the sheriff relieved him of two handguns, three derringers, a sleeve knife, a vest blade, and a boot pistol, we had a few hands of cards through the bars. I lost a couple on purpose, as I did not want to make him feel bad.

Between coughs, he said, "Looks like I won't be doin' you any good, Irish. That C. E. O'Day won't let me take the stand. Says a reference from me can only be bad. I was tempted to plug him." He rocked back in his chair and picked through his hand. "Two cards."

I dealt them out to him. "I stand pat. I'm sorry you've had the trip for nothing, Doc. It's fine to see you again, though. I never got a chance to thank you for this deck."

He bet fifteen matches and took a swallow from his flask. "This wouldn't happen in an Earp town."

I shoved more matches into the pile. "Call. What are you holdin'?"

He laid out a full house, kings over sevens. I had figured as much.

"Your pot," I said. "And I think you're wrong. Tombstone has got more politics than any other five places put together, Hanged Dog included."

"True," he allowed, "but in Cochise County we'd have shot all these goddamn witnesses before they had a chance to defame you."

The Earps did not come. I didn't really expect them to. Things were bad in Tombstone, but Virgil (who was still in office) sent a notarized statement attesting to my being more-or-less upright. In it, he also said that in his professional opinion, the mercantile fire in Tombstone was an accident, pure and simple, and that he did not consider me to be the arsonist type.

Prosecutor Starch made mincemeat of that, too.

The trial dragged on for near four weeks, and it was mid-September before Mr. Starch and Mr. O'Day finished their last addresses to the jury. You have never heard such grand and glorious speechifying as those summations.

Ignatius Starch hooked his thumbs in his wide vest and talked for a whole day, and threw in a lot of Bible verses and looks of despair laced with disgust. You could sure tell he wanted to be Territorial Governor.

He called me a "deviant personality" and a "detriment to society." He said I was old beyond my years and could not be thought of as a child. He demanded the death penalty and vowed that any civilized Christian person would not settle for less. He also pointed out (for about an hour and a half) as how, if the Territory wanted to show that it had got to be a fit place for decent people to raise up their families, the jury had better show good faith by making me into an example of how honest Arizona citizens dealt with scofflaws. By the time he got done, I would have voted to hang myself.

Mr. O'Day used up a day, too. He peeled down to shirtsleeves and suspenders, and talked softer and more fatherly. He called me a "poor unfortunate child" (with the *poor* lasting about three syllables) and a "victim of tragic circumstance." He made no claim to my innocence of the charges. Instead, he argued that if the citizenry really wanted to show the world what a civilized place Arizona Territory had become, they needed to demonstrate wisdom and mercy. He followed that up with a real moving plea for leniency on account of my tender years. Even though he had near half the onlookers in tears by the end, I did not think it was a very good defense. I don't think Will Fowler did, either, but by then Mr. O'Day had already said it.

The jury was only out a half hour. When they marched back in and the foreman took his feet and read down the list, adding "Guilty" after each charge, a thunderous cheer rose up in the courtroom.

Judge Patterson banged his gavel so hard the head flew

off and hit the bailiff in the elbow. Once the tumult subsided, he told me to stand up and face the bench, which was actually Pearl's old beat-up bartop.

He said, "Geneva Kincaid, some say it is breeding that makes a person, some say surroundings. It is my opinion that you have had the bad end of both of these. It is also my opinion that many others have had worse, but have come through it honest and upright. By the calendar you are a child. But by the list of your crimes, for which this jury has found you guilty on all counts, I can believe you nothing less than a hardened criminal with a seasoned and wicked heart, and no hope of redemption by man or God. Sorrowed though it makes me, that is how I must judge you. I hereby sentence you to hang by the neck until you are dead. Date of execution to be determined one week from today."

I heard Elma weeping, but I couldn't cry. I had made myself not cry all during the trial, at least in public; and now that I really wanted to weep, I couldn't. The newspapers made a big thing of it later, calling me icy and unmoved. The nicest ones said I was stoic.

Will and Elma came to see me the next day, and brought the news that there would likely be a stay of execution. For a minute I got kind of hopeful, but then Will explained it was because they were sending to Kansas City for the celebrated scientific hangman, Mr. Hammurabi O'Keefe, and intended to comply with his schedule.

Elma was teary, as usual. I do not think her eyes had been dry for longer than fifteen minutes at a stretch since the day she arrived in Hanged Dog. She blew her nose on an apricot-colored hankie and then handed me a little package bound with string. Inside were two books, both by Bartholomew Strump.

He had not been idle. One was titled *Terror in the*

Wasteland: Gini Kincaid and the Canyon of Mirrors. The other was *Flame of the West: Gini Kincaid Strikes Out for Justice*.

I could scarcely believe it. Counting the first, that made three whole books, all about me. Plus, on the inside cover of *Flame of the West*, it said:

Coming Soon!

The Life and Times of Gini Kincaid:

The Last Days of an Outlaw Princess

The Terrible Trial of a Western Heroine!
The Flame-Haired Angel of Arizona
at the
Mercy of Railroading Pettifoggers!
Excitement! Thrills! Adventure!
The Ending of an Era!
Only Ten Cents at Fine Retailers Everywhere

I shook my head and said, "Boy howdy! How could he write this last one? He wasn't even at the dang trial. But I guess I know now why Hanged Dog has turned into such a popular place. Why, this is almost as many books as were writ about Tuck Brennan!" Thinking about Tuck sent me off into wailing, and right then and there I commenced to make up for all the tears I had not shed in court.

Will got pretty flustered. He said, "Gini? Gini, are you all right? Elma, do something!"

Elma didn't answer him. She was crying, too.

Execution was set for nine o'clock on the morning of November fifth, which was the soonest the hangman could fit me into his schedule. It seemed like a long way off, which did not please me. I had grown weary of the mortal coil. I wanted to go be with Gam and Zack and Tuck and Mace. I wondered, sometimes, if Mace would still be so nasty to me up in Heaven.

There were more threats made against me, and rumors of lynching. Schoolkids (and some grown-ups) took to throwing rocks and vegetables and eggs at my cell window, so even more guards had to be added onto the town payroll. Doc Holliday left Hanged Dog, as did Will Fowler. I don't know where Doc took off to, but Will had his business to tend down in Tombstone. Elma stayed on, though. She came to visit with me every single day, though she managed to rig it so she never showed up at the same time as Pearl Scrimm. She did not approve of Pearl.

I read the two books Elma had brought me, and when *The Last Days of an Outlaw Princess* came out, I read that, too. Mr. Bartholomew Strump had made me famous for sure and certain; but for all my setting him straight, he had not got any of the facts even halfway right. He was at one end, trying to pass me off as a gun-toting, justice-seeking female saint, and the newspapers were at the other. They said I was a murdering prostitute, and that I had social diseases and no conscience or respect for Jesus. Finally, one of them said that it was rumored I had murdered Gam to get her house. That did it. The very next day I asked Elma Justice Fowler to bring me paper and ink, and I started setting down this story, stiff fingers or no.

I was about halfway through it and ten days from the hanging when I had a new visitor.

I heard him before I saw him. I stood on my cot and looked out the window, and I admit that when he came into sight I wept out of pure gladness. That old rig of his was still so festooned with bells that it fair sagged, and Grace and

Comanche had not changed one jot. By the time he pulled up beside the jail, half the town was following along holding their ears.

"Jingles!" I called, and waved to him.

"Great day in the mornin', girl! This here contraption for you?"

He meant the scaffold, which they were building in the lot next to the jail, and upon which two carpenters hammered from sunrise to sunset. He tied his team to it.

Deputy Riggs walked out then and the two of them and a couple guards had a go-round about disturbing the peace, during which Jingles warned three men and a kid with a dog to stay back from Comanche or face the consequences.

When they finally got it straightened out, he came in and sat a spell with me.

"Would have been here sooner, Gini-for-Short, except my Comanche pulled up lame about twenty miles north of Tucson and I had to lay over. That, and Gracie has been bad about sitting down. Say, I passed by that old graveyard you told me about. You were right: it has caved into the shaft something fierce. I wouldn't be surprised if the whole of it was warrened with badgers. What's all that paper?"

By then, I had three notebooks stacked up on my little table. They were not thick notebooks, but I guess it looked like a lot to Jingles. I said, "I am writin' my true life story. I don't think badgers cluster up like prairie dogs, Jingles."

He nodded, thoughtful-like, and said, "Am I in it?"

I figured he meant the story, and not some badger hole. I said, "You sure are. Comanche and Grace, too. And the bats and the bottle house."

"Make sure you get my name spelt right. That's Beldon with a *d*, not a *t*. My bats have finally gone away. Flicked 'em with nitro. They got weary and moved south, though they may only mean to stay gone for the winter. A person can't have too little confidence in bats."

We talked for a bit about his claim and Tombstone politics and his horses. He didn't ask me about Tuck or Mace or the trial. I guess he had read the papers.

Finally, I said, "Jingles, I am goin' to tell you where there is a lot of gold. You are the only one I am tellin'."

He took off his hat and rubbed the heel of his hand over his scalped place. "Why, I already know where there's a lot of gold. It's down to my claim, if I can ever blast my way back to the queen vein."

"No, I mean solid, refined gold. Bars. Well, they're likely melted some now. But there's a good bit of it." I told him about Mescal Mort and Spirit Kettle and Black Ear Cicero, and about that last night at Gospel Joe's cabin. "Tyrone took off with one of the saddlebags," I said at the end, "but there should still be two left, under the rubble and the burial mound. If you do not mind a little grave-shiftin', it's yours. Though I would appreciate it if you pushed some of it Elma and Will Fowler's way. I imagine they could use some for Will's schoolin'. Maybe you'd better not tell Elma where you got it. I doubt she'd approve."

He thought on that for several minutes, during which he paced up and down in front of my cell and whistled little snatches of "Daddy Popped His Buttons When He Heard He Had a Son."

At last, he sat down and leaned forward to push his face against the bars. "I am not keen on grave-robbing, Gini. I think that is a fact plain to anyone who has had my acquaintance more than four or five days. But I don't think Tuck Brennan would mind me rootin' around up there, under the circumstances. Are you—"

He broke off, for just then part of a tomato sailed through the bars of my window and went splat on the floor. Some fool was laughing it up outside, and then I heard footsteps and one of the guards shouting. Me and Jingles just sat there and stared at that squished tomato for about two minutes before Jingles looked up and said, "You sure you don't want me to break you out of jail? I have got a stealthy side you do not suspect."

I figured Jingles had about as much chance of being stealthy as I did of walking through walls, so I ignored the question. I drew him a map of how to get to what was left of Gospel Joe's place, and showed him the location of the gold. He thanked me, stuffed the map in his pocket, and took his feet.

I got up, too. "Will you be comin' back to see me again, Jingles?"

"Count on it," he said. "I believe I will go flush out your friend Miss Elma and pay my respects, but I'll stop by in the morning before I head up into the mountains." He shook my hand through the bars, patted his pocket, and hollered for a guard.

I said, "If they have not got any markers up there for Tuck and Mace, maybe you could see to it?"

"My privilege," he said as Deputy Riggs unlocked the door and let him out.

Over the next week, Hanged Dog's population swelled to four times the normal count, with more folks expected all the time. Merchants raked in landslide business. Most ranchers in the vicinity were packing in boarders at two and three dollars a head, on account of the hotel and the saloon and all the private houses in town being crammed full of gawkers. Along the streets and in empty lots, stands were built to sell sweets and tamales and roasted peanuts and such, and the streets were full of trash. The city fathers bought a load of fireworks, to be set off the night after my execution. I was sorry I would miss them, as I had never seen real skyrockets.

At least I didn't have to listen to any more hammering. They had finished the scaffold, as well as three tiers of board seats: four rows high and already reserved at five dollars a place. The whole business had been whitewashed and the gallows fitted with a new rope, courtesy of the Malone Bros. Mercantile.

About every other day Sheriff Russell squired me outside so some new fella or other could take my picture. A couple times they sat me on a horse, and once they made me put on a silly outfit with a fringed skirt and a vest and gave me a pair of unloaded eagle-butt Colts to hold, and then the photographer told me, "Look menacing, honey." But most times I was just made to stand on the sidewalk in front of the jail. If it was strong sunlight, they'd put my head in one of those braces to make sure I wouldn't move while they did a timed exposure. If it was clouded over, *pop!* would go the flash and there'd be black powder everywhere. You see little lights in front of your eyes for several minutes after a thing like that. I didn't mind so much. They reminded me of Tuck's stars, some of the ones I couldn't see from my cell.

The Malones were doing a fast trade in "Genuine Gini Kincaid Souvenirs": copies of those books Bartholomew Strump had writ about me, photographs, and even little bits of wall from what was left of Gam's old adobe. I heard they got a nickel extra for the really charred pieces.

The celebrated executioner, Mr. Hammurabi O'Keefe, arrived. He was short and portly and round-faced, and he wore a black frock coat and a stovepipe hat, like you see President Abraham Lincoln wearing in pictures. He was a scientific man, and was famous for his Apparatus of Death. There was no simple throwing a rope over a beam or limb for him: he had pulleys and cogs and contraptions, all designed for a "humane demise." I didn't see how any killing, legal or no, could be considered humane, but I kept my sentiments to myself.

I watched him rig his machine together along the high crossbeam. He turned up his nose at the rope the Malones had donated, having brought his own. It was extra long and of a special circumference, custom-made for the Apparatus. He announced to the gawkers that it was the same rope that had hanged Big Cletus Tobin and also Nacogdoches Bob. I had never heard of either of them, but a couple men in the crowd nodded like they were impressed. I felt a little cheated. To my mind, if a man is going to hang you, he can at least do it with new equipment.

Anyhow, he looped that rope every which way through slots and around big metal wheels, all the while making tiny adjustments to this cog or that. When he had it all assembled, it looked kind of like the inside of a watch, only big and with the last necktie of Nacogdoches Bob threaded roundabout through it.

The process drew a crowd. I guess it was pretty impressive, though I think I can be excused for not being too excited about it. I don't think Sheriff Russell was real overwhelmed, either. I saw him out there, hands on his hips, just shaking his head and muttering something about "tits on a boar-hog." I guess he did not have much time for science.

Anyhow, before he did his final adjustments, Hammurabi O'Keefe had some deputies escort me down to the feed store and weigh me on the scales. He was real fussy about his counterweights, on account of his Apparatus being a "delicate instrument." Another of those danged photographers followed us down and took my picture as I stood on the scale in handcuffs and leg irons. When I got off, I kicked his camera over and broke it. I was not sorry one bit.

I *was* sorrowful, though, when I heard the news about

recent goings-on down in Tombstone. Wyatt and some of his brothers and Doc Holliday had finally got fed up with the Cochise County gangs, and had faced off with the Clantons and McLaurys in the vacant lot by Fly's lodging house and the OK Corral. The papers were making a big case of it, and Earp stories were already pushing me off the front pages. I can't say I minded that, but I felt bad that Wyatt and the others would have to put up with lying reporters.

Late the night before my scheduled execution, I was still writing on this book, scribbling faster and faster because I was only up to the part where the bear stepped on my hand, when I heard "Psst! Psst!" outside my window.

I climbed up on the cot and peered out. They had hung bunting and lanterns and flags all over the gallows and polished up all Hammurabi O'Keefe's wheels and cogs and rope-guides to a high shine. I guess it looked kind of festive.

"Psst! Down here!"

"Jingles! Where you been so long? I was gettin' worried! Where's your team?"

He had a truly odd look on his face. He said, "They abide, Gini-for-Short. They abide."

"Did you get the gold?"

"Yes and no. Did some digging. Oh, I did some digging, all right. Found that old satchel of yours up a tree. Found a king snake, too. Biggest king snake I ever saw, and I have seen some big ones. They're good snakes, and I let it go. Pretty country up there. No bats. Found the last of a dead bear, too." He jabbed a thumb over his shoulder toward the old Mission. "How far away's that bell tower, you reckon?"

"I don't know. Maybe a hundred yards. But what about the gold? Did you find—"

"What's goin' on out here?" It was Deputy Riggs. He had a lantern in one hand and a sawed-off shotgun in the other.

Jingles doffed his hat. "Don't splatter me with that hog-leg, mister. I'm just payin' my respects."

Deputy Riggs scowled. "Pay 'em in the morning. Early." He shouted, "Harley! Harley Thorndike! Where in tarnation are you? You're supposed to be on guard under this window!"

Harley trotted up. His rifle was clamped under his arm and he was busy doing up his belt, so I guess he must have been at the outhouse. While he and Deputy Riggs had words, I whispered, "Come morning, Jingles, I'd appreciate it if you'd see to Elma Justice Fowler. I know she'll want to be with me, but I don't think a hangin' is the sort of thing a lady of her refinement ought to witness. Maybe you could lead her away before they pull the lever?"

Harley had himself put back together. He came over and laid a hand on Jingles's shoulder. "Move on, old-timer."

Jingles stepped away, but he called out, "Don't fear, Gini-for-Short. I won't let her see you hang."

Well, that is my honest and true story. It's well past dawn now, and I guess I've got about an hour left. Sheriff Russell brought me a big fancy breakfast, but I can't make myself put fork to plate.

I can already hear a goodly crowd outside. I hope they will not throw things at me as I walk to the scaffold. I hope I will not cry.

I guess I am scared. Of course, I'll be going to Gam and Tuck and the others, and that part makes me happy. It's just the getting there that has me worried. Tuck told me once about how folks in China and India believe you don't live just one life, but keep getting born and living and dying over and over again. I don't know about that. I think one life has been plenty for me.

I have asked to be buried next to Gam, and Pearl Scrimm

and Doc Ben promised they would see to my headstone. I hope that if you read this you'll think kindly of me, and see that I have not been a bad person, at least not on purpose. Maybe, if you ever visit Hanged Dog, you will come to the cemetery and say hello to me and Gam.

Maybe you could bring a flower for her.

18

Big Show at Hanged Dog

Well, I suppose the minute you finished the last chapter and saw there were more pages to go, you figured out I didn't get hanged, and you are right. This is how it happened.

They came for me at a quarter to nine. I was waiting with my notebooks tucked under my arm, hoping to pass them to Pearl or Doc Ben on the street. I had wrapped all the notebooks up together, marked in the right order and tied with string, with a note on top asking that they be sent to Mrs. Will Fowler of Tombstone. I figured if anybody would know how to get my story published it would be her.

Deputy Riggs, Hammurabi O'Keefe, and three guards stood outside the cell while Sheriff Russell cuffed my hands behind my back. Everybody was real solemn, none more than me.

Sheriff Russell took my parcel and then he took my arm and led me out the cell door. Two guards in front, Deputy Riggs and Hammurabi O'Keefe behind, and the sheriff at my elbow, we walked down the corridor, through the office, and out into the street.

The sun was real bright; I remember it hurt my eyes. The street smelled like a carnival, I guess because of the roasting peanuts and spun sugar and such.

The crowd was raucous, and mixed, too: white, colored,

Mex, and Chinese; men, women, kids, dogs. I guess an execution's the sort of thing to naturally bring folks together.

Somebody was playing a hurdy-gurdy. Kids darted through the throng, trailing red, white, and blue streamers, blowing candy whistles, and setting off strings of firecrackers. The marching ladies were back, and though I couldn't see them, I could see the bobbing tops of their placards and hear them chanting "Free Gini now! Free Gini now!" People were shouting and laughing and eating cotton candy and Indian fry bread, and when I was sighted they got even noisier. Temporary deputies were lined up double, so as to make a passage for us from the jail to the gallows. Folks pushed at them from behind, trying to reach out a hand to touch me.

I saw Pearl Scrimm in the crowd. She had a soggy handkerchief in one hand and a half-eaten tamale in the other. Doc Ben, already staggered with drink, was with her. Sheriff Russell stopped our procession till Pearl could get over to us, and he gave her my parcel of notebooks. I was real grateful to him for that.

We started up the steps. There were thirteen; I counted. Then we were up on the gallows. The boards gave a little under my feet. Sun glared hot off the Apparatus of Death. Another string of firecrackers went off right under us, and I jumped.

Hammurabi O'Keefe and Sheriff Russell had a short argument. Hammurabi O'Keefe said they had to put those heavy old leg irons on me, as I had been weighed with them and it would throw off his scientific calculations for the counterweights. Sheriff Russell replied that he had just about had it with science. He said all he knew was that it was sin enough to hang a child without adding leg shackles to the situation, and that we would just have to make do.

Hammurabi O'Keefe went kind of red and clenched his teeth and said he would not be held responsible.

I searched through the crowd for Jingles or Elma Justice Fowler, but I couldn't see them. I guessed they were gone, after all. I had not wanted them, Elma especially, to see me die, but I wished I could have looked on them one last time.

The crowd went still as Hammurabi O'Keefe took my shoulders and walked me forward to stand on the trapdoor, directly under all his fancy polished machinery. Some preacher I had never seen came up the steps and read a couple Bible verses over me. I can't say that I listened.

Hammurabi O'Keefe put the rope round my neck and snugged it up under my jaw, just so. I remember being surprised that he put the knot at the back of my neck instead of behind my ear.

Hammurabi O'Keefe took a step back. Sheriff Russell asked if I had any last words. I shook my head no. Somebody asked if I would like a hood to cover my face. I said no but I guess they did not hear me, as they put it on anyway. I hoped Hammurabi O'Keefe was not as stingy with his hoods as with his ropes, or that he had at least washed it since Nacogdoches Bob's last day.

I heard a fast slide of wood on wood, heard the *pops* of another string of firecrackers and the crowd's gasp as I fell. There was a terrible jerk that snapped my jaws shut and shot my brain full of red, then black.

The firecrackers kept popping, but slow, as if time had stretched like india rubber.

I dropped again. I wondered if maybe I had been wrong all along about the Lord being so forgiving. I wondered if that last drop would land me down in Hell.

I heard bells: thousands of bells, maybe millions, getting closer all the time.

I lit, and what I lit on wasn't hot enough to be Hades or

soft enough to be Heaven, though it seemed too shivery and shaky to be Earth. I was thinking maybe there was something to that Purgatory business when a voice said, "Gini? Gini!" Fingers tugged at my noose to loosen it, and I took a big gulp of air. A hand touched my shoulder, then tore away my black hood.

The bells were closer. I was trembling something terrible. It felt like my bones were buzzing. I shook my head and looked up. The rope was still round my neck, but there was a good two feet of slack in it, even with me sitting clear down on the ground beneath the scaffold. The crowd was scattering. Between the moving trunks of their legs and skirts I saw Jingles's rig thunder past, swaybacked Comanche at a hard lope and Grace galloping so fast her stumpy legs blurred. Elma Justice Fowler was on the seat, and she was crying, "Runaway! Help!"

A serape-clad, mustachioed man, his sombrero pulled low and his gun aimed directly at the head of Temporary Deputy Harley Thorndike, leaned down and jerked me to my feet.

It took me a second to recognize him. "You grew a mustache! How can you do that when you are dead?" I shouted as Elma and Jingles's rig clamored past.

"Not quite dead yet," Mace growled before I could say thanks; and leaving go of me, he seized hold of Harley's collar, pressed the gun to his head, dragged him out from under the gallows, and shouted, "Key!"

Sheriff Russell did not hesitate. He tossed it down just as, beneath our feet, the ground began to quake and groan in earnest.

A couple women screamed. Kitty-cornered across the street, the Malone Bros. Mercantile commenced to shake and shiver. People scattered, trampled each other, snatched up their kids. The lady marchers changed their chant to "Retribution now! Retribution now!"

A deep rumbling rose from the earth to overtake us. The gallows trembled in time with it. The tiered seats shook and creaked. People cried out and jumped clear, knocked each other sprawling.

Mace ignored them. He gave the key to Harley and had him unlock my handcuffs. My bones vibrated along with the ground. Shivering metal still dangling from one wrist, I grabbed the key from Harley and unlocked the other bracelet before I jerked the noose off over my head. There was sure a lot of play in that rope. I gave it a tug, and one of Hammurabi O'Keefe's big polished gears clattered down through the trapdoor. It would have banged me on the head if Mace hadn't yanked me out of the way.

"Get moving!" he yelled over the din. Poor Harley was craning his head like a chained owl at high noon, but Mace seized him again and dragged him through the mob, gun to his neck.

I followed as best I could, what with having to duck and dodge so many panicky people. "What's the matter with that rope?" I shouted. "We have got to help Elma! That team has run away on her, and—" I tripped over a coonhound that was trying to get out of town about as fast as I was, only in the opposite direction. It was a good thing I only went down to my knees, or I would have been trampled.

I glimpsed Mace for a half-second. He was scowling like I had fallen on purpose, just to cause him trouble. "Judas Priest!" I heard him holler over the tumult. "Will you just shut up and c'mon?"

Hanged Dog had gone to pure pandemonium. Sight-seers stampeded like lightning-spooked cattle. Frenzied horses ripped their ties, bolted through the throng. The lawmen could not shoot for fear of hitting poor Harley or an innocent citizen; and what deputies tried to follow us were cut off or bowled over by panicked spectators. Hammurabi

O'Keefe was the only one left up on the scaffold. Hat gone, he clung to the swaying rails. His fine Apparatus of Death was half-busted off the crossbeam and swinging wildly, caught in big loops of rope.

The mob's screams were drowned out by the crash and boom as the Malone Bros. Mercantile splintered, popped, collapsed, and sank straight into the ground. On either side, the earth opened in long, wide cracks, fell in on itself. The front half of Pinkerton's Café cracked, tottered, then went in. Part of the corral next to Swinbourne's Livery just dropped away. The whole of Nadine Pinchot's dress shop followed. The lady marchers ceased to chant, dropped their signs, and took off running. Something down in the hole exploded, and part of the mercantile roof sailed up out of the depths and landed across the street with a crash. A woman in a green dress ran past me, screaming, "Armageddon!"

I caught up to Mace at the Thirsty Buzzard's horse rail. "It's the Busted Flush!" I cried. "The old 'C' shaft's cavin' in!"

He grabbed me by the shirt and half-lifted me onto a horse. I scrambled the rest of the way up, which wasn't easy, since the horse was scared almost to death and kicking up a ruckus.

Doc Ben and Pearl Scrimm were in the saloon doorway, their mouths agape as they watched half the town disappear into the ground. Doc was hanging on to the doorframe for dear life. Pearl clutched at her heart. My package was still under her arm. I yelled for her to throw it to me. She looked real surprised to see me. Happy, too.

Mace handed me Harley's pistol before he shoved him away and hopped on the pony next to mine. I jammed the gun in my belt and got a good grip on my package.

Mace yelled, "Go, dammit!"

I did.

Even though nobody had the chance—or presence of mind—to shoot at us, it was not easy getting out of town. Agitated people darted every which way, and all of Hanged Dog was filled with the boom and crash of real estate going fast to ruin. Flames and black smoke shot up from the hole where the Malone Bros. Mercantile had stood two minutes before. The circus smells of peanuts and popped corn and tamales were gone, replaced by choking billows of white dust and dark, greasy smoke.

Nobody was exactly chasing us, but when we got to the open, we pushed those horses flat out. Mace led me north, then east toward the foothills.

We raced up into the mountains, wove between the trees, dodged low-hanging limbs. The horses were lathered and groaning. I hollered, "Got to slow down!"

He answered by pointing ahead, to the rocky crest of a ridge. There, against the pines, sitting on his old bay Zeus horse and watching us through his spyglass, was none other than Tuck Brennan. He lifted an arm and waved.

He started down toward us, leading Mace's horse and Filibuster and one other, which looked pretty winded. By the time we reached him, I was in a state. I jumped off my horse and he climbed down off Zeus, and I hugged and hugged him and cried like I'd never stop. When I could talk again, I said, "Tuck, are you sure I didn't die? Are you sure this isn't Heaven?"

He threw back his head and laughed so big it showed all those white teeth. He said, "We're all still among the living, Miss Gini. I hope you're not disappointed."

By way of an answer, I burst back into tears.

He gave me his handkerchief, then lifted my hair and peered at my neck. "Got yourself a bad rope burn, honey, but we'll get some salve on it and you'll heal up fine.

Swallow for me; tell me if it hurts around your Adam's apple."

I did as he said. "Not really, but my jawbone is awful achy. Under my ears. I have got kind of a headache, too."

He rumpled my hair. "Both temporary. Looks like that famous quick-kill hangman of yours isn't all he's cracked up to be. By Hera, Miss Gini, I believe you are indestructible. Blast go all right, Mason?"

Mace nodded. He had stripped the tack off the spent horses and turned them loose, and was busy saddling up his horse and Filibuster. "It went just like Jingles said, but I might have liked it a half-minute sooner. He get out safe?"

Gently, Tuck peeled me off him, though he kept his arm round me. He said, "I checked him on my way up. He was outside the shaft and setting off to retrieve his team from Mrs. Fowler. Said it was the best time he'd had since he fought off Chico Morales's gang up the Gila River in sixty-two. That's quite a friend you made for yourself, Miss Gini. Quite a pinpoint blaster, too." He transferred my old satchel, scorched but still sound, from his saddle to mine, then gave me a boost up on Filibuster.

"But what about Elma Justice Fowler? Will she be all right, Tuck? What if she and Jingles get into trouble because of me?"

With a soft creak of saddle leather, he swung up on Zeus. "I wouldn't worry about it. They have a good story worked out, should anyone think to ask."

"But what happened? Where were you and Mace all this time? How did you match up with Jingles? And if you two weren't burned in that fire, who was? It can't be Tyrone, as he is in San Francisco."

"That's my Pandora Kincaid," Tuck said with a grin. "Always brim-full of questions. The answers are fairly

simple. I'm afraid I got myself stove up pretty bad back at
Gospel Joe's place. Mace came to my rescue. Yours, too."

I looked to Mace and said my thanks.

He said, "The blast knocked you mostly clear. I just
dragged you a few yards away from the fire is all." He
shrugged and looked away, like he was embarrassed about
having done a gallant thing.

"As for yours truly," Tuck went on, "that bear did a good
job on my leg. The explosion broke the other one in two
places. Took a bad burning, too, on my back and arm."

"I could have made you a poultice for that."

"I don't doubt it for a second, honey. But you weren't
there, and Mace did the best he could, with some help from
Gospel Joe. It was Joe who helped Mace drag me up the
mountain to his friend's shack. The horses had run off, so it
took both of them to do it. When they went back for you, the
posse was already at Joe's cabin. Joe went on down and
Mace snuck back up to me."

"But the bodies!"

"Your friend Vince was one. As to the other, well . . .
Miss Gini, I once heard a story about some boys up around
Carson City who came on the lightning-struck and burnt-out
shell of a friend's cabin. Four of them, stone-cold sober and
in the full light of day, dragged out the cadaver and buried
it with full and serious Christian rites. Then, halfway
through the services, their buddy came strolling down out of
the trees and asked who the Sam Hill they were planting in
his front yard."

"Tuck, what does that have to do with—"

He chuckled. "Sorry, honey. I left out the most important
part. Seems that, the day before, this gent had shot himself
a half-grown bear and hauled the carcass into his shack. It
was that bear those boys found and buried. A bear and
human carcass have got a great deal in common, especially

when fire has sizzled off the fur and twisted the limbs into gargoyle postures. And a charred thing like that, especially if you have reason to believe it was once human, is not conducive to close study."

It was getting chilly, what with the altitude and all, and he turned up his collar. "I am deeply sorry we couldn't get you out before, child. I know what it's like to be locked in a cell and feeling hopeless. But in the beginning I was too crippled up to ride, let along pull off a rescue. And after that, they had so damn many guards on the place we couldn't figure a way to get in, much less get you out. When Mace ran across Jingles digging through our 'graves' and brought him on up to me, well, that's when I got the idea for this little show. Don't you want a coat?"

I twisted round and dug my old duster out of my satchel. It smelled of smoke, but it was warm. After I got wiggled into it, I said, "Gospel Joe is dead. Did you know that?"

"Yes. It was sad news. He was a good man."

Everybody rode along quiet for a bit. Finally I couldn't stand it any longer. I said, "What happened to my rope back there?"

Proudly, Mace said, "Tuck happened to it. He was up in the bell tower with a rifle, and then he rode out the back way to make sure your friend Elma got stopped all right. It was good shooting, Tuck."

I rubbed at my neck. I was pretty dang impressed. "Why, that's just like in some of my dime books, like the one where Smiley Carlisle gets saved by Panhandle Slim at the very last minute!"

Tuck chuckled and reached over to pat my leg. "I thought you'd appreciate the symmetry of it, Miss Gini. Unfortunately, I'm not such a talented marksman as your Panhandle Slim. I missed the rope entirely and knocked one of those big shiny flywheels akimbo. Second shot went there on purpose and knocked it all the way out. The gear behind it, too. Gave you about ten extra feet of rope all told, I imagine. In light of my being an inferior marksman on this occasion, I am grateful to those kids for popping off all those firecrackers. Also to Mr. O'Keefe for concocting such a preposterous mechanism. I may have to compose a note of thanks."

I said, "I don't know that you're a poor marksman, Tuck. I have seen you shoot. I think I should take some fault, as I was swingin' some. Now, if I'd known the plan, I'd have tried harder to stay still. Why, I don't guess even Buffalo Bill could hit a swayin' rope from that bell tower!"

We came to a little brook, entered the water, and began to ride upstream. "Stay to the center," Tuck said. "Looks like there's snow on the way, but we'd better cover our tracks the best we can and not rely on the whims of nature."

"Where are we goin'? And what about the gold? Did you get it back?"

Mace grumbled, "Will you just be quiet? I'd think, what with having that rope round it, your throat would be too sore to talk through. Honest to God if you aren't a pest!"

"Boy howdy, Mace! If I'm such a dang nuisance, why'd you bother in the first place?"

"I only did it because I owed you from back in Oro Tiempo," he snapped. "If it hadn't been for that, I would'a let you swing if for no other reason than to finally have some goddamn peace and quiet!"

I took a second to look at him, really look at him. He was all nerved up from the excitement in town and sparring for a quarrel; but he was a good man, all right, better than I'd ever bothered to credit him. A brave one, too, to come right up to the scaffold and practically into the arms of the law to rescue me. I guessed he must actually like me some, after all. I smiled and said, "You look real handsome in that mustache, Mace."

His jaw kind of opened, then snapped shut, and I'll be danged if he didn't color up. And Tuck? He just laughed like anything.

I will not go into the details of how we covered our tracks, but I will say we did a good job of it. Two days later we set up a temporary residence in the wilderness, and have thus far been here a little over a month.

Tuck told me he gave two gold bars to Jingles: one for himself and one for the Fowlers. I was glad to hear it, as it meant Jingles would be able to live in comfort—or at least buy himself enough dynamite to spend the rest of his days blasting to his heart's content—and that Will and Elma Fowler would be fixed fine to go back east, so Will could finish up his lawyer education. Tuck said if he'd known Will Fowler would use the gold to make himself a career as a "professional pettifogger," he might have thought twice about the gift. He smiled when he said it, though.

A trapper wandered by last week and stayed the night. We said we were a family of pilgrims down from Salt Lake, and I guess he believed it, especially after Tuck pulled out that old *Book of Mormon* and made a good show of trying to convert him to the Latter-Day Saints persuasion.

The trapper told us the news he had heard, one item of which was about the big cave-in in a little town called Hanged Dog, on the edge of El Despoblado. He said there had been a notorious female criminal there, but that, on the day she was to be hanged, vile calamity had struck. He told us about the ground opening and the buildings caving into the old Busted Flush Mine, and how they still hadn't figured out why that shaft had decided to give way all of a sudden. He said the only reason nobody was killed was because the entire populace was out on the street to watch the hanging.

He also said the lady they were about to hang stole away in the confusion, aided by a male accomplice some witnesses swore to be a Mex *bandido*. Nobody had seen her since, and now it was wondered if maybe she didn't get swallowed up in the ground along with six businesses, three water troughs, half a corral, and the back lot of Fillmore's Undertaking & Carpentry. I said, "Tsk, tsk, brother," and then I gave him another slice of roast venison and some extra biscuits. They were good, fluffy ones.

I end this story from my "writing room," which is a corner of our big cave high in the White Mountains. We are snowed in pretty good, and it looks like we will have to winter here. It's not so bad. I guess Tuck had figured this might happen, as he and Mace had stocked it pretty good beforehand with flour and salt and beans and canned goods and such, and grain and fodder for the horses. We have plenty of game. The cave has several chambers and is big enough to shelter both us and the horses with room left over, and there is a crack in the roof to let out the smoke of our fire.

We are not bored, either. Every night for an hour or three we say out stories. Tuck has read us a long and exciting one called *The Odyssey*, which has lots of battles and heroes and heroines and magic. I have said out the Ghost Ruggles book, plus that poem Gam liked so well about the old sailor and the albatross. Mace and Tuck liked it, too.

A mountain cave is not the coziest roost but, all things considered, it is a good place to be for now. Tuck and Mace put together some chairs and a table, and I am thinking I will take my red saloon dress and maybe one of the others and tear them into strips for a braided rag rug. That would make it more homey.

I am looking forward to spring. I've heard tell that, in certain parts of these mountains, the ladybugs migrate by the millions. Tuck says they cling to the trunks in such numbers that the forest turns red-orange, and the limbs dip down under their weight.

I would like to see that.

Postscript

I am pretty old now, I guess, having seventy-one summers under my belt, which is still just twenty-four inches around, thank you very much. I have seen sixteen U.S. presidents come and go: seventeen if you count Grover Cleveland twice. I have witnessed the advent of telephones and automobiles and radios; the Great War, Prohibition, and now the Great Depression.

I'm the last one left. Tyrone died in 1889, near Tucumcari, New Mexico. He was shot to death by some woman's husband, and he died in poverty, or at least that was what we heard. I guess he had lost all his gold at cards or roulette. I can't say I felt real bad about it.

Me and Mace married up about six months after I got sprung from the hoosegow. We were hid out in the White Mountains for that whole winter, and I guess we just got so used to each other we couldn't imagine splitting up, even though we hollered and scrapped almost nonstop the whole time.

Mace took a leaf from the Malones (probably the only good page in their whole book) and used our shares of the gold money to start up in the retail business in Denver. He did real good by us, even though he would never let me step

409

foot inside one of our stores till after he got rid of the last lamps and gas jets and got hooked up to the electricity. He thought that was real funny. He would.

Anyhow, we yelled and made up and yelled and made up again for near forty years: through one middling mercantile grown to three department stores, five houses (the first was six rooms; the last, thirty-four), and a sparker of a set of redheaded twin girls. The firstborn we called Mary-Elma. The Mary was for Gam, the Elma for Elma Justice Fowler. The second, who followed by twenty-six minutes, we named Martha, just because we liked it. Those girls were real firecrackers, I can tell you!

Mace and me got to be Mr. and Mrs. Dixon Peters. The Peters was in honor of his dead brother. I went along with it, but to this day, every time somebody calls me Mrs. Peters, I swear I catch a whiff of old Stinky Pete. The Dixon part came from Mace's middle name. I never knew that till after we got hitched. Mason Dixon Danahoe. His daddy must have had some sense of humor, all right.

Tuck came to visit us twice a year, sometimes three. He always brought toys or candy for the girls and a book or two for me. He loved telling long-ago stories to the youngsters and just sitting out on the porch, smoking his pipe, watching the stars, and talking soft about the old times.

He was going by Jacob T. Brennan then (that having been his true name all along), though our girls always called him Uncle Tuck. He had a big house over to Boulder, with gardens and a fountain and a library you could rope a steer in. He also hired a genuine chef from Paris, France, and finally grew himself a big, comfortable belly and a bushy beard to match. Idleness didn't suit him, though, and from 1885 till he died, he taught Ancient History at the University of Colorado.

It still tickles me sometimes to think what those eggheads

would have said if they found out their Esteemed Professor was the celebrated—and officially deceased—Boss Brennan, Hero of the Navajo Whoop-Up and longtime resident of Yuma Prison.

We heard that Elma Justice Fowler and her blue-eyed husband, Will, went back east. Later on, Will got to be a United States senator from his home state of Iowa, and he and Elma were powerful "Hawkeyes" indeed. Their pictures were in the papers and magazines sometimes. Usually it would be Will kissing a baby or orating with his arm swept out to emphasize a point, and Elma in the background with all her clothes matched up. I guess she never did get over that.

I never wrote her till after the Senator died. That was in 1918, during the influenza epidemic. I told her how sorry I was, both about her being widowed and my not keeping in touch. I wrote that I had always thought it wouldn't do Will's career much good if it got out his wife had been friends with the likes of me. I got a note from her daughter, Betsy, telling me Elma had passed on within a week of Will's death, but that my letter had made her mother very happy. I cried and cried.

We never heard from Jingles again, though I sent two letters to him in care of General Delivery, Tombstone. I like to think he took that gold bar and bought himself a place where Gracie would have lots of nice soft grass to sit in.

Tuck passed on in 1900. He was with us to see in the new century, and about five minutes after it arrived, he departed. The doctor said it was plain heart failure and old age, but I think Tuck just figured his time was gone, and he'd best go with it graceful-like. He died in my arms, his hand in mine.

Mace had a stroke in March of '24. It was a bad one, and he didn't last a week. After, I got so lonely I went out and got a ginger cat, just to have something to argue at. The cat didn't mind. We had an agreement. He'd just lie there and purr and wait for me to quiet down and give him his cream and steamed kidney. That was one fat, happy cat, though I think he gained weight as much on all the talk and holler as the kidneys and fried chicken and calf liver I fed him. Funny. When Mace died I cried for near six months solid, thought I'd never be so hollow-sad again. But that cat? I think his dying was harder on me than when Mace kicked.

Anyhow, after the cat died, I got kind of homesick for Arizona. I sold off the big house up in Denver and gave away the furniture. I let the servants go and headed back home.

There's not much left of Hanged Dog except the stone water trough that used to front the livery, a chunk of rusty pump here and there, and a partial foundation that was likely the back-alley side of the Thirsty Buzzard. Jingles's charge had been a real corker, for a deep arroyo runs right through the town, with a wide rubble-bottomed pit marking the space formerly occupied by the Malone Bros. Mercantile. The blast must have caved in the old Busted Flush shaft for a furlong in either direction.

I found Gam's headstone in what's left of the tumbleweeded graveyard, though it had pitched over backwards. It was way too heavy for me to budge, but I dusted it off so you could read the words some better, and I gathered up a few wildflowers to lay on it.

I went over to San Carlos, too, just to see if I could find out what became of Sees Silver. He was long dead, of course, Hell's Forty Acres not being a place to foster long life; but the lady at the office was real nice and tracked down his grandson for me. His name is John Henry Silver, and he's a schoolteacher there on the reservation. The two of us had a fine afternoon, me telling him the stories of my meetings with his fierce and handsome granddaddy, and

John Henry hanging on every word and asking all kinds of questions about the olden times. He asked, too, if he could talk to me again someday, and I said he sure could. You know, it may just be hope and wishing, but I believe there was a touch of Gam about him, around the eyes.

I tried to find Zack's grave, too, to tend it a bit. I even went out there thinking that maybe old Malachi might still be sitting by the cairn, blinking at the sun and waiting for me to scoop him up into my satchel. But the grave wouldn't be found and neither would Malachi, not even after I hired a bare-to-the-waist gum-cracking teenaged boy to drive me around out there all day long in his pickup truck. Nothing looked the same, though I am certain we were in the right vicinity. I knew the desert would have changed a good bit in fifty-five years, but I hadn't figured it could swallow up the whole of a good limestone marker, even if the years would have melted it down some. I finally gave the boy his money and told him to drive me back down to town. I think he thought I was just a crazy old lady, and maybe he was right.

I live in Phoenix now, out on the edge. I've got a fancy apartment—well, as fancy as it gets in Phoenix—brand-new and studded all around with too dang many palm trees. My daughter Mary-Elma came down and picked it out for me, said I was too old to have a house again. She said if I insisted on moving out to the middle of nowhere and refused live-in help, I had better have people around in case I lit myself on fire accidental or fell and broke a hip. She fussed a lot, but I think Mary-Elma was glad to see me go. She's embarrassed in front of her hoity-toity friends because I say just what I think.

I found a Mex lady to come in and clean for me twice a week. She's not much for windows or silver polishing, but she's as sassy as can be and talks right back. Also, her uncle rode with Pancho Villa, and she has some fine stories. I'd rather have a good confab than shiny silver any day.

I live right up on top of the building, and have the whole floor to myself: the penthouse, they call it. I have a good view of the desert and the mountains beyond. Some nights I sit up till two or three in the morning, just staring out at the land, thinking about how it was before the highway was there and watching the headlights snake along. They remind me of some story Tuck told the twins once. Dragon's eyes.

I ran across my jail notebooks when I was ridding out up in Denver. They were yellow and crumbly, not being writ on the best paper; but I got hold of a typewriter machine and I copied them all out. It was a good thing, because not one week later, Mary-Elma (who is Mrs. Highfalutin-Howard-Colter-the-Third-of-Denver and the mother of four of the most spoilt social climbers in the whole of Colorado) took the notebooks for rubbish and threw them out. I had a little talk with her, I can tell you!

But my copy is word for word, comma for comma, what I wrote in my jail notebook. Of course, I had that little accident with chapter 2 and a Zippo lighter my Community Pillar son-in-law, Mr. Colter, had forgot at my house. When they say those lighters never go out, they are not fooling. That chapter was only singed at the edges, though the parlor curtains went up in a hurry; but there was no need for that nosy Mrs. Wallace across the street to call the Fire Brigade again, as I had it all put out before they pulled up.

Anyhow, I carried the whole shebang down here with me to Phoenix, all the time thinking what to do, and I guess I have finally decided. Today I rented myself a safety deposit box, and salted it with a codicil that leaves a third of my estate to the Apache Nations, to be administered by Mr. John Henry Silver.

Tomorrow my story goes in, willed, in case of death, to my granddaughter, Lois. She lives in Hollywood, California, and sings in the movies and on the radio with the Bobby Briscoe Big Band, and she once got me the autograph of Mr. Clark Gable himself. Lois is the only daughter of my other girl, Martha, who is Mrs. Daniel Pykes of Chicago, Illinois. Martha used to play the big pipe organ in the Bijou De Luxe Theater there until the movies went to sound. Her husband, Mr. Pykes, owns that theater and several others, so do not think she did it because she needed the money. She just liked the playing. Anyway, where Mary-Elma got my temper, Martha got my music and passed it on to Lois.

Mace and me never told the girls who we really are. We always said we came from farm people in Virginia, which, if you take Gam into consideration, was not a total lie. I'll let the family decide, when I'm gone, what they want to do with my story. Maybe they'll burn this copy, too. I know Mary-Elma and her clan would. They are sure going to be shocked to find out their fine social position got started with stolen gold, and not just once-stole. By my count that gold was swiped six times, if you count Harlan Wilbeck digging it out of Apache land as the first thievery. And out of those six, I only stole it twice: once off Mescal Mort's dead mule, and once off Black Ear Cicero and his bunch. I guess that's not so bad, is it? But Mary-Elma is going to be shocked right out of her Patron of the Arts corset.

I think Martha and Lois might see it a little different. Oh, I forgot to tell you: Lois and her husband, Bill, have a little girl now: hair the color of flame, feisty as can be. Her name's Geneva, after me.

Boy howdy, when I was sitting in that cell in Hanged Dog and listening to them hammer up those gallows, I never thought I'd be a great-grandma!

Boy howdy! Been a long time since I said that, and it feels so good to say that I believe I'll do it again.

Boy howdy! Those sure were the times!

A native of Iowa, Ellen Recknor moved to Arizona in 1977. Today she resides in Scottsdale with seven reasonably placid cats, two enthusiastic teenaged whippets, and a kindly but vigilant greyhound, Dash Hammett Recknor, whose hobbies include barking at imaginary monsters in the air-conditioning ducts.